Extraordinary Praise for
Sophie Hannah's Hercule Poirot Mysteries

"We Agatha Christie fans read her stories—and particularly her Poirot novels—because the mysteries are invariably equal parts charming and ingenious, dark and quirky and utterly engaging. Sophie Hannah had a massive challenge in reviving the beloved Poirot, and she met it with heart and no small amount of little gray cells. I was thrilled to see the Belgian detective in such very, very good hands. Reading *The Monogram Murders* was like returning to a favorite room of a long-lost home."   —Gillian Flynn

"Perfect. . . . A pure treat."   —Tana French

"Does Sophie Hannah's Poirot live up to our expectations? Yes, he does, and markedly so. Set in London in the winter of 1929, *The Monogram Murders* is both faithful to the character and an entirely worthy addition to the canon. . . . The plot is as tricky as anything written by Agatha Christie. Nothing is obvious or predictable in this very difficult Sudoku of a novel. *The Monogram Murders* has a life and freshness of its own. Poirot is still Poirot. Poirot is back."
                                         —Alexander McCall Smith

"Terrific . . . uncanny. As Hercule Poirot himself would say, 'Bravo, Madame Hannah. Bravo.'"   —*Boston Globe*

CLOSED CASKET

Also by Sophie Hannah

Little Face
The Truth-Teller's Lie
The Wrong Mother
The Dead Lie Down
The Cradle in the Grave
The Other Woman's House
Kind of Cruel
The Carrier
The Orphan Choir
The Monogram Murders
Woman with a Secret
A Game for All the Family

CLOSED CASKET

A New Hercule Poirot Mystery

Sophie Hannah

wm

WILLIAM MORROW
An Imprint of HarperCollinsPublishers

For Mathew and James Prichard and family, with love

AGATHA CHRISTIE and POIROT are registered trademarks of Agatha Christie Limited.

A hardcover edition of this book was published in 2016 by William Morrow, an imprint of HarperCollins Publishers.

FIRST WILLIAM MORROW PAPERBACK EDITION PUBLISHED 2017.

Lillieoak floor plans by Nick Springer. Copyright © 2016 by Springer Cartographics LLC. Background art throughout © by MSSA/Shutterstock, Inc.

Library of Congress Cataloging-in-Publication Data has been applied for.

ISBN 978-0-06-245883-4

21   LSC   10 9

Contents

PART I

1. A New Will   3
2. A Surprise Reunion   13
3. A Particular Interest in Death   22
4. An Unexpected Admirer   30
5. Tears Before Dinner   38
6. The Announcement   42
7. The Reaction   51
8. A Stroll in the Gardens   59
9. King John   67
10. Open Casket   77
11. Overheard Voices   85
12. Sophie Points a Finger   92

PART II

13. Enter the Gardaí   99
14. Lady Playford's Two Lists   110
15. Seeing, Hearing and Looking   117
16. Down in the Dumps   122
17. The Grandfather Clock   128

18. Unrequited   134
19. Two Irises   139
20. Cause of Death   146
21. The Casket Question   154
22. In the Orangery   158
23. The Inquest   166

Part III
24. Sophie Makes Another Accusation   181
25. Shrimp Seddon and the Jealous Daughter   187
26. Kimpton's Definition of Knowledge   191
27. The Iris Story   197
28. A Possible Arrest   206
29. The Grubber   211
30. More than Fond   215
31. Lady Playford's Plan   225
32. The Kidnapped Racehorse   235
33. The Two True Things   240
34. Motive and Opportunity   247
35. Everyone Could Have but Nobody Did   259
36. The Experiment   267
37. Poirot Wins Fair and Square   279
Epilogue   294

Acknowledgments   301
Books by Agatha Christie   303

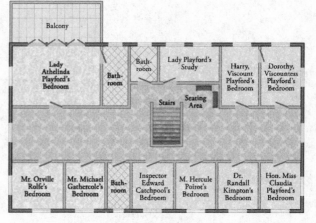

Lillieoak

Balcony

Lady Athelinda Playford's Bedroom

Bathroom

Bathroom

Lady Playford's Study

Harry, Viscount Playford's Bedroom

Dorothy, Viscountess Playford's Bedroom

Stairs

Seating Area

Mr. Orville Rolfe's Bedroom

Mr. Michael Gathercole's Bedroom

Bathroom

Inspector Edward Catchpool's Bedroom

M. Hercule Poirot's Bedroom

Dr. Randall Kimpton's Bedroom

Hon. Miss Claudia Playford's Bedroom

First Floor

To Servants' wing

Mr. Joseph Scotcher's Bedroom

Miss Sophie Bourlet's Bedroom

Bathroom

Cloakroom

Kitchen

Orangery

Dining Room

Stairs

French windows leading to gardens

Drawing Room

Entrance Hall

Library

Parlour

Terrace

Ground Floor

PART I

1

A New Will

MICHAEL GATHERCOLE STARED AT the closed door in front of him and tried to persuade himself that now was the moment to knock, as the aged grandfather clock in the hall downstairs stuttered its announcement of the hour.

Gathercole's instructions had been to present himself at four, and four it was. He had stood here—in this same spot on the wide first landing of Lillieoak—many times in the past six years. Only once had he felt less at ease than he did today. On that occasion he had been one of two men waiting, not alone as he was this afternoon. He still remembered every word of his conversation with the other man, when his preference would have been to recall none of it. Applying the self-discipline upon which he relied, he cast it from his mind.

He had been warned that he would find this afternoon's meeting difficult. The warning had formed part of the summons, which was typical of his hostess. "What I intend to say to you will come as a shock . . ."

Gathercole did not doubt it. The prior notice was no use to him, for it contained no information about what sort of preparation might be in order.

His discomfort grew more pronounced when he consulted his pocket watch and noticed that by hesitating, and with all the taking out of the watch and putting it back in the waistcoat pocket, and pulling it out once more to check, he had made himself late. It was already a minute after four o'clock. He knocked.

Only one minute late. She would notice—was there anything she did not notice?—but with any luck she would not remark upon it.

"Do come in, Michael!" Lady Athelinda Playford sounded as ebullient as ever. She was seventy years old, with a voice as strong and clear as a polished bell. Gathercole had never encountered her in sober spirits. There was always, with her, a cause for excitement— often such morsels as would alarm a conventional person. Lady Playford had a talent for extracting as much amusement from the inconsequential as from the controversial.

Gathercole had admired her stories of happy children solving mysteries that confounded the local police since he had first discovered them as a lonely ten-year-old in a London orphanage. Six years ago, he had met their creator for the first time and found her as disarming and unpredictable as her books. He had never expected to go far in his chosen profession, but here he was, thanks to Athelinda Playford: still a relatively young man at thirty-six, and a partner in a successful firm of solicitors, Gathercole and Rolfe. The notion that any profitable enterprise bore his name was still perplexing to Gathercole, even after a number of years.

His loyalty to Lady Playford surpassed all other attachments he had formed in his life, but personal acquaintance with his favorite author had forced him to admit to himself that he preferred shocks and startling about-turns to occur in the safely distant world of fiction, not in reality. Lady Playford, needless to say, did not share his preference.

He started to open the door.

"Are you going to . . . Ah! There you are! Don't hover. Sit, sit. We'll get nowhere if we don't start."

Gathercole sat.

"Hello, Michael." She smiled at him, and he had the strange sense he always had—as if her eyes had picked him up, turned him around and put him down again. "And now *you* must say, 'Hello, Athie.' Go on, say it! After all this time, it ought to be a breeze. Not 'Good afternoon, your ladyship.' Not 'Good day, Lady Playford.' A plain, friendly 'Hello, Athie.' Is that too much to manage? Ha!" She clapped her hands together. "You look quite the hunted fox cub! You can't understand why you've been invited to stay for a week, can you? Or why Mr. Rolfe was invited too."

Would the arrangements that Gathercole had put in place be sufficient to cover the absence of himself and Orville Rolfe? It was unheard of for them both to be away from the office for five consecutive days, but Lady Playford was the firm's most illustrious client; no request from her could be refused.

"I daresay you are wondering if there will be other guests, Michael. We shall come to all of that, but I'm still waiting for you to say hello."

He had no choice. The greeting she demanded from him each time would never fall naturally from his lips. He was a man who liked to follow rules, and if there wasn't a rule forbidding a person of his background from addressing a dowager viscountess, widow of the fifth Viscount Playford of Clonakilty, as "Athie," then Gathercole fervently believed there ought to be.

It was unfortunate, therefore—he said so to himself often—that Lady Playford, for whom he would do anything, poured scorn on the rules at every turn and derided those who obeyed them as "dreary dry sticks."

"Hello, Athie."

"There we are!" She spread out her arms in the manner of a woman inviting a man to leap into them, though Gathercole knew that was not her intention. "Ordeal survived. You may relax. Not too much!

We have important matters to attend to—after we've discussed the bundle of the moment."

It was Lady Playford's habit to describe the book she was in the middle of writing as "the bundle." Her latest sat on the corner of the desk and she threw a resentful glance in its direction. It looked to Gathercole less like a novel in progress and more like a whirlwind represented in paper: creased pages with curled edges, corners pointing every which way. There was nothing in the least rectangular about it.

Lady Playford hauled herself out of her armchair by the window. She never looked out, Gathercole had noticed. If there was a human being to inspect, Lady Playford did not waste time on nature. Her study offered the most magnificent views: the rose garden, and, behind it, a perfectly square lawn, at the center of which was the angel statue that her husband, Guy, the late Viscount Playford, had commissioned as a wedding anniversary gift, to celebrate thirty years of marriage.

Gathercole always looked at the statue and the lawn and the rosebushes when he visited, as well as at the grandfather clock in the hall and the bronze table lamp in the library with the leaded glass snailshell shade; he made a point of doing so. He approved of the stability they seemed to offer. Things—by which Gathercole meant lifeless objects and not any more general state of affairs—rarely changed at Lillieoak. Lady Playford's constant meticulous scrutiny of every person who crossed her path meant that she paid little attention to anything that could not speak.

In her study, the room she and Gathercole were in now, there were two books upside down in the large bookcase that stood against one wall: *Shrimp Seddon and the Pearl Necklace* and *Shrimp Seddon and the Christmas Stocking.* They had been upside down since Gathercole's first visit. Six years later, to see them righted would be disconcerting. No other author's books were permitted to reside upon those shelves, only Athelinda Playford's. Their spines brought some much-needed brightness into the wood-paneled room—strips of red, blue, green, purple, orange; colors designed to appeal to children— though even they were no match for Lady Playford's lustrous cloud of silver hair.

She positioned herself directly in front of Gathercole. "I want to talk to you about my will, Michael, and to ask a favor of you. But first: how much do you imagine a child—an ordinary child—might know about surgical procedures to reshape a nose?"

"A . . . a nose?" Gathercole wished he could hear about the will first and the favor second. Both sounded important, and were perhaps related. Lady Playford's testamentary arrangements had been in place for some time. All was as it should be. Could it be that she wanted to change something?

"Don't be exasperating, Michael. It's a perfectly simple question. After a bad motorcar accident, or to correct a deformity. Surgery to change the shape of the nose. Would a child know about such a thing? Would he know its name?"

"I don't know, I'm afraid."

"Do *you* know its name?"

"Surgery, I should call it, whether it's for the nose or any other part of the body."

"I suppose you might know the name without knowing you know it. That happens sometimes." Lady Playford frowned. "Hmph. Let me ask you another question: you arrive at the offices of a firm that employs ten men and two women. You overhear a few of the men talking about one of the women. They refer to her as 'Rhino.'"

"Hardly gallant of them."

"Their manners are not your concern. A few moments later, the two ladies return from lunch. One of them is fine-boned, slender and mild in her temperament, but she has a rather peculiar face. No one knows what's wrong with it, but it somehow doesn't look quite right. The other is a mountain of a woman—twice my size at least." Lady Playford was of average height, and plump, with downward slopes for shoulders that gave her a rather funnel-like appearance. "What is more, she has a fierce look on her face. Now, which of the two women I've described would you guess to be Rhino?"

"The large, fierce one," Gathercole replied at once.

"Excellent! You're wrong. In my story, Rhino turns out to be the slim girl with the strange facial features—because, you see, she's had her nose surgically reconstructed after an accident, in a procedure that goes by the name of *rhino*plasty!"

"Ah. That I did not know," said Gathercole.

"But I fear children won't know the name, and that's who I'm writing for. If *you* haven't heard of rhinoplasty . . ." Lady Playford sighed. "I'm in two minds. I was so excited when I first thought of it, but then I started to worry. Is it a little too scientific to have the crux of the story revolving around a medical procedure? No one really thinks about surgeries unless they have to, after all—unless they're about to go into hospital themselves. Children don't think about such things, do they?"

"I like the idea," said Gathercole. "You might emphasize that the slender lady has not merely a strange face but a strange *nose*, to send your readers in the right direction. You could say early on in the story that she has a new nose, thanks to expert surgery, and you could have Shrimp somehow find out the name of the operation and let the reader see her surprise when she finds out."

Shrimp Seddon was Lady Playford's ten-year-old fictional heroine, the leader of a gang of child detectives.

"So the reader sees the surprise but not, at first, the discovery. Yes! And perhaps Shrimp could say to Podge, 'You'll never guess what it's called,' and then be interrupted, and I can put in a chapter there about something else—maybe the police stupidly arresting the wrong person but even wronger than usual, maybe even Shrimp's father or mother—so that anyone reading can go away and consult a doctor or an encyclopedia if they wish. But I won't leave it *too* long before Shrimp reveals all. *Yes.* Michael, I knew I could rely on you. That's settled, then. Now, about my will . . ."

She returned to her chair by the window and arranged herself in it. "I want you to make a new one for me."

Gathercole was surprised. According to the terms of Lady Playford's existing will, her substantial estate was to be divided equally, upon her death, between her two surviving children: her daughter, Claudia, and her son, Harry, the sixth Viscount Playford of Clonakilty. There had been a third child, Nicholas, but he had died young.

"I want to leave everything to my secretary, Joseph Scotcher," announced the clear-as-a-bell voice.

Gathercole sat forward in his chair. It was pointless to try to push the unwelcome words away. He had heard them, and could not pretend otherwise.

What act of vandalism was Lady Playford about to insist upon? She could not be in earnest. This was a trick; it had to be. Yes, Gathercole saw what she was about: get the frivolous part out of the way first—Rhino, rhinoplasty, all very clever and amusing—and then introduce the big caper as if it were a serious proposition.

"I am in my right mind and entirely serious, Michael. I'd like you to do as I ask. Before dinner tonight, please. Why don't you make a start now?"

"Lady Playford . . ."

"Athie," she corrected him.

"If this is something else from your Rhino story that you're trying out on me—"

"Sincerely, it is not, Michael. I have never lied to you. I am not lying now. I need you to draw me up a new will. Joseph Scotcher is to inherit everything."

"But what about your children?"

"Claudia is about to marry a greater fortune than mine, in the shape of Randall Kimpton. She will be perfectly all right. And Harry has a good head on his shoulders and a dependable if enervating wife. Poor Joseph needs what I have to give more than Claudia or Harry."

"I must appeal to you to think very carefully before—"

"Michael, please don't make a cake of yourself." Lady Playford cut him off. "Do you imagine the idea first occurred to me as you knocked at the door a few minutes ago? Or is it more likely that I have been ruminating on this for weeks or months? The careful thought you urge upon me has taken place, I assure you. Now: are you going to witness my new will or must I call for Mr. Rolfe?"

So that was why Orville Rolfe had also been invited to Lillieoak: in case he, Gathercole, refused to do her bidding.

"There's another change I'd like to make to my will at the same time: the favor I mentioned, if you recall. To this part, you may say no if you wish, but I do hope you won't. At present, Claudia and Harry are named as my literary executors. That arrangement no longer suits me. I should be honored if *you*, Michael, would agree to take on the role."

"To . . . to be your literary executor?" He could scarcely credit it. For nearly a minute, he felt too overwhelmed to speak. Oh, but it was all *wrong*. What would Lady Playford's children have to say about it? He couldn't accept.

"Do Harry and Claudia know your intentions?" he asked eventually.

"No. They will at dinner tonight. Joseph too. At present the only people who know are you and me."

"Has there been a conflict within the family of which I am unaware?"

"Not at all!" Lady Playford smiled. "Harry, Claudia and I are the best of friends—until dinner tonight, at least."

"I . . . but . . . you have known Joseph Scotcher a mere six years. You met him the day you met me."

"There is no need to tell me what I already know, Michael."

"Whereas your children . . . Additionally, my understanding was that Joseph Scotcher . . ."

"*Speak*, dear man."

"Is Scotcher not seriously ill?" Silently, Gathercole added: *Do you no longer believe he will die before you?*

Athelinda Playford was not young but she was full of vitality. It was hard to believe that anyone who relished life as she did might be deprived of it.

"Indeed, Joseph is very sick," she said. "He grows weaker by the day. Hence this unusual decision on my part. I have never said so before, but I trust you're aware that I adore Joseph? I love him like a son—as if he were my own flesh and blood."

Gathercole felt a sudden tightness in his chest. Yes, he'd been aware. The difference between knowing a thing and having it confirmed was vast. It led to thoughts that were beneath him, which he fought to banish.

"Joseph tells me his doctors have said he has only weeks, now, to live."

"But . . . then I'm afraid I'm quite baffled," said Gathercole. "You wish to make a new will in favor of a man you know won't be around to make use of his inheritance."

"Nothing is ever known for certain in this world, Michael."

"And if Scotcher should succumb to his illness within weeks, as you expect him to—what then?"

"Why, in that eventuality we revert to the original plan—Harry and Claudia get half each."

"I must ask you something," said Gathercole, in whom a painful anxiety had started to grow. "Forgive the impertinence. Do you have any reason to believe that you too will die imminently?"

"Me?" Lady Playford laughed. "I'm strong as an ox. I expect to chug on for years."

"Then Scotcher will inherit nothing on your demise, being long dead himself, and the new will you are asking me to arrange will achieve nothing but to create discord between you and your children."

"On the contrary: my new will might cause *something wonderful* to happen." She said this with relish.

Gathercole sighed. "I'm afraid to say I'm still baffled."

"Of course you are," said Athelinda Playford. "I knew you would be."

2

A Surprise Reunion

CONCEAL AND REVEAL: HOW appropriate that those two words should rhyme. They sound like opposites and yet, as all good storytellers know, much can be revealed by the tiniest attempts at concealment, and new revelations often hide as much as they make plain.

All of which is my clumsy way of introducing myself as the narrator of this story. Everything you have learned so far—about Michael Gathercole's meeting with Lady Athelinda Playford—has been revealed to you by me, yet I started to tell the tale without making anybody aware of my presence.

My name is Edward Catchpool, and I am a detective with London's Scotland Yard. The extraordinary events that I have barely begun to describe did not take place in London, but in Clonakilty, County Cork, in the Irish Free State. It was on October 14, 1929, that Michael Gathercole and Lady Playford met in her study at Lillieoak, and it was on that same day, and only an hour after that meeting commenced, that I arrived at Lillieoak after a long journey from England.

Six weeks earlier, I had received a puzzling letter from Lady Athelinda Playford, inviting me to spend a week as a guest at her country estate. The various delights of hunting, shooting and fishing were offered to me—none of which I had done before and nor was I keen to try them, though my prospective host wasn't to know that—but what was missing from the invitation was any explanation of why my presence was desired.

I put the letter down on the dining room table at my lodging house and considered what to do. I thought about Athelinda Playford—writer of detective stories, probably the famous author of children's books that I could think of—and then I thought about me: a bachelor, a policeman, no wife and therefore no children to whom I might read books . . .

No, Lady Playford's world and mine need never overlap, I decided—and yet she had sent me this letter, which meant that I had to do something about it.

Did I want to go? Not greatly, no—and that meant that I probably would. Human beings, I have noticed, like to follow patterns, and I am no exception. Since so much of what I do in my daily life is not anything I would ever undertake by choice, I tend to assume that if something crops up that I would prefer not to do, that means I will certainly do it.

Some days later, I wrote to Lady Playford and enthusiastically accepted her invitation. I suspected she wished to pick my brains and use whatever she extracted in a future book or books. Maybe she had finally decided to find out a little more about how the police operated. As a child, I had read one or two of her stories and been flabbergasted to discover that senior policemen were such nincompoops, incapable of solving even the simplest mystery without the help of a group of conceited, loud-mouthed ten-year-olds. My curiosity on this point was, in fact, the beginning of my fascination with the police force—an interest that led directly to my choice of career. Strangely, it had not occurred to me before that I had Athelinda Playford to thank for this.

During the course of my journey to Lillieoak, I had read another of her novels, to refresh my memory, and found that my youthful judgment had been accurate: the finale was very much a case of Sergeant Halfwit and Inspector Imbecile getting a thorough ticking-off from precocious Shrimp Seddon for being stumped by a perfectly obvious trail of clues that even Shrimp's fat, long-haired dog, Anita, had managed to interpret correctly.

The sun was about to set when I arrived at five o'clock in the afternoon, but it was still light enough for me to observe my rather spectacular surroundings. As I stood in front of Lady Playford's grand Palladian mansion on the banks of the Argideen River in Clonakilty—with formal gardens behind me, fields to the left and what looked like the edge of a forest on my right—I was aware of endless space, the uninterrupted blues and greens of the natural world. I had known before setting off from London that the Lillieoak estate was eight hundred acres, but it was only now that I understood what that meant: no shared margins of your own world and that of anyone else if you did not desire it; nothing and nobody pressing in on you or hovering nearby the way they did in the city. It was no wonder, really, that Lady Playford knew nothing of the way policemen conducted themselves.

As I breathed in the freshest air I had ever inhaled, I found myself hoping I was right about the reason I had been invited here. Given the opportunity, I thought, I would happily suggest that a little realism would significantly improve Lady Playford's books. Perhaps Shrimp Seddon and her gang, in the next one, could work in cooperation with a more competent police force . . .

Lillieoak's front door opened. A butler peered out at me. He was of medium height and build, with thinning gray hair and lots of creases and lines around his eyes, but nowhere else. The effect was of an old man's eyes inserted into a much younger man's face.

The butler's expression was odder still. It suggested that he needed to impart vital information in order to protect me from something unfortunate, but could not do so, for it was a matter of the utmost delicacy.

I waited for him to introduce himself or invite me into the house. He did neither. Eventually I said, "My name is Edward Catchpool. I have just arrived from England. I believe Lady Playford is expecting me."

My suitcases were by my feet. He looked at them, then looked over his shoulder; he repeated this sequence twice. There was no verbal accompaniment to any of it.

Eventually, he said, "I will have your belongings taken to your room, sir."

"Thank you." I frowned. This really was most peculiar—more so than I can describe, I fear. Though the butler's statement was perfectly ordinary, he conveyed a sense of so much more left unsaid—an air of "In the circumstances, this is, I am afraid, the most I can divulge."

"Was there something else?" I asked.

The face tightened. "Another of Lady Playford's . . . guests awaits you in the drawing room, sir."

"Another?" I had assumed I was to be the only one.

My question appeared to repel him. I failed to see the point of contention, and was considering allowing my impatience to show when I heard a door opening inside the house, and a voice I recognized. "Catchpool! *Mon cher ami!*"

"Poirot?" I called out. To the butler I said, "Is that Hercule Poirot?" I pushed open the door and walked into the house, tired of waiting to be invited in out of the cold. I saw an elaborately tiled floor of the sort you might see in a palace, a grand wooden staircase, too many doors and corridors for a newcomer to take in, a grandfather clock, the mounted head of a deer on one wall. The poor creature looked as if it was smiling, and I smiled back at it. Despite being dead and detached from its body, the deer's head was more welcoming than the butler.

"Catchpool!" Again came the voice.

"Look here, is Hercule Poirot in this house?" I asked more insistently.

This time the butler replied with a reluctant nod, and moments later the Belgian moved into view at a pace that, for him, was fast. I could not help chuckling at the egg-shaped head and the shiny shoes, both so familiar, and of course the unmistakable mustaches.

"Catchpool! What a pleasure to find you here too!"

"I was about to say the same to you. Was it you, by any chance, wanting to see me in the drawing room?"

"Yes, yes. It was I."

"I thought so. Good, then you can lead me there. What on earth is going on? Has something happened?"

"Happened? No. What should have happened?"

"Well . . ." I turned round. Poirot and I were alone, and my suitcases had vanished. "From the butler's guarded manner, I wondered if—"

"Ah, yes, Hatton. Pay no attention to him, Catchpool. His manner, as you call it, is without cause. It is simply his character."

"Are you sure? It's an odd sort of character to have."

"*Oui*. Lady Playford explained him to me shortly after I arrived this afternoon. I asked her the same questions you ask me, thinking something must have occurred that the butler thought it was not his place to discuss. She said Hatton becomes this way after being in service for so long. He has seen many things that it would not have been prudent for him to mention, and so now, Lady Playford tells me, it is his preference to say as little as possible. She too finds it frustrating. 'He cannot part with the most basic information—what time will dinner be served? when will the coal be delivered?—without behaving as if I'm trying to wrestle from him a closely guarded and explosive family secret,' she complained to me. 'He has lost what judgment he once had, and is now unable to distinguish between outrageous indiscretion and saying anything at all,' she said."

"Then why does she not engage a new butler?"

"That, also, is a question I asked. We think alike, you and I."

"Well, did she give you an answer?"

"She is fascinated to monitor the development of Hatton's personality, and to see how he will further refine his habits in the future."

I made an exasperated face, wondering when someone would appear with the offer of a cup of tea. At that moment, the house shook, then stilled, then shook again. I was about to say "What on earth . . . ?" when I noticed, at the top of the staircase, the largest man I had ever seen. He was on his way down. He had straw-colored hair and a jowly face, and his head looked as tiny as a pebble balanced atop his planet-sized body.

Loud creaking noises came from beneath his feet as he moved, and I feared he might put one of them clean through the wood. "Do you hear that appalling noise?" he demanded of us without introducing himself. "Steps shouldn't groan when you stand on them. Isn't that what they're for—to be stood on?"

"It is," Poirot agreed.

"Well?" said the man unnecessarily. He had been given his answer. "I tell you, they don't make staircases like they used to. The craftsmanship's all gone."

Poirot smiled politely, then took my arm and steered me to the left, whispering, "It is the fault of his appetite that the stairs groan. Still, he is a lawyer—if I were that staircase, I would obtain legal advice." It was not until he smiled that I realized it was supposed to be a joke.

I followed him into what I assumed was the drawing room, which was large and had a big stone fireplace that was too near the door. No fire burned in the grate, and it was colder in here than it had been in the hall. The room was much longer than it was wide, and the many armchairs were positioned in a sort of messy row at one end and an equally untidy cluster at the other. This arrangement of furniture accentuated the room's rectangular shape and made for a rather divided effect. There were French windows at the far end. The curtains had not been drawn for the night, though it was dark outside—and darker for the time of day in Clonakilty than in London, I noticed.

Poirot closed the drawing room door. At last, I took a proper look at my old friend. He looked plumper than when I had last seen him, and his mustache seemed larger and more prominent, at least from across the room. As he moved towards me, I decided that in fact he looked exactly the same, and rather it was I whose imagination had shrunk him to a manageable size.

"What a great pleasure to see you, *mon ami*! I could not believe it when I arrived and Lady Playford told me that you were to be among the guests for the week."

His pleasure was evident, and I felt a pang of guilt because my own feelings were less straightforward. I was heartened by his good spirits and relieved that he did not seem in the least disappointed in me. In Poirot's presence, it is easy to feel that one is a disappointing specimen.

"You did not know I was coming until you arrived here today?" I asked.

"*Non*. I must ask you at once, Catchpool. *Why* are you here?"

"For the same reason as you are, I should think. Athelinda Playford wrote and asked me to come. It is not every day that one is invited to spend a week in the home of a famous writer. I read a few of her books as a child, and—"

"No, no. You misunderstand me. I chose to come for the same reason—though I have not read any of her books. Please do not tell her so. What I meant to ask was, why does Lady Playford want us here, you and me? I imagined she had perhaps invited Hercule Poirot because, like her, he is the most famous and acclaimed in his field. Now I know that cannot be so, for you are here also. I wonder . . . Lady Playford must have read about the business in London, the Bloxham Hotel."

Having no desire to discuss the business in question, I said, "Before

I knew I would meet you here, I fancied she had invited me to ask me about police matters, so that she can get the detail right in her books. They would certainly benefit from a more realistic—"

"*Oui, oui, bien sûr.* Tell me, Catchpool, do you have with you the letter of invitation?"

"Hm?"

"Sent to you by Lady Playford."

"Oh, yes. It's in my pocket." I fished it out and handed it to him.

He cast his eye over it and passed it back to me, saying, "It is the same as the one sent to me. It reveals nothing. Maybe you are right. I wonder if she wishes to consult us in our professional capacities."

"But . . . you have seen her, you said. Did you not ask her?"

"*Mon ami,* what sort of oafish guest demands of his hostess on arrival, 'What do you want from me?' It would be impolite."

"She did not volunteer any information? A hint?"

"There was barely time. I arrived only a few minutes before she had to go to her study to prepare for a meeting with her lawyer."

"The one who was on the stairs? The, er, rather large gentleman?"

"Mr. Orville Rolfe? No, no. He is a lawyer too, but the one with whom Lady Playford had a meeting at four o'clock was a different man. I saw him also. His name is Michael Gathercole. One of the tallest men I have met. He looked very uncomfortable about having to carry himself around."

"What do you mean?"

"Only that he gave the impression of wishing he could discard his own skin."

"Oh. I see." I did not see at all, but I feared that asking for further clarification would have the opposite effect.

Poirot shook his head. "Come, take off your coat and sit," he said. "It is a puzzle. Particularly when one considers who else is here."

"I wonder if it would be possible to ask someone to bring some tea," I said, looking around. "I would have expected the butler to have sent a maid by now, if Lady Playford is busy."

"I insisted upon no interruptions. I had some refreshments upon arrival, and soon drinks will be served in this room, I am told. We do not have long, Catchpool."

"Long? For what?"

"If you would sit, you would learn for what." Poirot gave a little smile. He had never sounded more reasonable.

With some trepidation, I sat.

3

A Particular Interest in Death

"I MUST TELL YOU who else is here," said Poirot. "You and I are not the only guests, *mon ami*. Altogether, including Lady Playford, there are eleven of us at Lillieoak. If one counts the servants as well, there are three more: Hatton the butler, a maid named Phyllis, and the cook, Brigid. The question is: ought we to count the servants?"

"Count them as what? Or *for* what? What are you talking about, Poirot? Are you here to conduct a study of the population of County Cork—how many inhabitants per house, that sort of thing?"

"I have missed your sense of humor, Catchpool, but we must be serious. As I say, we do not have long. Soon—within the half hour—someone will disturb us to prepare for the serving of drinks. Now, listen. At Lillieoak, apart from ourselves and the servants, there is our hostess, Lady Playford, the two lawyers we have talked about—Gathercole and Rolfe. There is also Lady Playford's secretary, Joseph Scotcher, a nurse by the name of Sophie Bourlet—"

"A nurse?" I perched on the arm of a chair. "Is Lady Playford in poor health, then?"

"No. Let me finish. Also here are Lady Playford's two children, the wife of one and the young gentleman friend of the other. In fact, I believe Mr. Randall Kimpton and Miss Claudia Playford are engaged to be married. She lives at Lillieoak. He is visiting from England. An American by birth, but also an Oxford man, I think Lady Playford said."

"So you got all of this from her?"

"You will discover when you meet her that she is able to convey much in a short space of time, all with great color and speed."

"I see. That sounds alarming. Still, it's comforting to know that someone in this house is capable of speech—given the butler, I mean. Have you reached the end of your inventory of people?"

"Yes, but I have not yet named the last two. Mademoiselle Claudia's brother, Lady Playford's son, is Harry, the sixth Viscount Playford of Clonakilty. He too I have already met. He lives here with his wife, Dorothy, who is referred to by all as Dorro."

"All right. And why is it so important that we list these people before we all gather for drinks? Incidentally, I should like to find my room and run a flannel over my face before the evening's activities get under way, so—"

"Your face is clean enough," said Poirot with authority. "Turn around and look at what is mounted above the door."

I did so, and saw angry eyes, a big black nose and an open mouth full of fangs. "Good gracious, what the devil is that?"

"The stuffed head of a leopard cub—the handiwork of Harry, Viscount Playford. He is a practitioner of taxidermy." Poirot frowned and added, "An enthusiastic one, who tries to persuade strangers that no other hobby is likely to provide the same satisfaction."

"So the deer's head in the hall must be his too," I said.

"I told him I do not have the necessary implements or knowledge for the stuffing of animals. He said I would need only some wire, a penknife, needle and thread, hemp and arsenic. I thought it judicious not to tell him that I would also need not to find the idea repellent."

I smiled. "A hobby involving arsenic would hardly appeal to a detective who has solved murders caused by that very poison."

"This is what I want to talk to you about, *mon ami*. Death. Viscount Playford's hobby is one that is all about the dead. Animals, not people—but they are still dead."

"Assuredly. I don't see what the relevance is, though."

"You remember the name Joseph Scotcher—I mentioned it a moment ago."

"Lady Playford's secretary, yes?"

"He is dying. From Bright's disease of the kidneys. That is why the nurse, Sophie Bourlet, lives here—to tend to his needs as an invalid."

"I see. So the secretary and the nurse both live at Lillieoak?"

Poirot nodded. "Now we have three people gathered here who, one way or another, are involved closely with death. And then there is you, Catchpool. And me. We both have encountered many cases of violent death in the course of our work. Mr. Randall Kimpton, who plans to marry Claudia Playford—what work do you think he does?"

"Does it involve death? Is he an undertaker? A chiseler of gravestones?"

"He is a pathologist for the police in the county of Oxfordshire. He too works closely with death. *Eh bien*, do you wish to ask me about Mr. Gathercole and Mr. Rolfe?"

"No need. Lawyers deal with the affairs of the dead every day."

"That is particularly true of the firm of Gathercole and Rolfe, which is well known for its specialism: *the estates and testamentary dispositions of the wealthy*. Catchpool, surely you see by now?"

"And what of Claudia Playford and Dorro, the viscount's wife? What are their connections to death? Does one of them slaughter livestock while the other embalms corpses?"

"You joke about this," said Poirot gravely. "You do not think it is interesting that so many people with a particular interest in death, either private or professional, are gathered here at Lillieoak at the same time? Me, I would like to know what Lady Playford has in mind. I cannot believe it is accidental."

"Well, she might have some sort of game planned for after dinner. Being a writer of mysteries, I imagine she wants to keep us all in suspense. You did not answer my question about Dorro and Claudia."

"I can think of nothing appropriate to our theme that applies to them," Poirot admitted after a moment.

"Then I call it a coincidence! Now, if I'm to wash my face and hands before dinner—"

"Why do you avoid me, *mon ami*?"

I stopped inches from the door. It had been foolish of me to suppose that, since he had not mentioned it at once, he would not raise the matter at all.

"I thought you and I were *les bons amis*."

"We are. I have been confoundedly busy, Poirot."

"Ah, busy! You would like me to believe that is all it is."

I glanced towards the door. "I am going to track down that silent butler and threaten him with all manner of mutiny if he does not show me to my room immediately," I muttered.

"You Englishmen! However strong the emotion, however fierce the fury, stronger still is the desire to smother it, to pretend it was never there at all."

At that moment the door opened and a woman of between—at a guess—thirty and thirty-five walked in, wearing a sequined green dress and a white stole. In fact, she did not so much walk as slink in, making me think instantly of a cat on the prowl. There was a supercilious air about her, as if walking into a room in an ordinary fashion would be beneath her. She seemed to be using every movement of her body to indicate her superiority over whomever else happened to be in the vicinity—in this instance, Poirot and me.

She was also almost unnaturally beautiful: exquisitely arranged hair of a rich brown color, a perfect oval of a face, mischievous catlike brown eyes with thick lashes, shapely eyebrows, and cheekbones as sharp as knives. She was an impressive sight to behold, and obviously aware of her charms. There was also a viciousness about her that communicated itself before she had spoken a word.

"Oh," she said, hand on hip. "I see. Guests, but no drinks. Would that it were the other way round! I suppose I am early."

Poirot rose to his feet and introduced himself, and then me. I shook the woman's chilly, elegant hand.

She did not respond with a "Delighted to meet you" or anything of that sort. "I am Claudia Playford. Daughter of the famous novelist, sister of Viscount Playford. Older sister, as it happens. The title landed on my younger brother and not me, simply because he is a man. Where is the sense in that? I would make a far better viscount than him. Frankly, a buttered teacake would make a better viscount than Harry. Well? Do you think it's fair?"

"I have never given it any thought," I said truthfully.

She turned to Poirot. "What about you?"

"If you were to have the title immediately, would you then say, 'Now that I have what I want, I am completely happy and content'?"

Claudia raised her chin haughtily. "I would say no such thing, for fear of sounding like a silly child from a fairy tale. Besides, who says I am unhappy? I am very happy, and I was talking not about contentment but about what is *fair*. Are you not supposed to have a brilliant mind, Monsieur Poirot? Perhaps you left it in London."

"No, it traveled with me, mademoiselle. And if you are one of the few people in this world who can sincerely say, 'I am very happy,' then I promise you this: life has been fairer to you than it has to most people."

She scowled. "I was talking about me and my brother and *nobody else*. If you cared about playing fair, you would confine your assessment of the situation to the two of us. Instead, you sneakily introduce a nameless crowd of thousands to support your argument—because you know you can win only by distortion!"

The door opened again and a dark-haired man entered, dressed for dinner. Claudia clasped her hands together and sighed rapturously, as if she had feared he might not arrive but here he was, to save her from some terrible fate. "Darling!"

The contrast between her demeanor now and her rudeness to me and Poirot could not have been greater.

The newcomer was handsome and clean-cut, with a ready and engaging smile and almost-black hair that fell over his forehead on one side. "There you are, dearest one!" he said as Claudia ran into his embrace. "I have been looking everywhere for you." He had the most perfect teeth I had ever seen. It was hard to believe that they grew naturally in his mouth. "And here, by the look of it, are some of our guests—how marvelous! Welcome, one and all."

"You are in no position to welcome anybody, darling," Claudia told him with mock sternness. "You are a guest too, remember."

"Let's say I did it on your behalf, then."

"Impossible. I should have said something quite different."

"You have been saying it most eloquently, mademoiselle," Poirot reminded her.

"Have you been divinely beastly to them, dearest one? Take no notice of her, gentlemen." He extended his hand. "Kimpton. Dr. Randall Kimpton. Pleasure to meet you both." He had a remarkable manner when speaking—so much so that I noticed it straightaway, and I am sure Poirot did too. Kimpton's eyes seemed to flare and subside as his lips moved. These wide-eyed flares were only seconds apart, and appeared to want to convey enthusiastic emphasis. One was left with the impression that every third or fourth word he uttered was a source of delight to him.

I could have sworn that Poirot had told me Claudia's chap was American. There was no trace of an accent, or at least not one that I could detect. As I was thinking this, Poirot said, "It is a great pleasure to make your acquaintance, Dr. Kimpton. But . . . Lady Playford told me that you were from Boston in America?"

"Indeed I am. I expect you mean that I don't sound American.

Well, I should hope not! I took the opportunity to divest myself of all the unsavory trappings the moment I landed at the University of Oxford. It doesn't do to sound anything but English at Oxford, you know."

"Randall has a talent for divesting himself of trappings, don't you, darling?" said Claudia rather sharply.

"What? Oh!" Kimpton looked unhappy. His demeanor had completely changed. So had hers, for that matter. She stared at him as might a schoolteacher at a disobedient pupil, apparently waiting for him to speak. Finally he said quietly, "Dearest one, do not break my heart by reminding me of my most reprehensible mistake. Gentlemen, I was once, momentarily, foolish enough—having gone to great lengths to persuade this extraordinary woman to become my wife—I was foolish enough to doubt my own wishes and—"

"Nobody is interested in your regrets and recriminations, Randall," Claudia said, cutting him off. "Apart from me—I never tire of hearing of them. And I warn you, you will need to reproach yourself a good deal more in my presence before I agree to set a wedding date."

"Dearest one, I shall do nothing but reproach, accuse and vilify myself from now until the day I die!" Kimpton said earnestly, eyes flaring. The two of them might have forgotten entirely that Poirot and I were there.

"Good. Then I see no immediate need to divest myself of you." Claudia smiled suddenly, as if she had only ever been teasing him.

Kimpton seemed to inflate with confidence once again. He took her hand and kissed it. "A wedding date *will* be set, my dearest one— and soon!"

"Will it, indeed?" Claudia laughed merrily. "We shall see about that. In any case, I admire your determination. There is no other man on earth who could win me over *twice*. Or, probably, even once."

"No other man would be as obsessed or devoted as I, my divine dearest one."

"That I can believe," said Claudia. "I did not imagine I could ever be induced to wear this ring again, yet here I am, wearing it." She took a moment to examine the large diamond on the third finger of her left hand.

I thought I heard her sigh then, but the sound was masked by that of the door opening a third time. A young maid stood in the doorway. Her fair hair was arranged in a bun that she patted nervously as she spoke. "I'm to prepare the room for drinks," she muttered.

Claudia Playford leaned towards me and Poirot and said in a loud whisper, "Make sure to sniff before you drink. Phyllis is as scatter-witted as they come. I can't imagine why we still have her. She wouldn't know the difference between port and bathwater."

An Unexpected Admirer

A PHENOMENON I HAVE had cause to notice time and again in both my professional and my social life is that when one meets a large group of people all at once, one somehow knows—as if by otherworldly instinct—which of them one will enjoy speaking to and which are worth avoiding.

So it was that when I returned, after dressing for dinner, to a drawing room full of many more people, I knew instantly that I should endeavor to end up standing next to the lawyer Poirot had described to me, Michael Gathercole. He was taller than even the average tall man, and stood slightly stooped as if to minimize his height.

Poirot was quite right: Gathercole did indeed look as if his physical self was a cause of discomfort to him. His arms hung restlessly by his sides, and each time he moved even slightly, it looked as if he was trying rather clumsily and impatiently to shake something off—something unfortunate that had attached itself to him, but that no one else could see.

He was not handsome in the usual sense of the word. His face made me think of a faithful dog that had been kicked too often by its owner and was certain it would happen again. All the same, he looked by far the cleverest of my new acquaintances.

The other newcomers to the drawing room were also as Poirot had advertised, more or less. Lady Playford was telling a complicated anecdote to nobody in particular as she entered. She made as imposing an impression as I had expected, with a loud, melodic voice and her hair in a sort of coiled leaning tower. After her came the planet-sized lawyer, Orville Rolfe; then Viscount Harry Playford, a blond-haired young man with a flat, square face and an amiable if distant smile—as if he had felt chipper about something once and had been trying ever since to recollect the cause of his good cheer. His wife, Dorro, was a tall woman with features that brought to mind a bird of prey and a long neck with a deep hollow at its base. One could have set down a teacup in that hollow and it would have nestled there quite satisfactorily.

The last two to arrive for drinks were Joseph Scotcher, Lady Playford's secretary, and a dark-haired, dark-eyed woman. I assumed she was the nurse, Sophie Bourlet, for she had pushed Scotcher into the room in a wheelchair. She had a kindly smile that looked, at the same time, efficient—as if she had decided that a smile of this exact sort would be suitable for the occasion—and a modest manner. Of everyone in the room, she was the one to whom one might go with a practical problem. She carried a bundle of papers under one arm, I noticed, and as soon as she had the chance, she put them down on a small writing desk by one of the windows. Having done so, she approached Lady Playford and said something to her. Lady Playford looked over at the papers on the desk and nodded.

I wondered if, in the face of Scotcher's declining vigor, Sophie had taken over some of the secretarial duties at Lillieoak. She was dressed more like a secretary than a nurse. All the other women wore evening gowns, but Sophie looked as if she had dressed smartly for a meeting at the office.

Scotcher was as light, in his physical appearance, as his nurse was dark. His hair was the colour of spun gold, and his skin was pale. He had delicate features, almost like a girl's, and looked dangerously thin: a fading angel. I wondered if he had been sturdier before his health failed.

I managed to put myself in front of Gathercole reasonably swiftly, and the usual introductions followed. He turned out to be friendlier than he had looked from a distance. He told me he had first discovered Athelinda Playford's Shrimp Seddon books in the orphanage that had housed him for most of his childhood, and that he was now her lawyer. He spoke of her with admiration and a little awe.

"You are evidently extremely fond of her," I remarked at one point and he replied, "Everybody is who has read her work. She is, I believe, a genius."

I thought about the profoundly unconvincing Sergeant Halfwit and Inspector Imbecile, and decided it would be injudicious to criticize the creative efforts of my host when she was standing only a few feet away.

"A lot of the big houses belonging to English families were burnt to the ground in the recent . . . unpleasant business over here."

I nodded. It was not something that an Englishman at the beginning of a week's holiday in Clonakilty cared to discuss.

"No one came near Lillieoak," said Gathercole. "Lady Playford's books are so well loved that even the lawless hordes could not bring themselves to attack her home—or else they were restrained by those better than themselves, to whom the name Athelinda Playford means something."

This sounded unlikely to me. What lawless horde, after all, would cancel its plans to wreak havoc on account of Shrimp Seddon and her fictional chums? Was young Shrimp really so influential? Could her fat, long-haired dog, Anita, bring a smile to the face of an angry rebel and make him forget all about the cause? I doubted it.

"I see you are unconvinced," said Gathercole. "What you forget is that people fall for Lady Playford's books *as children*. That sort of attachment is difficult, later, to talk yourself out of, no matter what your political affiliation might be."

He spoke as an orphan, I reminded myself; Shrimp Seddon and her gang were probably the closest thing he had had to a family.

An orphan . . .

It struck me that this was another connection between a guest at Lillieoak and death. Michael Gathercole's parents had died. Did Poirot know? Although of course Gathercole was already connected—by his firm's specialism, the estates of the wealthy. And—I was a fool!—everybody in the world has a relative who has died. Poirot's idea of a death-themed gathering was ludicrous, I decided.

Gathercole left me to go and refill his glass. Behind me, Harry Playford was talking enthusiastically to Orville Rolfe about taxidermy. I did not care to hear a step-by-step account of his method, so I crossed the room and listened instead to Randall Kimpton's conversation with Poirot.

"I hear you set great store by psychology in your solving of crimes, what?"

"I do."

"Ah! Well, if you will permit me, I should like to disagree with you. Psychology is so intangible a thing. Who knows if it is even real?"

"It is real, monsieur. Let me assure you, it is real."

"Is it? I do not deny that people have thoughts in their heads, of course, but the notion that one can deduce anything from one's assumptions about what those thoughts might be and why they are there—I'm not convinced by that, I'm afraid. And even when a murderer confirms that you're right—even when he says, 'Quite so. I did it because I was wild with jealousy, or because the old lady I coshed over the head reminded me of a nanny who was cruel to me'—how do you know the blighter's telling the truth?"

This was accompanied by many a triumphant eye-flare, each one seeming to revel in the superiority of Kimpton's arguments. The doctor sounded, furthermore, as if he was not about to drop or change the subject. I thought of what Claudia had said about him winning her over twice and wondered if there had been an element of browbeating involved. She did not seem the type who would allow herself to be coerced, but all the same . . . there was something frightening about the unswerving and arrogant determination exuded by Kimpton—to win, to prevail, to be right.

Perhaps, after all, it would be more relaxing to listen to Harry describing how he had removed the dead leopard's brain.

I was saved by Joseph Scotcher, who had been wheeled over to me by Sophie Bourlet. "You must be Catchpool," said Scotcher warmly. "I have so looked forward to meeting you." He extended a hand, and I shook it as gently as I could. His voice was more robust than his outward appearance had led me to expect. "You seem surprised that I know who you are. I have heard of you, of course. The Bloxham Hotel murders in London, February of this year."

I felt as if I had been slapped in the face. Poor Scotcher; he could not have known his words would have this effect.

"Sorry, I have neglected to introduce myself: Joseph Scotcher. And this is the light of my life—my nurse, friend and good luck charm, Sophie Bourlet. It is thanks to her and her alone that I am still here. A patient who has Sophie to look after him scarcely needs medicine." At these lavish compliments, the nurse looked overcome by emotion, and had to turn away. *She loves him*, I thought. *She loves him and she cannot bear it.*

Scotcher said, "Cunningly, Sophie keeps me alive by refusing to become my wife." He winked at me. "You see, I can't possibly die until she has agreed."

Sophie turned back to face me with pink spots on her cheeks and her sensible smile restored. "Pay no attention, Mr. Catchpool," she said. "The truth is that Joseph has never asked me to marry him. Not once."

Scotcher laughed. "Only because if I were to go down on one knee, it is unlikely I should be able to rise again. It's easy for the sun, but not so easy for me in my condition."

"Rising or setting, Joseph, you shine more brightly than the sun ever could."

"See what I mean, Catchpool? She is worth staying for, even though I have to contend with what I like to call my *deviled* kidneys."

"Excuse me, gentlemen," said Sophie. She walked over to the writing desk, sat down at it and busied herself with the papers she had put there earlier.

"What a selfish oaf I am!" Scotcher declared. "You don't want to talk about my kidneys, and I should far rather talk about you than about myself. It must be terribly difficult for you." He nodded in the direction of Poirot. "I was sorry to see the newspapers ridicule you so cruelly. It was almost as if they didn't notice the part you played in wrapping up that nasty Bloxham affair. I hope you don't object to the mention of it?"

"Not at all," I was obliged to say.

"I read all about it, you see. The whole story. I found it fascinating—and without your brilliant deduction in the graveyard, the case might never have been solved. It seems to me that everybody missed that aspect of the matter."

"They did, rather," I mumbled.

Scotcher had left me with no alternative: I was forced to think once again about the killings that were known at the time—and doubtless always would be—as the Monogram Murders. The case had been solved most ingeniously by Poirot, but it had also attracted much unfortunate publicity—unfortunate if you were me, at any rate. Poirot came out of it all very well, but I was not so lucky. Newspapermen had accused me of being inadequate as a detective and relying too much on Poirot to get me out of a tight spot. Naively, I had made some remarks when interviewed that were a little too honest, about how I would have been lost without Poirot's help, and these had appeared in the papers. A few letters were published asking why Edward Catchpool was employed by Scotland Yard if he couldn't handle the work without bringing in a friend of his who was not even a policeman. In short, I became an object of ridicule for a few weeks, until everybody forgot about me.

Since then—as I found myself telling Joseph Scotcher, who seemed truly to care about my predicament—my work had brought me into contact with another murder case, one that I was ultimately unable to solve, but this time I was praised for doing everything I could, and doggedly pursuing the elusive truth. I was astonished to read in the letters pages of the newspapers that I was a plucky hero; no one could have been braver or more conscientious than I had been—that was the general consensus.

I drew the only possible conclusion: that I was better off failing alone than succeeding with the help of Hercule Poirot. That was why I had been avoiding him (I refrained from sharing this particular revelation with Joseph Scotcher): because I could not trust myself not to ask for help with the murder I had failed to solve. There was simply no way to explain this to Poirot that would not lead to him demanding to know all the details.

"I'm sure many people noticed the shoddy way the newspapers treated you and thought it was jolly unfair," said Scotcher. "Indeed, I wish I had written a letter to the *Times* to that effect. I meant to, but—"

"You must concentrate on looking after yourself and not worry about me," I told him.

"Well, you should know that I admire you inordinately," he said with a smile. "I could never have slotted that piece of the puzzle into place the way you did. It would not have occurred to me, nor to most people. You evidently have an extraordinary mind. Poirot too, of course."

Embarrassed, I thanked him. I knew that my mind was nothing special and that Poirot would have solved the Bloxham Hotel murders with or without my solitary moment of insight, but I was nevertheless greatly heartened by Scotcher's kind words. That he was dying made it all the more touching, somehow. I don't mind admitting that I was quite overcome.

A hush began to spread across the room, like a flood of silence. I turned and saw that Hatton the butler was standing in the doorway, looking as if there was something important that he must on no account tell us. "Oh!" declared Lady Playford, who was standing with Sophie next to the writing desk. "Hatton has come to announce— or to hear *me* announce—that dinner is about to be served. Thank you, Hatton."

The butler looked mortified to be accused of almost saying something to so many people. He gave a small bow and withdrew.

As everyone moved towards the door, I hung back. Once I was alone in the room, I made for the writing desk. The pages laid upon it were handwritten and almost illegible, but I did see what I thought was "Shrimp" in several places. There were two inks, blue and red: red circles around blue words. It seemed that Sophie was indeed doing some secretarial work for Lady Playford.

I read a line that seemed to say "Shrimp a patch sever ration and the parasols." Or was it "parasite"?

I gave up and went in search of dinner.

5

Tears Before Dinner

I EMERGED FROM THE drawing room with not the faintest idea of where to go, though distant voices coming from a certain direction gave me a clue. I was about to follow the sound of laughter and chatter when I heard, from the other side of the house, a more disturbing noise: loud sobbing.

I stopped, wondering what was the best thing to do. I was famished after my long journey, having been offered nothing since I arrived, but I did not feel I could ignore a display of distress so close to where I stood. Scotcher's kind words to me in the drawing room—and the knowledge that he, a complete stranger, held me in such high regard and that therefore there might be other strangers out there who did not think too badly of me—had made me feel altogether jollier and more buoyant than I had for a considerable time. I was determined to hunt down and be similarly kind to whomever was crying so piteously.

Sighing, I went in search of the sobber and soon found her. It was the maid, Phyllis—the poor unfortunate described by Claudia as scatter-witted. She was sitting on the staircase, rubbing at her tears with her sleeve.

"Here," I said, passing her a clean handkerchief. "It can't be all that bad, surely."

She looked up at me doubtfully. "She says it's for me own good! Yells at me morning to night, she does—for me own good! I've had enough of me own good, if that's what it is! I want to go home!"

"Are you new here, then?" I asked her.

"No. Been here four years. She's worse every year! Every day, I sometimes think."

"Who are you talking about?"

"Cook. 'Get out of my kitchen!' she screams, when I've done nothing wrong. I can't help it, I says to her—I try, but I can't help it!"

"Oh dear. Well, look—"

"And then she comes after me, as if I've run away instead of been thrown out by her! 'Where the blazes have you got to, girl? Dinner won't serve itself!' She'll be after me any second now, you watch!"

Was Phyllis supposed to be serving our dinner, then? She did not seem in a fit state to do so. This alarmed me more than her tears and tirades. I was starting to feel light-headed from hunger.

"I *would* have run away by now if it weren't for Joseph!" Phyllis declared.

"Joseph Scotcher?"

She nodded. "D'you know about him, Mr. . . . ?"

"Catchpool. Know what about him? Do you mean his state of health?"

"He hasn't long. Crying shame, I call it."

"Indeed."

"He's the only one as cares about me. Why can't one of the others die? One of them as never so much as looks at me."

"I say, steady on. You really ought not to—"

"Nasty snooty-nosed Claudia or bossy Dorro—they all look past me like I don't exist, or talk to me like I'm dirt on their shoes! I swear it, once Joseph's gone, I'll be gone too. I couldn't stay here without him. He says to me all the time, he says, 'Phyllis, you have great strength and beauty inside you. Silly old Brigid's not half the woman you are.' That's Cook, that is—he calls her Brigid, which is her name. 'She's not a patch on you, Phyllis,' he says to me. He says, 'That's why she needs to shout and you don't.' It's the weakest as have to shout the loudest, make others suffer, he says."

"I expect there is some truth in that."

Phyllis giggled.

"Did I say something funny?" I asked.

"Not you. Joseph. He says to me, he says, 'Phyllis, I don't have a kitchen, but if I ever do, if I am ever the proud owner of a kitchen . . .'—because that's how he talks! Oh, it makes me laugh, the way he says things. And, d'you know, I think that pompous Randall Kimpton copies him, the way he comes out with things, but he's not got Joseph's charm and he'll never have it, no matter how he tries. 'If I am ever the proud owner of a kitchen,' Joseph says to me, he says, 'I hereby solemnly swear that I shall never throw you out of it. On the contrary, I should want you to be in it all of the time and not least because I cannot so much as poach an egg!' See what I mean? He's so kind, is Joseph. I only stay for him."

Joseph Scotcher appeared to know precisely what to say in order to make others feel better. It was jolly decent of him to take the trouble, I thought—with strangers like me who happened to be visiting; with the servants.

As for Phyllis's contention that Randall Kimpton had it in mind to copy Scotcher, I found that rather puzzling. Kimpton struck me as very much himself and the sort of purposeful, fully formed chap who had always been that same self. From what little I had seen of him, I could not imagine him changing course for anybody. Well, perhaps for his beloved Claudia—but certainly not for Joseph Scotcher. Still, I had to concede that Phyllis probably knew both men far better than I did.

I wondered how many ripples of discomfort at Lillieoak Scotcher had been skillfully smoothing away since he had arrived. How would the other inhabitants of the house manage after his death?

Some people were more virtuous and self-sacrificing than others, there was no doubt about it. Claudia Playford, for instance, struck me as a woman who would do and say nothing for the benefit of anyone but herself.

At that moment the floor beneath me started to shake. Phyllis leapt to her feet. "She's coming!" she whispered, frantic. "Don't say I've told you anything or she'll have my guts for garters!"

A short, compact barrel of a woman came into view, stomping towards us. She had a red face and curly iron-gray hair that formed a stiff sort of circle around her head, like a wire crown.

"There you are!" She wiped her chunky red hands on her apron. "I've got better things to do than run around looking for you! Do you think the dinner's going to grow legs and walk to the dining room on its own? Do you?"

"No, Cook."

"'No, Cook'! Then get in there and serve it like a good girl!"

Phyllis scuttled away. I tried to make my escape at the same time, but Brigid moved to block my way. After looking me up and down for a few seconds, she said, "Meeting with the likes of you, bottom of the stairs when there's no one about—just what that girl needs! On and on she goes about that Scotcher fellow—wasting her time, whichever way you slice it—but next time, not when I'm trying to get dinner started, if you don't mind."

I think my mouth might well have fallen open.

Before I could protest, Brigid was marching away at speed, shaking the ground as she went.

The Announcement

I HAD EXPECTED TO be last to the dining room, but I arrived to find everybody speculating about what had become of Athelinda Playford. Her place at the head of the table was unoccupied. "Were you not with her?" Dorro Playford demanded of me, as if I jolly well ought to have been. I told her that I had been talking to Phyllis and had not seen Lady Playford.

"Dorro, stop being a harridan," said Randall Kimpton as I sat down between Orville Rolfe and Sophie Bourlet. "Piece of advice, Catchpool: never answer one of Dorro's questions—she will quickly come up with another nineteen at least. Whistle and look the other way. It's the only sensible approach."

I took a sip from my water glass to avoid having to respond. I would have reached for one of the wineglasses, but they had not yet been filled.

"Well, I would like to know where she has disappeared to!" A flush had spread across Dorro's cheeks. "Was she not only just with us? We were all in the drawing room together. She was there. You all saw her! And I didn't notice her go anywhere else. Did anybody?"

Still looking at me, Kimpton said loudly out of one side of his mouth, "Do not answer, I warn you."

The door opened and Lady Playford entered the room with her hair in a different arrangement from before—one I could not begin to describe if I tried for a hundred years. She looked as elegant as the room we were in, which was perfectly square with a high ceiling and red and gold curtains and chandeliers. It was considerably more aesthetically pleasing than the drawing room. This must have been intended by the architect as the main room of the house, I thought. I wondered if Lady Playford agreed.

Harry waited until his mother was halfway to the table before saying, "Look, here she is! Hello, old girl."

"Yes. Here she is," said Claudia. "Isn't it fortunate that nobody panicked?"

"Panic?" Lady Playford laughed. "Who would panic, and why?"

"I simply wanted to know where you had got to," Dorro said stiffly. "Dinner is delayed, and we have had no explanation."

"Well, that's easy enough," said Lady Playford. "The cause of the delay is what it always is: Brigid and Phyllis have had another pointless squabble. I heard the distant and sadly familiar sound of a mewling maid and, since I knew it would mean no food for the foreseeable future, I took the opportunity to do something different with my hair. It was too tight before."

"Then why wear it in that style in the first place?"

"Is that another question, Dorro?" said Kimpton. "You know, I might keep a tally tonight. And every night. How else will we know when you set a new record?"

Dorro said quietly, "One day, Randall, you will learn that being foul and being amusing are not the same thing."

"Come now, let us not carp at one another," said Joseph Scotcher. "We have guests, after all—some who have not visited Lillieoak before. Monsieur Poirot, Mr. Catchpool, I do hope you are enjoying your stay so far."

I made the appropriate response. I certainly was not bored at Lillieoak, and I was pleased to encounter Poirot again now that I was over the shock of it, but was I *enjoying* this evening? I felt as if I would have had to stand outside myself and watch for clues in order to attempt an accurate answer.

Poirot replied to the effect that he was having the most wonderful time, and it was not every day that one received an invitation from a famous writer.

Lady Playford said, "I cannot abide the word 'famous.'"

"She prefers 'popular,' 'esteemed,' 'acclaimed' or 'renowned,'" said Kimpton. "Don't you, Athie?"

"I am certain that all of those adjectives apply." Poirot smiled.

"I prefer a simpler one," said Scotcher.

"Is that because using long words aggravates your kidneys?" Claudia asked him.

What an unpleasant remark! I thought. Vicious, really. Astonishingly, no one reacted to it at all.

"I prefer the adjective 'best,'" Scotcher went on as if nothing had happened, looking at Lady Playford.

"Oh, Joseph!" She pretended to scold him, but it was plain to see that she was delighted by the compliment.

I was startled to find Claudia staring at me. The longer she did so, the more I felt as if I had unwittingly fallen into a dangerous machine and might never climb out. She said, "Joseph has told us all that he does not wish to be treated as an invalid. Therefore, I treat him as I treat everybody else."

"Yes, appallingly," said Kimpton with a grin. "Sorry, dearest one—you know I don't mean a word of it. And your treatment of me is exemplary, so who am I to complain?"

Claudia smiled coquettishly at him.

I made up my mind: no, I was not enjoying myself.

While Scotcher explained to Poirot that it was an honor for a humble man like himself to be secretary to the great Athelinda Playford, Claudia rather pointedly started a conversation of her own with Kimpton. Dorro took the opportunity to berate Harry for having failed to intercede on her behalf when Kimpton had attacked her—"Steady on, old girl! Hardly an attack, eh? Little bit of harmless teasing!"—and soon we were not one large group but many small ones, all conducting separate conversations.

Mercifully, the first course arrived not long afterwards, served ineptly by a red-eyed Phyllis. I noticed that Scotcher made a point of breaking away from his conversation with Poirot and turning to thank her fulsomely as she put down his portion of what Lady Playford described as "good old traditional English mutton broth." The way she said it made me think it must be her favorite thing to eat in the world. It smelled delicious, and I tucked in as soon as was decent.

The conversation died down as we applied ourselves to eating. Beside me, a loud creak came from Orville Rolfe's chair as he adjusted his position. "Is your chair all right, Catchpool?" he asked. "Mine is wobbly. There was a time when a chap making a chair would build it to last. Not anymore! Everything made nowadays is flimsy and disposable."

"Many people say so," I replied tactfully.

"Well?" said Rolfe. It was evidently a habit of his to demand an answer immediately after receiving one.

"I agree with you," I said, hoping that would put an end to the matter. I felt as uncomfortable as I would have if we were discussing his size, and irritated that I should be embarrassed while he seemed perfectly all right.

He finished his soup before anybody else, looked around and said, "Is there more? I don't know why modern bowls are made so small—do you, Catchpool? This one's shallow enough to be a side plate."

"I think they are probably a standard size."

"Well?" Rolfe adjusted his position again, giving rise to more loud creaking. I prayed his chair would last for the duration of the meal.

Joseph Scotcher was still talking to Poirot about Lady Playford's books. "As a detective, you more than most will find them a delight," he said.

"I am looking forward to reading many during my stay here," Poirot told him. "It was my intention to read one or two before I arrived, but alas, it was not to be."

Scotcher looked concerned. "I hope you have not been unwell," he said.

"No, nothing of that sort. I was engaged to offer my opinion on a case of murder in Hampshire and . . . let us say, it became complicated and frustrating."

"I trust your efforts were successful in the end," said Scotcher. "A chap like you is surely a stranger to failure."

"Which novel of Lady Playford's would you recommend that I read first?" Poirot asked.

That was interesting, I thought. Like Scotcher, I could not imagine Poirot failing to solve a case, and I had expected him to say something about the business in Hampshire having reached a satisfactory conclusion. Instead, he had altogether changed the subject.

"Oh, you *must* start with *Shrimp Seddon and the Lady in the Suit*," said Scotcher. "It's not the first, but it's the most straightforward and, in my humble opinion, the best introduction to Shrimp. It's also the first one I read, so I am sentimental about it for that reason."

"No," said Michael Gathercole. He had been talking to Lady Playford and Sophie Bourlet, but now he addressed Poirot. "One must read them in chronological order."

"*Oui*, I think I would prefer to do so," Poirot agreed.

"Then, like Michael here, you must be frightfully conventional," said Lady Playford with a twinkle in her eye. "Joseph's clever theory is that it's *better* to read books in the wrong order, if they are a series. He says—"

"Let him tell us himself, since we have the benefit of his company tonight," said Claudia. "We will have plenty of time to remember his wise words once he's dead, after all."

"Claudia!" said her mother. "That is quite enough!"

Sophie Bourlet had covered her mouth with her napkin and was blinking away tears.

Scotcher, however, was laughing. "Sincerely, I do not mind. Laughing about a thing takes the sting out of it, I find. Claudia and I understand one another well."

"Oh, we certainly do." Claudia smiled at him. There was something about her smile too. Not exactly flirtatiousness, but something . . . knowing. That was the only way I could describe it to myself.

"And in fact, doctors and the terminally ill joke about death all the time," said Scotcher. "Is that not so, Kimpton?"

Kimpton said coldly, "It is. I tend not to participate, however. I believe death ought to be taken seriously." Was he chastising Scotcher for mocking the idea of his own demise? Or for being overly familiar with Claudia? It was hard to tell.

To Poirot, Scotcher said, "My theory is simply this: when you read the Shrimp books in the *wrong* order, you meet Shrimp and Podge and the gang not at the beginning of their story, but in the middle. Certain things have already happened to them, and if you want to find out more about their histories, you have to read the earlier books. Now, to my mind, this is much more faithful to real life. For example, here I am meeting the great Hercule Poirot for the first time! I know only what I see of him and what he says to me in the present moment. But if I find him interesting enough—and I most certainly do—then I will endeavor to learn more about his past adventures. That was how I felt about Shrimp Seddon after reading *The Lady in the Suit*. It's terribly ingenious, Poirot, and contains the best Shrimp moment of all: when she discovers that 'hirsute' is another word for hairy, and realizes there is no lady in a suit! There never was!"

"You have just given away the resolution of the mystery," said Gathercole impatiently. "Why should Monsieur Poirot read it now that you've spoilt it for him?"

"Don't be silly, Michael." Lady Playford waved away his objection. "There are many intricacies to that story about which Joseph has said nothing. I should hope that nobody would read one of my books only to find out the answer. Monsieur Poirot, I am sure, is no philistine. It's the working out, and the psychology, that matters."

"Not you as well, Athie," Kimpton grumbled. "Psychology! Hobby for degenerates—that's all it is."

Scotcher appeared to regret his words. "Gathercole is quite right. How cloth-headed of me to reveal such a pivotal moment. I am aghast at my own stupidity. I allowed my love for Lady Playford's work to carry me quite away. I forgot myself."

Gathercole, at the other end of the table, was shaking his head in apparent disgust.

Poirot said, "I am not a philistine, but I enjoy a mystery and I prefer to try to work out the solution myself. Is that wrong, Lady Playford? Surely that is the point of a mystery?"

"Oh, yes. I mean, it is, but . . ." She looked doubtful. "I do hope the chicken arrives soon," she said, glancing towards the door.

Dorro said very quietly and without expression, "Nothing Joseph does is wrong. The opposite rule applies to me." It was not clear whether she intended to criticize herself or her mother-in-law.

"Of course you prefer not to have the mystery ruined for you by a fool like me," said Scotcher. "What appalling carelessness on my part. A million apologies, Monsieur Poirot. Though I must insist that you withhold your forgiveness indefinitely. Some sins are not deserving of pardon."

Claudia threw her head back and laughed. "Oh, Joseph, you are a scream!"

"I wish Phyllis would clear away the first course and bring the entrée," said Lady Playford. "I have an announcement to make, but let us see dinner on the table first."

"I see—an announcement that requires an amply lined stomach, is it?" Kimpton teased.

As soon as Phyllis had served what we were told was Brigid's finest dish, Chicken à la Rose, Lady Playford stood up. "Please, do not wait," she said. "I have something to say to you all. Many of you won't like it one bit, and nothing is ever better on an empty stomach."

"I do so agree," said Orville Rolfe. "Well?" He set about his chicken with a ferocious enthusiasm.

Lady Playford waited until a few more knives and forks had started to move before saying, "This afternoon I made a new will."

Dorro made a choking noise. "What? A new will? Why? How is it different from the old one?"

"I assume that is what we are about to hear," said Claudia. "Do tell, dearest Mama!"

"Do you know about this, Claudia?" Dorro fussed. "You sound as if you do!"

"Most of you will be shocked by what I am about to say." Lady Playford's words sounded rehearsed. "I must ask you all to trust me. I have confidence that all will be well."

"Out with it, Athie," said Kimpton.

In the silent ten or so seconds that followed—perhaps it was not even as long as that; it certainly felt far longer—I was acutely aware of the jagged breathing of everybody around the table. Dorro's long neck twitched and she gulped several times. She seemed barely able to sit still.

Lady Playford said, "According to the provisions of my new will—made this afternoon and witnessed by Michael Gathercole and Hatton—everything I own is to go to Joseph Scotcher upon my death."

"*What!*" Dorro's voice shook. Her thin lips were twisted in terror, as if she had come face-to-face with a grisly specter invisible to the rest of us.

"By everything, you mean . . . ?" Claudia prompted. She appeared unruffled; Kimpton too. They had an air about them of people watching a pantomime and rather enjoying it.

"I mean everything," Lady Playford said. "The Lillieoak estate, my houses in London, everything. All that I own."

7

The Reaction

SCOTCHER ROSE TO HIS feet so quickly, his chair crashed to the floor. He looked suddenly pale, as if he had heard bad news. "No," he said. "I never asked or expected . . . Please . . . There is no need . . ."

"Joseph, are you all right?" Sophie stood, ready to hurry over to him.

"Here, give him this." Kimpton, on her left, handed her his water glass. "He looks as if he needs it."

The nurse was soon by Scotcher's side. She placed one of her hands under his elbow, as if to hold him upright.

"It's always so upsetting to discover a vast fortune is one day to be yours," Kimpton remarked drily.

"Has everybody gone mad?" Dorro said. "Joseph is *dying*. He will be dead and buried before he has a chance to inherit anything! Is this some sort of cruel trick?"

"I am entirely serious," said Lady Playford. "Michael will confirm it."

Gathercole nodded. "It is true."

Claudia smiled. "I ought to have been able to guess. I imagine you have wanted to do this for some time, Mother. Though I'm surprised you cut off Harry, your favorite child."

"I do not have a favorite, Claudia, as well you know."

"Not in the family, no," her daughter murmured.

"Golly, this is a bit of a surprise," said Harry, wide-eyed. It was the first comment he had made.

Poirot, I noticed, was as still as a statue.

Orville Rolfe took the opportunity to jab me in the ribs—if you could call it a jab, from so amply padded an elbow—and say, "This chicken is excellent, Catchpool. Superb. Brigid is to be congratulated. Well? Tuck in, I should."

I'm afraid I could not persuade myself to reply.

"Isn't it rather pointless to leave one's money to someone who is about to die, when one is not likely to die oneself for a good many years?" Kimpton asked Lady Playford.

"Randall is right," said Scotcher. "You all know my predicament. Please, Athie, you have been so . . . There is really no need . . ." A complete sentence appeared to be too much for him. He looked ravaged.

Sophie picked up the chair that Scotcher had knocked to the floor. Having helped him back into a seated position, she handed him the glass of water. "Drink as much as you can," she urged. "You will feel better." Scotcher was barely able to hold the glass; Sophie had to help him steer it towards his mouth.

I found the whole spectacle curious. Of course Lady Playford's news would come as a shock, but why should it distress Scotcher to such an extent? Would not a puzzled "How silly, when I will not live to inherit and we all know it perfectly well" have been more appropriate to the occasion?

Dorro stood up. Her mouth opened and closed, but no words came out. She clutched at her dress. "Why do you hate me, Athie? You must know that Harry and I are the only ones who will suffer, and I cannot believe you hate your own son! Is this punishment for my failure to bear a child? Claudia doesn't need your money—she is about to marry into one of the richest families in the world."

Kimpton caught me looking at him. He smiled as if to say, "Didn't know, did you? It's true: I am quite as rich as Dorro makes me out to be."

"So it must be *me* that you seek to harm!" she went on. "Harry and me. Have you not cruelly deprived us already of what was rightfully ours? I *know* it was your doing and not the wish of Harry's late father, God rest his soul."

"What nonsense you invent," said Lady Playford. "Hate you, indeed—rubbish! As for your reference to my late husband's will, you have, I am afraid, mistaken your own feelings of disappointment for cruelty on my part."

Kimpton said, "Dorro, surely if Scotcher dies before Athie, everything will go to you and Harry as before. So why worry?"

"Mr. Gathercole, is it true what Randall says?" Dorro asked.

I was still reflecting upon the mention of the late Viscount Playford's will. What was the story, I wondered. Even in the midst of this unusual scene and amid the airing of family grievances, one could hardly say to Dorro, "What did you mean about Harry's father's will?"

"Yes," Michael Gathercole confirmed. "If Scotcher were to predecease Lady Playford, it would be exactly as if the terms of the old will still applied."

"You see, Dorro?" said Kimpton. "No need to worry."

"I wish to understand why this change was made," Dorro insisted, still clutching at her dress. She would rip the skirt in a moment if she kept it up. "Why leave everything to a man who will soon be rotting in the earth?"

"Oh, now, that was bitter!" said Scotcher.

"I *feel* bitter!" Turning to Lady Playford, Dorro pleaded, "What will Harry and I *do*? How will we *manage*? You must put this right at once!"

"I for one am glad to have proof at last," said Claudia.

"I quite agree that proof at last is the grail," said Kimpton. "But proof of what, dearest one?"

"Of how little we matter to Mother."

"Apart from *him*." Dorro jabbed an accusing finger at Scotcher. "And he isn't even family!"

At that moment, I happened to glance at Gathercole. What I saw caused me nearly to fall off my chair. His face was a deep, mottled red, and his lips trembled. Evidently he struggled to contain a powerful rage, or it might have been great anguish. Never have I seen a man look more likely to explode. No one else appeared to have noticed.

"I'm an old woman, and you, Joseph, are a young man," said Lady Playford. "I neither wish nor intend to outlive you. I am accustomed to getting what I want, you see. Hence my decision. It is well known among the best doctors that the psychological has a profound influence upon the physical, and so I have given you something to live for—something that many would *kill* for."

"Psychology again!" grumbled Kimpton. "Now an improved mood can cure a pair of shriveled brown kidneys! We doctors are surplus to requirements."

"You are disgusting, Randall," said Dorro. "Whatever will our guests think?"

"Is it 'shriveled' and 'brown' that you object to?" Kimpton asked her. "Would you mind explaining why those words are more offensive than 'rotting in the earth'?"

"Shut up!" cried Sophie Bourlet. "If you could only hear yourselves! You are *monsters*, the lot of you!"

"It is human nature that is the monster, not anybody at this table," said Lady Playford. "Tomorrow you will come with me to *my* doctor, Joseph. There's none finer. He can cure you if anyone can. Don't protest! It's all arranged."

"But there can be no cure for me. You know this, dear Athie. I have explained."

"I shall not believe it until I hear it from my own doctor. Not all medical men are equally intelligent and capable, Joseph. It is a profession that risks attracting those who find sickness and weakness attractive."

"I know what must be done." Dorro clapped her hands together. "Joseph must make a will naming Harry and Claudia as the beneficiaries. Mr. Gathercole, Mr. Rolfe, you will assist with this, won't you? Can it be done, quickly? I don't see why it should not be done! You evidently do not wish to steal from this family, Joseph—and I believe it *would* be theft if you were to allow what is rightfully ours to be left to you without putting in place—"

"That is enough, Dorro," Lady Playford said firmly. "Joseph, please take no notice. Theft! The very idea! It is no such thing."

"And what of Harry and me? We will starve! We will have nowhere to live! Where will we go? Have you made no provision for us *at all*? Oh, do not bother to answer! It gives you pleasure, does it not, to see me squirm and beg!"

"What an extraordinary thing to say," Lady Playford observed mildly.

"This is about Nicholas!" Dorro babbled on, wild-eyed. "In your mind, you have turned Joseph into Nicholas—your dead little boy, come back to life! The resemblance is quite apparent: both fair-haired and blue-eyed, both weak and sickly. But Nicholas cannot be brought back from the grave by this new will of yours! Nicholas, I am afraid, is *stone-cold dead* and will remain so!"

All movement at the table ceased. A few seconds later, without a word, Lady Playford left the dining room, closing the door quietly behind her.

"All those children you never had, Dorro?" said Kimpton. "Lucky blighters, I should say."

"Indeed," said Claudia. "Imagine."

"Mr. Gathercole, Mr. Rolfe—go after her, please." Dorro gestured frantically towards the door. "Make her see sense!"

"I'm afraid I cannot do as you ask," said Gathercole tonelessly. Whatever inner crisis had gripped him before seemed to have passed; he looked composed once again. He averted his eyes as he addressed Dorro, as if she were a gruesome spectacle that, once seen, might haunt a fellow forever. "Lady Playford is certain of her wishes in this matter, and I am satisfied that she is of sound mind."

"Mr. Rolfe, you must tackle her, then, if Mr. Gathercole is too lily-livered to try."

"Do not disturb Lady Playford, please," said Poirot. "She will wish to be alone for a while."

Claudia laughed. "Listen to him! He only arrived this afternoon, yet he talks with such authority about my mother."

Harry Playford leaned forward and addressed Scotcher. "How do you feel about all this, old boy? Bit rum, what?"

"Harry, you must believe me. I neither asked for this nor hoped for it—ever. I do not want it! Though I am, of course, deeply moved to learn that dear Athie cares for me to this extent, I never imagined . . ." He grimaced and changed course. "I should very much like to understand what is behind it, that is all. I cannot truly believe that she envisages a cure for me."

"You say you do not want it—then write down your wishes on a piece of paper!" said Dorro. "That is all you need do! Write down that you want everything to go to me and Harry, and we will sign our names as witnesses."

"All to go to *you* and Harry?" said Claudia. "What was it you said to Joseph about not even being family?"

"I meant to you and Harry." Dorro blushed. "You must forgive me. I scarcely know what I am saying! All I want is to make this right!"

"You spoke of my wishes, Dorro," said Scotcher. "I have only one wish. Sophie . . . I would kneel if I could, but I am feeling particularly unwell after all this commotion. Sophie, would you do me the great honor of agreeing to become my wife, as soon as it can be arranged? That is all I want."

"Oh!" Sophie exclaimed, taking a step back. "Oh, Joseph! Are you sure you want this? You have had a shock. Maybe you should wait before—"

"I have never been more certain of anything in my life, my dearest one."

"That is what I call Claudia," Kimpton muttered. "Kindly invent your own endearments, Scotcher."

"What would *you* know about kindness?" Sophie turned on him. "What would any of you know about it?"

"We should all leave you and Mr. Scotcher alone, mademoiselle," said Poirot. "Come—let us give them some privacy."

Privacy! That was rich, coming from Poirot, the world's most zealous interferer in other people's romantic affairs.

"You are taking this proposal of marriage seriously, then, Monsieur Poirot?" asked Claudia. "You do not wonder what is the point of it when Joseph has only weeks to live? Surely a sensible invalid would rather not be concerned with arduous wedding preparations."

"You are as bad as Randall! You are heartless tormentors, both of you!" Loathing seemed to pour from Sophie's eyes as she stared at Kimpton and Claudia.

"Heartless?" said Kimpton. "Incorrect. I have the valves, the chambers, the arteries that make a heart. My blood is pumped around my body in the same way yours is." He turned to Poirot. "This is what your psychology does, my friend—it has us all speaking as if muscle tissue were capable of finer feelings. Believe me, Sophie, when you've opened up as many bodies as I have and seen the hearts inside them—"

"Will you stop talking about disgusting, blood-soaked *organs*, while our plates are heaped with meat?" Dorro spat at him. "I cannot bear the sight of it, nor the smell." She pushed away her plate.

None of us had managed to eat very much, apart from Orville Rolfe, who had wolfed his entire dinner within a few seconds of it being placed in front of him.

"Dearest Sophie," said Scotcher. "Randall and Claudia are right: I do not have long to go. But I should like to spend what time I have left with you, as your faithful and loving husband. If you will have me, that is."

The sound of a strangled cry, cut off at its midpoint, made everyone look up. It had come from nobody in the room.

"Which nosy so-and-so has his or her waxy lug-hole pressed up against the door?" said Kimpton loudly.

We all heard the flurry of footsteps as the listener ran away.

"Joseph, you know I love you more than anything," said Sophie. She sounded—and it struck me as rather odd—as if she was pleading with him. "You know I would do anything for you."

"Well, then!" Scotcher smiled. At least, I think it was a smile. He appeared to be in a certain amount of pain.

"Monsieur Poirot is right," said Sophie. "We should be sensible and discuss this in private."

Two by two, the rest of us filed out of the room. Claudia and Kimpton went first, then Harry and Dorro. Ahead of Poirot and me were Gathercole and Rolfe. I overheard Rolfe's complaint that he had been promised a lemon chiffon cake for pudding; how, now that he had been forced away from the table, was he to be served this cake, and could Mr. Scotcher not have been a little less inconsiderate and postponed his proposal until dinner was properly concluded?

As for me, I had completely lost my appetite. "I need fresh air," I muttered to Poirot. "Sorry. I know you find that incomprehensible."

"*Non, mon ami*," he replied. "Tonight, I comprehend it only too well."

8

A Stroll in the Gardens

The first thing I did, as Poirot and I stepped outside, was gulp in air as if I'd been starved of it. There was something stifling about Lillieoak, something that made me want to escape its confines.

"This is the best time of day to walk in a garden," said Poirot. "When it is dark and one sees no plants or flowers."

I laughed. "Are you being deliberately silly? No gardener would agree with you."

"I like to savor the smell of a garden I cannot see. Do you smell it? The pine, and the lavender—oh, yes, very strongly the lavender. The nose is as important as the eyes. Ask any horticulturist." Poirot chuckled. "I think that if you and I were to meet the one who created this garden, I would make the more favorable impression upon him."

"I expect you think that about anyone the two of us might meet, whether they were a gardener or a postman," I said curtly.

"Who was at the door?"

"Pardon?"

"Someone was listening at the door—someone who made an

unhappy exclamation immediately after Joseph Scotcher asked the nurse Sophie to marry him."

"Yes, and who then ran away."

"Who was it, do you think?"

"Well, we know it was nobody in the dining room—so not you, me, Harry, Dorro, Claudia, Kimpton. It wasn't the two lawyers, Gathercole and Rolfe. It wasn't poor old Joseph Scotcher, whose running days are over, and nor was it his nurse, Sophie. That leaves Lady Playford, who had left the room by then, Brigid the cook, Hatton the butler, Phyllis the maid. It could have been any of them. I am inclined to believe it was Phyllis—she is besotted with Scotcher. She told me so herself, before dinner."

"And that is why you arrived late to the dining room?"

"Yes, it was."

Poirot nodded. "Shall we walk a little?" he suggested. "I can see the path now. It goes all the way around the lawn and will bring us back to the house."

"I have no wish to be brought back," I told him. I did not want to walk a neat square on a paved path. I should have liked to stride out across the grass, with no thought about how or when I would return.

"You are wrong," Poirot told me as we set off on the safe route of his choosing.

"About what?"

"The listener at the door who ran away—yes, it could have been Lady Playford, or the maid Phyllis, or Hatton, but it could not have been Brigid the cook. I caught a glimpse of her when I first arrived. I doubt she could move so quickly, and her tread would be heavier."

"Yes. Now that I think of it, the footsteps had a light and nimble aspect."

"'Nimble' is an interesting word. It suggests youth."

"I know. Which makes me think . . . It must have been Phyllis. As I said: we know she is enamored of Scotcher. And she's young and sprightly, isn't she? No one else is—no one who might have been listening outside that door. Hatton and Lady Playford are both older and move more slowly."

"So it was Phyllis," Poirot seemed content to agree. "Let us move on to our next question. Why would Lady Playford decide to change her will in such a peculiar way?"

"She told us why. She hopes that Scotcher's unconscious mind will exert its powerful influence—"

"That is senseless." Poirot dismissed my answer, only half-expressed. "Kidney failure is kidney failure. The prospect of all the riches in the world cannot reverse a terminal illness that has nearly run its course. Lady Playford is a woman of considerable intelligence, therefore she knows this. I do not believe that was her reason."

He stopped walking in order to disagree with himself. "Although the ability of people to believe what they hope is true is without limit, *mon ami*. If Lady Playford loves Joseph Scotcher very much, perhaps . . ."

I waited to see if he would say more. When it was clear he did not intend to, I said, "I think you were right the first time. If there's one thing I know about Athelinda Playford from her books, it's that she thinks of all kinds of peculiar motives and schemes that no one else would ever dream up. I think she was playing a game at the dinner table. She strikes me as the sort who would enjoy games."

"You think it is not real, this will that leaves her entire estate to Scotcher?" We had started to move again.

"No, I think it is," I said. What did I mean? I considered it carefully. "Making it real is part of her game. She's serious, all right—but that doesn't mean she isn't toying with everybody."

"For what reason, *mon ami*? For revenge, perhaps? The desire to punish—though not so severely as she might? A most interesting allusion was made to the late Viscount Playford's will. I wonder . . ."

"Yes, I have been wondering about it too."

"I think I can guess what happened. Usually the family estate passes to the son, the new viscount. Yet in this instance that evidently did not happen. Lady Playford, as we heard this evening, is the owner of the Lillieoak estate and of several houses in London. Therefore . . . an unusual arrangement must have been made by the late Viscount Playford. It is possible that he and Lady Playford did not believe the young Harry to be capable of taking on such a responsibility—"

"If that was their worry, one could scarcely blame them," I interjected. "Harry does rather give the impression of having a suet pudding between his ears, doesn't he?"

Poirot murmured his agreement, then said, "Or perhaps the reluctance of Lady Playford and her late husband had more to do with their daughter-in-law, who has shown her vicious streak most clearly in the short time we have known her."

"What do you mean about Lady Playford wanting to punish, but not too severely?"

"Let us say that she does not wish to disinherit her children—that would be too extreme. At the same time, it infuriates her that they take her for granted. Perhaps they are not as attentive as they might be. So she makes a new will leaving everything to Joseph Scotcher. She knows he will not outlive her—her new arrangements make no difference to him, apart from as a gesture. Now her children and her daughter-in-law will be nervous for the remainder of Scotcher's life, in case she should happen to die before him—after all, accidents do happen. When Scotcher dies from his illness, they will all breathe a sigh of relief and never again take for granted that everything belonging to Lady Playford will one day be theirs. They might treat her more considerately thereafter."

"I don't like that theory at all," I said. "Accidents *do* happen, and I cannot believe that Lady Playford would make so imprecise a plan. If she wanted her estate to go to her children, she would not take even the tiniest risk. As you say, she could fall down the stairs and break her neck tomorrow and everything would go to Scotcher."

I expected Poirot to argue the point, but he did not. We walked for a while in silence. My legs were starting to ache from the effort of adjusting my pace to match his. Someone ought to make a competitive sport out of trying to walk excessively slowly; it tests muscles of which one was previously unaware.

"I have an outlandish hypothesis," I said. "Imagine that Lady Playford has reason to believe one of her children intends to kill her."

"Ah!"

"You've already thought of this, I suppose."

"*Non, mon ami.* Continue."

"She is worried about her dying secretary, Joseph Scotcher. As a sort of mother figure to him, which is very likely how she sees herself—he is an orphan, and she lost a child—she doesn't want to die while he is alive and needs her. She hopes to stay alive in order to be of help and comfort to him during his final illness. At the same time, she knows her power is limited; if Harry or Claudia—or Dorro or Randall Kimpton for that matter—is serious about killing her, she might not be able to prevent it."

"So she changes her will to ensure that her would-be killer waits until Scotcher is dead before killing her?" said Poirot.

"Yes. She calculates that they *would* wait, in order to make sure of getting their hands on her money, the houses, the land. Exactly. And after Scotcher is dead, why should she care if she lives or dies? Her husband has already passed on, and losing Scotcher will be like losing a child all over again."

"Why would Lady Playford not go to the police if she believed her life was in danger?"

"That is a good point. Yes, she would, most probably. Which makes my exciting theory pure bunkum."

I heard a little laugh beside me. Poirot, like Athelinda Playford, enjoyed playing games with people. "You give up too easily, Catchpool. Lady Playford is not a young woman, as we have discussed. Many at her age do not like to travel. So, she did not go to the police.

Instead, she brought the police to her. You, *mon ami*. And she did better than that: she brought to her home the great detective Hercule Poirot."

"You think there is something in my hypothesis, then?"

"It is possible. It would be hard for a mother to say of one of her children, 'He plans to kill me,' especially to a stranger. She might try instead to push away the unbearable truth and approach the matter in a less direct fashion. Also, she may be unsure; she may lack the proof. Did you notice any interesting reactions to the news of the changed will?"

"Knocked everyone for six, didn't it? Caused a great to-do, and I doubt we've heard the end of it either."

"Not everyone seemed knocked for the six," Poirot said.

"Do you mean Harry Playford? Yes, you're right. He appeared equally unmoved by his wife's distress, by her cruel words about his dead brother, Nicholas, and by his mother's anguished departure that followed. I should say that Harry Playford is an even keel sort of fellow who could find himself at the center of an earthquake and barely notice. He strikes me as neither bright nor sensitive. I mean . . . gosh, that sounded rather harsher than I intended it to!"

"I agree, *mon ami*. So we can put to one side for the time being Harry Playford's unusual reaction and say that it is probably not unusual for him. I suspect that he has come to rely on his wife to express all the emotion for the two of them."

"Yes, Dorro does enough fretting for twelve people," I concurred. "You asked about unusual reactions—I don't suppose you noticed Gathercole's? He seemed to be struggling to contain some terrible grief or fury that threatened to burst forth. There was a moment, I confess, when I feared his efforts would fail and it would all come out, whatever it was."

"You describe it very well," said Poirot. "However, it was not the announcement of the new will that upset Mr. Gathercole. Remember, he had known for some hours and was perfectly composed when we all sat down at the table. So what altered his mood?"

"I've been puzzling over that very question," I said. "What happened that he might not have been prepared for? I suppose Scotcher's reaction was unexpected: he did not seem glad of the new arrangements at all, did he?"

"Understandably, he did not. Scotcher is close to death. What can he gain from this new will? Nothing. He will not live to see the money, so it spells only trouble for him—resentment from Dorro, from Claudia . . . which is why I wonder."

"What do you wonder?"

"Lady Playford's intention—perhaps it is not to benefit Scotcher but to incommode him. To cause him distress and inconvenience. That, after all, is the effect that we observed, and Lady Playford seems to be a person whose aim would not miss."

"What if she and Joseph Scotcher have jointly concocted some kind of plot?" I said.

"Why do you suggest it?" asked Poirot. We had reached the far side of the lawn, the spot that offered the best view of Lillieoak. People were supposed to stop here and admire the house.

"Oh, I don't know. It's only that their behavior struck me as similar somehow. Lady Playford leaves everything to a dying man who will not benefit from her generosity. Joseph Scotcher proposes marriage to a girl who, if she accepts him, will get deathbed duty instead of the romantic dream, before becoming a widow. In both cases, the promise of everything—one's dreams come true—but a vastly different and more desolate reality."

"That is an interesting observation," said Poirot as we walked on. "Yet I can imagine the desire to marry the one you love growing more urgent as life departs. There is great consolation in the symbolic union."

"What if Nurse Sophie ends up with the lot?" I said.

"While I think of the grand romantic gestures, you think of practicalities, *n'est-ce pas*?"

"You have not considered it? If he marries her, and Lady Playford dies before he does, to whom would her estate go? To Sophie, as Scotcher's wife."

"Catchpool. What is that noise?"

We stopped. It seemed to be coming from the bushes to our right: the distinct sound of a person weeping that soon gave way to an intermittent hissing noise.

"What on earth is that?" I asked Poirot.

"Frenzied whispering. Lower your voice, or they will hear us, if they have not already."

It was obvious as soon as he said it that the hissing I had heard was the sound of a frightened person trying to communicate quietly but urgently.

"There must be two of them out here," I whispered. "Shall we look for them?"

"In these gardens?" Poirot made a dismissive noise. "It would be more profitable to look for a particular leaf—the first one you saw when you arrived here."

"People are easier to find than leaves," I said.

"Not when you and I are strangers to these paths and others are not. No, we will return to the house. There is work for us to do. We must make ourselves busy. Once we are inside, we will be able to see who is there and who is not. That is more productive than looking for the needle in the hay."

"What did you mean about us having work to do?" I asked. "What sort of work?"

"I know now why we were invited here, you and I. It was not for our congenial company. *Non, pas du tout.* We are here to use our little gray cells. It is all part of Lady Playford's plan."

Before I had a chance to ask "What plan?" Poirot added quietly, as if as an afterthought, "We are here in order to prevent a murder."

King John

HATTON ADMITTED US TO the house. Predictably, he said nothing, though his bearing suggested that all three of us might benefit from the pretense that Poirot and I had not ventured outside and then needed to be let in again.

We went first to the dining room, which was empty, then to the drawing room. Here we found Harry, Dorro, Claudia and Randall Kimpton. A fire blazed in the grate, yet the room was still cold. All were seated and drinking what looked like brandy, apart from Kimpton. He had been fixing himself a drink, but after filling the glass he handed it to Poirot, who raised it to his nose. Whatever it was, it did not meet with his approval. He set it down on the nearest table without taking a sip. Kimpton was busy pouring a drink for me and so failed to notice.

"Have you heard any news?" Dorro asked, leaning forward. Her anxious eyes flitted from me to Poirot and back again.

"News of what, madame?"

"Joseph Scotcher's proposal of marriage to Sophie Bourlet. We left them alone in the dining room—well, it seemed tactful—but we have not seen or heard from them since. I had assumed they would join us in here. I should like to know the outcome."

"How delightful that you care, Dorro," said Kimpton. He lit a cigarette. Harry Playford took a silver case out of his pocket and lit one of his own.

"She said yes, naturally." Claudia yawned. "I don't see how anyone can think it in doubt. They will certainly marry, assuming the grim reaper allows sufficient time. It's terribly like *The Mikado*, isn't it? Do you know it, Monsieur Poirot? The Gilbert and Sullivan operetta? Wonderful music—killingly funny too. Nanki-Poo wants to marry Yum-Yum, but the only way he can is if he agrees to be beheaded by Ko-Ko, the Lord High Executioner, after exactly a month. He agrees, of course, because he adores Yum-Yum."

"Good chap," said Kimpton. "I should marry you even if it meant having my head chopped off in a month, dearest one."

"And then I should have a dilemma—whether to keep your head or your body," said Claudia. "I think, all things considered, the head."

What an alarming and illogical remark, I thought. Kimpton, to whom it had been addressed, seemed charmed by it.

"Why not keep both, my divine girl?" he asked. "Is there a rule forbidding it?"

"I think there must be, or else it's no fun at all," said Claudia. "Yes! If I refuse to choose between lifeless head and bloodless body, both will be taken away and burned, and I will have neither. I choose the head!"

"My mind is flattered, at the same time as sending signals to my extremities of great offense taken. I don't mind telling you it's a tricky balancing act, even for a brain as sophisticated as mine."

Claudia threw back her head and laughed.

I found this entire exchange astonishing, and—if I am to be honest—rather repulsive.

Dorro seemed to agree with me. "Can you not stop?" She covered her face with her hands. "Can the two of you never stop? A terrible thing has happened. This is no time to be frivolous."

"I disagree," said Kimpton. "Frivolity is free, after all. Heiresses and paupers may enjoy it alike."

"You are *beastly*, Randall." Dorro stared at him with loathing in her eyes. "Harry, have you nothing to say?"

"We'll all feel better after a snifter or two," said Harry matter-of-factly, looking down at the contents of his glass.

Kimpton took his drink and crossed the room to stand behind Claudia's chair. He leaned down, kissed her forehead and said, "'He is the half part of a blessed man, left to be finished by such as she, and she a fair divided excellence, whose fullness of perfection lies in him.'"

Claudia groaned. "Shakespeare's infernal *King John*. It is endlessly tiresome. I prefer your ideas to Mr. Shakespeare's, darling— they are more original."

"Where are the others?" asked Poirot.

"All in bed, I expect," said Claudia. "Mr. Gathercole and Mr. Rolfe have said good night. I cannot *think* why they should wish to extricate themselves, when the Playford family fun has barely started."

"I heard Mr. Rolfe say he was feeling unwell," said Dorro.

"Poor Scotcher looked sick as a dog too," said Harry.

"I'm sure Sophie has tucked him up in his nice warm deathbed," Claudia said.

"Stop it! Stop it at once, I can't bear it." Dorro's voice shook.

"I shall say what I like," Claudia told her. "Unlike you, Dorro, I know when there is a funny side and when there is none. Harry, how would you like to stuff Joseph's corpse and stick him up on the wall?"

I saw Poirot recoil at this, and I could hardly blame him. Did Randall Kimpton, a doctor, seriously intend to marry a woman who thought a man's tragic death was something to laugh about?

Dorro slammed her drink down on the table beside her. She folded her hands into fists, but couldn't keep her fingers still; they wriggled like worms. "There is not a soul who cares about *me*," she cried. "Even you do not care, Harry."

"Hm?" Her husband inspected her for a few seconds before saying, "Buck up, old girl. We'll muddle along."

"You're a fine one to be offended by a little deathbed joke, Dorro." Claudia narrowed her eyes at her sister-in-law. "Mother is sobbing in her room, I am sure, thanks to *your* harsh words. You accused her of trying to turn Joseph into Nicholas and make a substitute son of him. That is quite untrue."

"Don't! I could tear out my tongue!" Dorro crumpled. No longer puffed up with indignation, she began to cry. "I was beside myself, and it . . . it came out of me. I did not choose to say it."

"Yet say it you did," said Kimpton cheerfully. "'Stone-cold dead,' I believe it was."

"Please, let us not speak of it!" Dorro begged.

"What, of 'stone-cold dead' as your description of Nicholas? I noticed at the time that you drew out each syllable to the length of two. It was as if you wanted the saying of it to last as long as possible. What interests me most is this: if you had said 'dead' without the 'stone-cold,' would Athie have fled as she did? I doubt it. To my estimation, it was the 'stone-cold' that did it."

"You are an unkind man, Randall Kimpton," Dorro sobbed.

Harry Playford finally sat up and took notice. "Look here, Randall, is there any need for these jibes?"

Kimpton smiled. "If I believed you really wanted an answer, Harry, I would happily supply one."

"Well . . . jolly good, then," Harry said doubtfully.

"Jolly, *jolly* good," said Kimpton, and Claudia laughed her brittle laugh again.

I can honestly say that of all the family gatherings I have attended, including my own, I have never encountered a worse atmosphere than the one in the drawing room at Lillieoak that night. I still had not sat down and was not inclined to do so. Poirot, who preferred to be seated whenever possible, stood by my side.

"Why do we allow words to have such power over us?" Kimpton asked of nobody in particular. He had started to walk slowly around the room. "They are lost in air the moment they leave our mouths, yet they stay with us forever if they're arranged in a memorable order. How can three words—'stone-cold dead'—be so much more upsetting than the wordless memory of a dead child?"

Dorro rose from her chair. "And what about the way Athie has treated her two living children this evening? Why have you nothing to say on *that* subject? How dare you portray me as the aggressor and Athie as the victim, as if she is a frail old thing. She is stronger than any of us!"

Kimpton had stopped by the French windows. He said, "'Grief fills the room up of my absent child, lies in his bed, walks up and down with me, puts on his pretty looks, repeats his words, remembers me of all his gracious parts, stuffs out his vacant garments with his form. Then have I reason to be fond of grief?' Are you familiar with Shakespeare's *King John*, Poirot?"

"I am afraid not, monsieur. It is one of the few that I have not read."

"It's sublime. Brimming with love for king and country, and without the dreary structural straitjacket that Shakespeare so often insisted on imposing. Do you have a favorite of his plays?"

"I can attest to the excellence of many, but if I had to choose one . . . I am fond of *Julius Caesar*," said Poirot.

"An interesting and unusual choice. I'm impressed. Do you know, it is only because my favorite is *King John* that I pursued a career in medicine. If it were not for Shakespeare, I would be a man of letters and not a doctor. If ever I meet a dissatisfied patient, I make sure to tell them to blame Shakespeare, not me."

"Those poor desperately bored corpses on your autopsy table, darling," said Claudia.

Kimpton laughed. "You forget, I encounter the living as well as the dead, dearest one."

"No one with a beating heart could find you unsatisfactory in any particular. I assumed the dissatisfied patients you referred to were the corpses, therefore—dissatisfied with their own personal outcomes. Luckily they are in no position to say anything about it."

"I do not want to think or talk about death!" said Dorro. "Please."

"In what way do you owe your career in medicine to the play *King John*?" Poirot asked Kimpton.

"Hm? Oh, that. Yes indeed. I could probably have gotten away with *Julius Caesar*. Yes, I think I could have. It's a respectable if uncommon choice. One would not have to suffer the condemnation of one's peers or participate in ceaseless arguments that can have no clear winner. As a Shakespeare scholar, I was told every day that *Hamlet* and *King Lear* and *Macbeth* were vastly superior to *King John*. I disagreed, but how could I conclusively prove I was right? I could not! My enemies were able to produce many scholars who agreed with them, as if an army of head-nodders were proof of anything. One only has to look at the political situation to see that it is not so. Vast numbers of people on this tiny island believe they would be better off as an entirely separate country—"

"Please, can we not discuss politics, after all that has happened tonight?"

"Bless you, Dorro," said Kimpton. "Present me with a list of topics I am allowed to refer to, and the authority by which you seek to enforce your restrictions—moral or legal, I will allow either—and I will give your document my full consideration. In the meantime, I will finish my explanation to Poirot. Many in the Irish Free State view the English not as an asset but as an antagonist—which tells us, in my opinion, that many people are fools. It does not, however, settle the matter in dispute. What I am trying to say—circuitously, I will admit—is that some things are subjective and cannot be proven in an absolute sense. Whether or not *King John* is William Shakespeare's finest play is one of those things."

"While medicine is not," said Poirot.

"Quite correct." Kimpton smiled. "As someone who likes to win and prefers each victory to be unambiguous, I realized that I was better suited to a different kind of work. I am pleased to say that I made the right decision. Now my life is much more straightforward. I say, 'If we don't amputate this chap's leg, he will die,' or 'This lady was killed by a brain tumor—here it is, the size of a melon.' Nobody argues with me because they cannot. There is the melon-sized tumor for them all to see, or the dead fellow—dead from gangrene, with both of his legs still attached, thanks to an idiot optimist who erred on the side of hope rather than caution."

"You chose a profession that enables you to prove you are right," Poirot summarized.

"I did, yes. The study of literature is for those who enjoy speculation. I prefer to *know*. Tell me—all these murderers you've caught . . . in how many cases did you have absolute proof that would have held up in court if the beggar in question had not confessed? Because a confession proves nothing at all. I will prove it: I, Randall Kimpton, murdered Abraham Lincoln. I was not born when it happened, but nevertheless . . . I'm an ambitious young cove, so I did not let that stop me. I killed President Lincoln!"

Claudia cackled in appreciation. It was an alarming sound, but Kimpton seemed to like it.

"There are mysteries, also, in medicine, and much that cannot be proven," said Poirot. "The tumor in the brain, the missing leg . . . you choose examples that serve your purpose. You do not mention the patients who come to you with pain for which you are unable to find a cause."

"There have been a few, I will grant you that. But generally, if a chap sneezes and has a runny nose and swollen red nostrils, I can say he has a cold and no one will waste hours trying to prove me wrong. That is why I would far rather do my work than yours, old boy."

"And I, *mon ami*, would rather do mine. If anyone can look at the running nose and take the temperature and see the influenza, what then is the challenge?"

Kimpton started to chortle to himself, and before long he was laughing so hard, his whole body was shaking. "Hercule Poirot!" he said when finally he had composed himself. "How glad I am that you exist and that you are here! How marvelous that, after all you have accomplished, you still welcome the challenge presented by uncertainty. You are a better man than I. To me, uncertainty is a pestilence. It is a plague. But I am glad you disagree with me."

I sensed that Poirot was struggling to maintain his composure. For my part, I could cheerfully have punched Kimpton right on his insufferably smug nose. He made Poirot look shy and self-effacing in contrast.

"May I change the subject, monsieur?"

"Oh, I'm not the one in charge of which conversational topics are permitted," said Kimpton. "Dorro, how's your official document coming along? We need guidance."

"Have the four of you been together since you left the dining room?" Poirot asked. "And did you come from there directly to here?"

"Yes," said Claudia. "Why?"

"None of you was out in the garden approximately ten minutes ago, or fifteen?"

"No," said Dorro. "We left the dining room together and came in here. No one has been off on their own anywhere."

They all agreed on this.

That ruled out Harry, Dorro, Claudia and Kimpton. Unless they were lying, none of them was the person crying in the garden, nor the person heard whispering.

"I wish to ask of you all a favor," said Poirot. "Stay here, together in this room, until I return and say you may leave it."

"Since it's where the drinks are, I imagine we will all be happy to comply." Claudia held out her empty glass in Kimpton's direction. "Fill me up, darling."

"Why must we be sealed away?" Dorro asked tearfully. "What is all this about? I have done nothing wrong!"

"I do not yet know what it is all about, madame, but I hope to find out soon. Thank you for your cooperation, all of you," said Poirot. "Come, Catchpool."

I followed him out into the hall. When we reached the bottom of the stairs, he whispered, "Find the butler, Mr. Hatton. Ask him to show you whose bedroom is where. Knock on the door of every person staying tonight at Lillieoak and make sure that all are safe and well."

"But . . . won't that mean waking them up? Lady Playford might already be asleep—anyone might be."

"They will forgive you for waking them when you tell them it is necessary. Once you have satisfied yourself that everybody is unharmed, your next task will be to position yourself close to Lady Playford's room, in the corridor. You must remain there all night to keep watch, until she comes downstairs in the morning."

"What? When will I sleep?"

"Tomorrow. I will take over from you first thing in the morning." Seeing my astonished expression, Poirot added, "I would not be able to stay awake all night."

"Neither will I!"

"I rose very early this morning—"

"So did I! I too have arrived from England today, remember?"

"You are more than twenty years younger than me, *mon ami*. Trust Poirot. The system that I have devised is the one most likely to ensure the safety of Lady Playford."

"So she is the one, is she? When you said we were invited here to prevent a murder . . . you believe Lady Playford to be the intended victim?"

"It is possible."

"You do not sound sure."

Poirot frowned. "According to Mr. Kimpton, it is not possible for one in a subjective profession such as mine to be sure about anything."

10

Open Casket

FOR HATTON, NO ORDEAL could have been more excruciating than having to tell me which bedrooms were occupied by whom. As a result,
the process took longer than necessary. I managed to coax from him
most of the information I needed, but he seemed unwilling to tell me
where I might find Sophie Bourlet—so much so that I began to feel
uneasy. After nearly a full two minutes, I was finally rewarded with
a barely audible "Adjacent to the only other that's not upstairs, sir."

I knew what he meant at once: Sophie's bedroom was next to
Scotcher's—which made sound good sense, since it was she, presum-
ably, who wheeled him to breakfast every morning. There was no
reason to suspect that anything of an improper nature was going on
between them, and the possibility would not have crossed my mind
if Hatton had not folded and unfolded his lips so many times before
coming out with it, as if there were a shameful scandal to be covered
up. Silly fellow!

I went first to the servants' wing. Disturbing people when they
do not wish to be disturbed is not much fun, I discovered. Brigid

Marsh, in a hairnet and a dressing gown with large pink buttons, took the opportunity to launch a verbal assault against me by way of retaliation. For a reason I could not fathom, this involved shouting the provisional menus for tomorrow's lunch and dinner at my face until I backed away.

Phyllis was in her room. She took some time to come to the door, and when she did, she had a thick layer of white goo spread all over her face, which gave me a start. Harmless and pointless, I imagined— and insufficient to conceal two red, tearful eyes.

"I'm doing my face," she said, pointing at her chin.

I nodded. Why any person with umblemished skin should wish to daub herself with such a substance—or, having done so, to open her door so that others might see it—was a mystery to me. I had no doubt that the poor gullible girl's complexion would look the same tomorrow as it had earlier today; if she was hoping that this magic skin potion would make Joseph Scotcher decide he wanted to marry her and not Sophie Bourlet, she was almost certain to be disappointed.

I apologized for disturbing her, and withdrew.

Hatton I had only just spoken to, so I returned to the main part of the house, where I knocked on Joseph Scotcher's door first. There was no answer. I knocked again. Nothing.

He had looked distraught at dinner, and no doubt needed his rest more than most. How much would Poirot want me to wake him up? I wondered. Should I seek him out and ask?

No, I would leave Scotcher alone, I decided. It wasn't as if he was the person Poirot was worried about. Although the more I pondered it, the more I wondered if we *ought* to be concerned for Scotcher's safety. If Poirot was right and Lady Playford had invited the two of us to her house in order to prevent a murder, surely an obvious possible victim was the beneficiary of the new will.

I knocked again at the door, and this time it was opened imme-diately. "Yes?" Scotcher said in a weak voice. He wore navy blue and gold striped pajamas and a navy dressing gown, and he looked dreadful—worse than at dinner.

"I'm so sorry," I said. "Did I wake you?"

"No. I heard your first knock, but I'm afraid I can't get to the door as I once could. Even being on my feet . . ." He broke off, grimacing in pain.

"Let me help you."

"There is no need, really," Scotcher said, leaning against me. "I'm better alone. I shall be stronger in the morning. It is only the shock that has turned me for the worse. Why has she done it?"

"Lady Playford? I'm afraid I can't help you. I don't know her at all."

"No, of course not."

I helped him back to his bed and he thanked me fulsomely—I was in possession of a rare kindness and a generous spirit, apparently. The praise was excessive, but I could not help liking the man. It was rare to meet an overly appreciative person.

"Good night, Catchpool." He closed his eyes. "You too should get some sleep. You have had a long journey—all the way from London."

I assured him that I was fine, and moved on to Sophie Bourlet's room, cursing Poirot for the task he had assigned me, and my own weakness in agreeing to do his bidding.

When I knocked on Sophie's door, it swung open. It must not have been fully closed. "Miss Bourlet?" I called out. The wallpaper was pale blue with spirals of pink roses and there was a basin in the corner. The curtains were neither fully open nor fully closed.

When I did not get a reply, I entered. Sophie was not there, only her possessions in tidy piles, meticulously arranged as if ready for inspection.

Again I wondered what to do. Should I find Poirot and tell him the nurse was not in her bedroom? Should I search the house for her? If she was not here and not attending to Scotcher in his room, where could she be?

In the end, I decided I would check on the people upstairs before going back to Poirot, for I did not know how many bedrooms would turn out to be empty. There was a chance I might stumble across Sophie Bourlet, Michael Gathercole and Athelinda Playford all playing cards together, and I wanted to be properly apprised of the position before I reported back.

Lady Playford opened her door immediately. "Yes?" she said. I asked her if she was all right and she said drily, "Edward! Yes, thank you, I'm fine," with a silent "And you are the last person who would be able to help me if I were not" added at the end—unless I imagined it.

No, I had not. She had sounded cavalier and impatient, which, if she feared there was about to be an attempt on her life, was not the tone one would expect her to strike.

I knocked on Gathercole's door. Nothing. Sighing, I knocked again. I tried the handle to see if it would open, and it did. I walked into the room, which was in darkness. After a little stumbling, I found myself at the window. Pulling back one of the curtains let in enough light for me to see that Gathercole's bed was neatly made. The lawyer was nowhere in evidence.

I left the room, closing the door behind me, and moved on to Orville Rolfe's bedroom, which was next to Gathercole's. This was the last one to check, thank goodness. Harry, Dorro, Claudia and Kimpton were all downstairs in the drawing room.

Orville Rolfe opened his door wearing striped flannel pajamas. A sheen of perspiration covered his forehead. To my astonishment, he grabbed my forearm with his beefy hand. "Oh, Catchpool, the pain! It is agony! I cannot find a comfortable position. Where is the doctor chap, Kimpton? Fetch him at once, will you? Tell him I have been poisoned."

"Goodness. I'm sure you haven't been poisoned, Mr. Rolfe, but—"

"Well? Poisoned, I tell you! What else could it be? Will you go for Kimpton before it's too late?"

Had Poirot and I been invited to Lillieoak to prevent the poisoning of Orville Rolfe? Anything seemed possible.

"Yes, yes, all right. Wait here."

"Where else would I go? I am bent double in agony! Look at me! If you can't find Kimpton, bring that nurse! She'd be better than nothing."

I fairly leapt down the stairs, praying that Kimpton would not turn out to have disappeared, like Sophie Bourlet and Gathercole.

Were they together? Why had Gathercole looked so anguished at the dinner table, as if he was being torn apart inside? Did it have something to do with Sophie—perhaps with Scotcher's proposal of marriage to her? No, that had not happened until later. It could not be that.

Kimpton, thankfully, was still in the drawing room with Poirot, Claudia, Harry and Dorro. "Orville Rolfe is in great pain!" The words tumbled out of me. "Says he's been poisoned!"

Claudia let out a weary sigh and Kimpton laughed heartily. "Does he indeed? Well, I suppose it's been an unusual evening, so I shouldn't take anything for granted, but you needn't look so abject, Catchpool. Did you see how quickly he demolished his chicken? Trapped wind's all it is—feels like a thousand devils tearing at your gut, but I'll wager I can cure it in seconds with a sharp poke of my finger to the right part of his anatomy!"

"Afterwards, please make sure that finger keeps its distance from *my* anatomy," said Claudia, and Dorro scolded her for being vulgar.

"Dr. Kimpton, please go to Mr. Rolfe without delay," said Poirot. "Catchpool, you go with him."

"I will, but that's not all: Gathercole and Sophie Bourlet—both are not in their rooms. I don't know where they are."

"Viscount Playford and I will look for them," said Poirot. "And you two ladies, you will please stay together in this room. Yes?"

"If you insist," said Claudia. "But really, don't you think you are being a little hysterical? Nothing has actually happened apart from

Mr. Rolfe eating too much. Is there any reason to suppose Gathercole and Sophie have come to harm?"

"I pray that they have not," said Poirot.

As I followed Kimpton upstairs, I heard Claudia say to Dorro, "*I* should be the one searching the woods, while that demented Belgian waits in the drawing room and fusses like a girl!"

By the time Kimpton and I reached him, Orville Rolfe's skin had taken on a ghastly yellow sheen. He lay on his back, stretched out across his bed, with one leg dangling off it. So alarmed was I that I found myself saying to Kimpton, "Could it be poison?"

"What else is it likely to be?" Rolfe groaned. "I'm a goner! I can't breathe!"

"Poison my eye!" said Kimpton briskly, taking Rolfe's pulse. "You'll be quite all right in no more than an hour—that's my prediction. Can you turn over and lie on your side? And then bring your knees up to your chest? The more you can alter your position, the better."

"I can't move, I tell you!"

"Hm." Kimpton rubbed his chin thoughtfully. "I don't suppose you'd allow me to sit on your stomach, would you?"

Rolfe yowled like a wounded animal. Then his eyes widened and he tried to sit up. The attempt failed; he fell back down on the bed. "I heard them!" he said.

"Whom did you hear?" Kimpton flexed the fingers of both hands as he approached the prone lawyer, as if he were about to sit down at a piano and play a concerto. To me he said, "The problem is knowing where to apply the much-needed sharp jab. In a patient of a normal size, the skin is much closer to the organ."

"I heard them talking about it," Rolfe mumbled as perspiration dripped from his brow onto the pillowcase beneath him. "*He* said I had to die, that it could not be helped. And they talked about my funeral!"

"If you would consider eating less, and more slowly, there'd be no need for anybody to discuss your funeral for a good long while," said Kimpton, bending to examine Rolfe's right side. He flexed his fingers again.

"Wait," I said. "Mr. Rolfe, what exactly did you hear, and who said it?"

"Well?" Rolfe yelled at me. "Had to be open casket, that's what they said. 'Open casket: it's the only way.' Poison, you see. That's how I know. If you poison someone . . . Oh, the agony! Do something, Kimpton—are you a doctor or not?"

"Most certainly am!" With that, Kimpton thrust his index finger at great speed into the southerly region of Rolfe's middle section.

The lawyer let out a frightful howl. I took a step back. Voices were coming from outside: the sound of two people talking. "Ha!" Kimpton declared triumphantly. "First time lucky, I believe. You should feel better very soon, old boy."

I opened the window. "Poirot? Is that you?" I shouted into the night.

"*Oui, mon ami.* I am with the viscount."

"Hallo up there!" Harry Playford called out cheerfully—like a man who had forgotten that he had been disinherited earlier in the evening.

"Come quickly. Rolfe might have been poisoned."

The lawyer had not completed his sentence, but I thought I knew what he had been trying to say: that if you wanted or needed to give somebody an open casket funeral, poison was a method of murder that left the face intact.

"Utter rot, Catchpool." Kimpton sounded disappointed in me. "My diagnosis was correct: trapped wind. Look, he's stopped sweating, you will notice. Soon there will be no pain to speak of. Not very observant, are you?"

"I hope that I am," I said coolly.

"Well, you have failed to notice this: nothing that happens to Orville Rolfe is ever in any way attributable to Orville Rolfe. His chair creaks because it is poorly made; his feet ache because modern shoe-making techniques are lacking; his stomach pain is the fault of a mysterious poisoner and nothing to do with his determination, against the odds, to inhale an entire chicken in a fraction of a second. Look at him now!"

On the bed, Rolfe had started to snore.

Dorro and Claudia Playford appeared in the doorway. "What is that foul smell?" asked Dorro. "Is it cyanide? Doesn't cyanide smell vile like that?"

"There is no cyanide, and Mr. Rolfe is fine," said Kimpton. "And my index finger is the hero of the hour, though far too modest to draw attention to its own stellar performance." He wiggled it in the air.

Harry Playford appeared, out of breath. "Poison!" he announced to his wife. "Rolfe has been poisoned. Catchpool said so."

"What? But he's sleeping peacefully," said Dorro.

"He said something strange," I told them all. It appeared that Kimpton's diagnosis was correct on this occasion, but it was beyond me how anybody could feel triumphant about the release of some gas while ignoring Rolfe's peculiar story about the people who had discussed his death.

Nobody asked me to expand upon what I had said. They were all too busy laughing about Randall Kimpton's finger, or backing away from it in mock disgust, or (in Harry's case) staring at it with great admiration, as if it were the poet laureate. Not that Harry would have any interest in the poet laureate, I expect, unless there was a chance of stuffing his head and mounting it on a wall.

Where the devil was Poirot?

11

Overheard Voices

POIROT FINALLY APPEARED AND his face was a picture! Never had I seen a mere expression so full of urgent questions. Before he could ask any, I started to tell him what he needed to know. "He's recovering fast. Cried poison at first, which gave me a bit of a fright. Why should anybody wish to harm Orville Rolfe? It turns out that maybe they did not. Look, he's regained some color in his cheeks. Kimpton says all is well, and he's the doctor."

"Though my credentials were questioned by the patient," said Kimpton. "Ungrateful cur!"

I walked over to Poirot and said in whisper, so as not to be over-heard, "Rolfe said something that worried me." I was determined to tell this story to someone who would take it seriously.

"Wait, *mon ami*. Have you checked on Lady Playford?"

"Yes. She was perfectly well. And, really, her room is only across the landing. With all of us up here attending to Rolfe, no one would go anywhere near Lady Playford if their intention was to murder her and get away unnoticed. Besides, I don't think any of us has been alone for a moment."

"Some killers work in pairs, don't they?" said Kimpton, looking gleeful about having managed to eavesdrop successfully. Confound the man!

"Although, I grant you, it is hard to imagine that level of cooperation and shared purpose at Lillieoak," he added.

"Continue, Catchpool." Poirot dismissed the doctor's frivolity with a cold look.

There was no point trying to keep this part quiet, since Kimpton had heard it himself. "Rolfe said something odd about an open casket," I told Poirot. "He said—"

"Wait a moment, please. Viscount Playford, Dr. Kimpton—go outside, please, and look for Michael Gathercole and Sophie Bourlet. Both are still unaccounted for."

"Will do, old boy," said Harry. He left the room at once.

"I am going to bed," said Dorro. "It has been a horrible, exhausting evening."

Kimpton said to Poirot, "Gathercole and Sophie might be unaccounted for, but they are both grown-ups who may do as they please. As may I, now that Mr. Rolfe's digestive problems are happily resolved. And what I wish to do is take my dearest one here and exchange a few sweet nothings before retiring for the night. Is that permitted, Poirot? I don't understand why you and Catchpool have decided to proceed as if a murder is imminent, but you can hardly expect us all to play along with the charade, if I may be blunt—which I'm afraid I just have been."

"You must do as you choose, monsieur."

"Jolly dee! Well, good night, then!" He took Claudia's arm and steered her out of the room.

Poirot and I were left alone with Rolfe. Small snorting sounds came from him at regular intervals and his eyelids fluttered.

Finally I was able to tell Poirot what Rolfe had said about the open casket argument. Poirot listened carefully. Then, without a word by way of response, he crouched down by the side of the bed and gave one of the lawyer's large pink cheeks a slap.

Rolfe's eyes opened. "Steady on, old fellow," he said.

"You must wake up immediately," said Poirot.

This provoked a look of confusion. "Am I not awake now?"

"You are, monsieur. Do not fall asleep again, please. Catchpool tells me that you overheard someone saying that you must die, and that you must have an open casket funeral. Is that true? Did you hear this?"

"I did. That's why, when I thought I might have been poisoned . . . but the discomfort has eased considerably, so I am content to bow to Dr. Kimpton's expertise. It was not poison after all."

"Please repeat to me the exact words you heard, about the open casket," said Poirot.

"*He* said I must die, and that there was no other way. And they talked about my funeral—it had to be open casket, that's what they said."

"Who is 'he'?"

"I don't know. I could not hear clearly. A man—that is all I can tell you. A man saying I had to die. And a woman . . ." Rolfe stopped, frowned, carried on. "Yes, yes, a woman was trying to talk him out of it. I think it was only the man who wanted me dead."

"Did you recognize the voice of the woman?" Poirot asked.

"No, I'm afraid not."

"When did you hear this conversation?"

Rolfe looked a touch afraid to offer yet another disappointing answer. "I couldn't tell you. Sometime this afternoon. They were talking in the parlor, in lowered voices. They did not know I was in the library at the time, reading the newspaper."

"Is the library close to the parlor?" asked Poirot.

"Adjoining. There's a door between the two rooms. It was ever so slightly ajar. And it was not a conversation, it was a passionate disagreement. The woman disagreed about the need for an open casket. She was angry, and then he got angry too, and she said, 'Would you be so severe with *her,* or do you love her too much?' And then he said . . . oh dear!"

"Why 'oh dear,' monsieur?"

"No, blast it, I shall carry on," said Rolfe. "He assured her that nothing could be further from the truth, that she was his one and only true love."

My mind filled with names—possible pairings. I'm sure Poirot's did too. Harry and Dorro, Claudia and Randall, Joseph Scotcher and Sophie Bourlet. My fourth pair was more of a stretch: Michael Gathercole and Sophie Bourlet. I had no reason to assume there was any kind of romantic bond between them; it was only that they were the two people missing.

"I remember that phrase distinctly: 'my one and only true love,'" Rolfe said. "But I do wonder . . . The more I think about it, the more I wonder if I might have imagined it all."

I feared Poirot might slap him again, and harder this time.

"Imagined?" he said ominously.

"Yes. You see, I remember hearing all that, but not *thinking about* having heard it. I don't recall saying to myself, 'Who might that be? I wonder if I could take a peek and see who it is.' Surely I would have been keen to know, after all that talk of murder. Though all the overblown romantic rubbish sounded so silly, I might have dismissed the rest on its account, I suppose." Rolfe looked perplexed. "What if I was so delirious from the pain that I imagined the whole thing?"

"Do you think you imagined it?" I asked him.

"Well? I don't know! I rather suspect something might have distracted me. I wonder if . . . Yes, I do now recall that I had some terrible pain in my right foot earlier in the day. It set me thinking that the chaps who make shoes nowadays are really *criminally* remiss . . .

I remember the days when a shoe would give a man's foot some support. Not anymore!"

Poirot looked dissatisfied. "You did not, I suppose, tell anybody about what you overheard?"

"No."

"How did you know that the man and the woman were talking about you when they spoke of the open casket funeral?" Poirot asked. "Did either of them say, 'Mr. Orville Rolfe'?"

The lawyer's eyes widened as he considered this.

"I don't believe they did, no. I simply assumed it was me they were talking about because I was the one who had been poisoned—or so I thought. No, they definitely said 'he' and 'him,' with no name mentioned. I suppose they might have meant anyone. Any man, at least." Rolfe yawned. "I am about ready to drop, gentlemen—not from poison, but from fatigue. Might I . . . do you think?"

"We will leave you in peace," said Poirot. "Two final questions, if I may: apart from the pain in your stomach, did you have any reason to think someone might want to poison you?"

"No. Why? Do *you* think somebody wants to poison me?"

"I do not know. All in this house are strangers to me, and I to them."

"I suppose someone might want to kill me," Rolfe said phlegmatically.

"Why?"

"No reason I can think of. But one never knows if one is popular. People are generally polite, especially if one is a person of some influence, as I am."

Poirot nodded. "Mr. Rolfe, I would like to ask you about the late Viscount Playford's will. Dorro Playford referred to it at dinner."

"She did, and not for the first time—oh, not by *any* means for the first time. It's a rather long and involved story. Might you ask Gathercole? I cannot remember feeling as tired as I do now . . ."

His eyes had closed again. "We should let him sleep," I said.

Poirot and I left the room and closed the door behind us. I suggested that I might go outside and help Harry look for Gathercole and Sophie Bourlet.

"First bring me a chair—one with arms and a back that is comfortable," said Poirot. "I will sit here until you return, directly in front of the door of Mr. Rolfe. Then you will take my place so that I can go to bed. I shall, no doubt, fall asleep—but it does not matter. If anybody wishes to enter, they will first have to move me!"

"Enter Rolfe's room? So you have changed your mind about the intended murder victim, then? You think it is Orville Rolfe and not Lady Playford?"

"You heard what Mr. Rolfe said, Catchpool. 'He.' The person who needs to be disposed of is a man. And why the talk of poisoning if no poisoning has occurred? It is possible that Orville Rolfe might be in danger, but I do not know. I know considerably less than I need to know in order to act effectively. It is extremely frustrating."

Tentatively, I said, "I suppose there is an outside chance that Kimpton is right and no one at Lillieoak intends to harm anyone else. Rolfe might have dreamed up the open casket memory while unwell—delirious, as he said himself. And Lady Playford might have invited us here for another, entirely innocent, reason. For all we know, she will tell us tomorrow that she wishes to consult us about an idea for a book."

"It is possible, yes, that the situation might be less dangerous than I imagine," Poirot conceded. "Tomorrow I shall insist that Lady Playford reveals her true purpose in bringing us here. But remember, it is also possible that the danger is not to one person but to two."

I liked the way he said, "Remember . . . ," as if this were something I had once known.

Poirot explained: "If Orville Rolfe was the victim of a botched poisoning—a possibility I do not yet rule out—then he is in danger on account of what he heard when he was in the library. And if the 'he' of the open casket disagreement was *not* Mr. Rolfe, then that is somebody else who is in danger."

I knew what two potential murder victims meant: no sleep for me for the foreseeable future. The prospect made my eyelids feel twice as heavy as I made my way to the garden to look for Michael Gathercole and Sophie Bourlet.

12

Sophie Points a Finger

I FAILED TO FIND a single soul anywhere on the grounds, and would have called my search a waste of time were it not for the fact that the bracing wind and sheeting rain had between them driven away my drowsiness.

If Harry was still out here, I had seen no sign of him. I had shouted his name, and Gathercole's, and Sophie's, until my voice was hoarse. No luck.

Eventually I gave up and returned to the house. I headed upstairs and saw that Poirot had predicted the future with a good deal of accuracy: he had fallen asleep in the chair I had put there for him. He seemed at first to be snoring twice—a deep booming bass alternating with a light buzzing sound. It was an illusion: the louder, lower noises were coming from behind Orville Rolfe's bedroom door.

I took some pleasure in shaking Poirot until he opened his eyes. His hand went automatically to his mustache. "Well?" he demanded.

"I'm afraid I found neither Gathercole nor Sophie Bourlet," I said. "I didn't see Viscount Harry out there either. Did he come back inside, do you happen to know?"

"I could not say," said Poirot vaguely, and I decided he must have fallen asleep moments after I left him.

He turned around and looked at the closed door behind him. "What is that terrible noise Mr. Rolfe makes? It is like something from a nightmare."

"I'd say that din means nobody needs to guard his door. If he were to stop breathing—and snoring—we would know in seconds. We could dash over here and catch his killer red-handed."

Poirot stood up and pushed the chair out of the way. He opened the door and walked into Rolfe's bedroom.

"What are you doing?" I whispered loudly. "Come out of there!"

"You come in," he said.

"We cannot walk into the bedroom of a sleeping—"

"I am in already. Do not complain. Come in."

Reluctantly, I followed him. Once I was in, he closed the door. "Out there, someone could hear us," he said. "Mr. Rolfe will not mind us talking next to his bed. I do not think he will be easy to wake."

"Poirot, we simply can't—"

"So the lawyer, Gathercole, and the nurse, Sophie, are both vanished. Interesting. They might be lovers, I suppose. Sometimes, lovers make plots together . . ."

"No, I doubt that very much," I said, more firmly than I had intended to.

"Why? You know nothing about either of them."

"They might be plotting murders together for all I know. I meant that, in my opinion, they are not lovers. I cannot exactly tell you why, but . . . don't you sometimes get a feeling about people? Anyway, Sophie can hardly tear herself away from Joseph Scotcher."

"Why should it matter so much, the open casket funeral? What difference could it make, open or closed?"

"I can think of only one reason: so that someone attending the funeral could see the body and check that the person was really dead, or that the right person was in the coffin. With a closed casket, that would not be possible."

"Maybe someone has said, 'I will give you this or that amount of money if you kill him—but I need to see him with my own eyes, to know that he is dead,'" said Poirot.

"I'm sure all will become much clearer when you speak to Lady Playford in the—"

I was interrupted by a piercing howl that seemed to come from below my feet. It soon turned into a full-blooded scream. The voice belonged to a woman.

I hurried to the door and threw it open.

"Downstairs!" Poirot said, behind me. "Quickly! Do not wait for me—you are faster."

I ran without thinking, once nearly tripping. The screaming stopped for a few moments, then started up again. It was an unbearable noise—like an animal having its heart ripped out. In the gap—the small silence—I had heard exclamations of shock from upstairs, and doors opening.

Once downstairs, I ran to the drawing room and found it empty. Then I realized that the screaming sounded more distant now than it had from the landing; it had to be coming from the other side of the house.

I dashed back to the hall and saw Poirot and Dorro Playford hurrying down the stairs. I heard Poirot murmur, "The parlor," as they hared off towards the dining room. I followed, and soon located the source of the screams. It was Sophie Bourlet. She had her hat and coat on. She was not facing the dining room, but the room opposite. I assumed this was the parlor—in which the contentious conversation about an open casket had taken place between a man and a woman, if Orville Rolfe was to be believed.

Tears poured from Sophie's eyes as she wailed and shrieked, as if staring at a horror that could scarcely be imagined. She was standing outside the room, looking in. I could not see what she was looking at, but from her expression and the noise she was making, it must have been some sort of hellish vision.

Soon Poirot was at her side. "*Mon Dieu*," he muttered, trying to move the screaming nurse away from the doorway. "Do not look, mademoiselle. Do not look."

"But . . . that is *horrible*! I cannot understand why . . . and I mean, who . . . ?" Dorro looked around. "Harry! Harry! Where *are* you? Something unspeakable has happened in the parlor!"

I too was at the parlor door by now, and looked in, unable to imagine what I might see there. I shall spare the reader of this account a full and gruesome description. Suffice to say that Joseph Scotcher lay on the carpet beside his wheelchair, his body strangely twisted. He was dead; of that there could be no doubt—murdered, in a most appalling way. A club made of dark wood lay next to his body. It had his blood and brains all over its wider end. There was blood on the carpet, and very little left of poor Scotcher's head, only his lower jaw, which revealed a mouth twisted in agony.

Harry appeared behind me. He said to Dorro, "I'm here, old girl. What the devil is all the shouting about?"

"The devil," said Poirot quietly. "You are quite right, Viscount Playford. This is his work."

I had a sense, by now, of everybody having joined us. Many people were standing around me—in front or behind, or by my side. Claudia and Harry, and Lady Playford in a yellow silk dressing gown. Behind her, Randall Kimpton and Orville Rolfe stood side by side. Kimpton looked as if he was trying to say something—perhaps to take charge of the situation—but whatever instructions he was attempting to issue were inaudible in the chaos. Brigid and Hatton and Phyllis hovered behind Lady Playford. At the very back was Michael Gathercole. He too had on a coat, I noticed. Had he and Sophie been in the garden together all this time? Were they lovers?

Lady Playford covered her mouth with her hand, but nobody screamed apart from Sophie.

"Joseph!" she wailed. "Oh, no, no, my darling Joseph!" She broke free of Poirot's hold on her, ran to Scotcher's body and lay down beside it. "No, no, this cannot be, this cannot *be*!"

Lady Playford laid a hand on Poirot's arm. "Is it him, Poirot?" she asked. "Is it definitely him? His head . . . I mean, how can one be sure?"

"It is Mr. Scotcher, madame," said Poirot. "He is recognizable from his face—what is left of it—and from the thinness of his frame. No one else at Lillieoak is quite so thin."

"*Damn* you!" Lady Playford growled. A moment later she said, "I am so sorry, Poirot. This is not your fault."

Randall Kimpton murmured something, of which I missed the beginning: ". . . the jewel of life, by some damn'd hand, was robb'd and ta'en away." From Shakespeare's *King John*, no doubt.

I looked for Gathercole. He appeared serious but composed, and almost peaceful. Not in a state of extreme distress, I thought.

"She killed him! I saw her!"

Hearing these unlikely words, I turned back to the parlor. Sophie, who had made the accusation, was on her knees beside Scotcher's body, staring wildly at the rest of us.

Poirot took a step forward. "Mademoiselle, be very careful how you answer this question," he said. "You are understandably distraught, but you must tell the truth, and concentrate for a moment on the facts. Are you saying that you saw who killed Mr. Scotcher?"

"I saw her do it! She had the club in her hands and she . . . she beat him over the head with it. She wouldn't stop! He begged, but she wouldn't stop. She murdered him!"

"Who did, mademoiselle? Whom do you accuse of murder?"

Slowly, Sophie Bourlet rose to her feet. With a shaking arm, she pointed.

PART II

Enter the Gardaí

The following morning, the real murder detectives arrived. By "real," I mean the ones who were authorized to make arrests in County Cork, not the ones from England—and, if one wanted to be pedantic, from Belgium—who happened be lurking in the vicinity of the murder disguised as houseguests.

In the Irish Free State the police are known as "garda." This is an abbreviation of "Garda Síochána," of which a literal translation is "the guardian of the peace." One of the two policemen sent by the commissioner in Dublin to investigate the suspicious death of Joseph Scotcher fitted that description perfectly. Sergeant Daniel O'Dwyer—with a face as round as any clock's and spectacles that sat slightly askew on the bridge of his nose—contributed to harmonious relations by agreeing with whatever was suggested to him. He seemed to have nothing in his repertoire but unconditional assent.

He was the junior officer, however. The man in charge, Inspector Arthur Conree, was a trickier customer. In his middle fifties, with hair that did not move but loomed over his forehead like a large gray outcrop of rock, he had the peculiar habit of pressing the underside of his chin against the top of his chest when he listened, and raising it only slightly when speaking.

The first thing Conree did upon arrival at Lillieoak was deliver a small lecture that I think he intended as an introduction of sorts, but which came across more as a stern ticking-off. "I did not ask to be sent here," he told us. "All of the asking that took place was on the other side. 'It has to be you, Arthur,' they said. 'No one else would be quite suitable. This is an important case—none more so.' So I spoke to my wife. I can tell you that she did not want me to come all the way to Clonakilty any more than I wanted to take on the journey or the responsibility myself, at my age, and holding in consideration the various other burdens placed upon me."

"Strange, then, that you have ended up here, Inspector," Poirot remarked mildly.

Sergeant O'Dwyer nodded at this and said, "It is strange—you're right there, Mr. Poirot."

The inspector was not finished. "But my wife said, 'Arthur, they want it to be you, and if that's what they want, well, they must have their reasons. And let's face facts, now—who would do a better job? Why, there's not a man who could!' I have never made any such claim upon my own account, you understand, being a modest man; I am merely relating my wife's opinion. So we put it to our three lads— grown-up as they all are now . . ."

The story of what happened after Inspector Conree's sons joined the fray was conveyed at length and with a solemnity befitting a speech at a king's funeral. In summary: the junior Conrees, like Mrs. Conree, were worried that the esteemed head of their family might collapse under the strain of having to do his job, but all were agreed that without his expert leadership, there could be no resolution or justice.

"So," Conree concluded at long last. "Here I am. I shall be here until this distasteful matter is resolved, and I must insist that *everyone* in this house remains here too. Anyone who has work obligations must consider them canceled! You will all remain under this roof for as long as is necessary. I insist upon it. And I must insist upon something else before we go any further." He raised his right hand, which he had arranged into the shape of a gun—index finger pointing upward, thumb pointing back. He was in the habit of using the gesture for emphasis, we soon discovered.

"I must insist that the arrangements are as follows: I will be in charge of this investigation. I am the one who will assign duties and tasks—the *only* one."

Sergeant O'Dwyer's nodding had accelerated.

"Nothing will happen that I am not informed about," Conree went on. "Nothing will happen without my express permission. No one will go off to pursue any investigations without my say-so, based upon little *bright ideas* of their own." As he said "bright ideas," he made a most bizarre gesture with his hands near his head—as if he were trying to sprinkle imaginary confetti into his ears. "Your reputation goes before you, Mr. Poirot, and I will be glad of your cooperation in this matter, but you must follow my instructions to the letter. Is that clear?"

"Of course, Inspector." Poirot's presentation of his most charming and compliant façade in the face of Conree's provocation (I called it provocation, though I suppose it might simply have been his personality) made me suspicious. What was he up to?

"Good. As I say, I have no desire to be here. If there had been anyone else who could have handled this unpleasant business . . . Regrettably, there was not."

"Am I permitted to ask a question, Inspector?" Poirot asked, his every word and gesture oozing unconvincing deference. I tried not to laugh at his performance. "I am? Thank you. I should like to know if you intend to start by arresting Mademoiselle Claudia Playford? You have been informed, I believe, that the nurse Sophie Bourlet—"

The inspector waved Poirot's words away as if they were an

unpleasant odor. "I have no intention of arresting the daughter of Viscount Guy Playford simply because a nurse of no particular distinction has made a wild accusation against her," he said.

Poirot acknowledged the response to his question without commenting upon it.

Conree wasted no time in telling us all what to do. O'Dwyer was to stay at Lillieoak and supervise the local gardaí, who were on their way to comb the house for fingerprints and anything else they could find by way of evidence. The medical examiner would also be along to have a look at Scotcher's body.

My role—for I too was to remain at Lillieoak—was to keep the Playford family and their guests and servants out of the way of the police and, at the same time, get as much information from them as I could.

I found myself nodding as these instructions were barked at me. Then I wondered what kind of a chap Sergeant Daniel O'Dwyer had been when he had arrived for his first day at work. Proximity to Conree could make an ardent nodder out of anyone, I feared.

"Mr. Poirot, you and I will take this nurse, this Sophie person, to the garda station at Ballygurteen, where *you* will ask her questions and do your best to get to the bottom of her tale about seeing Claudia Playford taking a club to Scotcher's head. We must find out what is behind it."

"The nurse Sophie telling the truth might be behind it," said Poirot, wearing his most innocent face. "We must at least consider the possibility, despite her not being of the nobility. If I may say, Inspector . . . Mademoiselle Claudia denies the charge against her most emphatically, as she would if she were guilty or innocent, but what bothers me is the precise . . . what is the word? Ah, yes: the precise *flavor* of her denial. She is not afraid, or enraged. She shows no sign of confusion. She merely says with a mischievous smile, 'I did not do it.' She speaks as if she is confident of getting away with murder—yet here is the puzzle! I do not think she is guilty of that crime. No, I do not think so. She has the confidence, *bien sûr*, but . . ." Poirot shook his head.

"We must not speculate in this way," said Conree fiercely. "It achieves nothing. Let us see what the nurse has to say. I shall allow you to ask whatever questions you see fit, Poirot. I will do no more than listen."

So speculation was banned, I thought glumly. That was unfortunate, for there was rather a lot to puzzle over. Since pointing a shaking finger at Claudia, Sophie had spoken not a word, declining to repeat or withdraw her accusation of murder. Tears seemed to be all the young nurse could produce, and plenty of them.

Poirot, I should say—if I am allowed to jump ahead a little—returned from the Ballygurteen garda station in quite a foul temper. "The inspector asked *nothing*, Catchpool," he told me later that evening. "He made no contribution. It was I who asked all the questions."

"Did that not suit you?" I dared to say. "You normally want to ask all the questions. Besides, you knew that was the plan."

"I did not mind asking the questions. I objected only afterwards, when Conree told me that the listening was the most important part. His part! The words, sometimes, are neither here nor there, he said. What stupidity! The words, they are here *and* there! He does not recognize the illogic! To what does one listen if not the words? If one matters, then so must the other! Also, I too have ears! Does he imagine that Hercule Poirot does not listen adequately because he also speaks?"

"Oh dear, Poirot!"

"What, 'oh dear'?"

"However infuriating and pompous he is, we're stuck with him, so you might as well calm down. Learn to nod, like O'Dwyer and me. Now, stop griping and tell me what happened at Ballygurteen."

Poirot had started, he told me, by asking Sophie a series of questions at which she was unlikely to take fright:

"Do you think, mademoiselle, that you will stay on as private secretary to Lady Playford?"

Sophie had looked surprised at this. "I . . . I do not know." She, Poirot and Conree were in a small low-ceilinged room with windows that rattled when the wind blew. ("There was the illusion of being inside a building rather than outside, but that is all it was—an illusion," Poirot complained bitterly later. "The weather was in that room with us.")

"It is only that I notice you have been doing tasks that are . . . clerical, secretarial, for Lady Playford. Oh! I mean that you performed these tasks before the death of Mr. Scotcher. Of course, you have done no work since, and nobody would expect it."

Sophie said almost inaudibly, "I understood what you meant." Her tears had stopped as soon as the car had departed for Bally-gurteen, since when she had been as a ghost trapped among the living, devoid of hope and vitality, but resigned to her fate. Her clothes looked as if she had slept in them, and her hair hung untidily around her face. She was the only one whose outward appearance was dramatically altered.

"Am I right in surmising that you did the work that Mr. Scotcher was supposed to do for Lady Playford, once his illness advanced beyond a certain point?" Poirot asked her.

"Yes."

"And, at the same time, you nursed Mr. Scotcher? You were nurse and secretary combined?"

"I was able to manage it all."

"Has Lady Playford spoken to you, then, about staying on as her secretary?"

"No." Sophie produced the word after nearly half a minute and apparently with great effort. "Nor will she. I have accused her daughter of murder."

"Do you stand by the accusation you made against Mademoiselle Claudia?"

"Yes."

"Please describe exactly what you observed."

"What is the point? They will all say I did not see it, that it never happened. I must have murdered Joseph myself, they will tell you—even Athie will say it, because she is Claudia's mother and, compared with a daughter, I am nothing to her."

"I should still like to hear your account," Poirot assured her. "What, may I ask, was Claudia wearing?"

"Wearing? Her . . . her nightdress and dressing gown. You saw her, didn't you?"

"I did. That is why I ask. The last time I saw her before you started to scream was around twenty or twenty-five minutes after nine. Then, she was wearing the green evening gown she had worn all evening. Your screams did not summon us all to the parlor until ten minutes after ten. So, Claudia would have had time to change, of course—ample time. *But the dressing gown she was wearing when we all gathered downstairs after hearing you scream was white.* Plain white. I saw no blood on it—not a tiny splash or drop. If a person wearing white attacks with a club the head of a man, causing blood to flow all over the rug beneath him, there would also, I am certain, be blood on the attacker's clothing."

"I cannot explain everything that does not make sense," said Sophie quietly. "I have told you what I saw."

"Did Mademoiselle Claudia wear gloves?"

"No. Her hands were bare."

"To whom did the club belong?"

"It was Guy's—Lady Playford's late husband. He brought it back from one of his trips to Africa. It's been in the cabinet in the parlor since I first came to Lillieoak."

"Let us go back," said Poirot. "I would like to hear what happened after dinner. Start from when you and Mr. Scotcher were left alone in the dining room. Please include any detail you can remember. We must try to put together the complete sequence of events."

"Joseph and I talked. It was strange to find ourselves alone, after his public proposal of marriage. He was eager to have my answer."

"Did you give it to him?"

"Yes. I accepted without hesitation. But then Joseph wanted to talk about our wedding, and the arrangements, and how soon we could do this, that and the other—and all I could think of was how sickly he looked, how dreadfully weak. The business of Athie's will was a great shock to him. He needed to rest. I could see that even if he could not. I told him we would talk more tomorrow, not knowing . . ." She came to an abrupt halt.

"Not knowing that for him there would be no tomorrow?" Poirot suggested gently.

"Yes."

"So you persuaded him to retire to bed?"

"I did. I got him settled for the night and then I went out into the garden."

"For what purpose?"

"To be away from everybody. I wanted to run away, far from Lillieoak—but only to remove myself from the pain, not from Joseph. I would never have left him. And yet, it was unbearable."

"His illness, do you mean?"

"No." Sophie sighed. "It doesn't matter."

"Mademoiselle, please continue," Poirot urged.

"Even if Joseph and I had made it as far as the altar, what then? Our joy would soon have been snatched away. Lasting happiness was impossible."

In the corner of the room, Inspector Conree seemed to be trying to squash the knot of his tie with the underside of his chin.

"Pardon the impertinence, but did you cry when you were in the garden?" Poirot asked Sophie. "Loudly, so that someone might have overheard?"

She looked surprised. "No. I walked and walked."

"Did you encounter any other person on the grounds?"

"No."

"You did not whisper to anybody?"

"I did not."

"I was in the garden also, with Catchpool. We spoke at length."

"I heard nothing," said Sophie. "Only leaves rustling, and the wind."

"What time did you go outside and what time did you return to the house? Do you remember?"

"I went out a little after everybody left the dining room—everybody but Joseph and me, that is. I don't know what time that was, I'm afraid."

"It was five minutes before eight o'clock," Poirot told her.

"Then Joseph and I must have left the room at around ten minutes after eight. I helped him to prepare for bed for another fifteen or twenty minutes, and then I went outside. It must have been around thirty minutes past the hour when I went out."

"Then you left the house as Catchpool and I returned from our walk in the garden. We did not see you."

"I was quite unaware of the time. Perhaps I was five minutes later, or earlier."

"And what time did you return to the house?"

Sophie said angrily, "Why do you ask questions to which you know the answers? You all heard me scream. You all came running."

"But I do not know how long you had been inside the house when you screamed, mademoiselle. You started to scream at ten minutes after ten o'clock—that I know."

"I had come in from the garden no more than five minutes before that. I heard the shouting immediately. No one upstairs would have heard it, but I did, clearly, as soon as I closed the back door and shut out the wind. I heard Joseph begging for his life."

"What precisely did he say?" Poirot asked.

"I cannot bear to think of it! I must, I know. He said, 'Stop, stop! Please, Claudia! You don't have to—' He knew she would kill him. I should have flown at her as soon as I saw the club in her hand, but it did not seem possible . . . And then, the shock! I was paralyzed, Monsieur Poirot. It is my fault that Joseph is dead. If I had thrown myself on Claudia, I might have stopped her. I could have saved his life."

"Was it only Monsieur Scotcher that you heard speak? Did Claudia Playford say anything?"

Sophie frowned. Then suddenly her eyes widened. "Yes! Yes, she spoke of a woman named Iris. 'This is what Iris should have done,' or something like that. She said it while she was attacking Joseph."

"Please be as accurate as you can," Poirot urged. "It is important that I know her words."

"'This is what Iris should have done'—I'm certain of that part. And then, I think, 'But she was too weak—she let you live, and so you killed her.' Or maybe it was 'she let you kill her.' I was frozen. I could do nothing but scream and scream. I did not . . ." Sophie's voice cracked. "I did not attempt to save Joseph's life."

"Who is Iris?"

"I have no idea. Joseph never mentioned her in my presence."

"Yet Claudia Playford believes that he killed her," said Poirot.

"Joseph would not harm a soul. Claudia is a demon."

"Why were you so long in the garden on such a cold night?"

"I was too ashamed to return to the house. I was not myself at all.

"Capable Sophie, strong Sophie—that's how they all see me. Always on hand to take care of Joseph and Lady Playford and everybody. I needed some respite from being the person that everybody mistakes for me."

"I understand," said Poirot. "What did Claudia Playford do once she had finished attacking the head of Mr. Scotcher?"

"She dropped the club on the floor and ran from the room."

Inspector Conree raised his chin and said, "Claudia Playford and Randall Kimpton tell a different story. They say they were together in Dr. Kimpton's room from when they left the bedroom of Orville Rolfe until you started to scream downstairs."

"Then they have told you a lie," said Sophie simply.

14

Lady Playford's Two Lists

WHILE POIROT AND INSPECTOR Conree were in Ballygurteen with Sophie Bourlet, Sergeant O'Dwyer and I were in Lady Playford's study at Lillieoak. Since Scotcher's death she had refused to come downstairs. The luncheon tray on her desk had not been touched, I noticed, and her face looked markedly thinner, though less than twenty-four hours had passed since the tragedy.

"I left the dining room and went straight to my bedroom," she told Sergeant O'Dwyer. Her manner suggested that his question and any that might follow were a distraction. I had the distinct impression that she was trying to work something out on her own, and regarded interventions from others as a hindrance. "I did not eat dinner. You would find out anyway, so you might as well hear it from me. Mr. Catchpool might already have told you."

I indicated that I had not.

"My daughter-in-law, Dorro, made a remark that upset me. You must not think badly of her. She is a kind person who worries excessively, that is all. There is nobody in this house who is unkind or wicked, Sergeant. Even my daughter, Claudia, who has a punishingly sharp tongue sometimes . . ." Lady Playford straightened her back in preparation for what she was about to say. "Claudia is no more a killer than I am a pirate on the high seas. It's absurd."

"Then you believe that Sophie Bourlet is lying?" I said.

"No," said Lady Playford. "Sophie would not falsely accuse a person of murder. She has a good heart."

"Then . . ."

"I do not know! Believe me, I quite see the problem! I insist upon two things—that my daughter is not a murderer and that Sophie Bourlet would not falsely accuse her of murder—and those two things are irreconcilable."

"If I might just kindly ask, your ladyship . . ." Sergeant O'Dwyer seemed to introduce all his questions with these words. "You returned to your room—and did you leave it again, or did you stay in it, or what did you do after that?"

"I stayed in my room, alone, until I heard Sophie's distant screams and people running along the landing. In all that time I was disturbed only when Mr. Catchpool knocked at my door. He wanted to check that nothing terrible had happened to me."

"Poirot asked me to make certain of everybody's safety," I told O'Dwyer. "I found that all were safe and well except for Sophie Bourlet and Michael Gathercole, who were nowhere to be found, and Joseph Scotcher and Orville Rolfe, who were in their rooms but not at all well."

"If I might just kindly ask, your ladyship . . . Scotcher was dying of Bright's disease of the kidneys, is that right, now?"

"That is correct."

"And the upsetting remark that your daughter-in-law made. I should like to hear about it, if you don't mind."

"She said that I was trying to pretend that Joseph Scotcher was my son Nicholas, who died as a child. She described Nicholas as 'stone-cold dead.' As of course he is. I know that perfectly well. What upset me was not the unpleasant reality, which I accepted long ago, but that Dorro would choose to say such a thing to me."

"She regretted it soon afterwards," I could not help saying. "She was terribly upset later, in the drawing room, and wished she could take it back."

"Yes," said Lady Playford thoughtfully. "One ought not to use words carelessly, or even spontaneously. Once they are launched, they cannot be called back. I have been unhappy on many occasions, but never once have I used a word or words that I have not carefully chosen."

"I'd agree with you there," said O'Dwyer. "If anybody has a talent for choosing words, it's you, your ladyship."

"And yet, thanks to me, poor Joseph is dead." Tears shone in her eyes.

"You must not blame yourself," I told her.

"Now there Inspector Catchpool and I are of one mind," said O'Dwyer. "Whoever is to blame for Mr. Scotcher's demise is the one that coshed him over the head with the club."

"It's kind of you to try, gentlemen, but you will never convince me this was not my fault. I changed my will in a way that was designed to provoke. I made a theatrical spectacle of the announcement, over dinner."

"Yet you did not expect Joseph Scotcher to be murdered a few hours later," I said.

"No. Had I considered the possibility, I would have concluded it was out of the question. Shall I tell you why? Because the only sensible motives for this murder belong to those who would never commit the act. My son Harry—unthinkable! As for my daughter, Claudia . . . You might not believe this, Edward—may I call you Edward?—but the psychology is all wrong. It cannot be Claudia."

"What makes you so sure?"

"A violent murder is the last resort of a person whose passionate rage or burning resentment has been locked inside them for too long—for a lifetime!—with no means of escape," Lady Playford said. "Finally, the cork pops. The glass shatters! My daughter's simmering fury—which has been with her since childhood, despite having no discernible cause—has garnered quite an audience in the daily run of things. Far from keeping it stoppered up all her life, she has broadcast it far and wide, to anyone who crosses her path. Bitterness emanates from her as she stomps around the house feeling aggrieved on her own behalf, and she gives full vent to it. I am sure you have noticed, Edward."

"Well . . ."

"You are too polite to say so. Claudia could lay waste to an army simply by opening her mouth and speaking her mind. For her to pick up a club and batter a man's head with it . . . words would first have to fail her, and I assure you, no such thing has happened."

"And Dorro?" I said.

"Are you asking if Dorro might have killed Joseph? The idea is laughable! Oh, she was in a bate at the prospect of inheriting nothing, but Dorro is a fearful woman. More importantly, she is a pessimist. She could not commit murder without feeling that discovery, conviction and execution were almost guaranteed, and that trio of unfortunate consequences would deter her. Anyhow, why should Sophie pretend she saw Claudia doing it if Dorro was the one she saw?"

"What about your daughter's young man—Randall Kimpton?" I asked.

Lady Playford looked surprised. "Why should Randall wish to kill Joseph? His only motive would be money, and he already has it in abundance."

It was all very well her insisting that this, that and the other person could not possibly have murdered Scotcher. Someone had. That was beyond doubt. "Whom do you suspect?" I asked.

"Nobody. 'Suspect' suggests a firm belief, and I have none. I have two lists in my mind, and nothing more."

"Lists?"

"Those who are innocent beyond all doubt, and the rest."

"When you say 'beyond all doubt'—"

"From my knowledge of their characters."

"Might we hear the two lists, your ladyship?" asked O'Dwyer.

"If you must. The innocents are: Harry, Claudia, Dorro, Michael Gathercole, Sophie Bourlet. The others are—forgive me, Edward— Edward Catchpool, Hercule Poirot—"

"I beg your pardon? Poirot and I are on your list of potential murderers?"

"I have every confidence that neither of you murdered Joseph, but I do not *know* it," Lady Playford said with a hint of impatience. "I cannot say that you, or Poirot, would *never* commit murder. If it makes you feel any better, I could not say it of myself. In the right circumstances . . . For instance, if I knew who had killed Joseph, I might well find the largest, sharpest knife in the house and stick it into them. I should enjoy it too!"

There was a knock at the door.

"I don't want to speak to anybody else," Lady Playford said urgently, as if speaking to me and Sergeant O'Dwyer were quite enough of an ordeal. "One of you shoo them away, whoever it is."

It was Hatton, the butler. The crisis conditions at Lillieoak seemed to have restored his ability to speak when necessary. "There is a message for you from Monsieur Poirot, Mr. Catchpool," he whispered efficiently, leaning forward to aim the words directly at my ear. "He telephoned. He wishes you to ask everybody if they know a woman by the name of Iris."

I wondered if Inspector Conree shared this wish of Poirot's.

"Hatton, Brigid, Orville Rolfe—and Randall Kimpton in some circumstances, though *never* for money," said Lady Playford once the butler had gone. "They are all on my list of possible murderers. The person who poses the gravest problem is Phyllis. She *adored* Joseph—hung on his every word. I do not believe she would have harmed him. On the other hand, she is slow-witted, and it is never difficult to persuade that sort of person to do the wrong thing."

"If I could trouble you to answer one more question, your lady-ship," said O'Dwyer. "It's about your new will."

"I thought it might be."

"Why did you decide to change it in the way that you did, with Mr. Scotcher so close to death's door? Did you not believe he was bound to die before you?"

"I have answered that question already," said Lady Playford wearily. "I do not wish to repeat myself yet again. Edward here will be able to tell you."

I nodded, remembering her impressive performance in the dining room. Physical health is affected by psychology, therefore Scotcher might be persuaded to last a little longer if he knew he would one day inherit a fortune. I had not been convinced at the time and I was no more convinced now.

"I wonder if you would mind talking a little about your late husband's will, Lady Playford," I said hesitantly, half expecting her to shout at me to be quiet and stick to the subject at hand.

"Guy? Oh—you mean because of what Dorro said at dinner? No, I don't mind in the least. It was not an easy decision to make, but my husband and I knew it was the right one. You've seen Harry. If Lillieoak and everything that was Guy's had passed to him in the customary fashion, it would not have been him making the decisions and running things, it would have been Dorro, and—"

Lady Playford broke off abruptly. After making an impatient noise she continued. "I might as well finish, now that I have started, whatever you will think of me. I love Dorro well enough, but I do not trust her. Neither does Claudia—and Lillieoak is her family home as much as it is Harry's. And, really, the fact that things are habitually done a certain way does not mean they must always be done that way. I am Guy's widow—frankly, I don't see why I should be pushed aside any more than Claudia should be. Why should I leave my home that I love and let Dorro take over? And Harry and Claudia receive allowances that *are* generous and cover all their needs, whatever Dorro's opinion might be. Guy quite agreed," she added as an afterthought.

I was glad this was the sort of problem I was never likely to have. "Do you know a person by the name of Iris?" I asked Lady Playford.

"Iris? No. Whom do you mean?"

I wished I knew.

"No. I know of no Iris."

Her denial was convincing. All the same, I could not help thinking that if anyone could tell a lie and make the world believe it, that person was surely Athelinda Playford.

15

Seeing, Hearing and Looking

WHILE SERGEANT O'DWYER CONFERRED with the police doctor, and organized the local gardaí who were charged with searching Lillieoak, I went in search of Gathercole. I wanted to speak to him alone, and guessed that I would miss nothing that mattered if I left O'Dwyer to his own devices for the time being. After the gardaí, Orville Rolfe was next on his list. Rolfe was the one person who could not have killed Joseph Scotcher, as far as I could see. Between when I knocked on Scotcher's door, finding him alive, and when I knocked on Rolfe's and encountered him in his unwell state, there were no means by which Rolfe could have gotten downstairs without passing me, and I would certainly have noticed if he had done so.

He did not. And after that, either I or Poirot was with him, or else confining him to his room by means of a large chair outside his door, until Sophie Bourlet screamed. That seemed conclusively to rule out Orville Rolfe.

I searched the house for Gathercole and did not find him, so I went outside to stroll around the gardens. After about ten minutes of walking wherever the fancy took me, I saw him in the distance. He was standing with his hands in his pockets, staring down at a row of rosebushes. I approached slowly so as not to scare him away.

He looked up and almost smiled at me, then turned quickly to glance up at the house. Was he looking at a particular window, or at the house in general? I could not tell.

He stared at the building for some seconds before turning back towards me. At that moment, I was struck by an interesting notion. It was watching Gathercole that had put it into my mind.

"Are you all right?" he asked me.

"Would you mind awfully if I tried out an idea on you?" I said. "I had it only a moment ago, and I shall find it hard to think about anything else until I have discussed it with someone."

"By all means."

"When you looked up at the house just now, I remembered something that Lady Playford said when Sergeant O'Dwyer and I spoke to her."

"Go on."

"It was a question: why should Sophie Bourlet pretend she saw Claudia Playford murder Scotcher if in fact Dorro Playford was the one she saw?"

"Dorro? I don't understand. Has it been suggested that Dorro—"

"No. The opposite," I assured him. "Lady Playford was telling us that Dorro was on her list of those who are innocent beyond doubt. In support of this, she asked her question: why should Sophie say she had seen Claudia clubbing Scotcher to death if in truth it was Dorro that she saw? Lady Playford asked this as if the answer were so obvious, it should not need stating: 'Well, of course she would not!' That was what Sergeant O'Dwyer and I were supposed to think, and I duly did. Until a few moments ago."

"And now what do you think?" Gathercole asked.

"Shall we walk?" I suggested. He shrugged, but followed me when I started to move.

I decided it could do no harm to share my ideas with him. I might even tell Poirot later that I had done so. "Let's assume Sophie saw *someone*—we do not know whom—lift a club and bring it down once, twice, three times, maybe more, on poor Scotcher's head. She is so horrified by the sight that she screams and screams, bringing everyone rushing down the stairs to see what is amiss."

"That is what she says happened," Gathercole agreed as we walked between two rows of lime trees.

"Imagine the horror of witnessing such a thing happening to the person you love. Anyone might scream uncontrollably."

"I daresay."

"Imagine this too: in your state of shock, you make an almighty din. You can't help it. Straightaway, you hear footsteps and cries of 'What on earth is that?' Soon they will all be upon you, and you will have to explain that you witnessed a murder . . . and that's when it dawns on you!"

"What?"

"That the person you saw clubbing Scotcher to death is *someone you cannot bring yourself to name as his killer*," I said. "Someone you want to protect, would want to protect no matter what they had done. What do you do? Why, you tell as much of the truth as you can, and you simply substitute someone you dislike and regard as dispensable—Claudia Playford—for the real murderer. This was my brain wave when I saw you looking up at the window of Lady Playford's study! I *saw* you, you see. There would have been no use in telling me you did not look, because I know you did."

Why had he? I wondered. Did he want to make sure Lady Playford was not watching before he embarked upon a conversation with me?

"In exactly the same way, *we all heard Sophie Bourlet witnessing the murder of Joseph Scotcher*," I went on. "She screamed because she could not help herself—but having done so, she could not pretend that she had *not* just seen someone kill Scotcher. There she was, frozen by the door, with his dead body in front of her! And if she was unwilling to name the true culprit, and decided to lie and say it was Claudia, well, then it might have been anyone. And the answer to Lady Playford's question—why accuse Claudia if she saw Dorro do it?—is then perfectly simple: Sophie wanted to save the true murderer from the gallows."

Gathercole came to an abrupt halt. "Will you pardon me if I point out an error in your reasoning?"

"Please go ahead."

"If Sophie wanted to protect Scotcher's killer, she needn't have admitted she witnessed the murder. Her screams were adequately explained if she had simply found the battered body of the man she loved. We would all have accepted that without question."

"Indeed we would. But in her state of extreme shock and distress, that might not have occurred to her."

"Perhaps not," Gathercole conceded less than wholeheartedly.

"Did you come down the stairs?" I asked him as we began to walk again.

"I beg your pardon?"

"When Sophie started to make her commotion—did you come down the stairs with the rest of us? Suddenly you were there, but you were dressed for outdoors, as I recall. And before that, I had been unable to find you."

"I went out. Walked all the way down to the river and back. I find water calming. Our evening so far had been . . . less so."

"If you don't mind my asking, where were you when you heard Sophie scream?"

"At the front door. I had returned to the house mere seconds before. I made my way to where the noise seemed to be coming from and there you all were. I think I was the last to arrive."

Nervous about what I wanted to say next, I did my best to appear casual about it. "I say, do you mind if I ask you something else? It's been on my mind since we all sat around the dining table together."

"What would you like to know?"

"After Lady Playford left the room, there was a moment when you looked . . . well, quite beside yourself. Utterly desolate. It was as if something had upset or enraged you. I only wondered . . ."

"I was concerned about Lady Playford," said Gathercole. "She had left the room in response to Dorro's unkindness—which was unforgivable."

I did not believe him. His voice had changed to something less natural than before.

"Unforgivable? Dorro regretted saying it soon afterwards, you know. She was also in a state of shock, and frightened about her future, and Harry's."

"Yes," Gathercole said briskly. "I might have judged her too harshly."

He was withholding something important. The faster he walked, and the longer he kept his head turned away from me, the more certain I became.

I decided to take a risk. "Listen, I work for Scotland Yard. My job, whatever the crime, is to suspect everybody. In this case, I am guilty of negligence: I suspect everybody except you."

"Then you are foolish," he said. "You know nothing of my character."

"I believe I do. And I believe there is something you are keeping back, something relating to your expression of despair in the dining room—"

"Expression of despair! You are too fanciful. May we please change the subject?"

I decided we might as well, since I was getting nowhere. "Do you know, or know of, a woman called Iris?" I asked him.

He pulled a handkerchief out of his pocket and used it to wipe his face. "No," he said. "I do not."

16

Down in the Dumps

It was vexing to have to ask everybody about Poirot's Iris without knowing who she was, or why he thought her so important. When Sergeant O'Dwyer and I sat down with Harry and Dorro Playford in the library, I decided to get her out of the way first.

"Iris is a pretty name," said Harry Playford. "Not sure I know any Irises. Do you, Dorro? Although, wait a second! What about the lady who made that hat for Mother? You know, with the pink lace. She had a little white terrier—Prince, was it? Yappy thing." Harry's demeanor was relaxed and jovial. Murder in his home had not put a crimp in his mood, it seemed. If he was afraid of falling under suspicion, or if he was mourning the demise of Joseph Scotcher, he showed no sign of either.

His wife, by contrast, twitched like a frightened mouse. Her eyes would not keep still; it made me dizzy to look at her. "The hat lady's name was Agnes," she said. "Did you mean Agnes, Mr. Catchpool? Or is it definitely an Iris you want? Who is she? I can think of no one by that name. Has Athie talked about an Iris? Is she someone Joseph Scotcher knew?"

"I'm afraid I know as little as you do," I told her. It was true that Agnes sounded a little like Iris. Could Hatton have misheard Poirot, or did Poirot mishear somebody else? It was safer not to assume it.

"The dog was Prince, though, what?" said Harry. "Or was it Duke?"

No answer came from Dorro, only a stampede of questions aimed at me. "Is it true what Sophie said—that she saw Claudia kill Joseph Scotcher? I have to say that I cannot see Claudia doing that at all. If she were to kill a person, she would not do it where anyone might wander in and see her. Tell them, Harry."

"Tell them what, old girl?"

"That Claudia is innocent! That Sophie must be lying!"

"I have never known Sophie to lie," said Harry thoughtfully. "Never known my sister to kill a man either. All very out of character," he concluded.

"There is something that nobody seems to have considered, apart from me," said Dorro.

"Tell us," I said.

"If Claudia hangs for murder, Harry would then stand to inherit Athie's estate in its entirety. I fear that an accident would then almost certainly befall him! He would become the killer's next mark. Can you gentlemen truly not see what is happening in plain view?"

O'Dwyer opened his mouth to answer, but was cut off by more frenzied babbling from Dorro. "Joseph Scotcher was to be the sole beneficiary, but he was murdered—mere hours after Athie changed her will in his favor! Then the next thing we hear is that *Claudia*, of all people, has been caught red-handed, clubbing him to death. Attempted murder by hangman, that's what it is! And if it succeeds, who is left? Harry! I have no doubt that the killer would find a way to dispose of him without delay—and what I want to know is, why are you not finding out who would inherit if Harry and Claudia and Joseph Scotcher *are all dead*?"

"Steady on, old girl." Harry looked dazed.

"Ask that Michael Gathercole fellow and see what he says." Dorro sounded far from steady. "I don't like him one bit. I shouldn't be surprised if he were next in line. Athie is awfully fond of him. I can't think why. But that is how you will find the murderer. I should not be surprised if it were Gathercole, or fat Orville Rolfe. Fat people are as greedy about money as they are about food, more often than not. It must be one of those two lawyers that did it, and you need to prove it. I cannot do it—what resources do I have at my disposal? Meanwhile, Claudia must be shown to be innocent. As soon as the killer sees that there is nothing but Harry standing between him and a vast fortune . . ." Dorro buried her face in her hands and started to cry, and at last we were given some respite from the endless flow of words.

Her determination that Claudia be kept alive as protection for Harry meant, of course, that she would proclaim Claudia's innocence whether she believed in it or not. Her theory left a lot to be desired, I thought. I was no aspiring murderer, but if I had been, I should certainly have had a go at Harry before Claudia. She was much more likely to be on her guard, whereas I imagined one might stroll up to Harry and say, "Any objection to getting murdered, old boy?" and be met with an appreciative guffaw.

He placed his hand on his wife's arm. "Remembering old Prince has started me thinking," he said. "Would it be jolly to have a little dog running about the place? I rather think it would."

Dorro shook him off.

"Where were you both on the evening that Scotcher was killed—between when we all left the dining room and when his body was found?" I asked.

"We were with you!" Dorro said indignantly.

"Not all the time," I reminded her.

"Let me see," said Harry. "Well, first Mother shocked us all with her news, and nobody could really get to the bottom of it. Then there was a bit of a to-do, as you'd expect, and then Scotcher knocked us all sideways by asking Sophie to marry him. That was unexpected! Fellow only has a few months to live and he thinks about taking a wife. That's love for you, I suppose."

"A few months?" I said. "I had heard it was only weeks."

"I think you might be right," said Harry. "One never knows with an illness."

"Could you describe the to-do, Viscount Playford?" asked O'Dwyer.

"I daresay . . . let me see . . . Scotcher was terribly upset."

"He was pretending to be upset," Dorro said. "Do you want to know why he took such pains, always, to appear so concerned for the welfare of others? It was pure selfishness that drove him. Athie could never see it, but I saw it!"

"Come now, darling. I'm not sure that—"

"*I saw it,* Harry. As my husband you ought to take my word for it! Joseph Scotcher was a shrewd character if ever I met one. He had worked it all out, you see: appear to want nothing and people want to give you everything. It worked on Athie, like a charm. Of course he had to seem shocked and distressed at the announcement of the new will. What else could he say? 'Oh, tip-top—this is what I have planned for all along'? And there is another one made in the same mold as Scotcher: Michael Gathercole! All his dutiful service over the years—self-interest is behind that, I can promise you."

"Dorro, you must not think the worst of everybody," said Harry firmly.

"Not everybody, Harry. Take Brigid Marsh. I would trust Brigid with my life. Hatton the butler, and that ghoulish Phyllis—they are quite another matter, but Brigid is one in a million. And I have already said that Claudia is innocent. I could not say the same of Randall Kimpton with any certainty. Do we know how much of the

Kimpton family fortune is at his disposal? I don't mind admitting that I can picture Randall committing murder with no difficulty whatsoever. My family, the Sawbridges—we were wealthy land-owners once. Did you know that, Sergeant? Mr. Catchpool?"

Silently, we shook our heads.

"My father contrived to lose the lot, silly old fool that he was! Harry might well have broken off his engagement to me. If he had had any sense—"

"Wouldn't hear of it!" said Harry. To O'Dwyer and me he said, "Randall Kimpton could not have killed Scotcher. He was with me, Dorro and Claudia the whole time. We left the dining room with him, went to the drawing room with him. He only left us when summoned by you, Catchpool, to go and attend to Mr. Rolfe."

"But who knows what happened after he and Claudia retired for the night?" said Dorro. "He could easily have slipped downstairs to murder Joseph Scotcher."

"So could you, old girl." Harry grinned, as if he had scored a point in a game we were all playing.

"Harry, have you gone *mad*? You can't honestly believe that I would ever—"

"Club a chap to death? Ha! Not a bit of it! I only meant that when you went to bed, I went outside for a while. Poirot asked me to. You could have scuttled off downstairs and done poor old Joseph in. I don't believe you did, but you had as much of an opportunity as Randall did."

Dorro's face crumpled. "How can we bear this?" she muttered. "Suspecting each other like ... like ..." She had started to rub her hands together as if trying to wear the skin away. "I wish I could take back every word I have said! You must pay no attention to me, Sergeant, Mr. Catchpool. None at all. Of course Harry is right. Randall—dearest Randall! Oh, I feel dreadful. I have accused half the household of murder, when really I don't believe it of any of them. Nice sensible Mr. Gathercole—I must have taken leave of my senses thinking ill of him. It's only that I'm so *afraid*. I am not myself at all. You have no idea what it's like! Athie is the only Lady Playford ever addressed or thought of as such. I too am Lady Playford, yet no one ever calls me that—oh, no, around here I am just plain old Dorro! I have no children, so I am accorded no respect or consideration. Lillieoak should be *ours*, mine and Harry's. *She* arranged it all to thwart us! It would not have occurred to Guy in a hundred years to do such a thing—to humiliate us in this way! Athie underestimates Harry—she always has. And she had poor gullible Guy wound round her little finger. But that is the last word I shall say against anybody—I'm too kindhearted, you see, to think ill of those I love for very long. Please, forget everything you have heard me say. *Please*."

"It is unthinkable that anybody in this house is secretly a murderer," said Harry.

"And yet Joseph Scotcher was murdered, Viscount Playford," said O'Dwyer. "Somebody must have done it—someone who was here at Lillieoak that night."

A shadow of something—it might have been anger, anxiety or any number of things—passed across Harry Playford's face. "Yes," he said finally, with a sigh. "Because, after all, Scotcher was alive when we all sat round the dinner table together." He nodded, as if subjecting the fact to a process of internal verification. "And then, only a handful of hours later, he was . . . well, he was *dead*."

"Exactly," I said. "Which means somebody here, in this house, killed him."

"Quite," Harry agreed. "When one approaches the matter from that angle, it's rather hard not to be down in the dumps about it. We shall all need cheering up after this, that's for sure." He turned to Dorro. "What about the idea of a dog, old girl? A dog like Prince—or was it Duke? House like this needs one, or else it feels empty. I don't know why Mummy hasn't . . . Oh, well, I suppose she's so busy now. But when I was a boy there was always a dog dashing about the place—there could be again!"

The Grandfather Clock

SERGEANT O'DWYER AND I spent the next two hours finding no trace of an Iris. Poirot had still not returned from Ballygurteen to explain why we were supposed to be looking for her. Orville Rolfe knew of no woman or girl by that name, and neither did Brigid or Hatton.

Nonetheless, our conversations with the two longest-serving members of Lillieoak's staff were the most helpful we'd had so far. I had an opportunity to agree with Sergeant O'Dwyer, rather than the other way round, when he said, "I almost wish we had spoken to Hatton and Mrs. Marsh first of all. Between them, they have painted a clear picture of the movements of the night in question."

"They have—assuming we can rely on their testimony," I said.

"Brigid Marsh strikes me as an impressive character if ever there was one." O'Dwyer patted his stomach. "If her word is as good as her mutton soup, then I am in favor of relying on it."

I said nothing. The mutton soup might have been near flawless, but as for the word or words . . . Brigid had said something to me earlier in the day that I had found inexplicable. Happening upon me in the hall, she narrowed her eyes at me and said, "I knew I was right—you've got that look about you!" I asked the obvious question, to which she answered, "The look of a man who drinks water all through the night!" She said this as fiercely as if she were accusing me of baby farming or some equally heinous crime, then pointed to her mouth and said, "Dry lips—I can see from here!"

As if all this were not quite galling enough, I was then subjected to a long and confusing story about her nephew, who had stolen some peppermints from a bowl that was a family heirloom, and broken the bowl in the process. He had then needed to lie about breaking it—which was an accident—because if he had confessed, Brigid would have known he had stolen the sweets—which was deliberate and pernicious.

I never drank water in the night, and I did not understand what analogy she was trying to make, but before I could say any of this, she had stomped off in the direction of the kitchen.

"What about Hatton?" I asked O'Dwyer. "Are you inclined to believe him too?" Asking questions was the way to get the best from O'Dwyer. Make a statement and he would agree, but ask a question and he would happily produce an opinion of his own, as he did now.

"Well, as I see it, Inspector Catchpool—"

"Edward, please."

"As I see it, Edward, the butler told us nothing that made us more likely to think of anybody as guilty. And if he himself were the murderer, he would surely benefit from a cloud of suspicion lingering over somebody else."

"He observed a remarkable number of comings and goings that night," I said. "I daresay it is his job to monitor the activities of the house in that way."

I started to list, mainly for my own benefit, the things Hatton claimed to have witnessed on the night of the murder. Working with Poirot in London earlier in the year had left me with an appetite for listing things. As a method of clarifying one's thoughts, I had found that it helped enormously.

Things Hatton saw on the night of the murder:

1. Lady Playford left the dining room in the middle of dinner. She appeared to be in a state of high emotion. She ran upstairs to her bedroom, closed the door and stayed there as far as Hatton was aware.
2. The next people to leave the dining room were Claudia Playford and Randall Kimpton. They were followed closely by Harry and Dorro Playford. All four went straight to the drawing room.
3. After that, the next to leave the dining room were Michael Gathercole and Orville Rolfe, who also left the room together. The latter was complaining of feeling a little unwell. Gathercole said something about feeling better after a good night's rest. The two men entered the drawing room briefly to take their leave of the others, and then ascended the stairs. Each went to his room.
4. Next to leave the dining room were Hercule Poirot and Edward Catchpool, who went outside together.
5. Gathercole emerged from his bedroom ten minutes later. He went downstairs, put on his overcoat, and left the house by the back door.
6. Approximately five minutes after Gathercole had left the house, Joseph Scotcher and Sophie Bourlet came out of the dining room. Scotcher appeared to be in some discomfort. Sophie pushed him in his wheelchair to his bedroom. Once she had settled him for the night, she went to her own room, put on her coat and went out into the garden.
7. Roughly fifteen minutes later, Poirot and Catchpool returned to the house and proceeded to the drawing room.

8. At about twenty minutes to ten, Hatton retired for the night. As the grandfather clock in the hall was striking ten, which happened to be just as he was getting into bed, Hatton glanced out of his bedroom window and saw Sophie Bourlet walking through the garden in the direction of the house.

9. Ten minutes later the screaming started. Hatton put on a dressing gown, left his bedroom and went in search of the noise. When he reached the hall, he encountered Michael Gathercole, who was walking in through the front door at that moment. Together, they moved in the direction of the parlor to see what the noise was about.

"We cannot eliminate Sophie Bourlet and Michael Gathercole as suspects," said O'Dwyer. "Either might have done the deed, then gone outside, and made sure as they were seen coming in again."

"What about Claudia Playford?" I said. "Brigid Marsh swears that as she ran from the servants' quarters to the parlor, she saw Claudia with Randall Kimpton at the top of the stairs, outside Lady Playford's study, on their way down like everyone else. It's rather baffling."

"What is?" O'Dwyer asked.

"Hatton mentioning the grandfather clock in the hall has made me think about the chronology of it all—and it doesn't make sense. Listen: Sophie Bourlet is outside. She returns to the house—she is seen to do so by Hatton. Almost immediately upon entering, she witnesses Claudia Playford beating Joseph Scotcher to death with a club. She starts to scream. Claudia drops the club and runs upstairs to the landing, where she is seen soon afterwards by Brigid Marsh. *How can Claudia have gotten herself from the parlor to that landing without using the main stairs?* There is no other way up to the landing outside Lady Playford's study."

"You're right, there is not," said O'Dwyer.

"Remember, Sophie is still screaming all this while. Upstairs, Poirot and I and others are opening bedroom doors and rushing towards those very same stairs. I think I was the first there—I did not see Claudia Playford coming up and I saw no one on the landing. My question is: could Claudia Playford have reached the safety of Randall Kimpton's bedroom, or her own, between Sophie starting to scream and me opening the door of Orville Rolfe's room and stepping out onto the landing?"

"Well, could she?" said O'Dwyer eagerly. "Only you can answer that. Are you minded to say that it was impossible, and that therefore she could never have been downstairs murdering Mr. Scotcher in the first place?"

"Unless my memory of events is distorted . . . Yes. I should say it was quite impossible. Which means either Brigid is mistaken about seeing Claudia on the landing while Sophie was screaming, or . . ."

"Or else Sophie is lying," said O'Dwyer.

"She might have killed Scotcher, then gone out into the garden—hidden the clothes she wore to commit the murder, which would have been covered in blood—and then made sure she was seen returning to the house, ready to scream in false shock, as an innocent party would on discovering the battered body of the man she loved."

"What about Phyllis the maid?" O'Dwyer said. "Did you know that she was enamored of Mr. Scotcher? Brigid thinks it was Phyllis that killed him. She told me so quite bluntly. I have to say, I was as persuaded by her account of Phyllis's passion for the deceased young gentleman as I was by her muffins, which are delicious. If Phyllis knew that Scotcher loved Sophie and not her, there's no telling what she might have done, Brigid said. Oh, she had a thing or two to say, so she did! 'What species of fool goes and falls head over heels for a man who's as near dead as he is alive, when Clonakilty's full of big, strapping lads?' She's not wrong there! And what I want to know is, if Phyllis was missing from the kitchen when she should have been helping Brigid, then where was she? Mr. Hatton did not mention seeing her, not in any shape or form."

"Let us find her and ask," I said.

18

Unrequited

WE WAITED IN THE hall until Phyllis was produced by Hatton. Her posture brought to mind a reluctant gladiator—forced, terrified, into the arena. She sniffed, shuffled her feet and said, "I never did it. I never did nothing wrong! I'd not have hurt Joseph, not for anything!"

"Nobody is here to accuse you of wrongdoing, miss," said O'Dwyer. "We need to talk to you, is all."

"I'm innocent," Phyllis protested. "Me, a murderer? That what Cook's told you? Ask anyone who knows me, they'll swear I could never."

"Shall we find somewhere a little more private to sit and talk?" I suggested.

"No." Phyllis recoiled as if I had laid a trap for her. "I've work to do. Haven't I always? Ask what you want to know and I'll answer. I'd as soon have it over with."

"Do you know anybody by the name of Iris?"

"Iris?" Phyllis looked around wildly. "Iris? I've never known an

Iris. I knew an Eileen—from Tipperary, she was—and a Mavis, as used to work here at Lillieoak. Who are you talking about? What Iris?"

"Never mind," I said.

"There is no need to fret, miss," said O'Dwyer. "We only need to know what were your movements on the night that poor Mr. Scotcher met his untimely end."

Phyllis's face twisted. She started to sob, and sank to the floor in a heap. O'Dwyer crouched down beside her. "There, there, miss. You were fond of Mr. Scotcher, were you?"

"He was the only one I cared about! I wish I had died instead—I truly wish it, I do! They can bury me alongside him!"

"Now, now, miss. You're a grand young lady. I should think that plenty of fellows will—"

"Don't say it! Don't!" Phyllis wailed. "Don't speak to me of anybody else. As if Cook in me ear all the time isn't bad enough! I was a silly fool, like she always said I was. Joseph was so nice to me—just being kind, as he was, no one kinder—and I got it all wrong. I should've known. Me a servant and him a book-learned sort. I wanted to believe he could love me the way I loved him. And then I heard him ask Sophie to marry him, and . . . and . . ." She dissolved into weeping.

O'Dwyer made comforting noises and patted her on the back. I guessed he was a married man. My father was forever patting my mother in the same way.

"Did you say that you *heard* Scotcher ask Sophie to marry him?" I asked Phyllis.

She was too much beside herself to answer with words, but her ardent nodding was unambiguous.

"You were not in the dining room when Scotcher made his proposal of marriage, Phyllis. I was. I was at the table. You had left the room some time before it happened. So if you don't mind my asking, how did you hear what you claim to have heard?"

"I listened outside the door, and no more than that! Doesn't mean I murdered anyone! Nice girl like Sophie—course he'd sooner marry her than the likes of me, a drudge without a penny to my name."

"If I might inquire, miss . . . ," O'Dwyer began. "When you were listening outside the door, did you happen to hear of Lady Playford's alterations to her will?"

Phyllis shook her head. "I heard all the talk afterwards, but I didn't hear her say it. I only went listening at the door after I heard it slam and saw Lady Athie rushing upstairs. Trying not to cry, she was—and her the steadiest of folk, normally."

"So you wondered what had happened to make her abandon her dinner and her guests?" I said.

"That's right. And when I heard them all talking, well, I could scarcely believe it! Joseph was to inherit the lot, everything Lady Athie had to leave! Nobody was happy about it—him least of all. And what sense did it make, leaving it all to a dying man?"

"No sense whatsoever," I agreed.

"And then I heard Joseph ask the question that broke my heart. I knew he was fond of Sophie, but I never thought he saw her that way. I thought I was his special one. He'd see me coming along the hall and he'd say, 'Here she is—Phyllis, light of my life.'" She had taken off her apron and was dabbing at her eyes with it.

"Not all men are as responsible as they ought to be in their dealings with the ladies," O'Dwyer said soberly.

"Phyllis, may I ask you something?" I said. "After you heard what you heard, did you run off?"

"I did! Didn't want to be caught in floods of tears, and Mr. Kimpton was making nasty jibes about someone listening at the door, so I ran."

That explained the stifled sobs we heard, and the running footsteps.

"Where did you go?"

"I started off to the kitchen, but Cook would have had plenty to say and I didn't feel strong enough to hear it. She'd have taunted me for being foolish and tried to persuade me to step out with her nephew, Dennis. That's her plan for me, but I don't like Dennis! His breath smells foul as anything. So I ran past the kitchen, out the back door and down to the river. I was minded to toss myself in, I might as well tell you. If I'd had more courage, that's what I'd have done. Wish I had!"

"What did you do instead?" I asked.

"Walked up and down a bit, then came back up to the garden. Sat on the grass by the big pond, hoping I'd get wet and catch a chill and die of it."

"While you were in the garden, did you hear two men talking?"

"Do you mean you and Mr. Poirot?" said Phyllis. "Oh, yes, I heard you right enough."

"Good. That's one mystery solved," I said with relief. "And . . . you were crying at the time?"

"Thought I'd never stop," Phyllis confirmed.

"Were you alone? It's only that, in the same way that you heard us, we heard you, and then we heard a sort of whispering or hissing sound."

"That was me talking to meself. 'Quiet, Phyllis, you stupid girl,' I said, but it did no good. Nothing could stop me crying. I heard you saying that you might come looking for me, so I made off back to the house. Straight to my room, I went. I locked the door, lay down on the bed and cried and cried. And the worst thing was . . ." Phyllis's mouth wobbled and more tears poured forth. "Joseph wasn't even dead then! He was still alive, and I was that upset about him marrying someone else, and now . . . well, now I'd do *anything* to have him back and to have things as they were before, even if that meant him marrying her and not me."

I believed that her regret was real, and I said as much once she had taken her leave of us. O'Dwyer lost no time in agreeing. "So you'd be after crossing her name off the list, would you?"

"Not a bit of it," I said.

"No? I could have sworn that you said only a moment ago—"

"One regrets nothing so much as the unfortunate things one has done oneself that cannot be undone—don't you find?"

Immediately, I felt as if I had accused Phyllis of murder, when I had intended merely to refrain from eliminating her from my mental list of suspects.

I then felt duty-bound to say, "I am sure Phyllis is not the killer," when the truth was that I was not sure at all.

19

Two Irises

AN HOUR LATER, UNABLE to find Claudia Playford in the house or the gardens immediately around it, I walked to the highest point I could find on Lillieoak's grounds, which was also the most exposed. Up here, the wind hit the skin like something solid and hard. For some reason, I found myself thinking again about Phyllis's claim that Randall Kimpton had copied Scotcher. I was torn between concluding that this imitation must have been obvious enough to be noticeable to Phyllis, since she had noticed it, and thinking that if Kimpton had set out to copy anybody, he would surely have done it more successfully.

Really, he and Scotcher were not at all alike. Fundamentally, they were opposites. Scotcher's defining characteristic, it seemed to me, was that he tried hard, always, to make others feel better about themselves and about life in general, whereas Kimpton sought only to make himself feel better and appear superior.

I don't know how long I stood there pondering, but in due course I heard a voice behind me: Claudia's. "Have you been looking for me?" she asked.

"Oh!" I exclaimed, startled. How the devil had she got up here without my seeing her? Had she been up here already? "Sergeant O'Dwyer and I wanted to speak to you, yes."

"Then why hide away here where the wind might blow you away? I assume you wish to know if Sophie Bourlet is telling the truth about what she says she saw me do? You will have heard what I have told others, but you wish to put the question yourself, and watch my expression as I answer."

"Yes."

Claudia smiled. She seemed to enjoy making me wait for her answer. "Sophie is not telling the truth," she said eventually. "It's a lie—unless someone else dressed in my clothes and wore a wig, and kept their face turned away, and Sophie saw that person attacking Joseph and assumed it must be me. Have you thought of that?"

"No. Did you like Joseph Scotcher, Miss Playford?"

She laughed. "Like him? Not at all. I did, however, *enjoy* him. I found his presence at Lillieoak wonderfully entertaining. It's going to be awfully colorless without him here."

"You mean that he was a talented raconteur?"

"He had a singular way with words—but no, I meant that everybody was in love with him and it was quite funny to watch. Phyllis slobbered over him like a helpless creature, and Sophie fainted with desire every time he looked in her direction. And then there was Mother, of course. I found it fascinating to observe how Joseph did it, how he reeled them in and kept them all adoring him while he felt nothing for any of them, really. He loved the idea of everybody falling in love with Joseph Scotcher more than he loved any real people."

"You counted your mother among Scotcher's admirers," I said. "Surely you mean she loved him in a motherly way?"

"Oh, heavens, not you as well! You must pay no attention to Dorro and her ridiculous substitute-for-dead-child theory. Everything is about babies for Dorro, ever since she failed to have any herself. If you listen to her, a boiled egg looks like a baby! Mother might be an old bird but there is plenty of pep left in her. She loved Joseph the same way that Phyllis and Sophie loved him. Oh, she would die rather than admit it. She knew the feelings she ought to have had for him were those of a mother figure, so she pretended they were. Not for the sake of convention, you understand—Mother loves to be unconventional—but to avoid being spurned and laughed at. She is a very proud woman." Claudia's eyes narrowed. "I see you are not convinced."

"Well . . ."

"You are aware that I am not as fond of her as a daughter ought to be of her mother, and so you wonder if I am simply being cruel. I would too, in your position. I assure you, this is my clear-eyed assessment of the facts. I shall be cruel about Mother a little later, perhaps—I do so enjoy it, and she amply deserves it—but at the moment I am trying to help you understand. Mother was desperately in love with Joseph. Why else do you think she changed her will to leave him every last penny? He was due to die of Bright's disease in the very near future."

"Scotcher did not respond well to the news of the new will," I said. "He became severely agitated."

Claudia made an impatient noise. "He *pretended* to be aghast, but that's all it was: a charade. What would you expect him to do: leap up and shout, 'Hip hip hooray, I'm going to be divinely rich!'?"

"He was not going to be rich unless Lady Playford predeceased him and, even if she had, he would then only have been rich for a few weeks or months."

Claudia laughed. "Which was it—weeks or months? I take it you are an expert on Bright's disease?"

"Far from it."

"Well, then."

"Scotcher's distress that you call a pretense was as convincing as any true distress I have witnessed," I said.

"Well, of course it was," said Claudia. "That's why I'm sorry he is no longer around. Joseph was a magician!"

"Do you mean that he lied habitually?"

"Oh, no—nothing as ordinary as that. *Everybody* lies habitually. Oh, look—Monsieur Poirot is here."

I looked down through the branches of a cluster of hawthorn trees to the sweep of Lillieoak's driveway. Claudia was right: Poirot, Inspector Conree and Sophie Bourlet had returned from Ballygurteen.

"Joseph really was a marvel," Claudia went on. "He cast powerful spells with nothing more than words. If he were here now, he could convince you in less than five minutes that you are not a Scotland Yard policeman but a lion tamer escaped from a traveling circus. Oh, Mother lost no time in falling in love with him. She too is a words person, you see. Until she met Joseph, she had not encountered anybody who was as adept with words as she herself was."

"Do you know of a woman named Iris?" I asked.

"Iris Gillow?" said Claudia at once. "Iris Morphet?"

I blinked several times. "You know of *two* Irises! Nobody else has been able to suggest any."

"You have not asked Randall, then?" said Claudia.

"Not yet, no."

"I see. Iris Morphet and Iris Gillow are the same person. Were. She died. Randall will be able to tell you all about her. I could tell you myself, but it's his story. You ought to hear it from him. Look, here he comes now!" The burst of joy in her voice suggested that a savior had arrived from on high. Kimpton was still some way off too. The mere sight of him in the distance was apparently enough to send Claudia into raptures.

"What are you thinking about me?" She eyed me with suspicion. "Perhaps you have trouble believing that I love Randall as much as I seem to, when I do nothing but denounce and deride everybody else."

"I have no trouble believing that you are as fond of him as

you purport to be. It is obvious that you love him very much. I suppose . . ."

Claudia tilted her head and almost smiled. "There is something you would like to ask me?"

"The first time we met, you mentioned that Dr. Kimpton had won your affection twice."

"Yes. And my affection is not easily won."

"I can imagine."

"It took him *years* the first time. I knew I would accept him eventually—I *adored* him from our first conversation—but if I succumbed too readily, I feared he might stop trying. And Randall trying—a man of his intelligence and single-minded determination— well, there is nothing more satisfying than watching him put every effort into his campaign to win me over." Her smiled faded, and was replaced by a more mundane expression. "But of course I had to let him succeed in due course, and I did. And then five—no, nearly six years ago—his manner towards me suddenly changed. He seemed to have lost his confidence—it was repulsive! Confidence is the nature of a man like Randall. It is his essence. I did not want him without it— he was no longer himself, I thought—and so I called for its return."

"What happened?"

"He confessed to uncertainty about whether he wanted to marry me. Doubts!" Claudia waved her diamond ring in front of my face. "I took this off and threw it at him. Naturally, I told him I never wanted to see him again as long as I lived. But the very next day, there he was, outside my window. Oh, not at Lillieoak. I lived in Oxford then. I was one of the first women to matriculate at the university there—I don't suppose anyone bothered to tell you that, did they? My achievements are recognized by nobody but me. I moved back here to get away from Randall—who was desperately sorry and regretting his moment of doubt. 'Well,' I thought to myself. 'I intend to make you regret it a hundred times more than you could ever manage on your own.' That was when I moved back to Lillieoak. It didn't deter Randall. He was always cluttering up the drawing room, weeping and begging to be forgiven, brandishing his diamond in the hope that it might prove to be a lucky charm."

Claudia glanced at her ring. "It was pathetic. *He* was pathetic and I told him so. I was so foul to him, it made him angry and almost tyrannical in his insistence that I would wither and perish without his love. He said that I must choose him or nobody, because he would surely throttle any other man I chose. I liked him a little bit more once he stopped crying and drooling over me and started trying to lay down the law. He insisted that I would end up marrying him whether I wanted to or not. It struck me that I probably did want to, in fact. Randall is adorable when he's fierce, and he had never been more so."

The sort of mutual unpleasantness she was describing sounded nothing like love to me, but I was wise enough not to say so. "So you forgave him and became engaged to him a second time?"

"After *years* of making him suffer the torments of the damned, yes. And he is still suffering, every day. I have not yet agreed to set a wedding date. Perhaps I never will. One doesn't *absolutely* need to, you know." Claudia laughed at my shock, which I must have done a poor job of concealing.

Not caring if I approved of her or not, she went on, "One can still have fun and be just as deeply in love, without any danger of it wearing thin. Besides, Randall and I can't marry until we've decided where we would live. I mean, live for the most part—we would have more than one house, of course. Randall can't wait to get out of Oxford. He insists he will find a new job in County Cork and join me at Lillieoak, but I rather like Oxford. In Oxford, there are things to do besides stare at trees and sheep. Or we might try London—that would be thrilling! Do you enjoy living in London? Darling! You're here at last!"

"Hello, divine creature." Kimpton strode towards us. "I wish I could linger, and spend the rest of the day covering your beautiful face with kisses. But I can't. Catchpool, make haste—you are needed."

"By whom?" I asked. Something about his tone told me it was important.

"By me, though I suppose I ought to say: by Joseph Scotcher most of all. Poirot, Conree and O'Dwyer await us in the parlor—or they will, by the time we get there."

"The parlor?" I echoed.

"Yes." Kimpton turned on his heel. I hurried after him towards the house.

"Count yourself lucky to be invited," he said over his shoulder. "That puffed-up pest Conree did all he could to persuade me I should leave you and Poirot out of it and speak only to him and his half-wit toady. I told him: if he wants to hear what I've got to say, he had better not stand in the way of you and Poirot hearing it too. If I'm to perform, I would like to have at least a couple of decent brains in the audience."

"Perform? Kimpton, what is all this about?"

"About? Why, Joseph Scotcher's murder, of course," he said. "You're all quite wrong about it—all you crime-solving chaps. Very, very wrong—and I shall prove it to you."

20

Cause of Death

SCOTCHER'S BODY HAD BEEN removed from the parlor. I assumed it had been taken to a nearby mortuary, though all Conree was willing to offer us was the word "removed." Having been forced by Kimpton to include Poirot and me in this little gathering, he was retaliating by withholding as much mundane information as possible—like a more virulent counterpart of Hatton, the butler.

Though Scotcher was gone, his wheelchair was still in the same spot, forlorn in the absence of its former occupant. The bloodstain on the oriental carpet marked where his head had lain, or what was left of it.

Poirot, Inspector Conree and Sergeant O'Dwyer sat on the chairs furthest from the blood, like tense audience members waiting for a show to begin.

"I am confident that I know what this is about," Conree said as Kimpton and I entered the room. "You have my permission to raise the matter, Dr. Kimpton. Poirot, Catchpool, I hope I can rely on your discretion."

Stepping directly over the bloodstain, Kimpton approached Scotcher's wheelchair and put his hand on it. "'Here I and sorrows sit,'" he murmured. "'Here is my throne, bid kings come bow to it.'"

"A quotation from Shakespeare's *King John*?" Poirot asked him.

"At a time like this, old boy, I would draw upon no other dramatic work."

"You saw Scotcher's wheelchair as a throne?"

"Not really. Do not be so literal-minded. Ha!" Kimpton's eyes flared to underline the irony. "I, of course, am a fine one to talk!"

"But you saw Joseph Scotcher as a king—the king of Lillieoak?" Poirot persisted.

Kimpton smiled faintly. "Heir to Athie's kingdom, yes. Monarch-in-waiting. I like that! You are quite right, Poirot. The crime is regicide, though no newspaper will report it as such."

"Would you have been a loyal subject of King Joseph, I wonder," Poirot mused aloud.

"Wonder away, old stick. Have fun with your psychological con-fabulations. What harm can it do? Though I'm afraid I have brought us all here to talk about rather more pedestrian matters of fact."

"Come to the point," ordered Inspector Conree.

"I shall. The bloodstain—look at it. Does anything strike you?"

"Well, you may accuse me of fearing the worst, if you wish," said O'Dwyer, "but I can see it never coming out of that carpet. Lady Playford will need a new one."

"Quiet, O'Dwyer," Conree growled at him.

"Oh, yes," the sergeant agreed, as if keeping quiet were next on his list of activities, and always had been.

"Anything else?" Kimpton looked at Poirot and me. "Shall I tell you? All right, then. I would swear to it that there is not enough blood for a murder committed in the way we have all been assuming it was committed. All except me, I should say. I wondered as soon as I saw Scotcher lying there. But it was only once his body was removed that I became sure."

"Sure of what?" said Poirot.

"That Scotcher wasn't clubbed to death. Yes, somebody smashed his head to pieces with a club, but that was not what killed him. He must already have been dead when it happened."

"Well, I never," said O'Dwyer quietly.

"If I had to guess, I'd say that he'd been dead around an hour by the time the club got to him," said Kimpton. "Sergeant O'Dwyer, did the police doctor say something similar? I saw you talking to him. Frankly, I find it hard to credit that any medical man would miss it."

"It would have been improper for Dr. Clouder to say anything before performing the postmortem," Inspector Conree huffed. His mood was deteriorating fast in the face of Kimpton attempting to take charge. "I discouraged him from speculating. There is to be an inquest, and, since we cannot anticipate its verdict, it would be indecorous of any of us to try."

"Indecorous?" Kimpton guffawed at the ludicrous pronouncement. "Tommyrot—unless you are set on impeding your own investigation, Inspector."

He walked around the wheelchair, positioned himself in front of Poirot and said, "If Scotcher had been killed by the blows from the club, there would be twice as much blood on the carpet as there is."

"Are you saying that Mr Scotcher died from his illness, and his murderer was unaware that he was dead already?" O'Dwyer asked. "Now, if you are—and I'd be the first to allow that strange happenings are more common than people would think, but having said that—"

"I do not believe Scotcher died from any illness," Kimpton cut him off impatiently. "Poirot, how well do you remember the scene as we saw it on the night of the murder? We ran down the stairs and were confronted by a monstrous sight. Scotcher's head had taken a pretty thorough beating. There was not much left of it, but it was not entirely destroyed, if you recall."

"The lower part of his face was still intact," I said. "His mouth was fixed in a terrible grimace of pain."

"Full marks, Catchpool," said Kimpton. "I'm pleased you mentioned the grimace."

"*Mon Dieu,*" Poirot said under his breath. "I have been a fool—a blind fool."

"Here, gentlemen, is my guess," said Kimpton. "It has as its foundation certain observations I have made in the course of my work as a pathologist. I have performed many postmortems in cases of suspicious death, at the behest of the police. In one such case—a murder—the cause of death was poisoning. Strychnine."

Inspector Conree hauled himself to his feet, red in the face. "We must stop this at once. I am in charge of—"

"The victim of a strychnine death dies with what looks like a ghastly grin on his face," said Poirot as if Conree had not spoken. "Yet I did not think of it. *Je suis imbecile!*"

"Indeed, the facial muscles spasm," said Kimpton. "That's what causes the grimace or grin. It is also said of strychnine deaths that one ends up with a back so arched that both one's head and one's feet are on the floor. That's an exaggeration, but there is some truth in it."

"Scotcher's body lay in a most unnatural position," said Poirot. "Both were present: the arched back, the grin. I am ashamed that I did not see straightaway what must have occurred."

"Well, I didn't think of it, and I'm a doctor," Kimpton said. "It was only once the body had been removed and I was able to look at the amount of blood left behind that I was certain."

"Come along, O'Dwyer," said Conree. "You and I will not be part of this unsavory exercise." He marched from the room, having first reattached his chin to the top of his chest. O'Dwyer shrugged helplessly before following him.

"Test every liquid you can find in Scotcher's bedroom," Kimpton called after them. To Poirot and me, he said, "What an insufferable fustilugs! Might Sergeant O'Dwyer chop off his head with an ax, do we think? Here's hoping. Back to Scotcher, now that we can speak freely. The inquest will tell us that he died from strychnine poisoning. What it won't tell us is why somebody clubbed him about the head postmortem. Rather a waste of time, expending all that energy trying to murder someone who is already dead, I should say. Any theories, Poirot? I have one if you don't."

"I am interested to hear yours, monsieur."

Kimpton smiled. "You must promise not to hold it against me if I turn out to be wrong."

"Naturally. Even Hercule Poirot is, on the very rare occasion, wrong."

Kimpton walked over to the window and looked out. "I think our club-wielding culprit is Sophie Bourlet," he said. "That would explain her eagerness to blame it on Claudia. She must have believed she could fool the garda's medical examiner. She wrongly assumed that he would see a mess of blood and brains, and conclude that the cause of death was obvious, and there was no need for a postmortem or an inquest. Unpardonably foolish of her. As a nurse with a modicum of medical knowledge, she should have known better than to leave the lower part of Scotcher's face intact. The strychnine grin is a well-known phenomenon."

"Why should she wish to mislead anyone about the cause of death?" I asked.

"*Because . . . ,*" Kimpton began with a sigh, as if my question were idiotic and the answer as plain as day, ". . . it was common knowledge that Sophie was in charge of administering all Scotcher's medicines and tonics and whatever else he took. If she had wanted him dead, it would have been the easiest thing in the world for her to slip something into one of those bottles of his. If he'd turned up dead and it was a clear case of poisoning, the first name in everybody's mind would have been Sophie's. She had the opportunity several times each day."

"So, if you are correct, Sophie Bourlet did two things in order to divert suspicion from herself," said Poirot. "First, she bludgeoned Scotcher with a club after killing him with poison, in order to disguise the method that would suggest her as the most likely killer. Second, she took the further precaution of pretending to have witnessed Mademoiselle Claudia attacking him with the club."

"Quite so," said Kimpton.

"Sophie claims to have heard as well as seen certain things," Poirot told him.

"Heard?"

"*Oui.* A conversation between Mademoiselle Claudia and Mr. Scotcher, immediately before she attacked him with the club."

A heavy sigh came from Kimpton. "Which must be a lie if Scotcher was already dead when the attack took place. Do continue, Poirot."

"Sophie swears that she heard Mr. Scotcher beg for his life, and that, in response, Mademoiselle Claudia said, 'This is what Iris should have done.'"

"Iris?" Kimpton spun round to face us. "Iris Gillow?"

The same name I had heard from Claudia Playford. Who was she?

"I do not know which Iris, and Sophie Bourlet told me she did not know either," said Poirot.

"What else did she hear?" Kimpton demanded.

"She did not recall precisely the words. 'This is what Iris should have done.' And then 'But she was too weak. She let you live, and so you killed her.' Or something similar. Does this mean something to you, Dr. Kimpton? Who is Iris Gillow?"

Kimpton had lowered himself into an armchair and dropped his head into his hands. "I shall tell you, but . . . please, give me a moment to gather my thoughts," he murmured. "Iris. After all these years . . . But this is nonsense!" He sounded, for the first time since I had met him, uncertain and confused. "Claudia was with me upstairs. Whomever Sophie Bourlet heard talking about Iris, it cannot have been her. It must have been someone else."

Poirot smoothed his mustache with the index finger and thumb of his right hand. "Then you do not believe that Sophie lied about the words she overheard? Surely if she is capable of administering lethal poison, and of lying about seeing Claudia murder Joseph Scotcher, she might also lie about other things?"

"The words she claims to have heard have a ring of truth to them," Kimpton said darkly. Rallying, he added, "That means nothing, of course. The best lies always sound true."

I had been waiting for a while to raise something that was bothering me. Now seemed the perfect moment. "Dr. Kimpton, if your suspicions about Sophie Bourlet are correct, was it not rather reckless of her to leave the lower part of Scotcher's face intact?"

"She might have intended to obliterate the strychnine grin, but something prevented her from doing so," said Kimpton. "What if she heard footsteps and suddenly found herself with less time to set the scene than she had anticipated?"

"That is possible," Poirot agreed. "The trouble is that everything is still possible. Dr. Kimpton, if you believe that Sophie Bourlet murdered Joseph Scotcher, please tell me: what do you think was her motive?"

"Motive?" Kimpton snorted, as if the discussion of such a thing were unworthy of him.

"Yes, the motive. Scotcher had proposed marriage to her that very evening. Why should she murder the man she loved, who was, in any case, dying from an illness?"

"I don't know and I don't much care," said Kimpton. "Make her admit she did it and then ask her why. Motive! You persist in your folly of imagining that human beings can be made to make sense, Poirot."

"I do, monsieur."

"There is no sense. There is no consistency. I am living proof: I accuse Sophie Bourlet of lying, but I am convinced, for no good reason, that she heard the words she says she heard, about Iris. And I am considerably more rational than most people, I assure you."

"Who is Iris Gillow?" I asked.

Kimpton's mouth set in a hard line. "I should very much like to tell you about her. And tell you I shall—immediately after the inquest."

"Why not now?" Poirot asked.

"It is easier to wait," said Kimpton. He made to leave the parlor, then stopped at the door. "Prepare yourselves for a surprise, gentlemen. A big one."

"Do you mean the surprise of the cause of death being poison?" I asked.

"No. Something quite other. I will say no more, for I might be wrong. But I don't think I am." And with that, Randall Kimpton left the room.

The Casket Question

THE NEXT MORNING AFTER breakfast, Poirot indicated that he wished to talk to me alone, and suggested a walk by the river. I foolishly assumed that we would first walk *to* the river, only to discover that this was not what he had in mind. A motorcar would take us to the bank of the Argideen; Hatton had already arranged it, and we would be there within the hour.

In due course a driver presented himself and we set off. As we drove the long way round, circling away from the house at first and going in what I maintained was the wrong direction, given that we could have walked a straight line from Lady Playford's front door to the river, I said to Poirot, "Joseph Scotcher's murder cannot have been anything to do with the new will. That was only announced at dinner. Surely the poison must have been put into his medicine bottle before dinner."

"The strychnine was not necessarily in his medicine, *mon ami*. It might have been in his mutton soup. We do not know."

"Even if it was, we ate the soup before Lady Playford told us her news. The motive must have been something else. Unless the murderer is Gathercole or Lady Playford. They were the only ones who knew the terms of the new will before dinner. And here's another thing to consider: we can no longer be certain that Orville Rolfe is in the clear. He could be the poisoner just as easily as anyone else. Also—you'll think this a stretch, I'm afraid—Orville Rolfe was the person who brought up the subject of poison. He had it on his mind—which is interesting."

Poirot smiled. "Everything that you say, I have thought of already," he said. I think he meant it as a compliment. "But you neglect to mention the main puzzle in all of this."

"Which is what?"

Poirot indicated that he did not want to expand upon his words until we were alone, so we passed the rest of the journey in silence.

Eventually we arrived at our destination. "Here's the Argideen, genullmen," said our driver, leaning his elbow over the back of his seat. "Coulda walked it in a quarter o' the time. "I'll stop here for when you want taking back, will I?"

We thanked him and stepped out into the blustery day. The river was steely gray and noisy, in a state of unrest. I started to walk, but soon had to double back. Poirot was standing fixed to the spot, staring at the water. This, apparently, was his idea of a walk.

"Consider the account given to us by Orville Rolfe, Catchpool— the argument he overheard about a funeral, and whether the casket was to be open or closed. It is true that he might have imagined the whole thing while delirious from pain, or he might have lied to us, but I do not think so. It is too much of a coincidence."

"I don't understand. What coincidence?"

Now Poirot looked as gratified that I failed to grasp his meaning as he had been pleased before that I was thinking his very thoughts. I wished he would make up his mind whether he preferred me clever or stupid.

"Joseph Scotcher is already dead, from poison," he said. "Why, then, attack his head with a club until there is almost nothing left of it? One reason—the one proposed by Randall Kimpton—is that an obvious poisoning would have drawn suspicion to Sophie Bourlet, who was responsible for administering Mr. Scotcher's medicine. *Bien sûr, c'est possible, mais . . .* I favor a different possibility."

"I think I know what you're about to say. If you are poisoned, your face and head remain intact. An open casket at the funeral is possible. Orville Rolfe nearly said it himself, while writhing in agony, when he believed he had been poisoned. By contrast, if your head is reduced to pulp by a club, the only choice would be a closed casket."

"*Précisément!* And Orville Rolfe told us he heard a man say that it would have to be open casket—that was the only way. A woman argued with him. Do you see how it fits together?"

"Yes. Yes, I do. *That* is why the woman—perhaps Claudia Playford—would take a club to the head of a man already poisoned to death. Because she did not want him to be able to have an open casket funeral."

Poirot's expression was distant and contemplative. "Do you remember when we walked in the garden after dinner?" he said. "We imagined: what if Lady Playford believed that one of her children might be planning to kill her?"

"I remember it very well," I told him.

"Let us now try a variation of that hypothesis. What if Lady Playford knew for some time that her son or daughter, or maybe both of them together, plotted to murder Joseph Scotcher, or wanted him dead? That would explain the new will, would it not? She makes an elaborate show of leaving everything to Scotcher and depriving her own two children of their inheritance. She does so in the presence of two lawyers, one Scotland Yard policeman, and the famous *Hercule Poirot!*" He threw up his hands as he said this. I smiled to myself, half expecting the Argideen river to cease its frothing and foaming in deference to his greatness.

"This would explain perfectly the otherwise inexplicable actions of Lady Playford." Poirot started to walk up and down—tiny footsteps, back and forth. I tried to walk alongside him, but it proved rather difficult, so I stopped.

"Joseph Scotcher will not live to inherit—Lady Playford knows this," he went on. "So why does she make the revision of her will? Could it be that she wants to give her two children a very visible motive for committing murder—in front of the law, the police, the expert in solving crimes? Suddenly, Harry and Claudia Playford find themselves in a most alarming position. If they proceed with their plan to kill Scotcher, they are the obvious suspects because of this new motive given to them by their mother, so glaringly apparent to all! The same is true of Dorro Playford, and, to a certain extent, of Randall Kimpton."

"Would it not have been simpler for Lady Playford to summon the gardaí and say, 'I believe my son and daughter might be hatching a plot to murder my secretary'?"

"I do not think so, no. If she did not have incontrovertible proof, would she risk the accusation? It is more subtle, I think, to drape the enormous motive around the necks of Harry and Claudia in front of many people—as a deterrent."

"An ineffective deterrent," I pointed out. "Joseph Scotcher is dead—don't forget that. Besides, why should Harry or Claudia or anybody go to lengths and risk their neck to murder a man who is about to die of a kidney disease? And why should it matter to anybody whether Joseph Scotcher has an open or a closed casket?'

Poirot turned away from the river and started to walk back to where the car awaited us. He was busy arranging himself on the seat when I climbed in nearly a minute later. Only once we had set off back to Lillieoak did he say, almost inaudibly, "Once we know the answer to the casket question, we will know everything."

22

In the Orangery

BACK AT THE HOUSE, Hatton was waiting for me with a message. "Mr. Gathercole awaits you in the orangery, sir," he said. I wondered if his ability to speak freely would endure once Scotcher's murder was solved. Then I worried it might never be solved, and wondered if Poirot shared my anxiety on this score.

"The orangery?" I said. I had seen no such place at Lillieoak. If it existed, I did not know how to get to it, and I said so. What a strange place for Gathercole to choose.

"Follow me," said Hatton, before demonstrating that not only his speech but also his ability to show me which rooms were where had been significantly enhanced by the tragic circumstances.

The orangery turned out to be a large wooden structure attached to the back of the house, full of orange and lemon trees. In spite of the cold and windy weather, everything in here was lush and in full bloom. The heat was at first pleasant and then, after only a few seconds, uncomfortable; I found Gathercole mopping his brow with a handkerchief.

"Did you hear that the inquest into Scotcher's death will take place next Wednesday?" he said.

"No. Who says so?"

"O'Dwyer."

"And . . . this news disturbs you?" The evidence that it did was before my eyes. Gathercole looked considerably more uncomfortable than I felt, and I was certain it was not only the heat affecting him.

"Inspector Conree keeps insisting that no one leave Lillieoak," he said. "It's not healthy, all of us being penned in here under the same roof, after what's happened. Not safe. I am worried that . . ." He stopped and shook his head.

I decided to be bold. "Are you afraid the truth will come out at the inquest, about the poisoning? You maybe did not bank on it happening so soon." Bold and indiscreet. Conree, if he had heard me, would have been furious.

Gathercole looked confused. Indeed, his confusion appeared to interrupt his agitation.

I said decisively to myself: "If poison was the murder method, then Michael Gathercole did not kill Joseph Scotcher."

"Whatever do you mean?" he said. "Are you suggesting that Scotcher was *poisoned* as well as beaten about the head with a club? That is rather unlikely!"

"Yes. People are rarely killed twice." I smiled. "Nothing is clear at this point. We ought to wait for the inquest to tell us how Scotcher died. Did you want to speak to me about something? Hatton gave me to understand . . ."

"Yes. Yes, I did. There is something I must tell you, as soon as possible."

"Might I ask why I am the one you wish to tell?" I said. "Surely Inspector Conree or Sergeant O'Dwyer would be a better choice?"

Gathercole looked piercingly at me. "Not for me. I should hate for you to think me a liar, Catchpool. There are things, important things, that might have a bearing on this matter. Has anybody else approached you?"

"Of whom are you thinking? Approached me about what?"

He seemed not to have heard my questions. "It might be better if we talk *after* the inquest," he said. "I know nothing for certain. I *cannot* know, as much as I might feel sure."

"Please tell me what's worrying you," I urged him. "I should like to help if I can."

Two people had now promised further elucidation after the inquest: Gathercole and Randall Kimpton. I found this remarkable. Surely it would make more sense for them to cough up whatever they were withholding long before their hand was forced by a public revelation.

Gathercole turned this way and that, unable to keep still. He said, "You asked me if something upset me—in the dining room, on the night Scotcher died. I ducked the question, for fear that you would think me foolish to be so concerned about a family to which I do not belong. Athelinda Playford is no relation of mine. I am her lawyer, and that is all. Well, not quite all," he corrected himself. "According to the new arrangements she has put in place, I am also her literary executor."

"I should not have thought you foolish," I told him. "Many of us form our most profound attachments to those who are not kith and kin."

"As you know, I have no family," he said curtly. "In any case, what undid me at the dinner table—made me want to seize a knife and use it to inflict serious damage on most of those present—was that nobody thought to ask about Lady Playford's own health."

"I am not sure I follow." As I said this, an ominous crunching sound came from beneath me. I looked and saw that I had stepped back and put my right heel down on a shovel that was lying on the floor of the orangery, full of jagged pieces of glass. What was left of a broken jam jar stood proudly beside the shovel. I realized at that moment that I had a distaste for orangeries and conservatories and the like for this very reason: with their fancy names, they masqueraded as desirable additions to a house, but their true purpose, often, was to provide a home for rubbish that no one could be bothered to throw away. In a proper room, if one broke a jam jar, one would clear away its remains, not leave them lying around for hapless visitors to stand on by accident.

"Why would a woman who is not sick herself make a will leaving everything to a man whom she knows will die in a matter of weeks?" Gathercole said. "The most likely reason, as far as I can see, is that she has recently learned that she herself has even less time left than he does. That was my fear, when Lady Playford made the request in her study that afternoon for a new will. I could not contain my anxiety, and rather impertinently asked her if she expected to predecease Scotcher. She assured me that she was as fit and healthy as she appeared, and I believed her. It was a profound relief. But *none of them thought of it!*"

Gathercole's words came out loud and hard. "None of them asked! I could not bear it, Catchpool: the proof, unfolding before my eyes, of the selfishness, the sheer base unworthiness of the whole lot of them. They do not deserve Lady Playford's hospitality or generosity. And Scotcher . . ." Gathercole spoke his name with venom. "At that moment, I should have enjoyed murdering him very much indeed."

"What you enjoyed was the fantasy," I told him. "You would find the reality of committing a murder most unpleasant."

"I would have expected no better of Claudia, who is a vicious little cat, or Harry, who could hardly be more obtuse, but Scotcher was a clever man, and one who would have had us all believe he was devoted to Lady Playford. Yet he too failed to make the most rudimentary inquiry about her health. I am not normally intemperate, but truly,

I felt that I might explode with fury. None of them *deserve* her."
A moment later he added, "Deserved, I should say, in the case of
Scotcher."

"Thank you for telling me," I said.

"Yes, well." My gratitude had embarrassed him. "The only reason
I didn't straightaway is that it reveals my own . . . envy is what it
must be, I suppose."

"You thought to yourself that if you were the child of Lady
Playford, you would care more for her than for whatever you might
inherit from her."

"I know I would! If I were her child, or, for that matter, her
secretary. The only reason I am *not* her secretary is Joseph Scotcher."

"I beg your pardon?" I laughed, wondering if I had heard wrong.
"Lady Playford's secretary? You? But you are a partner in a firm of
solicitors."

"Yes. Disregard what I said, please."

"Wait a minute. Are you saying—"

"We have more important things to discuss than my feelings
about my profession! I told you a lie. You and Poirot, the gardaí."

"What lie?"

Gathercole turned towards me and laughed. "Your face is a
picture. Are you waiting for me to confess to murder? You needn't
worry—I did not kill Scotcher. The lie I told relates to my alibi."

"Walking in the garden, alone, with no one to vouch for you?"

"I was neither in the garden nor alone, and somebody can vouch
for me: Athelinda Playford. I was in her bedroom."

"In her *bedroom*? When, precisely?"

"After Rolfe and I went upstairs. We said good night at his door,
and once he was safely out of the way, I went to Lady Playford's room."

"To see that she was all right? That she had not taken Dorro's
cruel words too much to heart?" I knew I ought not to put words in
his mouth.

"No. I went to her bedroom by prior agreement, before Dorro spoke those words." Gathercole had closed his hand around an orange. He held it as if he were thinking about pulling it free, then let it go. The strong smell of citrus fruits combined with the heat was making me feel light-headed.

"It was the last thing she asked of me at our meeting earlier that afternoon," Gathercole said. "She told me that, later that same night, an attempt might be made on her life. Her plan—one that involved me, though she had made it without my participation—was that she should retire to bed and go to sleep as usual. Meanwhile, I should conceal myself behind the thick curtains, ready to pounce if I heard someone come into the room—and ready, otherwise, to stay awake and on guard all night."

"This is quite impossible," I said, afraid I was being taken for a fool. "Hatton saw you go outside into the garden ten minutes after Orville Rolfe retired to his room."

"He saw no such thing," said Gathercole. "Lady Playford explained to him that I was with her throughout the relevant period of time, and that, if asked, he was to say that he had seen me on my way to the garden. It was all arranged."

I did not know what to think. I wanted to believe him.

"I suppose it's useful to know that I should not depend upon the word of the butler," I said.

"Oh, Hatton's as trustworthy as they come. Unless specifically instructed by Lady Playford to do otherwise, he would tell the truth. He is . . ." Gathercole stopped and smiled. "Strangely, I did not consider him when I spoke of the selfishness of those at Lillie-oak. I think Hatton cares more for Lady Playford than either of her children does, in his own quiet way."

"That is commendable, but I am hoping to find at least one person who cares most about solving the brutal murder of Joseph Scotcher."

"I have no right to ask this of you, but if you could refrain from mentioning Hatton's . . . misleading testimony to either Inspector Conree or Sergeant O'Dwyer, I should be most grateful and I know that Lady Playford would too."

I was glad he had not asked me to keep it from Poirot. "What about your coat?" I said. "When we all gathered round to see the horrible sight in the parlor, you were wearing a coat."

"I was," Gathercole agreed.

"Yet you maintain that you did not set foot outside?"

He made an impatient noise under his breath and started to walk in a circle around me. "Do you have any idea how chilly it is next to the window of Lady Playford's room?"

I told him that I was ignorant on this score. "She does not invite all her guests to hide behind the curtains while she sleeps," I added drily.

"Anyone not invited to do so is lucky," said Gathercole with feeling. "Trapped in a veritable vortex of cold air with the panes rattling in your ears. I did not think of the inclement October weather, but Lady Playford did when she made her plan. She declared that I might catch pneumonia if I did not have my coat, so I put it on and was grateful for it."

"I see. And did anyone come to Lady Playford's door while you were positioned behind the curtain?"

Gathercole smiled sadly. "I suppose I should have expected you to test me. After all, here I am, admitting that I lied to you—why should you believe me now? Yes, someone came to Lady Playford's door: you did."

"Then I don't understand. There you were, ready to spring out and save Lady Playford—yet when she opened her door, you did nothing. How did you know I wasn't about to plunge a meat skewer into her heart?"

Gathercole looked away.

"Oh—now I understand!" I said. "You knew it was not *I* who might kill her. Which means that she expected a particular person to make an attempt on her life—and you know that person's name, don't you?"

Gathercole's face had taken on a sullen cast.

"Please tell me at once," I urged him.

"You ought to speak to Lady Playford," he said. He repeated the instruction several times, and would tell me no more.

23

The Inquest

THE INQUEST WAS HELD at Clonakilty Courthouse, an edifice as unprepossessing as any I had ever seen. It smelled of dark things that had been locked up for too long. The windows were narrow, with water rolling down their misty panes. I stood outside for as long as I could, thinking about the contrast between this building and Lillieoak, where I was prepared to reside temporarily, in spite of a murder having been committed there. Yet I would not spend as much as one night in this courthouse.

There were no chairs, only long wooden benches that filled the large room. Harry and Dorro Playford inserted themselves between me and Poirot as they hurried inside. Instead of dropping back to wait for me, Poirot took the opportunity to leave me behind. I was irked by this until I tumbled to his plan. He was trotting off in the direction of Lady Playford and . . . goodness me, he was elbowing Randall Kimpton out of the way in order to put himself next to her! I was not accustomed to seeing him move with such speed.

I smiled to myself, knowing his intention only too well. I had recounted to him everything Gathercole had told me, including his recommendation that I speak to Lady Playford if I wished to know more. This had proved impossible; she had done an excellent job of hiding herself away in the intervening days. And now here she was among us—approachable at last. I wondered how thorough an interrogation Poirot would be able to fit into the time before the inquest started.

A man I assumed was the coroner, with a small, knobbly head that made me think of a peanut, had walked in a moment ago, with Inspector Conree at his side. Sergeant O'Dwyer followed close behind, chattering away to a man with thin, sandy hair that seemed to lie in wispy horizontal sheets atop his head, and a bottom lip that curled downward when in a resting position, as if he had just said, "Look at this ulcer I have on my gum," and was attempting to display it.

Kimpton barely noticed Poirot as he snuck in next to Lady Playford. The motorcar containing Claudia had arrived moments earlier, and he was looking over his shoulder with his arm outstretched. "There you are, dearest one," he said, and she ran to him as if they had been separated for weeks instead of less than thirty minutes.

I secured for myself a spot on the bench behind Poirot, hoping I would be able to hear the conversation if he attempted to have it.

He wasted no time. "Lady Playford . . ."

"Lady Playford, Lady Playford! It's interminable! Will you *please* call me Athie?"

"Of course, madame. Please accept my apologies."

"What did you want to say?"

"Is it true what I hear about Mr. Gathercole, on the night of Joseph Scotcher's murder?"

"What have you heard, and from whom?"

"From Mr. Gathercole himself, though I did not hear his words. His words, ah . . . let us say they went over the houses to reach me."

"Around the houses. And it's the wrong phrase in any case. You might say 'reached me by a circuitous route,' but you would only say 'around the houses' if you wanted to imply that the communication had been inefficient. As this conversation is. What is it that you would like to know?"

"Mr. Gathercole claims that he spent most of the evening of Joseph Scotcher's murder hiding behind your bedroom curtains in case someone broke in and made an attempt on your life. Between leaving the dining room with Orville Rolfe and when Sophie Bourlet started to scream downstairs, that is where he insists he was: hiding behind a curtain. He also says that you asked Hatton the butler to lie and say that he saw Mr. Gathercole coming in from outside."

"Yes. That is all true. Don't blame poor old Hatton—he is too loyal for his own good. I wanted to protect Michael, who had done nothing wrong. I knew he had an alibi, and I decided it wouldn't matter if it were not precisely the same alibi given to the police. All that matters, really, is that we all know he could not have murdered Joseph." Lady Playford smiled, but without enthusiasm. There was an air of weariness about her, as if she was put out to have to explain.

Poirot had lapsed into silence. I imagined that he took a dim view, as I did, of her unscrupulous assessment of the matter. A famous and imaginative novelist she might be, I thought to myself, but she failed to realize that her testimony was worthless now that she had admitted how readily she was prepared to lie. Her fame must have gone to her head, I decided; she was too accustomed to being the sole arbiter of what everybody in the story said and did and thought.

"So you suspected that, as a result of your announcement at dinner, you would be murdered?" Poirot asked her.

"Oh, no!" She chuckled, as if the idea were absurd.

"Then I do not understand. Mr. Gathercole told—"

"Oh, do stop. Stop!" Lady Playford waved away Poirot's words. "Instead of pelting me with endless questions, allow me to tell you properly. I shall make sure to include all the relevant details, and I will be kind enough, in addition, to arrange them in the correct order."

At the front of the room, the man with the curled-down bottom lip and the sandy hair was pulling back a chair and sitting where the coroner ought to sit. I had got it wrong, then: he must be the coroner, and the other man with the knobbly peanut-like head was somebody else. Who? And why had he arrived with Conree and O'Dwyer? He wasn't the police doctor—who, I noticed now, was not here. I had caught a brief glimpse of him as he left Lillieoak. He was a disheveled fellow with things spilling out of his pockets and out of the battered brown leather bag he carried.

With the exception of Brigid Marsh and Hatton, everyone from Lillieoak was here. Poirot and Athie Playford were sitting in front of me, as I have said, and everyone else behind: Claudia Playford and Randall Kimpton were side by side, with Phyllis Chivers on Claudia's other side and Sophie Bourlet on Kimpton's. Harry and Dorro were seated together on the bench at the very back, and . . . That was peculiar. Why were Gathercole and Rolfe not sitting together? Had they exchanged unfriendly words?

Then I realized: they *were* sitting together—or at least as close together as they could get, given the girth of Rolfe. From where I sat, however, it looked as if they had made a point of positioning themselves so that there was a sizeable distance between them.

"All right, then," Athie Playford said to Poirot. "I shall tell you—but we will probably be interrupted. Yes, I asked Michael to do me the considerable favor of concealing himself behind my curtain for the whole night. I asked him to forgo a night's sleep, and he was kind enough to agree without hesitation to be my protector. I thought there was an outside chance that someone might panic, and try to kill me while I slept. I might be old, but I am not yet ready to die, if only because I have the most *delightful* idea for my next bundle. Shall I tell you? I haven't quite worked out all the particulars, but it has to do with a disguise."

"Madame—"

"It must be one that covers the face. A veil, I think. Anyway, somebody suspects that beneath this disguise lurks Mrs. So-and-so, and we see them suspecting it, and we also see others going to great pains—"

"Madame, I am sure this story is fascinating, but I am more interested in the other," said Poirot. "Did you fear that this attempt on your life would come from a particular person?"

"Yes. I had a definite name in mind. Is it not obvious to a great detective who that person must have been? Make an effort, Poirot! Would you like a clue? Though I am certain they both loathe me at the moment, neither Claudia nor Dorro would harm me, and as for Harry and Randall . . . well, you only have to look at Harry, don't you? And Randall is too much of a contrarian."

"What do you mean?" Poirot asked.

"Oh . . ." Lady Playford sighed. "It is most tiresome. He derives boundless pleasure from saying, doing and caring about wholly ridiculous things. It cannot have escaped your notice. He attacks psychology because he knows you set great store by it. His favorite Shakespeare play is *King John*—he abandoned a successful career because he couldn't bear the proximity of those who believed that *King Lear* was a greater masterpiece—which of course it is! Unquestionably!"

"Do you believe that Dr. Kimpton thinks so too, and simply pretends to disagree?"

"No. That is why it grates on the nerves. He is frustratingly unlike other people. He *should* have been furious with me about the will, if only for Claudia's sake—and so, of course, he was not! He is rich, but he would be equally happy poor. And yet once when he received a Christmas card—a very ordinary card with no important or interesting message—and could not read the signature on it, and couldn't think who might have sent it or work it out from the postmark . . . well, he was in *torment*. Absolutely coming apart at the seams, and that is no exaggeration. He marched around the circumference of his *entire* social and professional circle until he tracked down the culprit."

"He was then satisfied?"

"Oh, yes. But I mean, a normal person would have raised an eyebrow at the indecipherable signature and said, 'I daresay I shall never know.' And left it at that."

"Do you remember who sent Mr. Kimpton that Christmas card?" Poirot asked.

A peal of laughter burst from Lady Playford. "Oh, you are wonderful, Poirot. Ever the detective! Yes, as it happens, I recall it very clearly, because I shamelessly stole the poor fellow's name and put it in the bundle of the moment. Jowsey—Trevor Jowsey. He was a former teacher of Randall's—not a schoolteacher, a chap who taught him medicine. I reinvented him as David Jowsey, goods train driver."

At the front of the room, the coroner cleared his throat and patted the pile of papers before him. Any moment now the inquest would start.

Lady Playford leaned in close to Poirot's ear and whispered loudly, "Let me quickly tell you the rest of my idea—you of all people will appreciate it. The baddies suspect this disguised person of being Mrs. So-and-so. Shrimp and her friends help her to conceal her identity, and they insist that she is a different woman. In fact, the disguised woman is *not* Mrs. So-and-so, who is safely elsewhere. And Shrimp is telling the truth, but her *intention* is to mislead. Isn't that splendid? One can, you see, insist that the truth is true in a way that makes it appear a lie."

"I see that, as a plotter, you are without parallel," Poirot told her. "Tell me this: why might a murderer—in a story—be determined that his intended victim should have an open casket at his funeral and not one that is closed?"

"That sounds a most intriguing scenario," she responded enthusiastically. "My first thought is that it must be something to do with the face—but one *never* stops at the first thought. One asks oneself instead: what would make it so much more *interesting*?"

Did this mean, I wondered, that Lady Playford was unlikely to have been the woman Orville Rolfe overheard arguing with a man on the day of the murder? She sounded entirely innocent—as if she had never given the matter of caskets any thought whatever, and certainly not whether they ought to be open or closed.

"From whom did you ask Mr. Gathercole to protect you, Lady Playford?" By now, Poirot's voice sounded rather steel-edged.

"Why, from Joseph, of course," she said.

"Joseph Scotcher?"

"Yes. I had just told him that he would inherit an immense fortune if I were to die."

"But . . ."

"Most people would not leave everything to a man they imagined might murder them—is that what you are thinking?"

Poirot admitted that it was.

"You are quite right." Lady Playford sounded pleased with herself.

"I am thinking other things also. Such as: why would a dying man wish to murder you? For the money? That does not convince me—not when he would have it for such a brief time only, and when he would be too sick to make a nice use of it. I assume that all of Mr. Scotcher's needs in relation to his illness were taken care of?"

"Oh, yes. I made sure Joseph had the best of everything. No expense was spared."

"Then what other reason would there be for him to kill you? So that he could quickly marry Sophie Bourlet and leave her a rich woman after his death?"

"I am sure you will have great fun trying to work it out," was Lady Playford's reply.

"You are a talented storyteller. Would it not be fun for you to tell me?"

"There are things I am only prepared to speak of after the inquest—once we leave this courthouse."

I could well imagine Poirot's frustration; I felt it myself. Neither he nor I had the authority to compel anyone to talk to us who did not wish to do so. Conree had all the power, and there was no way of knowing if he was asking any of the right questions. From what I had seen of the way he conducted himself, I feared that he was not.

Poirot was not so easily defeated. "Tell me this one small thing," he said. "Why did you not lock your bedroom door if you feared a murderous approach from Mr. Scotcher? It has a lock. I have checked."

"After the inquest, I will happily tell you."

"Remarkable!"

"What is remarkable?" Lady Playford asked.

"Randall Kimpton said the very same thing, and also Michael Gathercole. Everybody promises to talk after the inquest. Why not before?"

"That really is a *very* silly question, Poirot. If I were prepared to answer it . . . Ah! It seems that we are finally about to start."

She was right. The curl-lipped man introduced himself as the coroner, Thaddeus Coyle, and proceedings were under way.

We listened attentively as the facts that only some of us already knew were revealed to all. The peanut-headed man turned out to be the superior officer of the police doctor, and his representative. The disheveled Dr. Clouder had mislaid the keys to his motorcar, we were told, and so could not attend.

Scotcher had died of strychnine poisoning, and it was the opinion of the garda's medical expert that the poison was ingested between five in the afternoon and half past seven in the evening, depending on how much poison was swallowed. Death was estimated to have occurred between nine and thirty minutes past. The evidence suggested that Scotcher was moved to the parlor postmortem, where his head was almost entirely destroyed by a club that had belonged to the Playford family, on which his blood, brains and bone fragments had been found.

The coroner listened to Sophie Bourlet's account of having witnessed Claudia Playford inflict the damage to Scotcher's head, after which Inspector Conree was called upon to present the fingerprint evidence. The club, he told us, chin raised only slightly from his chest, was covered in fingerprints, some of which belonged to Claudia Playford. However, the fingerprints of Athelinda Playford, Frederick Hatton, Phyllis Chivers, Randall Kimpton and Harry Playford were also found to be present. This was simply explained: the club was an easily accessible household ornament and many had touched it at one time or another.

Of the bottles in Scotcher's bedroom, only one was completely empty, and it was this one—the only one that was blue—that had been found to contain traces of strychnine as well as of a harmless herbal remedy, while the other bottles contained an assortment of herbal tonics but no poison.

I was surprised to hear about the tonics. I would have expected the bottles in the room of a dying man to contain various chemical concoctions, but perhaps Scotcher was too far gone for conventional medicines to be beneficial to him.

Sophie Bourlet testified that the blue bottle had been closer to full than to empty when she had last given any of its contents to Joseph. Asked when this was by the coroner, she replied, "It was that same day, the day he died. I gave him two spoonfuls at exactly five o'clock. I always do."

This too puzzled me. Believing in the efficacy of such things as herbal tonics was one thing, but why on earth should it matter at what time of day a person drinks lavender root or eucalyptus tincture or whatever it was?

I should probably, at that point, have had a premonition. Poirot later confessed to me that he had—though of course Randall Kimpton would say that his word alone is no evidence at all.

The coroner ruled that the cause of Joseph Scotcher's death was murder by person or persons unknown. Then, instead of drawing the inquest to a close, he stood up and cleared his throat.

"There is something else that I must say, and this will form part of the official record of today's proceedings. Having informed myself most thoroughly with regard to Inspector Conree's ongoing investigation into Mr. Scotcher's death, I am aware that one of the more, if you will permit me to use the word, *mysterious* aspects of this matter is the question of why anyone should bother to snuff out the life of a man with so little time left to him. Additionally, I have considered, and Inspector Conree has considered, that a possible motive for murder was the new will made by Lady Playford, which named the deceased, Mr. Scotcher, as the sole beneficiary. Therefore, another puzzle was this: why change one's will in favor of a man who is soon to die? In the light of these still unanswered questions, and after long and careful consideration, I have decided it is my duty to make public an aspect of this unfortunate business that both Inspector Conree and I believe might prove to be significant. It has nothing to do with the physical cause of Mr. Scotcher's death, but it might be pertinent nonetheless. As it is not, strictly speaking, a medical matter but what I believe would have to be called a *human* matter, I made the decision to tell you about it myself rather than have it presented alongside the police doctor's report."

"I wish he'd just say it," Lady Playford hissed impatiently.

Did she know what was coming? I wondered. My sense was that she did. I felt an uncomfortable prickling sensation all over my skin.

"Joseph Scotcher," said the coroner, *"was not dying."*

"What? Not dying? What do you mean, not dying?" It was Dorro, needless to say, who protested first. "You surely do not mean that he was *never* dying? He's dead, is he not? After he swallowed the poison, he must have been dying. So what precisely do you mean?"

"Good lord, we shall be here until Christmas," Randall Kimpton murmured.

"Silence, please!" The coroner sounded more astonished than angry. Perhaps Randall Kimpton was the first person ever to make a joke during one of his inquests. "I am presiding over these proceedings, and nobody speaks without my permission. Let me be clear: until he ingested strychnine, Joseph Scotcher was not dying. He was not suffering from Bright's disease of the kidneys, or from anything else."

Sophie Bourlet cried out, "That is not true! The doctor would be here to say it himself if it were true!"

Mr. Peanut stood up and said, "I am afraid it is quite true. I have read Dr. Clouder's postmortem report, and spoken to him about it at length. Mr. Scotcher's kidneys were as plump and pink and healthy as ever two kidneys could be."

"Which is why I said that it was not a medical matter," explained the coroner. "A fatal disease that is *present* is one thing. The absence of Bright's disease, on the other hand . . . well, in one who has told everybody that he is soon to die of that very illness, I would call that a matter of psychological interest."

I turned to survey the room—in time to see Randall Kimpton sneer at yet another mention of psychology. His eyes met mine and he smiled in a manner that anyone would have deemed excessive; he looked almost enraptured. The signal was clear: he wanted me to know that he had known, but was there any need to look so gleeful and self-satisfied about it? Of course he was more likely to have tumbled to the truth than I was; he had been acquainted with Scotcher for years, no doubt, and I for only one day.

He was not the only one who had known, it seemed. Claudia had that same look, a mixture of triumph and relief: "So now the truth is revealed," it seemed to say. "I have known all along."

Michael Gathercole looked guilty rather than triumphant. He glanced at me apologetically. "I knew as well," was the message. "Sorry I said nothing about it."

Sophie Bourlet sat perfectly still. Silent as tears rolled down her face. Phyllis, Dorro, Harry and Orville Rolfe clucked at one another like flustered chickens: "How the . . . ? What a . . . ! Why on earth . . . ? But what the devil . . . ?" None of them had suspected for a moment that Scotcher was not dying.

I sat, dumbstruck, as the coroner's words echoed in my head: *Joseph Scotcher was not dying. He was not suffering from Bright's disease of the kidneys, or from anything else.*

Poirot, in front of me, was shaking his head and murmuring to himself. Lady Playford turned to inspect me as I had inspected the others. She too had known. "People are peculiar little machines, Edward," she whispered to me. "Considerably more peculiar than anything else in the world."

PART III

24

Sophie Makes Another Accusation

AFTER THE INQUEST, POIROT and I traveled with Sophie Bourlet, Inspector Conree and Sergeant O'Dwyer to the Ballygurteen garda station. Conree had sprung this plan on us with his customary charmlessness as we were leaving the courthouse in Clonakilty. He had made it clear, furthermore, that this time he would be asking all the questions and the rest of us were forbidden to speak.

Not speaking was the approach favored by all, it seemed. On the steps of the courthouse, no one had said a word or even looked at one another. I said nothing myself, though my thoughts were louder than ever:

Joseph Scotcher's kidneys were healthy before he was murdered. Pink and flawless. No sign of Bright's disease, or any physical ailment likely to kill him. Yet Scotcher was introduced to me as a man who would face death in the near future. He himself spoke of his imminent demise . . .

How could it be? For what possible reason would a healthy man pretend he was dying? Had somebody misled Scotcher deliberately—

an irresponsible or malicious doctor? Randall Kimpton's name leapt to my mind. He was a medical chap, and I could see him being both irresponsible and malicious. But, no, he could not be Scotcher's doctor. Kimpton lived in Oxford, Scotcher in Clonakilty.

Nevertheless, there was something unsettling here. I felt as if I was circling it, but could not quite catch a glimpse.

Scotcher had told everybody that he was about to die of a disease. And then he had died—from strychnine poisoning. Then his head was smashed in to indicate a third cause of death.

How many ways did Joseph Scotcher need to die in order to please . . . whom? I liked this question very much, and decided it might be a useful one to ask in all kinds of ways, though I did not know what those ways were. The presence of Conree, O'Dwyer and Sophie Bourlet was rather an irritant. All I wanted was to talk to Poirot alone. I would have given one of my own pink kidneys to know what his thoughts were.

At the garda station in Ballygurteen, Conree led us to a room at the end of a long, narrow corridor that made me think of a schoolroom the moment I walked into it. There were chairs, and a board on the wall; only the desks were missing. On the seat of one chair there was a dusty glass vase with some long-dead flower stalks in it, bound tightly by a pale green ribbon. There was no water in the vase, and the stalks had no flower heads atop them. Water damage had turned the ceiling brown in one corner.

"Well?" Conree fired the word at Sophie Bourlet. "What have you to say for yourself? You were his nurse—you must have known there was nothing wrong with him."

"Your Doctor Clouder is a cruel man," Sophie said bitterly. "He is a wicked liar! If I believed him, I might imagine I could have had a long and happy life married to Joseph, if only he hadn't been murdered. What good would it do me to think that?"

Beneath his mustache, Poirot's lips were moving, though no sound emerged. It would not be long, I guessed, before he intervened; he would not be able to help himself.

"Dr. Clouder has told no lies," said Conree. "It is you, Miss Bourlet, who are the liar."

"Monsieur Poirot, Mr. Catchpool, tell him! Joseph was dying of Bright's disease. His kidneys had almost no life left in them. They must have been brown and shriveled. It is impossible that they were pink!"

"Did you see these shriveled brown kidneys with your own eyes?" Conree asked.

"You know I did not. How could I have seen them? I was not present at the autopsy."

"Then you have no right to accuse the doctor who performed the postmortem of lying."

"I have every right! Joseph was dying. You only had to look at him! Did you see these two pink, healthy kidneys yourself? No, you did not."

"As it happens, I did," said Conree. "Clouder summoned me immediately. I stood by his side and he pointed them out to me."

Sophie opened her mouth, then closed it without speaking.

"Your husband-to-be was a dishonorable liar, Miss Bourlet, and so are you."

"I am not a liar, Inspector," said the nurse. "Neither am I heartless, as you are. Please, continue to speak your mind with no consideration for my feelings. There could be no better demonstration of the difference between your character and mine."

"You were Scotcher's nurse for how long?" Conree asked her.

"Two years."

"And that whole time he was dying, was he?"

"No. At first there was the possibility that he might, but . . . we hoped and prayed. And then, a little over a year ago . . ." Sophie covered her mouth with her hand.

"A little over a year? Tell me, did you ever read up on Bright's disease?"

"I did. Every word I could find, the better to help Joseph."

"Did you miss the part about how long it takes to kill, once it has become terminal? A person would be lucky to last two months!" Conree turned to me and Poirot. "Gentlemen, I have read the testimonials Miss Bourlet offered to Lady Playford when she sought employment. I don't mind telling you, they appeared a little too exemplary. I suspected they were falsified."

"You are ridiculous," Sophie told him. "This is slander."

Conree made the gun shape with his index finger and thumb. "I know now that I was wrong about that," he said. "I sent one of my men from Dublin to speak in person to those who recommended you for employment. That is how I know you are a fine nurse—among the best the profession has to offer."

"And this is how you reward me, by suggesting—"

"Shut up!" Conree bellowed.

O'Dwyer muttered something under his breath. It sounded as if it ended with the word "draw."

"You have something to say?" the inspector asked him.

"Oh, no, not at all. It was only that it occurred to me . . . But it's not important."

"Out with it," barked Conree.

With a look of what can only be described as terror on his face, O'Dwyer said, "When I was a boy, my brother and I used to fight like rats in a barrel. Our mammy would watch us kick and punch the stuffing out of one another and she'd not say a word, but if one of us ever told the other to shut up—well, her face would be a picture! There was no difference in her mind between 'Shut up' and the foulest obscenities. Sir, I swear, this has nothing to do with—"

"Continue," Conree ordered.

"Well, we didn't want our mouths washed out with soap, but we still longed to tell each other to shut up as much as we ever had, so we found a way round it. We would say, 'Shut up the drawer, without the drawer.' If Mammy heard us, we pretended we were only talking about a drawer that one of us had left open. But we both knew what we really meant. 'Shut up the drawer, without the drawer' leaves you with plain old 'Shut up.' It was you saying those words that made me think of it, sir."

I released the breath I had been holding for several seconds.

Conree behaved in every respect as if O'Dwyer had not spoken. He said to Sophie, "You pushed Scotcher around in a wheelchair, knowing he could walk as easily as anyone. You gave him medicine that turns out not to be medicine at all—"

"I did not know that! The bottles were labeled by Joseph's doctor in Oxford."

"Oxford?" Conree responded, as if she had spoken of the planet Mars.

"That is where Joseph lived before he came to Lillieoak," said Sophie.

"And why did he not find himself a doctor in Clonakilty once he settled there?"

"He was fond of his Oxford doctor, whom he knew well."

"What was the fellow's name?" Conree asked.

"I . . . I do not know," said Sophie. "Joseph did not like to talk about him."

"I'll bet he didn't! How often did he travel to Oxford to see this chap?"

"Once or twice a year."

"Did you go with him?"

"No, he preferred to make the journey alone."

"Naturally—because he was a lying scoundrel through and through." Conree raised his chin so that it could take a good old run at his chest for greater impact, then slammed it down. "A dying man who needs a nurse to move him from one room of a house to another, but who hares off to Oxford on his own with no trouble at all, to visit a doctor who doesn't exist! The same doctor sends labeled bottles of herbal nonsense, pretending to be medicine. *Do you still deny that you knew the truth all along?*"

Sophie looked him in the eye. "I knew, and know, the truth. Joseph was dying of Bright's disease. He would not have lied to me."

"He would and he did," said Conree. "Of that there is no doubt. And by lying to me, you are helping his murderer to escape justice."

"On the contrary." Sophie rose to her feet. "I told you that I saw Claudia Playford bring down that club on Joseph's head until there was nothing left of it but blood and splinters of bone. I told you straightaway who the murderer was, yet you have not arrested her. And you wonder why I disbelieve your doctor? Your ever-so-proper inquest? I almost pity you."

Sophie walked slowly towards Inspector Conree. "If you care about catching Joseph's killer, you will listen to me as I say this one last time—and then I am finished with you. *I heard Joseph speak to Claudia Playford,* when he was supposed to have been already dead an hour from strychnine poisoning. He was not! He was alive! He begged Claudia not to kill him, as she stood with the club raised above her head. I do not deny that he might have had strychnine in his system, but Dr. Clouder's report that was read out at the inquest *cannot be true.* Why do you trust a man who cannot button his own shirt correctly? Whose shoelaces are untied, whose belongings spill out of his pockets as he walks?"

Conree turned to O'Dwyer. "Take this liar away," he said.

25

Shrimp Seddon and the Jealous Daughter

THE JOURNEY BACK TO Lillieoak by car was not a pleasant one. I sat beside Poirot and opposite Sophie Bourlet. It had started to rain and the sky was slate gray. Darkness was descending. I do not mind the nights in London; I scarcely notice them. There is always a sense that the next day is girding up to get going, and none too patiently. My feeling about Clonakilty is that the opposite seems true: it can be broad daylight and still there is the suspicion that the impending night is ready to pounce and smother when the time is right.

Poirot was fidgeting next to me, continually adjusting his clothing and his mustache. Every time the motorcar went over a bump in the road, he moved to restore to their correct position hairs that had not been displaced. Finally he said, "Mademoiselle—might I ask you something?"

It took Sophie a few seconds to break free of the cocoon of silence in which she had wrapped herself. "What is it, Monsieur Poirot?"

"I do not mean to add to your unhappiness, but there is something

I would like to know. How would you describe your relationship with Mademoiselle Claudia?"

"It has deteriorated since I accused her of murder."

"And before that, did you like her? Did she like you?"

"You ought to have asked the second question first. I had no opportunity to decide how I felt about her before it became obvious that she loathed me from every angle. So . . . it was then hard for me to think well of her and treat her kindly."

"You make it sound as if you tried."

"I did. Claudia has some admirable qualities. And it was uncomfortable living in a house with someone who detested me. I have always firmly believed that the best remedy, when someone dislikes you, is to be relentlessly friendly and generous-spirited towards them. It works nearly every time."

"Not with Claudia, though?"

"Decidedly not. She was determined to despise me on principle."

"What principle?" Poirot asked.

"Lady Playford approved of me, and soon grew fond of me. We both loved Joseph and talked a lot about how best to care for him. It strengthened the bond between us."

"And Claudia was jealous?"

"I think she saw me as the good daughter to Lady Playford that she had never been."

"Did Claudia like Scotcher?" I asked.

"She liked to have him around, certainly," said Sophie. "Him and Randall Kimpton, whom she dotes on—they were the only two people she ever showed any interest in."

"Why do you think Mademoiselle Claudia killed Mr. Scotcher if she liked to have him around, as you say?" asked Poirot.

Sophie pressed her eyes shut. "I have asked myself that question . . . oh, you have no idea how many times! I cannot think why she did it. There seems to be no reason, apart from maybe something about this Iris person she mentioned. Have you found out about her yet—who she is and what she was to Joseph? He never once spoke of her to me."

"Do you think Mr. Scotcher asking you to marry him might have had something to do with it?" Poirot said. "Again I wonder about jealousy. It is a most dangerous emotion."

"No. Claudia was not remotely interested in Joseph as a romantic prospect. Randall Kimpton is her sun, moon and stars. No other man holds any appeal for her." Sophie bit her lip. She said, "It's going to sound as if I'm contradicting myself, but . . . I don't think it was me that Claudia envied. I think she did her damnedest to make herself believe it was me, but I suspect she was jealous of a far more powerful rival than I could ever be."

"Who?" Poirot and I asked in unison.

"Shrimp Seddon. Lady Playford's detective heroine. I suspect that, as a young child, Claudia was hurt by her mother caring so much for Shrimp and spending so much time with her. One need only listen to the way Lady Playford talks about her writing to know that it excites her in a way that nothing else does. And Shrimp is clever enough to be fictional, and therefore beyond the reach of Claudia's capacity to punish, so a substitute is needed—someone on whom all the pain of childhood neglect can be vented. I think I fitted the bill very nicely."

"Mademoiselle, I should like to ask you one more question," said Poirot. "Please would you go over once more for me your discovery of Joseph Scotcher's body—what you saw when you returned to the house that night?"

"I have told you everything already," said Sophie.

"Please."

"I came in. I heard raised voices, a man and a woman. I moved towards the parlor, where it seemed to be coming from. I saw Claudia and Joseph. Joseph was on his knees, begging for his life."

This was the same Joseph Scotcher who had died at least an hour earlier from strychnine poisoning, I reminded myself.

"And Claudia said all those things about Iris: 'She should have done this, but she didn't, and you killed her,' or something like that. And then I started to scream, and Claudia dropped the club and ran—through the door to the library. Why must I go through all of this again? It's horrible."

I could not help but feel proud when Poirot put a question to Sophie that he had first heard from me.

"Claudia Playford was seen on the upstairs landing with Randall Kimpton, mademoiselle, when everybody was coming down the stairs in response to your screams. I see only one way she could have gotten there, and that is by running up the stairs very quickly after attacking Mr. Scotcher, before anyone opened their door. Did you, by chance, hear the footsteps of Claudia Playford running up the stairs? You would, I think, have heard her in the hall when she emerged from the library. That floor is tiled, with no carpet. You might perhaps have wondered if she planned to escape, this murderer of the man you loved. That might have made you more aware of her movements."

Sophie's eyes darted back and forth as she tried to think. "No," she said eventually. "I heard nothing. As you say, Claudia must have run upstairs, but . . . I did not hear her. I heard only my own screams."

26

Kimpton's Definition of Knowledge

As soon as we drew up outside Lillieoak, Sophie Bourlet flung herself out of our vehicle as if Poirot and I had conspired to imprison her in it against her will, and ran for the house.

"Everything is altered, Catchpool," Poirot said with a heavy sigh, as he and I stepped out into the cold air.

"Indeed. Two pink, healthy kidneys, and no getting away from it."

"Speaking of getting away . . . Whatever Inspector Conree might say now that the inquest is behind us, I must ask you to remain at Lillieoak until I have solved this case. Having you by my side, it assists with the flow of my thoughts. If it would help for me to speak to Scotland Yard on your behalf . . ."

"There is no need. Yes, I shall stay." I didn't tell him I had telephoned my boss that morning, before the inquest, and that the mere mention of the name "Hercule Poirot" had been sufficient to achieve the desired result. I had no intention of going anywhere, with the matter of Joseph Scotcher's murder unresolved.

"I will solve it, Catchpool! Do not be in doubt of that."

"I am not." I had utmost faith in him—as little as I had in Conree, and as much as my Belgian friend had in himself.

He sighed. "This case is full of apparent contradictions. Scotcher was dying of Bright's disease, but then no! He was not dying—he was healthy! Scotcher was bludgeoned to death with a club—but he was not! He was poisoned. There are two things about Mr. Joseph Scotcher that we first believed were true. *Eh bien,* both turn out to be false."

I didn't know I was going to say it until the words came out of my mouth: "Iris Gillow—what if she is the key to all of this?"

"What do you know about her?" asked Poirot.

"Only that Randall Kimpton needs to tell us who she is—because it seems to me that she must be a vital part of this story."

"Not really." The voice came from behind us as we stood outside Lillieoak's front door.

I turned. It was Kimpton, strolling towards us with his hands in the pockets of a long gray coat. "I do not deny that Iris is important, but she is not *relevant.* There is a difference. Shall we go inside? I said I would tell you after the inquest, and enough time has been wasted already."

No lights were on inside the house; it was as if we had entered the mouth of a cave. "'Here walk I in the black brow of night, to find you out,'" said Kimpton in a tone of exasperation. "Except it's not yet night and it would be nice to be able to see where one was going."

Once we were in the library with the lights lit, Poirot said, "Dr. Kimpton, you knew, did you not?"

"Knew what?"

"That Mr. Scotcher was not dying at the time of his murder. That he did not suffer from Bright's disease of the kidneys, or any other illness."

"Well . . . that depends on your definition of knowledge."

We waited for him to say more. He, in turn, appeared to be waiting for us to speak, with his usual charming smile in place. After a few seconds, he adjusted it to a frown. "Strong suspicion is not knowledge, as any detective will tell you," he said. "I see that you are uninterested in this line of inquiry, so I will abandon it. Yes, in the sense that you mean, I knew. I did not believe for a moment that Scotcher was dying, or that there was anything the matter with his kidneys. I never believed it."

"Why did you not tell me this immediately, monsieur?"

"Do you mean immediately after Scotcher was murdered, or immediately upon your arrival at Lillieoak?"

"The former," said Poirot.

"Conservation of energy."

"Would you care to explain what you mean by that?"

"I did not wish to have an argument, or waste my time trying to persuade you," said Kimpton. "Why should you have believed me if I'd told you Scotcher was no more dying of a fatal kidney disease than you are or I am? Most people do not encourage everyone of their acquaintance to believe they are about to meet their maker when they are not. I knew that if I told you, you would go to Athie for confirmation, or Sophie, or both, and I knew what both would say: that *I* was the liar. You would have said, 'Come, come, Dr. Kimpton, you have let your imagination run clean away. Don't be cruel. Nobody would do such a thing,' or words that conveyed the same meaning. Let me tell you, Poirot: somebody would *always* do such a thing, no matter how wildly implausible the thing. Anyway, happily we do not need to have this argument because the truth is now revealed. At long last."

"What about Mademoiselle Claudia? Did she believe in Scotcher's illness?"

"Claudia?" Kimpton laughed. "Not a bit of it. Neither did Athie, or Sophie, or Hatton, or anybody with a shred of sense."

"Sophie Bourlet assures me that Scotcher was dying," Poirot told him. "She accuses the police doctor of lying about the state of his kidneys. What do you say to that, Mr. Kimpton?"

"It's bunkum. As a doctor, I can tell you that no nurse—and Sophie is, I believe, a very good one—could have spent as long as she did tending to Scotcher's every need and not tumble to the truth of the matter. You are not a scientific or medical man yourself, Poirot—I quite see that—so let me explain: Scotcher talked a lot about his impending death, and he was thin. In every other respect, he and the dying had little in common. He was never too weak or in too much pain to be witty, considerate and charming. Ask any doctor or nurse about their death's door patients and you will find that flattering their interlocutors is generally not among their priorities. Yet for Scotcher, it was, always."

Kimpton pulled a chair away from a highly polished round table and sat down. "Sophie Bourlet is no fool," he said. "She is a shrewd and perceptive woman. She knew Scotcher was a fraud, but it didn't stop her loving him. Now she is lying to protect his reputation."

"What about Viscount Playford and his wife?" asked Poirot.

"Harry and Dorro? Oh, they would have believed Scotcher, absolutely. I daresay that numbskull Phyllis believed him too."

"I do not understand," said Poirot. "If Lady Playford knew that Mr. Scotcher was deceiving her so shamelessly, why was his employment at Lillieoak not terminated?"

"Aha! That is an excellent question. You must ask her. I should be interested to hear her answer."

"Did you never ask her? Did Claudia not ask—Lady Playford's own daughter?"

"No. Neither of us referred to it."

"Why not?"

"We had different reasons. I will tell you mine first. I gave the matter careful consideration and decided that Athie was every bit as clever as I am. She also spent much of each day in Scotcher's company. She therefore had the capacity and the opportunity to suspect him, and, what is more, I was certain that she did. So! What would have been the point of telling her that I shared her suspicion?

She had evidently decided not to act on it—to retain Scotcher in employment and to talk to us all about his illness as if it were real—which, to my mind, meant that she too was a liar.

"She then took it further: she engaged Sophie Bourlet to cater comprehensively to Scotcher's nonexistent invalid needs. Now she was almost an equal partner in Scotcher's edifice of lies! Oh, no, I was not about to issue any challenges—not without certain knowledge. Athie would have defended Scotcher to the hilt and taken against me. That would have upset Claudia dreadfully. She enjoys savaging her mother, and does not realize how much under Athie's influence she remains. I do not believe she would ever marry a man of whom her mother seriously disapproved."

"And what was Mademoiselle Claudia's reason for failing to speak to Lady Playford about Scotcher's lies?"

"Sport." Kimpton grinned. "It's always sport with Claudia. She adores two things: drama and power. In that respect, she is an exact replica of Athie. She dropped just enough hints to let Athie know that she knew—"

"Aha!" Poirot said triumphantly. "So Claudia knew, but you only suspected?"

Kimpton sighed wearily. "I am disappointed in you, Poirot. How could Claudia have *known* any more than I did? She had her suspicions, however, and she made the most of them. Imagine that Claudia had faced Scotcher across the breakfast table one day and said, 'Your illness—it's a great big whopping lie, old bean!' in front of Athie and everyone. What would have happened? Scotcher and his collaborators in deception would have denied it, and Claudia and I would have insisted that we did not believe them, and that would have been that. There would have been no way to settle the matter, no more suspense infusing every conversation at Lillieoak, no more mystery to enliven our humdrum lives. Most of all, there would have been no more scope for Claudia to drift menacingly around the place as if at any moment she might spill the beans and cause the most almighty scene. My impression was that Athie feared she might one day, which gave her a certain power. My dearest one *adores* power. Do you understand at all, Poirot? Catchpool? I expect our ways seem very strange to you."

"No stranger than the ways of anybody else," said Poirot.

"Oh, I would not say that," said Kimpton. Something about his tone conveyed a sense of a warning. "Tell me this: have you ever before met a man who *pretended to be dying any day now when in truth he was perfectly healthy*?"

"That precise pretense? No, I have not."

"There you are, then."

"Although I did encounter a criminal several years ago, a man who very much wished to avoid playing chess—"

"Incidentally, whoever murdered Scotcher . . ." Kimpton interrupted Poirot's reminiscences. "That person is not *why* he died. He died because, quite needlessly, he invited death into his life. I have never been more convinced of anything. Death had not spotted him, nor sought him out—it was, for the time being, steering clear of him, but then he dangled the bait in front of death's nose, with all his lies, and death repaid him by snatching his life away. That is what I think."

"That does not sound very scientific," said Poirot.

"I will concede: it does not," Kimpton agreed. "There must be a little of the Shakespeare scholar still left in me. And, as if that were not enough, there is also Iris. She is the reason why no opinion I offer about Scotcher could ever be objective."

"Iris Gillow?" asked Poirot.

"Yes." Kimpton stood up and walked over to the window again. "Though her name was Iris Morphet when I first met her. Shall I tell you about her?"

27

The Iris Story

"I met Iris Morphet when I was studying at Oxford. That is also where, and when, I met Joseph Scotcher. I cannot resist adding, though it is quite irrelevant, that I met them on the very same day, although they did not until later meet each other.

Do I wish they had never met? That is a tricky question! How does one choose between the present and what was once a possible future? Very hard indeed.

In college, Scotcher and I had rooms that were adjacent to one another. We met one day after both popping out of our little doors at the same time, like the man and woman from one of those old German weather houses! We soon became friendly. Scotcher flattered me most determinedly, and I lapped it up, rotten egotistical creature that I was in those days. I felt that befriending him was the least I could do. At the risk of sounding pleased with myself . . . well, it was clear to me that everything I was, he desired to be: rich, handsome, confident.

You think Joseph is handsome, I suppose? Pretty perhaps—

altogether too delicate-looking for a man. And you think he is confident, I daresay? Well, not in those days, he wasn't. Timid as a mouse! Hung on my every word. In due course, I noticed that a lot of his words were in fact mine. I once heard him tell a mutual friend about something amusing that had happened to him in Sevenoaks, in Kent—except it was an incident that had happened to me, not to him. I'd told him about it and, not knowing I was within earshot, he retold it as if it were his own experience.

I soon started to question whether anything I heard from him was the truth. Was it really his grandmother who had once dropped a hairnet into a bowl of rice pudding or was it some other chap's? Was it Scotcher's childhood home that had flooded, destroying all his treasured possessions, or that of a train porter who had once carried his suitcase? Was there ever a flood at all? Who could tell?

What? No, I never challenged him. Oh, I don't know. I felt sorry for him, I suppose. I hoped that he mostly told the truth—perhaps he had only got carried away on that one occasion, I told myself, because my caper in Sevenoaks had been such a riot!

Then there was the flattery. I wrote something for my tutor that had Scotcher in *raptures*. He asked my permission to have copies made, at his own expense, so that he could share it with his mother and his brother, both of whom would love it, he told me. I thought it rather lumbering and uninspired myself, but a few weeks later Scotcher told me that his brother had declared it to be simply the best prose he had ever read, and what cogent arguments, and what intellectual brilliance . . .

Gentlemen, please remember this brother of Scotcher's, for I shall mention him again in due course. His name is Blake. Scotcher and he grew up in Malmesbury, and Scotcher was the older of the two— and that is the sum total of what I learned about my new best friend at Oxford, who was remarkably reluctant to talk about himself or his family. I had the sense that they had no means to speak of, and that Scotcher was rather ashamed of them—but, at a distance of this many years, I can't recall whether he told me anything of the sort. My imagination might have filled in the gaps.

It was about two months after I met Scotcher that he first raised the subject of his health. He returned from a trip to the doctor, or what he told me was a trip to the doctor, and announced that he had bad news: there was something wrong with his kidneys—so wrong that it might kill him. Well, I duly felt even sorrier for him! Who wouldn't? There was I, stepping out with the lovely Iris Morphet . . .

I'm supposed to be telling you about her, aren't I? Not Scotcher. The trouble is, other people's romantic histories are so tedious, and the man I was then is not the man I am today. Besides, I'm eager to get to the exciting part of the story. I must, however, lay the foundations.

I was in love with Iris and she with me—that is all that needs to be said about that! She was not a beauty like Claudia, and neither did she have Claudia's alluring quick-wittedness that I find so irresistible, or her sharp tongue. My dearest one is a minx, is she not? I do adore a minx! Iris was more the good girl sort, I suppose, and unfailingly kind. She had big red lips that needed no paint, flawless skin like a statue made of marble, and flaming red hair. There was something comforting about her. She was calm and serene, but passionate too: as if she had claimed and tamed the fire. She seemed to the young Randall Kimpton to be the very essence of womanhood. Once again, quite different from Claudia.

I'm convinced that Claudia is merely disguised as a beautiful young woman and is in fact a cruel Roman emperor, fixated upon revenge. She is never happier than when she decides the world has done her a grievous wrong—which is every day, as reliable as the rising of the sun. Iris was different: grateful for a smile or a pleasant word, rarely angry or ill-tempered.

You might think it strange that I was drawn to two so different women. I disagree. Opposites attract, as everyone knows—but there is also something satisfying about meeting the female version of oneself. Claudia is, quite simply, a version of me that I wish to defile in all the usual enjoyable ways. Really, what could be better?

Do I shock you, gentlemen? I apologize. It's only that I'm rather keen on the truth. If it's true, then one ought to be able to come out and say it. I don't give a fig for virtue—who can say what that is, anyway?—but without truth, we are all doomed to live out our days in darkness. And all this talk of truth brings me back to Scotcher.

The news he brought back from his medical consultations grew progressively worse. Many people in Oxford knew about his kidney condition by now, but I was closer to him than anybody in those days, and no one else monitored him in quite the way I did. What? Oh, yes, he had met Iris by now, many times. And I do her an injustice by saying that *I* was closer to Scotcher than anyone else. Iris took more of an interest in his ailing, failing kidneys than I did. She was always fussing over him—our poor, sick friend—always fetching things for him and inflicting her sensible advice on him: he must be stoical and optimistic, but at the same time practical; he must make sure to have fun and enjoy life, but not *too* much fun—on and on ad nauseam. It reached the point where I was sick of hearing about Scotcher's blasted kidneys.

Being an observant fellow, I couldn't help noticing that having the most wretched kidneys on this fair isle—*that* fair isle, I should say, since I'm talking about England—never stopped Scotcher from doing any of the things he most wanted to do. Whereas it regularly prevented him from undertaking life's more tedious tasks. I won't bore you with the details. Suffice to say, I became suspicious. I shared my suspicions with several friends and one university official, and quickly learned that most people would much rather not know an inconvenient truth—and besides, what was I able to prove? Scotcher by now was flattering everyone he met, it seemed, where once he had only bothered to flatter me, and nobody wanted to think ill of him. Think ill—oh, the irony! Most people did not want to consider that he might be perfectly well and thoroughly dishonest. They preferred to take their Joseph Scotcher sick and saintly.

I said nothing about any of this to Iris, which was silly of me, but she was forever telling me I ought to be softer, kinder, more like her.

One day I followed Scotcher, without his knowledge, to what he had told me was a meeting with his doctor. Unsurprisingly, he went nowhere near a surgery or hospital. He met the wife of the master of . . . well, I won't say which college it was, for I have no wish to cause trouble for the lady in question. The point is, while Scotcher was supposed to be consulting a kidney specialist—a man—he was strolling through the botanic garden, exchanging confidences with another man's wife.

Naively, I assumed that if he was busy with her, he would not also be busy with Iris, but I was wrong. I had not yet proposed marriage to Iris. Like a damned fool, I took too long about it, waiting for some sort of sign that she was the right girl for me. Imagine my shock when one day she announced that Joseph Scotcher had proposed to her and she had accepted him! Scotcher needed her so much more than I did, she explained tearfully. I was strong, whereas he was weak.

You're going to ask me if I told her then of my suspicions. I did not. I had not done so before, and to announce them now, suddenly, would have made everybody question my motives and my honor. Iris would have thought I was prepared to say anything to discredit Scotcher. I did not wish to lower myself, and, as I have already said, I did not know for certain. What if I was wrong? I would have looked like a prize blockhead! Surely no one would tell a lie of such enormity, I kept trying to persuade myself.

To be frank, I was so angry with Iris that I found the idea of her marrying a complete charlatan rather entertaining. She and Scotcher deserved one another, I thought.

Scotcher threw himself upon my mercy. All I had to do was ask, he said, and he would explain to Iris that he could not marry her after all, though they were desperately in love. Ha! Called his bluff,

I did! 'I should very much like you to call off your engagement and return my young lady,' I told him. You should have seen the look on his face. He started to splutter. He assured me that once I thought about it, I would realize that I could never be truly happy with a woman who had betrayed me—and with my closest friend too.

He was right. I told him he was welcome to Iris, and she to him. As for me, I wanted nothing to do with the pair of them and I made sure I got what I wanted. I successfully avoided them both thereafter, with the exception of a few chance glimpses in town.

A few months later, I received a letter from Iris. She was no longer engaged to be married to Scotcher, she wrote, though of course she would not allow herself to hope that I might forgive her and take her back. I did not bother to reply. I wondered if she had come to suspect him as I had. Her letter made an oblique reference to trust . . . oh, I can't remember the details. I tore the infernal thing into many pieces and threw them on the fire.

Shortly after Iris's letter, another one arrived—this one was from Scotcher's younger brother, Blake, requesting a meeting with me. How could I resist? Surely the man's own brother would know if he were truly ill, I thought.

Blake Scotcher suggested we meet at the Turf Tavern. I objected to his choice—dreadful place!—and named Queen's Lane Coffee House instead. He agreed, and a date was fixed.

I'm not sure how to tell you what happened next. It matters, doesn't it, *how* you tell a story. One has sometimes to make a random choice and hope for the best.

Well, when I arrived for our meeting, he was already there. My first thought was, 'Strong resemblance, though this one has a darker complexion, and a coarser accent. There's no doubt he and Scotcher come from the same stock, but why on earth does the man not trim his beard?' It was an appalling growth, red in the middle with gray outer edges. It looked like the sort of thing you might see on a pirate! I soon forgot about his excessively whiskered face when he told me that his brother, Joseph, was dying, and that what he wanted most in the world was my forgiveness. He should not have allowed his friendship with Iris to develop in the way that it had, knowing she was mine, or almost mine.

I asked if it was his kidneys. The brother told me that it was. I asked how much time Scotcher had left and the answer was, 'Months. A year at the outside.'

I can honestly say that for the first and last time in my life, I did not know what to do. I had been wrong about Scotcher, I realized—gravely wrong; I must have been. Filial loyalty was one thing, but surely no man of honor would agree to tell a stranger that his brother was dying if it were not so.

But, wait (I argued with myself)—that was a feeble contention if ever I had heard one. If one Scotcher brother could be a shameless blackguard, why could not another be cut from the same cloth? I soon saw that my theory did not hold water.

As I was pondering all this, Blake Scotcher started to speak more quickly. This is odd, I thought to myself.

I am trying to tell the story exactly as it happened to me, but it's very hard. I must try, though.

It was as if something had suddenly made Brother Blake nervous, but what could it have been? Was it that I appeared to be thinking a little too long and hard? Was it that he had come to meet me assuming that I would rush with him to Scotcher's bedside, crying, 'All is forgiven,' and I was showing no sign of doing so?

'If you cannot bring yourself to pay Joseph a visit, would you consider writing him a letter?' asked Brother Blake, who appeared to be in more of a hurry with each word he spoke. 'I hesitate to ask, but it would mean so much to him. Even if you do not feel able to say that you forgive him—you might simply wish him a peaceful passage from this world to the next. Only if you were to feel comfortable doing so, of course. Here, take my card. You may send your letter to me and I will see that Joseph gets it.'

And with that Blake Scotcher was gone—*if he was ever there in the first place*. Which of course he was not!

Don't look at me like that, gentlemen. If I had told you too soon, I would have undermined the dramatic impact of the story. I wanted you to experience the incident as I did. Imagine *my* shock when Brother Blake handed me his card and his sleeve rode up his arm a little to reveal a wrist and lower forearm that were a quite different color from his hands, neck and face. The beard, the dark skin and the coarse voice were a reasonable disguise, but as I sat at the table and went over everything that had happened, *I became absolutely convinced that the man who had just left Queen's Lane Coffee House was not Blake Scotcher, but his devious older brother*—Fake Blake, as I have thought of him since, with great affection.

The eyes, the bony frame, the shape of the neck . . . Oh, yes, it was Scotcher all right! *Joseph* Scotcher. I would have suspected it much sooner than I did, were it not for the fact that only one in ten thousand men would consider impersonating his brother in order to lend credence to a fabricated tale of his own imminent demise.

I heard some months later that Iris had married a chap by the name of Gillow, Percival Gillow—an insalubrious cove by all accounts, a violent drunkard, never too far away from destitution. No doubt Gillow had found a way to engage Iris's sympathy, as Scotcher had.

Iris wrote to me once more after her marriage, asking if we could meet. She had something she needed to discuss with me, she said. Once again, I did not reply. Two weeks after her letter arrived, I heard news of her death. She had fallen under the wheels of a train in London. Her husband had been with her at the scene of the crime—or the accident, depending on your point of view. There was talk of Gillow having pushed her, but the police decided finally that there was no case for him to answer. Mr. Gillow is presently an inmate at the workhouse in Abingdon, near Oxford. Charming place, I am sure!

Well, that concludes my sorry tale. It won't have escaped your notice that I fairly stand out as the only body on the premises whose possible reasons for wanting to murder Joseph Scotcher could make a bumper edition of some sort.

I did not, however, kill the scoundrel. Neither did Claudia—which means Sophie Bourlet lied. In my book, that makes her the murderer! It's dashed peculiar, though—she was about to marry Scotcher and become, in due course, an exceedingly wealthy woman. Now that he's dead, everything once again goes to Harry and Claudia, and Sophie will get nothing. Yet if she is innocent, why did she lie and blame Claudia?

Dashed peculiar—that's what it is."

28

A Possible Arrest

THE FOLLOWING DAY, INSPECTOR Conree and Sergeant O'Dwyer arrived at Lillieoak a little before nine in the morning. Poirot and I were summoned by Hatton—not to a room where the four of us might talk, but to the front door. Inspector Conree was apparently intent on conducting the conversation on the doorstep.

"I am here to inform you both, as a courtesy, that I will shortly be making an arrest for the murder of Joseph Scotcher," he said.

Poirot straightened his back and moved forward. Conree retreated, looking down at his feet as if to check that the desired distance between himself and Poirot had been preserved to the inch.

"You think, then, that Sophie Bourlet is guilty of this crime?" Poirot asked.

"I do," said Conree. "I have from the start."

"Inspector, if I might make a request," said Poirot. "I strongly believe that the nurse is innocent. Soon I hope to know for certain. I entreat you, therefore—"

"You are going to ask me not to arrest her," said Conree.

"Yes—at least not yet."

"If you had listened patiently instead of interrupting me, you would know by now that I am not here to arrest Miss Bourlet."

"You are not?" Poirot looked at me, understandably puzzled. "You said that you were here to make an arrest, Inspector. I assumed—"

"Your assumption was incorrect. I am here to arrest Miss Claudia Playford."

"What?" I said. "But you just said that you suspect Sophie Bourlet."

Conree nodded to O'Dwyer, who said, "There is no proof that Miss Bourlet harmed Scotcher. In the case of Miss Claudia, we have the evidence we need to make an arrest."

"What evidence?" Poirot spluttered. "There is no evidence against Claudia Playford!"

I stood close behind him, fearing he might keel over, ready to catch him if he did.

"There is the testimony of Sophie Bourlet, who says that she saw Claudia Playford battering the head of Mr. Scotcher with the club, and that she heard the man beg for his life, to no avail," said O'Dwyer.

"*Nom d'un nom d'un nom!*" Poirot turned to Conree. "Inspector, please explain this nonsense!"

"I am not obliged to explain myself to you, Mr. Poirot. I am in charge of this investigation. You are merely a guest in the house where the murder took place. The same goes for your friend Catchpool."

I said to O'Dwyer, "Sophie might have witnessed the clubbing, but we know that was not the murder. Scotcher died from strychnine poisoning at least forty minutes earlier. So even if Sophie Bourlet saw Claudia Playford smash up his head—"

"Inspector, I implore you," said Poirot. "Think before you act. Whyever would you arrest a woman whom you believe to be innocent of murder, based on an account given by the woman you suspect is the real killer? Nothing has ever made less sense to me!"

"Claudia Playford is the daughter of a viscount and the sister of a viscount," said Conree.

"She is—and when you first came to Lillieoak, this same fact was the reason you gave for why you were *not* going to arrest her. You said, 'I have no intention of arresting the daughter of Viscount Guy Playford simply because a nurse of no particular distinction has made a wild accusation against her.' Yet now you propose to do that very thing!"

"Now is not the same as then," said Conree. "If we arrest Claudia Playford, things will start to happen, and soon enough we will know who we're after. O'Dwyer agrees with me that this is the correct course of action."

"I do," the sergeant confirmed. "The way I see it is this: Sophie Bourlet may well be a liar, and maybe a killer too—*but she says she saw Miss Claudia going at Mr. Scotcher with the club*. And no one else has come forward to say that they saw anybody other than Claudia Playford carrying out that brutal attack, now, have they? So if anyone at all was seen doing it, it was Miss Claudia. I hope you follow me?"

"Sergeant, I hope very much that I do not," said Poirot. He turned to me with a weary look in his eye. I understood what he wanted from me—to take over. This was something I could take care of on his behalf. No displays of brilliance were needed, only the relaying of what ought already to have been logically evident.

"You are on the verge of making a grave error," I told the two gardaí. "First, you assume that the person who assaulted Scotcher with the club must also have been his poisoner, but there is no reason to assume that. In a case as distinctive as this one, it is impossible to make such an inference, not without knowing the motive—or both motives, come to think of it. Why did someone want Scotcher dead? And why did someone then, after he was dead, want it to look as if he was killed in a different way—bludgeoned, not poisoned? We could well be talking about two different people. I should say we probably are! And as for your point, O'Dwyer, about no one but Claudia Playford having been seen attacking Scotcher in the parlor with a club, well, that could be argued in quite the opposite way!

"Listen: nobody else has been accused of clubbing Scotcher, nor allegedly witnessed in the act. That means everyone else might or might not have done it. Meanwhile, Claudia Playford features in a story in which she did it, but we know that other parts of that story are entirely untrue. Scotcher cannot have begged for his life; he was already dead. If Sophie's account is the truth, how on earth did Claudia Playford get to the landing outside Lady Playford's study without being seen running upstairs? Why were there no traces of blood on the white dressing gown that Sophie claims Claudia wore to attack Scotcher?"

I paused for breath, then said, "Claudia Playford, gentlemen, is the only person who features in a story about her bludgeoning Scotcher *that we know to be full of lies.* Can you truly not see that this makes her less likely than anyone to be the killer?"

"Catchpool is right, Inspector," Poirot said solemnly. "Please do not make this arrest. I know considerably more now than I knew before the inquest—the little gray cells of Poirot, they are always busy!—but still I have not assembled the full picture. I need to make a journey to England. There are people I must speak to urgently, and Catchpool also—he has many pressing questions to ask of those at Lillieoak in my absence.

"When I return to Clonakilty, if I have had good luck on my travels, I will know everything. Please, Inspector . . . allow me a few days, and make no arrests until I return. Action without proper foundation could be catastrophic."

"England?" Conree growled. "On no account! I forbid it!"

It was the first I had heard, too, about a trip to England; I could only assume Poirot had made some progress in his deliberations since the day before. Ah, well—I would miss him at Lillieoak, but if it was necessary for him to go then I would simply have to soldier on without him for a few days.

Poirot produced a rather sharp-edged smile for Conree, by way of retaliation. "Inspector, for how long do you intend to keep this . . .

restriction in place? You surely do not suspect me, Hercule Poirot, of murder? *Bien!* I wish only to be of assistance in this matter. If you order me not to go, I will not go!"

"Inspector Conree, I'm afraid I shall have to contradict my good friend," I said. "If he wishes to go to England, then go he must. Poirot is not one to dash about the place and tire himself out unnecessarily. He prefers to solve whatever is his case of the moment by sitting in a comfortable armchair and giving it thorough consideration. I assure you, he would not conceive of making the journey to England if it were not absolutely necessary. Since he is too polite to lay out the facts, allow me to do so: if you prevent him from going, he will be unable to obtain vital information. Joseph Scotcher's murder will remain unsolved and you will return, disappointed, to Dublin, where you will no doubt face the even greater disappointment of your superior officers. Will they look favorably upon your efforts, do you think, when they learn that you refused the help of Hercule Poirot? Or would you rather return triumphant to Dublin, able to say that you enlisted the help of the great Belgian detective and that your faith in him was thoroughly vindicated?"

Conree ground his chin against the collar of his shirt. "Very well," he said tightly after a moment or two. "You may go, Poirot."

"*Merci*, Inspector." He was gazing fondly at me as he said it.

Conree caught the look, and said, "But don't come crying to me when you fail and we end up arresting Claudia Playford for murder! The tactics that you have employed today ought to be beneath you, Poirot. I warn you—they will not work on me again."

"To which tactics do you refer?" I asked with a deliberate and cool formality. "We have used nothing more than reason and solid good sense."

"It is useless to argue with him, Catchpool," Poirot murmured as Conree and O'Dwyer climbed back into the car that had brought them to Lillieoak. "Good sense appears the most underhand of tactics to a man who has no reserves of his own to draw upon."

29

The Grubber

Late the following afternoon, I received a telephone call.

"It is I, Catchpool—your friend Hercule Poirot."

"No need for such a formal introduction, Poirot. I recognized your voice immediately. Besides, an uncharacteristically garrulous Hatton told me it was you when he summoned me to the telephone. How is England treating you?"

"Better now that I have been moved to a more suitable room in the hotel and I have *un sirop* beside me. The first room that they tried to put me in was not well appointed. Usually I would not complain about disadvantageous accommodation—"

"Of course you would not." I smiled to myself. "I can imagine you doing no such thing."

"—but having come today from *the grubber,* it was important to me to make myself comfortable." The down-at-heel colloquialism combined with Poirot's impeccable European accent made me laugh. He sounded as if he was trying it out to see if a chap of his sort could get away with saying it more regularly.

"The grubber? You mean the workhouse? Which workhouse, and what on earth were you doing there?"

"That I will tell you in a moment—but first I should like to ask what *you* are doing, Catchpool. What have you done since I left Lillieoak?"

"Me. Well . . . not an awful lot, really. I had a rather wonderful sleep this afternoon after lunch. It was most refreshing. Aside from that . . . I have tried to keep myself to myself. It's not very jolly around here without you to brighten up the place. When are you coming back?"

"I knew it! Stop at once the keeping of yourself to yourself! Do the opposite. Find occasions to start conversations with people—the servants too. Talk, listen, and notice what is said to you, every word. The more people talk, the more they reveal. You cannot waste the opportunity, Catchpool. Me, I do not waste a moment. I have been talking, and listening."

"At the grubber, you mean?"

"Yes. The one at Abingdon, in Oxford. It is presently the home of Percival Gillow, the widower of Iris Gillow. I had a very interesting conversation with him about the death of his wife. Once I am finished in Oxford—which is not quite yet—I will travel to Malmesbury."

"Malmesbury? Why on earth . . . ?"

"It is the birthplace of Thomas Hobbes—did you know that, Catchpool? The author of *Leviathan*."

I had not known. "And what has *Leviathan* to do with the murder of Joseph Scotcher?" I asked.

"Nothing at all. Though there is, as it happens, a work of literature about which one might say the opposite. Oh, yes."

"Whatever do you mean, Poirot?"

"All in good time, *mon ami*. Let me first tell you about Mr. Gillow."

I pulled a chair over to near the telephone and sat down to listen to the story.

Percy Gillow had apparently found the presence of a man of Poirot's class and elegance at the workhouse as comical as I did. He had chuckled when his unlikely-looking visitor was brought to the small, narrow room that was his, and said, "Don't much see your kind in here. Sure you didn't get lost on yer way to yer tea party?"

"I have come to speak to you, monsieur. I hope you do not mind?"

"I don't. Seems as you do, is all. Looking at the walls, weren't you? Bit of paint's all they need. There's not much room here, but it's enough. Food's better'n it used to be. And they take us to the picture house once a week—bet you didn't know, did you?"

"It sounds most agreeable. Monsieur . . . you married a girl by the name of Iris Morphet?"

"I did." Gillow sounded pleasantly surprised that Poirot, ignorant of workhouse outings as he was, should turn out to know anything at all. "I married her, all right. I was a gentleman then, like you—no, you won't believe it, but it's true. I fit in wherever I find myself—that's the secret. That's how to play it. Funny, you asking about Iris. She died. Never wanted to marry me in the first place, she didn't."

"Why do you say that she did not want to marry you?"

"She loved another man: Randall Kimpton. Won't never forget that name. She'd let him go—gone off with some wrong 'un who'd talked a pretty tale—and couldn't get the right one back. So she picked another wrong 'un: Percival Gillow Esquire!" He grinned broadly, revealing cracked and blackened teeth, and pulled a small snuffbox with a jeweled lid out of a pocket. His fingertips were the same color as the box's contents.

"I am acquainted with Dr. Kimpton," Poirot told him.

"Mention me, did he? And Iris? That why you're here?"

"Dr. Kimpton said that there was a rumor about Iris's death—that she did not fall in front of a train by accident."

"He weren't no doctor in them days."

"About Iris's death, Mr. Gillow?" said Poirot patiently.

"Weren't no accident. Murder, it was. That what Kimpton told you?"

"He suggests that you might have pushed your wife in front of the train."

"Nah, not me." Percy Gillow did not take offense at being

suspected of murder, and continued to pack his nose with snuff. "Woman dressed as a man, it were. In disguise! I told them that—the police—but they took one look at me and decided not to listen. What could a feller like me tell 'em that was worth listening to?"

"So you saw it happen? You saw this disguised person push your wife onto the tracks?" Poirot asked.

"No, sir. What I saw was this. I saw Iris fall—that was the first thing. Bam! Nowt I could do! Seemed to jolt forward for no reason, she did. Train was racketing towards her. She was crushed." Gillow shook his head and held up his snuffbox. "She gave me this. Not that day, mind. But I can't look at it and not think of her. She had a good heart, Iris. Good brain too—not that she used it much, and never where men were concerned. I was always the same with the girls. We were peas in a pod, Iris and me. But she never could see that I was the one for her, even once we were married. She kept wanting better."

"I see. So you saw her fall and then . . . ?"

"I looked away. Didn't want to see what was in front of me, so I turned round and there he was—I suppose I should say 'she.' Hat, suit. Beard—red in the middle, gray around the outside. Reminded me of a pirate's beard from a storybook. Not a bad disguise, but it didn't fool me."

"A pirate's beard. That is interesting," Poirot murmured.

"It fell off," said Gillow.

"What fell off?"

"The beard. As I was looking, it fell clean off! Now, I've never had one meself but I know they don't just drop off your chin. That's when I knew for sure it was a woman in disguise, see. She hooked it—which to my mind was a clear sign of guilt. But you try making the police pay attention when you've had too much ale and you've no profession to speak of, and your wife's just ended up under the wheels of a train!"

Poirot nodded, though he found it difficult to imagine himself in a predicament of that particular sort.

More than Fond

At Lillieoak, first thing the next morning, and bearing in mind Poirot's instruction to talk and listen as much as I could, I went in search of Lady Playford. As it turned out, she was also looking for me, and claimed it as her victory when our paths crossed. "Edward! Found you at last! Did you speak to Poirot on the telephone last night? I don't suppose he told you when we might expect him back at Lillieoak? It's funny, I scarcely know the man, but he turns out to be one of those people who changes a place for the worse once he leaves it—don't you find?"

She wore a long kimono with an intricate pattern in pale blue, gold and orange. It was rather magnificent, but made me think only of *The Mikado*. Claudia had compared the plot of the Gilbert and Sullivan operetta to Sophie Bourlet's prospective marriage to Joseph Scotcher—which, as it turned out, need not have been short-lived because Scotcher had not been dying after all, but could no longer happen because he was now murdered.

I told Lady Playford that I was at her disposal, and that Poirot would return as soon as he could.

"He had better, or I shall enter his name in my little black book." She took me by the arm and steered me through the hall. "It's not a real book—only in my head. It's what I call my list of those who have wronged me and are not to be forgiven! Oh, I keep a meticulous record. You would do well to ensure that your name is never added to the list, Edward."

"I shall make it my life's work."

She laughed.

"Where are we going?" I asked.

"To the parlor."

I stopped walking and freed my arm from hers. "The parlor?"

"Yes. That is where I thought we would have our talk."

"But . . ."

"It is also where Joseph's body was found?"

"Yes." It was one thing going in there with Randall Kimpton to look at the bloodstain—that could not have happened anywhere else, whereas Lady Playford and I could talk in any room at Lillieoak.

"The stained carpet has been removed," she said. "The gardaí gave their permission. I have Arthur Conree just where I want him. I told him that of course he would want to *withhold* his permission, and did I mention how *wonderful* he was at forbidding us all to breathe air, and how right he was to do so—and naturally he became as biddable as a little lamb. So, the carpet was dealt with yesterday. We will find no trace of murder in the parlor today, I promise you."

"I see."

She gave me a stern look. "It is a room in my home, Edward— one that gets more of the morning sun than any other at Lillieoak. I refuse to allow it to become a shrine to death. While I do not wish to sit in it this morning any more than you do, we must do it. Over and over again, until we no longer do so reluctantly."

"That is the wisest way to approach the matter," I had to agree.

"As it turns out, of course, Joseph was not even murdered there."

I followed her into the parlor, expecting to see bare floorboards, but another carpet had been laid in place of the old one: blue, green and white, with an elaborate pattern of birds in trees.

"Sit, Edward." Lady Playford pointed at the chair she had chosen for me. It was the furthest from the spot where Joseph Scotcher's ruined head had lain; I was grateful for that. She arranged herself on the chaise longue opposite me.

"There is much that you wish to ask me, and much I would like to tell you," she said. "Shall I start? It's only that, for so long, I have had a story—the most compelling story I have ever known—and I could not share it with anybody. Now that Joseph is dead and the inquest has made plain what I have known for a long time—that he was not ill, and certainly not dying—I can talk openly at last. There is nothing I must withhold. The relief is overwhelming!"

"I can imagine," I said dutifully.

"I thought I might never be able to tell this story," said Lady Playford. "I had resolved to protect Joseph's good name, but now, with him dead—*murdered*—I am duty-bound to tell you everything. If I want to help catch his killer, I have no choice. Tell me something, Edward: how well do you recollect the conversation at dinner on the night that Joseph was killed?"

"I think I recall most of it," I said.

"Good. Then you will remember that I offered an explanation for what must have seemed an extraordinary act on my part. Why should I disinherit my own children and leave everything to my secretary? I said to Joseph in front of you all—quite likely in these very words, for I had prepared my speech in advance—'It is common knowledge among good doctors that the psychological can and often does have a profound influence over the physical.' I said that I wanted to give Joseph something to live for—a vast fortune—in the hope that his unconscious mind would then work its magic and cure his bodily ailments. Do you recall all of this?"

"I do."

"Good. I also said that I was no longer prepared to give Joseph's doctors free rein, and that I intended to take him the very next day to see *my* doctor, who is the best of the best. That part is true—I have an excellent doctor. The rest, I am ashamed to say, was a lie. To be more precise: it was a *probable* lie. I did not know absolutely for certain. That was my dilemma, you see."

"I'm not sure I do," I admitted.

"Well, it was true that I was no longer willing to leave Joseph's doctors to get on with it as they wished—assuming his doctors were real and not a figment of his imagination. And I would definitely have taken him to see my own wonderful doctor the following morning *if nothing had happened in the night to change things*—but I had a feeling that something would." Lady Playford flinched as she added, "Though, naturally, I had no idea that Joseph's murder would happen. If I had suspected that somebody would kill him, I should never have done any of it—the new will, the announcement at dinner. For that error of judgment, I shall never forgive myself. It was unjustifiably conceited of me to imagine that I could foresee every possible consequence of my actions."

"Only Scotcher's murderer is responsible for his death," I told her.

She smiled. "That is nonsense—but comforting nonsense, so I will do my best to make myself believe it."

I waited in silence for her to say more. Eventually she sighed, like a train emitting a large puff of steam, and said, "I did not believe that Joseph was dying. Oh, I probably did for a very short time after he told me—and I was distraught, truly distraught. I had grown fond of him very quickly. More than fond. Within days of his arrival at Lillieoak, I was offering profound prayers of thanks to the Lord for sending him my way. Did you have the chance to talk to him at all, Edward? Then you will know what it felt like: as if no one in the world had ever understood you so well as he did; as if no one had ever cared so much."

"He did seem unusually thoughtful and interested in others," I said.

"Yes, and insightful," said Lady Playford. "Every time I spoke to him, it was as if he had a magic key that could open up my mind and reveal my own thoughts to me—wisdom I did not know I had. I should have objected most strenuously if anyone else had occupied my head in that way, but Joseph understood me so completely. No one else ever has. And he was so *clever*! And of course one always had such tremendous fun with him. He was the most stimulating company imaginable. When he expressed an opinion about a matter—and many of his opinions would have been too irregular for conventional tastes—I found myself agreeing with him *absolutely*. He always knew the right thing to say, and just how to say it."

She was not finished. "This will sound fanciful, Edward, but at times I almost believed that someone must have taken a piece of my soul and used it to create Joseph. After he arrived at Lillieoak, I could scarcely muster the will to speak to anybody else. They were all so dreary compared to him."

Lady Playford adjusted her position on the chaise longue so that she was sitting up straight. "I tell you all this only so that you will understand what comes next. When Joseph first told me that he was seriously ill with a kidney problem, I was surprised. I had noticed nothing untoward—he had been doing all that was required of him, and he did not look unwell. I was horrified to hear that he might not survive. Grief-stricken! There is no other way to describe it. The thought of losing him was *unbearable*."

She stopped for a moment and closed her eyes. What had been a thought was now a reality. The thing about realities, I reflected, was that one bore them because one had no choice.

"Immediately, I hired the best nurse for him that I could find: Sophie. I tried to make him see my doctor, but he was adamant that he did not wish to do so. By the time he came to me with the news that his affliction was terminal Bright's disease, and that he would not live much longer . . . Well, let us say that by then I was already suspicious. Even so, in spite of my doubts, I was moved by Joseph's apparent lack of concern for himself. He seemed to care only about comforting me. He assured me that he was a fighter, that he was determined to stay with me for as long as possible. I thought, 'How can this poor dying man be so selfless as to worry so much more about me than himself? He must be a saint!' I suppose—and I am ashamed to admit it—I must have thought, in that moment, 'How could I ever have doubted him? Pretending to be gravely ill is one thing, but surely no healthy person would claim to be *dying,* with no hope of a cure.'

"Common sense introduced itself again soon afterwards, of course. I realized that Joseph could afford to be saintly and think primarily of the effect upon me, because he knew he had no health worries to speak of."

"When did you start to suspect that he was lying about his illness?" I asked.

"I don't think he *was* lying. If I tell a lie—and I do sometimes, if it suits me, like the time I told Edith Aldridge that I had sent her a thank-you letter and it must have gotten lost in the post. It was a lie, and I knew it. Joseph, I believe, did not know when he was lying—or not in the same way, at least. He somehow convinced himself that it was all true."

"You think he sincerely believed himself to be ill?"

"No, not exactly. I simply mean . . . I think his lies were not so much a decision as a compulsion. There must have been something about the reality of his life or himself that was abhorrent to him, so he retreated into a fiction—one that he could bear. I am convinced that he did his best to make himself believe it so that he could live more effectively in accordance with it. Does any of this make any sense to you?"

"Not an awful lot, no."

Lady Playford shook her head. "Nor to me. But I believe I knew Joseph better than anyone—the *real* Joseph, insofar as a man like him can be so described, since in many ways I think he felt no more real than any of the tales he told. Possibly you have never come across anybody like him, Edward. If you had, you might understand. I would swear that it was himself Joseph wished to deceive as much as anyone else. That is why I cannot judge him as harshly as I would otherwise. His motivation was a deep psychological need of some kind. I am keen to discuss it with Poirot, for I know psychology is one of his interests."

"When did you start to suspect that Scotcher was not at all sick?" I rephrased my original question.

"I couldn't tell you precisely, but between two and three weeks after he first told me of his illness. There was a doctor's appointment he canceled for a rather trifling reason—that struck me as odd, given the supposedly perilous nature of his condition. He never seemed sickly at all. From my observation of his behavior, he appeared as healthy as Harry or Randall or any other young man. He was painfully thin—but then some people are, and there's nothing to do about it. Many of them, you find, eat like horses. It's their constitution. Then, on another occasion, Joseph went off to England to see a particular doctor whose expertise made it worth the journey, apparently. Well, *that* did not ring true at all! Why did he not need a doctor who was nearer and could see him more often? Why did no doctor ever come to the house?

"Joseph could not be persuaded to tell me this eminent English chap's name, and changed the subject whenever I asked. By sheer chance, Claudia was there at the same time—in Oxford to visit friends, and to indulge in her favorite activity of reminding Randall that she would never forgive him and never again give him house-room; what nonsense that turned out to be!

"The point is, Claudia *saw* Joseph at ten minutes after three o'clock on the day that he was supposed to be seeing the doctor. Instead, he was having tea with a woman with dark hair and one long eyebrow that went all the way across her face, Claudia said. Really, there is no need for such ugliness—these things can be easily attended to. She was a much older woman than Joseph. Oh, it was not an assignation or anything of that sort. Claudia saw them together through the window of the Randolph Hotel. The woman was eating a Chelsea bun."

"And you concluded from Scotcher's meeting with this woman that . . . What did you conclude? What bearing did it have upon his illness?"

"He had happened to mention the time of his doctor's appointment: three o'clock. A mere ten minutes later, he was at the Randolph Hotel. Now, if you are about to say, 'What if his doctor's appointment was over and done with in five minutes and it only took him another five to walk to the hotel?' then you underestimate me. The moment Claudia alerted me—the clerk at the Randolph was kind enough to allow her to use their telephone—I asked her to put the general manager on so that I could interrogate him. He was soon able to tell me that a table for afternoon tea for two had been booked for *three o'clock sharp* by one Joseph Scotcher!"

"I see. So when Claudia saw him with this woman, we can assume they had met at three and had already spent ten minutes together."

"Precisely. Of course, I might have wondered if Joseph had an eccentric doctor who insisted on meeting all his patients in fashionable hotels instead of at his surgery if Claudia had seen him at the Randolph with a man, but it was definitely a woman. Which means Joseph lied to me about the appointment."

"That is shocking," I said. "Knowing how fond you were of him, to allow you to believe that you might soon lose him to a terrible illness . . . and then to go on to confirm that falsehood!"

"It *was* shocking, but I was not shocked," said Lady Playford. "My initial reaction, once I had got it firmly stamped upon my mind that it was most unlikely that Joseph was dying or even sick . . . well, I had several responses. One was joyful relief: I would not lose him! He would live!" Her eyes filled with tears. "It is unbearable to think now about how I felt then. I'm sorry." She pulled a handkerchief out of the pocket of her kimono and dabbed at her face.

"There is no need to apologize," I said.

"That is kind of you, but I can't abide public displays of emotion. I prefer to analyze it *un*emotionally. To that end . . . aside from joy and relief, I was also immensely puzzled by Joseph's behavior. *Why should a man who could make the whole world fall at his feet choose to conduct himself in such an extraordinary way? I was intrigued— and I was grateful to be so.*"

"Grateful?"

"Does that sound strange to you? I am an only child. My parents were dull, quiet people. As a girl, if I wanted something interesting to happen, I had to invent it myself. So I turned my teddy bears into villains and my dolls into heroes and staged the most amazing dramas in my bedroom that no one else knew about. I have been inventing ever since—characters and dramas, mysteries and romances. As time went by and I got older, I met people who were far more interesting than my parents—*but never any who were more interesting to me than the characters I made up myself.* Until . . . ?"

She seemed to want me to complete her sentence. "Until you met Scotcher?" I said.

She nodded. "Joseph was more wonderfully baffling and be-wildering than any mystery I could ever hope to invent. Oh, yes, I was grateful to him. And . . . well, there was something rather *thrilling* about it all. I joined in with the game! The peculiar thing was, Sophie did too. She fell in with the pretense of sickness because she had fallen in love with Joseph and did not wish to expose his fabrications. Like me, Sophie wanted to protect him. Think of the damage to his reputation if the truth had got out!"

"Many would think that Scotcher would have deserved every bit of that damage," I said. I was one of the many. "Incidentally, Sophie Bourlet insists that she believed he was ill—that she still believes it. She accuses the police doctor of lying."

Lady Playford said, "Sophie has not the courage to confess that she colluded in a pretense of such enormity. She knew her patient was a fraud within a week of arriving at Lillieoak, I'll wager. Oh, she will never admit it. The truth offends her pride, so she insists it is otherwise. You must bear in mind, Edward, that the vast majority of people are disinclined to confront anything that is messy or peculiar. Most people are scared of most things—never forget that! It is really only writers and artists who can cope with the puzzling ambiguities—and those with an investigative inclination. I am sure Hercule Poirot would be fascinated by all of this."

"Did Sophie Bourlet know that *you* knew the truth about Scotcher's health?" I asked.

"I sincerely hope that she believed me to be fooled all the way along," Lady Playford said. A mischievous smile appeared, then vanished just as quickly. "After all, why would I waste money on a live-in nurse for a man who is not sick?"

Why indeed? I did not ask for an explanation. Lady Playford thought she had already supplied one, and, although I fully believed her, her reasoning in this matter would never satisfy me. It was unpardonable insanity as far as I was concerned.

"Claudia guessed the truth, of course, and so did Randall. I feared it was only a matter of time before one of them blurted it out in a way that was designed to wound Joseph as much as possible. Subtly taunting him would not have satisfied Claudia forever, and her jibes were escalating. It was that fear that led me to put together my quite brilliant plan."

Lady Playford's face creased in distress. "Except it was not brilliant at all. I was a vain old fool, thinking I could control everything. If I had done and said nothing, Joseph would still be alive today."

"What was the plan?" I asked her. "Or is it only what you have already told me, about taking Joseph to see your doctor?"

"Oh, no, there was a lot more to my plan than that. Much, much more."

Apprehensive about what I would hear next, I asked her to tell me the rest.

31

Lady Playford's Plan

"Catchpool—it is I, Hercule Poirot."

"I would never have guessed, old chap. Particularly since you telephoned at precisely the same time yesterday. Let me guess—do you have a *sirop* in your hand?"

"I wish it were so. No, *mon ami*. I am in the hospital."

I sat bolt upright. "Oh, dear—what has happened? Are you all right? Which hospital? In Oxford?"

"*Oui*. I am waiting to see a most eminent doctor—but do not worry, my friend. I am not here because of any injury to my person. I am here only to ask questions."

"I see." I chuckled in relief. "And this eminent fellow is a kidney specialist, I daresay."

"He has no more interest in kidneys than in any other part of the human body."

"Oh! Then he is not Scotcher's doctor. If Scotcher even had one," I added hastily. Sometimes the brain forgets what it has more recently discovered, and reverts to prior false knowledge of what turned out to be untrue.

"I am not here to talk about Joseph Scotcher but about a different matter altogether," said Poirot. "Oh—hello, Doctor!"

"Has the chap arrived?"

"No, it is a different doctor that has come in now—please stay on the line, Catchpool."

Less than five minutes into our conversation and I was losing track of all the doctors. I hoped I was right in thinking that so far there were three: Scotcher's (who might or might not exist), the one Poirot was waiting to see, and the one who had just walked into whatever room Poirot was in.

I listened and waited.

"Indeed—thank you, Doctor," Poirot was saying. "I asked the nurse to explain to you that I need to talk at length to my friend Edward Catchpool of Scotland Yard. It is a most private conversation, yes. Is there perhaps a different office you could use until . . . There is? Excellent. *Merci mille fois.*"

"Poirot, have you booted some poor chap out of an office that is rightfully his?"

"That is not important, Catchpool. I am eager to hear anything you might have to tell me."

"Are you?" I sighed. This was going to be difficult. "Before I start, I have a question for you. Your hotel in Oxford—what is its name?"

"The Randolph."

"How strange. I had a sort of feeling you would say that."

"Why is it important?"

"The story I'm about to tell you features the Randolph Hotel."

"Tell it to me," Poirot urged.

I started to summarize all that Lady Playford had told me, then broke off in frustration. "But, Poirot, I strongly advise you to talk to her yourself. She has a way of telling a story that . . . well, she brings it all to life and makes it make a funny kind of sense. My account is flat and colorless in comparison."

"Do not worry, *mon ami*. I will imagine how Lady Playford might have relayed the facts. My mind will add the color and the . . . bumps to eliminate the flatness."

I put aside my reservations and continued. My voice was sounding rather hoarse by the time I said, ". . . and then I asked her if that was the extent of her plan: taking Scotcher to see her own doctor. And she told me it was not. What came next was . . . well, it was rather extraordinary."

"Tell me," said Poirot eagerly.

"Well, you see, Michael Gathercole turns out to have applied for the position of private secretary to Lady Playford. That is how he and Scotcher . . . Wait, let me think. I wonder if this is the best place to start."

"Gathercole the lawyer? Applied to be the secretary of a novelist?"

As I gave Poirot the information he wanted, I felt as if I was translating from a foreign language. It was peculiar, but I would have found it easier to play the part of Lady Playford, as if on a stage, and recite the story as she had told it to me, than I did to retell it in my own words. I have decided, therefore, that any reader of this account should have the benefit of the best version. Poor Poirot had to make do with a rather more stilted version.

"I must bring Michael Gathercole into the story now," Lady Playford told me. "He is my lawyer, and an excellent one too, but he was not always a partner at the best and most exclusive firm in London. It was I who asked Orville Rolfe to take Michael on and to take him seriously, and Orville—whose family firm, Rolfe and Sons, had handled my father's affairs and my husband's—did not let me down.

"I first met Michael when he wrote to apply for the position of private secretary that I had advertised. He was a solicitor's clerk at the time, much too well qualified, and far brighter than his employment required him to be. Lacking in confidence as he was, he intended to remain as a clerk for the rest of his days. Then he saw my advertisement. He had so loved my books as a child, and he could not resist applying. I don't mean to boast, but it was clear from his letter of application that my books were all that had got him through a quite dreadful childhood. So of course I invited him for an interview.

"Joseph Scotcher also applied for the same position. His letter was impeccably polite, but not as personal. Before I met them both, I was certain that I would choose Michael over Joseph, but I did not want to choose without meeting them, so I asked both men to come to Lillieoak for an interview. I'm afraid I kept them both waiting an unpardonably long time—and the one who is not to be forgiven for that is Hatton, confound him! He was determinedly refusing to tell me something that day, so much so that I grew rather anxious, imagining it might pertain to either Michael or Joseph—and if it had, I would of course have wanted to know it *before* I interviewed them.

"It turned out to be no more than a need to rearrange the tuning of all the clocks—or whatever it is that one does to clocks—that had been planned for the following day. Well, I had to gather myself for thirty minutes or so after that—oh, I was fit to strangle that wretched butler of mine! So . . . a needless delay, during which time Michael and Joseph sat outside my study and talked. At length. You will understand shortly why that matters.

"I saw Joseph first. Well, there are no words to describe how he impressed me. His every sentence was full of references to Shrimp's adventures—he seemed to know my entire oeuvre by heart and in the most minute detail, and he had *theories*. It was as if he had delved into the depths of my creative essence and seen things there that I had not recognized myself.

"And so I chose Joseph. Anyone would have. You too, Edward. He was a sparkling, irresistible creature. It pained me that I had to allow him to leave the building; I wanted to keep him at my side from that moment on, but of course I had to show good form and think of the appearance of things. I had to let him go home, and I had to give Michael a fair hearing, having dragged him all the way to Clonakilty from London.

"I'm afraid I barely listened to Michael, barely noticed him. He was nervous, and did not make the best first impression. I was too busy, in my mind, rehearsing the letter that I would write to Joseph. Oh, I had chosen him before Michael entered the room, I am ashamed to admit. Michael is a lovely man and he deserved better from me. He is not dazzling, as Joseph was, but he is trustworthy. All right, I will say it: he is trustworthy *as Joseph was not*.

"I employed Joseph as my secretary, and awarded Michael a kind of consolation prize. I felt sorry for him, so I dropped a word or two in the ear of Orville Rolfe, as I said, and the result was more than satisfactory. I did not really think about Michael Gathercole again after that—until one day, some years later, I made a silly joke to Joseph that anybody who had read even one of my Shrimp books would have understood without difficulty. I don't suppose, Edward . . . ? Oh, you *have*? Why on earth did you not say so? Never mind. Let us put my conclusion to the test. If I said to you 'milk bottle top,' would you know what I was talking about, apart from an actual milk bottle top? There you are, you see! Of course you would. In *every single* Shrimp book, she makes the milk bottle top joke. But Joseph, it was plain, had not the faintest idea what I was talking about, which I thought was odd, because I could have sworn he made that very joke to *me* when I interviewed him for the job.

"I was confused. To put him to the test, I made two or three more coded references to my work, and again he looked quite at a loss. At that moment, it became apparent to me that he had read *none* of my books, having claimed to have read them all, passed them on to his family, bought extra copies and pressed them upon strangers on the street, attempted to start a new religion using the Shrimp books as holy texts—I am exaggerating, but not as grotesquely as you might imagine.

"At the exact moment that the extent of Joseph's dishonesty became clear to me—falsehoods about his relationship to my books as well as about his health—something else struck me too. A memory surfaced from the dimmest recesses of my brain. I had not imagined the 'milk bottle top' remark that had been made to me while I was interviewing possible secretaries. I had heard it, but not from Joseph—no, it came from *Michael Gathercole*. Unfortunately, I had been so taken with Joseph that I had attributed Michael's remark to the wrong man. Very unfair of me. Of course, it was not deliberate. But I worried . . . and I wondered . . .

"The next day, I wrote to Michael and asked him to come and see me again. He did so. I fired questions at him. In *Shrimp Seddon and the Painted Egg*, what quality of character does Shrimp's father say is the most important? In *Shrimp Seddon and the Fireman's Hat*, what gives Mrs. Oransky's scarf a peculiar smell? And so on. Michael got every single answer right. I then asked if he could recall any of what passed between him and Joseph as they waited together outside my study to be called in for their interviews. This embarrassed him, but I insisted he tell me. Lo and behold, out it all came, though more awkwardly and less eloquently than Joseph had presented the same insights—*but they were Michael's ideas, Michael's theories*. It was Michael who knew Shrimp's adventures inside out. Joseph had simply repeated what the other applicant for the job had been kind enough to tell him while they waited together to be interviewed.

"I felt terrible. You are thinking that I ought to have fired Joseph on the spot, but I had no desire to do so—no, not even after this latest discovery. Once again, Edward, you fail to take into account the need to *know*. What is the point of life with no mystery to solve? And so I kept asking myself: who *was* this dazzling young man? Was his name Joseph Scotcher, or was he somebody else altogether? Why did he think his life would be easier if he invented everything and told the truth about nothing? I wanted to *help* him. Because, you see, one thing about Joseph *was* true: he spent his every waking moment thinking of ways to make me happy, and help me, and keep me entertained. It seemed to be his only concern. No, I would not give up on him.

"First, though, I had to make it up to Michael. I told him that thenceforth he was to be my lawyer. Another firm had been dealing with my affairs, but I was not especially attached to anybody there, and I was happy to make a change. On hearing this news, Orville Rolfe invited Michael to become his partner in a brand-new firm, and Gathercole and Rolfe came into being. My conscience in relation to Michael was satisfied. I also resolved to talk about my new ideas for Shrimp always with Michael and never with Joseph. That was how I dealt with the matter.

"How to help Joseph, meanwhile . . . That was much harder. I did not want to accuse him, expose his dishonesty, scare him away from Lillieoak. I wanted him to feel absolutely safe with me . . . which meant pretending to believe him. I agonized over how best to help him in a way that would allow him to save face, and came up with nothing sensible or practical, and so, in desperation . . . well, the new will idea was a last resort.

"Oh, I had no intention of permanently disinheriting Harry and Claudia. If all had gone as I had hoped, I would have made yet another will as soon as the Joseph situation was taken care of. My plan for my third and final will was to divide my estate into three equal parts. Harry would inherit one, Claudia another, and the third would be shared between Joseph and Michael Gathercole. Dorro would have grumbled terribly, the ungrateful baggage—a third of my estate should be more than enough for anybody, and it isn't as if Harry and Dorro have children to think of!

"My will leaving everything to Joseph was designed so that it might work in two possible ways. If Joseph was truly sick, I hoped that news of a substantial inheritance might induce his unconscious mind to persuade his body to buck up and last a bit longer. And if he was not sick? Well . . . this is where it gets a little complicated. Don't worry, Edward, I will explain it all clearly. That is the main criticism leveled at my Shrimp books, incidentally—that they are sometimes too convoluted. Stuff and nonsense! I mean, if my plots were simpler then people would guess, wouldn't they? And you can't have people guessing. I'm afraid I don't write for dimwits and nor will I, ever. I write for those capable of rising to an intellectual challenge.

"I formulated my Joseph plot in exactly the way that I plan a book. Plotting is a skill like any other, and I regard myself as an expert after all these years of practice. I see you are agog to hear what I came up with. I will tell you . . .

"First, I would change my will and announce the change to everybody. Now, imagine Joseph—having put about the fiction that he is soon to die of Bright's disease—imagine him hearing this news. I say that I have left everything to him, and that the very next day I intend to take him to see my doctor. That would induce a state of panic in him, no? He cannot very well refuse me in the circumstances—I might change my mind about leaving everything to him, which I doubt he would wish to risk; the honest and the dishonest are equally keen on large amounts of money and land, I have found. And my doctor would of course take one look at him and say, 'A fine, healthy specimen.' The game would be up! I might send him away from Lillieoak in disgrace! Of course, I would do no such thing, but he was not to know that, was he? He believed his fibs had fooled me good and proper.

"With the visit to my doctor looming the very next day, Joseph had one night only—mere hours—to think of a way out of the pickle he had created for himself. As far as I could see, there were only two routes of escape for him. He could try to kill me, or he could throw himself upon my mercy and tell me everything. What? Of course I would have forgiven him! Wholly and completely. What? No, no little black book entry for Joseph! If he had only decided, finally, to be completely truthful with me, I believe I could have cured him—of whatever was wrong with his *mind* that made him feel the need to indulge in these fabrications.

"I notice you don't ask if I would have forgiven him if he had crept into my bedroom with a length of piano wire and had a go at strangling me! I would have. Absolutely. We are all capable of acting unwisely when forced into a corner. If Joseph was desperate enough to resort to murder, prompted by my mischievous new will, then that was my fault. I was not, however, prepared to be murdered, so I asked Michael Gathercole to conceal himself behind my bedroom curtain that night, so that if Joseph were to creep in and try to smother me in my sleep, Michael would be there to stop him.

"What you must understand, Edward, is that Michael was there, hiding in my room, in order to save not only me, but Joseph too. *Mainly* Joseph. Picture the scene: Michael springs out from behind the curtain and seizes the knife or gun or whatever it might be from Joseph's hand. I sit up in bed and am told by Michael what has occurred. What would Joseph do then, once he had been caught in the act of trying to kill me—his employer, his friend? Perhaps *then* he would admit all and beg to be forgiven, and then I could help him.

"You see, in the normal run of things, people who lie as easily as they breathe never admit to it. They have an endless capacity to invent new lies to explain the old ones. It is not a moral problem, in my opinion, so much as a mental illness. I see that you disagree, Edward, but I am right about this and you are wrong. In any event . . . catching Joseph red-handed and on the verge of committing murder was perhaps the only way to force the truth out of him, I thought. Because, you see, he might then have offered up his long-standing deception and his desperation to conceal it as mitigating factors, once he was accused of attempted murder—*which is so much more serious than lying.* He may have been willing, at that point, to say anything to make me believe he wasn't simply a callous killer who wanted to get his hands on my money as soon as he could. And then, once he had admitted to his true problem, he and I could have addressed, *together,* the unhappiness that must have been plaguing him for so long. With my help, Joseph Scotcher could have become the man he was destined to be. But instead . . .

"My plotting proved inadequate, as we now know. I never dreamt that anyone would . . . that anyone would . . . kill my darling Joseph.

"I must say, Edward, I had not anticipated that you would prove quite so unsympathetic an audience. Can you not understand that Joseph, for me, was like a magician? He transformed my whole life, using nothing more than his words. Even his big lie, once I tumbled to it, felt like the most amazing feat of magic. Ah—you are confused. Well, I guarantee you will look at me as if I am a lunatic when I explain, and who knows? Maybe I am! All right, then: quite simply, Joseph had cured a fatal illness *for which there was no cure.* The world's most brilliant kidney specialists had failed to find one, but Joseph Scotcher—my devoted, talented secretary—had succeeded! Do you see? He cured his Bright's disease *by turning out not to have it after all*!

"Don't! There is no need to tell me that turning out to be a liar is not the same as curing an illness. I know that as well as you do. I merely mean to say that *the effect upon me* was that one minute I was in anguish because I was about to lose my beloved Joseph, and the next I learned that he was not dying after all and was very likely in perfectly sound health! It was *as if* he had cured a fatal illness. I meant it as a metaphor, not as a summary of the facts of the matter.

"Look at your disapproving face, Edward! I wonder if you are angry with Joseph for misleading you too, in the short time that you knew him. Please try to see: he did not lie to you, or to me, or to anybody in particular. He simply . . . altered the truth, because he felt more comfortable doing so. And now I shall never get to the bottom of it. I shall never understand why he did it."

32

The Kidnapped Racehorse

"My very first suspicions about Scotcher's integrity and decency, or lack thereof?" said Michael Gathercole. It was the next day. He and I had left Lillieoak and ventured as far as O'Donovan's Hotel in Clonakilty. It was a great relief to be able to sit and talk and drink tea in a room where we would not at any moment be ambushed by an aggrieved Claudia or a fretting Dorro.

The lounge at O'Donovan's smelled musty and was stuffed too full of faded furniture. The curtains had lost any color they had ever had, but the tea and cakes could not have been better and, in all honesty, I would cheerfully have sat on a packing crate in order to spend an hour or two in a relaxed and pleasant atmosphere. I could tell that Gathercole felt it too: as if something dark and heavy had been temporarily removed. He seemed more at ease than usual.

"I remember the very moment," he said. "For a long time, it made no sense to me. Now it does. Scotcher said something about one of the Shrimp books—this was while the two of us were waiting to be interviewed by Lady Playford—and it was incorrect in every particular. He said, 'Which is the book about the racehorse that gets kidnapped? The title escapes me.' I thought it odd, because he had said only a moment before that he knew all of Lady Playford's books by heart, and I had told him I did too—and the thing is, there is no Shrimp book about a kidnapped racehorse, so he must have known that I would know that. Much later, I tumbled to what he was up to. He knew I would assume it was a mistake, albeit a rather inexplicable one. No civilized fellow would turn to a chap he's only just met and say, 'That's a lie. You're a liar.' And actually, I *did* assume it was a mistake at first."

"So did you set him straight?"

"I tried to, yes. I said the only Shrimp book featuring a horse—in a very minor way—is *Shrimp Seddon and the Voyage Around the World*. The shipbuilding chap, Sir Cecil Devaux, has a horse named Sapphire, and Shrimp solves the mystery when she realizes that Mr. Brancatisano, being Italian, pronounces Sapphire's name incorrectly—'fear' for the second syllable instead of 'fire,' making it sound like Sphere, Sir Cecil's shipbuilding company, and causing no end of bother and confusion."

"Do you know, I think that is one of the Shrimp books I've read," I told him.

"It's one of the very best."

"Is there a dreadful person in it called Higgins, who ends up falling into the sea, never to be seen again?"

"That's the one!" Gathercole smiled. "Well, you know more about Lady Playford's books than Scotcher did when I first met him. I can see now that he asked his question about a kidnapped horse to draw me out. In correcting him, and in the conversation that followed, I provided him with enough detail to pass himself off, during his interview with Lady Playford, as someone who knew more about Shrimp Seddon and her exploits than anyone else in the world. Do you know what he said after I told him all that about Sapphire and

Sphere and Sir Cecil Devaux? He said, 'Oh, yes—of course.' *That* was when I first suspected he was not so much an odd chap with a poor memory as a bit of a scoundrel. Only suspected, you understand. But an honest man would have said, 'Golly, I got that quite wrong, then, didn't I? I wonder how I could have misremembered so badly.' Instead, Scotcher's 'of course' implied he had known all along, and simply needed to be reminded. Tripe and twaddle! Anyone who had read *Voyage Around the World* would not have misremembered it in that particular way."

Gathercole seemed to want to say more, so I waited. A young woman came to ask if we would like more tea, and I told her that we would.

"By then it was too late. I had already told Scotcher too much about Lady Playford's work and all my bright ideas about it. When the time came for me to be interviewed, she barely asked me anything. I had to sit and listen as she told me about Scotcher—how awfully perceptive he was, and wasn't it clever of him to notice this and that about the structures and the themes of her novels? All, needless to say, were things he had heard from me an hour or so earlier. Oh—did I not say? His interview lasted a full hour. Mine took only twenty minutes."

"But . . . did you not tell Lady Playford what had happened?" I said.

"No. I do not like to disparage others, and I have never forgiven myself for not speaking up—for failing to protect Lady Playford from that fraud Scotcher. Still, I doubt she would have listened to me."

"She most certainly would not have," I assured him.

"Well, in any event, I was duly sent away after my short interview, and Scotcher got the job. And then four years later—no, almost five—Lady Playford summoned me and said, 'I did not give you a fair chance, Michael. I see that now. I should like you to become my lawyer and handle my affairs henceforth—that is how I intend to make it up to you!' I was delighted, naturally. She had already arranged for Orville Rolfe to employ me, almost immediately after not giving me the job as her secretary."

"Yes, she told me."

"I owe everything to her." Gathercole frowned. "Everything. She also told me, that same day, that even though I was to be her lawyer and nothing to do with her writing, she intended to test out her Shrimp stories on me from now on—me and *nobody else*. The way she said 'nobody else' so pointedly made me think that she was referring to Scotcher. And . . . well, now, many years later, I know that is precisely what she meant. 'You are my number one, Michael'—that is what she said. I believe she meant it. Scotcher was her secretary, but he was not the one she confided in about her books. Never."

I nodded, seeing that this was important to Gathercole.

"That same day, she told me about Scotcher's Bright's disease, only she related the news in a most unusual way. Instead of saying, 'He is dying,' she said, 'Joseph has told me that he is dying.'"

"She wanted to indicate to you, without saying so explicitly, that she did not believe him."

"Yes, and I am afraid I could not restrain myself," Gathercole said. "You will think me petty, but I was as sure as I could be that Scotcher had *still* not read a single word Lady Playford had published, nearly five years after becoming her secretary. He could easily have read them all as soon as he got the job, but he did not. He preferred to fool everybody. I believe he reveled in his own dishonesty, though I have no evidence, just a feeling. Do you remember at dinner, the night he died, when he revealed the solution of *The Lady in the Suit* in front of Poirot, who had not read it?"

"'Hirsute,' not 'her suit,'" I said. "How could I forget?"

"That alone ought to be all the proof anyone needs that Scotcher cared not one jot for Lady Playford's books! No one who cares about mystery stories would reveal a solution in such a cavalier fashion. And his advice to Poirot about reading the books in the wrong order, not chronologically, because that would be more akin to real life? I have no proof, but Joseph was forever producing fascinating insights and theories about the Shrimp books that cannot have been his own. I strongly suspect he got them from letters, which he then destroyed."

"Letters to Lady Playford?" I said.

"Yes—as her secretary, Joseph dealt with all her correspondence. He saw all the letters that came from readers before she did. Her publisher sends them in sacks. Joseph waded through them all—until he became too pretend-sick and Sophie took over. My uncharitable guess is that he stole those that were particularly interesting, memorized the opinions contained therein, then burned the originals. I recall walking into the drawing room once and catching him throwing a pile of paper on the fire. He looked startled and began to stammer about something quite irrelevant."

"You said that you could not restrain yourself, when Lady Playford told you about Scotcher's allegedly fatal illness," I reminded him. "What did you do?"

"What did I . . . ? Oh, yes, that. I said, 'Forgive me, Lady Playford, but what do you mean "*If* Joseph dies"? Is he going to die or is he not?'"

"How did she reply?" I asked.

"She smiled sadly and said, 'That is the question, Michael. Oh, indeed, that is the question.'"

The Two True Things

POIROT RETURNED TWO DAYS later, in the morning. I had overslept, and was woken late by the sound of rapping on my bedroom door. I put on my dressing gown, went to open it, and found Poirot outside on the landing. "You're back! Thank goodness."

This greeting seemed to please him inordinately.

"I am back, *mon ami, oui*. And we can once again make progress. What do you have to tell me since we spoke on the telephone?"

I told him about my conversation with Gathercole. Then I asked him if he had found what he was looking for in Malmesbury.

"Yes—I learned much that was relevant and interesting, but I suspected most of it already. Get dressed, *mon ami*. I shall await you in the library. There we will talk. I have left out the copy of Shakespeare's *King John* that I have been reading."

"Why are you reading it?" *King John*—could that be the work of literature to which Poirot had alluded, the one that he thought relevant to Scotcher's murder?

"Dr. Kimpton has been trying to draw it to our attention since we arrived," he said. "You have not thought to read it yourself while I have been away?"

"No. If you wanted me to do so, you should have said so."

"Never mind, *mon ami*." With that, he turned his back on me and started to move towards the stairs.

I washed and dressed quickly, and joined him in the library twenty minutes later. He was ensconced in an armchair in the corner, with *King John* on the table beside him.

"Well, here I am," I said. "Tell me, then: why Malmesbury?"

"It is where Joseph Scotcher's mother lives. With the help of the local police, I was able to find her."

"What does she look like?"

"It is interesting that you ask that. Would you not expect the mother of Scotcher to be beautiful, like a delicate angel? This woman was not. She was not pleasing to the eye. Also, she had . . ." Poirot pointed to the top of his nose.

"One eyebrow that went all the way across her face?" I guessed aloud.

"Yes. Like . . . a mustache above her nose instead of below!" Poirot sounded delighted to have found the perfect description. I could not help smiling. "How did you know, *mon ami*?"

I told him the one detail that I had omitted to mention over the telephone: that the woman Claudia Playford had seen in Scotcher's company at the Randolph Hotel had appeared to have one long, continuous eyebrow.

Poirot threw up his hands. "Did I not ask you to tell me everything? And you leave out this piece of the story? *Sacré tonnerre!*"

"Accidentally," I told him, unwilling to feel remiss when I had done nothing but cooperate. "You *deliberately* did not tell me why you were at the hospital or who this eminent doctor was. Incidentally, how many patients died in the corridors after you commandeered that office to talk to me for an hour?"

"Died?" Poirot frowned in puzzlement. "No one died. Now,

I have made some important discoveries. I will tell you. Blake Scotcher, the younger brother of Joseph. He is real."

"Then it was not Joseph Scotcher in disguise who met Randall Kimpton at Queen's Lane Coffee House?" I said.

"On the contrary, I am certain that it was. And if I am wrong . . . well, whoever it was that met Mr. Kimpton, it was not Blake Scotcher, the younger son of Ethel Scotcher of Malmesbury."

"How do you know?"

"Because he died when he was six years old, from influenza."

"Goodness!"

"Mrs. Scotcher, having lost one son already, is beside herself with grief at losing another. This is made worse by the guilt that for so long she has felt on Joseph's account. She neglected him as a child, she told me. He seemed always to be well and happy, while his brother, Blake, was sickly and needed her attention. He was forever coming down with one illness after another."

"I say!"

"*Oui*. And Dr. Kimpton says that the psychology cannot be proof of anything!"

"Anything else from Mrs. Scotcher?"

"No. But interesting details from elsewhere. I went to Balliol College in Oxford, where both Kimpton and Scotcher studied—where they met, also. Did you know that before Scotcher took the position as Lady Playford's secretary, he was what you might call 'a Shakespeare man'?"

"What? Like Kimpton was, before he went into medicine?"

"*Précisément*. Many at Balliol remember both young men very well. The consensus of opinion is that Scotcher idolized Kimpton, and modeled himself upon him."

So Phyllis had been wrong about the direction of mimicry: she had naturally assumed that the man she loved was, as it were, the original, and Randall Kimpton the imitator—but it had been the other way round.

"That must be the reason Kimpton changed course and moved over to medicine," I said. "Especially when you think about Scotcher snatching Iris from under Kimpton's nose as well. What if that was about Kimpton more than Iris?"

"You mean that Scotcher did not so much want the girl as he wanted to *be* Randall Kimpton? He could not be someone he was not, but having Iris by his side helped him to believe that he could?"

"Something like that, yes. If Scotcher wanted Iris purely because Kimpton had her, and if he became a Shakespeare scholar only because Kimpton was one, that must have been enraging for Kimpton. No one could bear to be imitated in that way. And Kimpton's story about giving up Shakespeare because others in the field disapproved of him for liking *King John* better than the other plays—that always struck me as claptrap."

"But Scotcher could have followed him also into the study of medicine, *non*? And maybe he would have, if he had not thought of something even better. Kimpton, once Iris was, as you English say, 'out of the picture,' transferred his romantic attention to the dazzling Mademoiselle Claudia Playford, aloof and apparently unattainable, daughter of a viscount and a famous novelist. Kimpton works hard and eventually succeeds in convincing her to become engaged to be married to him. Scotcher, who moves in the same circles in Oxford, sees that Kimpton has, after much effort, won the heart of this young beauty—and, as luck would have it, Claudia's mother, the authoress, is at the same time advertising for a secretary . . . oh, yes, this has much more appeal for Scotcher than the pursuit of a career as a doctor. Speaking of doctors . . ." Poirot shook his head.

"Are you going to tell me at last?"

"When we spoke on the telephone, you said that perhaps Scotcher did not have a doctor at all. Well, he was neither sick nor dying, but while he lived in Oxford, he was on the patient list of a doctor. I visited this man at his home. What I learned from him was fascinating. It made so many things so clear. Only there is a problem: what is now clear to me . . . unfortunately, it is also impossible."

"Please explain," I said without much hope.

"Now is not the time for explanation, Catchpool. Now, Poirot must think hard. I advise you to do the same."

"What is clear to you, and what aspect of it seems impossible? For pity's sake, Poirot, what is it that you would like me to think hard *about*?"

I was surprised when he answered willingly. "How can it all be made to fit together? Sophie Bourlet swears that Joseph Scotcher was alive—begging for his life—until the moment that Claudia Playford attacked him with a club in the parlor. Yet the inquest gave the cause of death as poisoning, and the time as considerably earlier. And Kimpton and Claudia tell us that they were together upstairs at the time the clubbing took place. Additionally, Brigid, the cook, saw them together on the upstairs landing when we were all hurrying downstairs in response to Sophie's screams. But . . . if my theory about who killed Scotcher and why is correct, then Sophie must be telling the truth about what she saw in the parlor that night. She would have no reason not to."

"Please tell me your theory," I said.

"Let me finish, Catchpool. If my theory about who killed Scotcher and why is correct, then, also, it makes perfect sense that Claudia would club the head of the already dead Scotcher."

"It does?"

"*Oui.*"

"Do you mean because she wanted Scotcher to have a closed casket funeral for some reason?"

"Not at all. His funeral turns out to be irrelevant. But, oh yes, it makes perfect sense that Mademoiselle Claudia would do this clubbing of Scotcher's corpse. *What makes no sense, however, is that Scotcher, who should have been dead from strychnine poisoning at that point, was apparently not dead at all!* So who is lying? Sophie

Bourlet? No, I do not think so. Claudia Playford? No! If Scotcher had been still alive in the parlor, *she would have had no reason to club him around the head, therefore she would not have done so.*"

"If you had said all of that in Ancient Greek and jumbled up the word order for good measure, it would have been no more incomprehensible to me," I told him.

I stood up, walked over to the window and opened it. The sight of the smooth green lawn bordered by trees calmed me; one can only stare at the ever-alert green eyes of Hercule Poirot for so long, I have found, without starting to feel dizzy.

I thought for a few moments, then said, "From what little I managed to understand of all that . . . you seem to be saying that you believe Sophie Bourlet, but you also believe Claudia Playford?"

"Yes, I believe the nurse Sophie. But I also believe the findings of the inquest."

"In that case, it seems rather obvious that . . ." I paused, wondering how to put it into words. "When you know two things are true, and those two things seem to go against each other, instead of telling yourself one must not be true, shouldn't you ask yourself what third thing that you have not yet thought of would allow both true things to be true at the same time?"

Poirot looked as if he had gritted his teeth behind his mustache. "That is a nice idea, Catchpool, but unfortunately it cannot be true that Joseph Scotcher was both dead *and* alive when he was attacked with the club."

"Of course not. The two apparently irreconcilable true things I had in mind were, number one, Sophie Bourlet telling the truth, which you are convinced she is, and, number two, Claudia Playford having no reason to smash Scotcher's head to smithereens with a club if he were not already dead."

"Catchpool!" Poirot cried out, startling me.

"Yes? Are you all right?"

"Be quiet. Close that window! Come and sit." He seemed very

agitated. I returned to my chair as instructed, hoping that I had not been too forthright.

We sat in silence for nearly five minutes. From time to time Poirot murmured something inaudible. I could have sworn that at one point I heard him whisper, "Shut up the drawer, without the drawer," but he would not confirm it.

I waited. It became rather tiresome. I was on the point of objecting when he stood up, walked over to me, grabbed my head with both of his hands and kissed the top of it. "*Mon ami*, without knowing how I might apply your suggestion, you have solved the riddle in my mind! I am indebted to you, more than I can say. At last, the full pattern reveals itself to Poirot!"

"Jolly good," I said coolly.

"But, if I may make a small criticism . . . it is beyond me, quite beyond me, that you could say what you have said and *still not see what is now so clear*. Never mind! We must make haste. Send word to Inspector Conree that Hercule Poirot, he is ready! And then find Sophie Bourlet and bring her to the parlor, as soon as you can. Hurry, Catchpool!"

Motive and Opportunity

THREE HOURS LATER, SERGEANT O'Dwyer and I had managed to shepherd everybody into the drawing room. It was a tense and terse gathering even before Poirot opened the proceedings. Inspector Conree was furious to have been ousted as leading man. He had abandoned his ongoing chin-erosion project and allowed his head to hang at an angle that would have suggested a broken neck to those unfamiliar with his habits.

Apart from Conree, O'Dwyer, Poirot and me, the others gathered in the room were Lady Playford, Harry and Dorro, Randall Kimpton and Claudia, Michael Gathercole and Orville Rolfe, Sophie Bourlet, Hatton, Phyllis the maid and Brigid the cook, who was the first to speak.

"What's all this fuss, then?" she asked, glaring at each of us in turn. "I don't sit about in the middle of the day! Meals wouldn't get cooked if I did! I hope no one thinks I've time for this idleness, because I haven't. Want to starve, do you? You'll let me go if you don't." Her muscly arms looked ready to propel her out of the chair at any moment.

Claudia said, "I will dance naked in front of Buckingham Palace if you didn't cook tonight's lunch *and* dinner between five and eight this morning, Brigid. Go on—admit it."

"Oh! Be a good sort and convince her that you didn't, Brigid." Kimpton winked at the cook, who responded with a huff of disapproval. "Meanwhile, I must work on getting myself hired as His Majesty's head gardener."

"Ladies and gentlemen." From the front of the room, Poirot gave a small bow. "I will detain you all no longer than is necessary. Dr. Kimpton, I would be grateful to encounter no interruptions. What I have to say to you all is important."

"I don't doubt it, old boy," said Kimpton. "Quick word in my own defense before you get under way: by any reasonable definition of 'interrupt,' I did not interrupt you. When I spoke, you had said nothing and requested nobody's undivided attention. I believe I have . . ."—Kimpton made a show of counting heads—". . . fourteen witnesses who will support my claim if necessary. But point taken and over to you, Poirot. I'm hoping you might be able to enlighten us in the matter of Joseph Scotcher's murder."

"That is my intention, and why we are here."

Through all this I stood by Poirot's side in front of the unlit fire, wishing I knew what he was about to say.

"This is not by any means the first murder I have investigated," he began. "It is, however, one of the most straightforward. So many questions I have wrestled with, and yet the solution to this puzzle is breathtakingly simple—almost alarmingly so."

"We are hardly in a position to agree or disagree with that," said Claudia. "Why don't you tell us what you have discovered, and then we can all reflect together upon the character of the crime?"

"Do not interrupt, dearest one," Randall Kimpton murmured.

"Straightforward, Poirot?" Lady Playford's voice came from the back of the room, where she sat in front of the French windows.

"A man's head smashed in with a club, and then it turns out he was poisoned before that, and you call it straightforward?"

"Yes, Lady Playford. Conceptually and in theory, this was an orderly and . . . yes, I would be forced to say that it was an elegant crime. The reality was quite different. The murderer had to adapt to changing circumstances and unforeseen events. All did not go as planned, but if it had . . ." Poirot's face was grave. "When evil makes itself orderly, the danger is severe. Most severe indeed."

I shivered. If only Hatton or Phyllis had thought to light the fire. It was a cold day—the coldest for a while.

"With any murder, one must consider motive and opportunity," said Poirot. "Let us start with opportunity because that part is simple. It would seem that, apart from Inspector Conree, Sergeant O'Dwyer and Catchpool here, anyone in this room could have murdered Joseph Scotcher. For the moment, we will put to one side the clubbing in the parlor. I will return later to that, but first let us address the murder itself. We know that traces of strychnine were found in the blue bottle in Scotcher's room, and we know that, in the presence of Sophie Bourlet, Scotcher took whatever medicine— or supposed medicine—was in that bottle at five o'clock every day, including on the day that he died. His death was caused by strychnine poisoning, as we heard at the inquest."

There was a murmur of agreement from some.

"Apart from the three exceptions I have named, *there is no one among you who could not have entered Scotcher's room before five o'clock that day and put strychnine into the blue bottle*," said Poirot. "So, we move on to motive. Most of you had a reason to want Scotcher dead. If I may start with you, Viscount Playford?"

"What?" Harry looked up, apparently confused. Then he rallied and remembered his manners. "Righto, yes. With you, old chap. Do go ahead. My pleasure."

"As the sixth Viscount Playford of Clonakilty, you naturally expected to inherit a portion of your mother's estate. You expected it as any son would. You were already unhappy about the terms of your late father's will, perhaps—your wife certainly was. Then one night at dinner you hear that there is to be no provision for you at all—you have been supplanted by Joseph Scotcher. If he were to be removed, however . . ."

"Of course Harry expected his fair share!" said Dorro. "Didn't you, Harry? What son would not?"

"And you, madame, as Viscount Playford's wife, you too had this expectation." Poirot smiled at her. "The property of the husband is the property of the wife. This gives you, also, a motive to kill. I would suggest that your motive differs from your husband's quite markedly, however. In your case, the new will is the beginning and end of it—fear of poverty, an insecure future, a need to see to it that the money comes to you. Not so your husband."

"No? I say!" said Harry. He and Dorro both looked surprised. "Out with it, then! What was my motive for wanting poor old Scotcher out of the way?"

"You knew what would happen to your wife if Scotcher were to survive," Poirot told him. "How bitter she would become and how obsessed. She would talk of nothing but the new will, and your straitened circumstances, you feared. You would be doomed to listen to her relentless discontent for the rest of your life, with little or no money to spend on enjoyable distractions."

Dorro stood up. "How *dare* you speak of me in that manner! Harry, do something. This is nonsense! If the poison was put in the bottle before five . . . well, Harry and I didn't know about the new will until dinner, which was served at seven!"

"Please sit down, madame. What you say is quite correct, but remember: for now I speak only of motive."

"Thank you for admitting I'm right, at least!" Dorro sounded furious, and not grateful in the least.

Poirot turned to Harry, who was easier to deal with in every respect. "Viscount Playford, I have demonstrated that both you and your wife had a motive. You did not, however, murder Joseph Scotcher. Neither one of you did it."

"That's the ticket!" Harry nodded. He reached over and patted Dorro's knee with a hearty "Ha! Good-oh!"

"Mademoiselle Claudia . . . ," said Poirot.

"Am I to be next? How thrilling."

"In spite of your engagement to Dr. Kimpton, your mother's altered will would, I believe, have been a sufficient motive for you too. Perhaps you did not need the money or the land, but you are a person preoccupied by injustices. You think it unfair that your brother inherited your father's title. Why not you, as the eldest child? And then to learn that Joseph Scotcher was to take something else that you saw as rightfully yours—"

"You need not continue," Claudia cut him off in a bored voice. "Of course I had a motive—anyone can see it! Though *I* should have killed Mother, not Joseph. After all, it was hardly his fault. Blame is something one ought to be very *precise* about, don't you think?"

"I believe one ought to be very precise about everything," said Kimpton.

"There is also the small matter of execution," said Claudia. "Oh!" She giggled. "I don't mean *that* sort of execution—the deathly sort. I mean the carrying out of one's plans. No murder planned by me would involve poisoning *and* bludgeoning. Whoever is responsible made a dreadful muddle of it all. Bungled the whole show, as far as I can see."

"You are lying!" Sophie Bourlet spat the words out. "I saw you with the club in your hand!"

"Oh, dear. Must we have this argument again?" Claudia raised her eyes to the ceiling. "I did not kill Joseph—tell her, Poirot, for heaven's sake." To Sophie she said, "I found him awfully compelling company, you know. And I care far too much about self-preservation to kill anybody in a way that would get me caught. If I ever killed a person—and I must stop imagining it or I might be tempted; *so* many deserve it—I would ensure that I did not fall under suspicion even for a second. If that proved impossible, I would leave the wretch alive, much as it might pain me to be merciful."

"Fighting talk, dearest one!" Kimpton clapped his hands together in appreciation. Michael Gathercole turned away in disgust.

"Claudia Playford did not murder Joseph Scotcher," said Poirot. "And so we move on to Randall Kimpton."

"Aha! I must pay attention," said Kimpton.

"You, monsieur, had more reasons to kill Scotcher than anybody else here—persuasive ones, all of them. Scotcher stole your first love, Iris Morphet. And now he was about to steal, as you would see it, Lady Playford's estate in its entirety. What an injustice! Your wife-to-be, to whom you are devoted, cut off altogether! That might have been motive enough for you on its own, even without the matter of Iris Morphet."

"Ample motive," Kimpton agreed easily.

"Let us talk a little more about Iris," said Poirot. "She deserted you in order to marry Scotcher, you told me, but that did not happen. Instead, her relationship with Scotcher came to an end. We can speculate about how and why this happened, but we do not know for sure. All we know is that she regretted her decision—but it was too late. You would not take her back."

"Would you have, in my place? A woman who has left me once already, for a man many times my inferior? A man who *imitated* me, who tried to replicate my mannerisms in order to make himself more popular? I do not see what you hope to achieve by going over this, Poirot. I have no more to say about Iris. I thought we were going to talk about all my excellent reasons for murdering Scotcher."

"That is what I am trying to do, *mon ami*. Please, be patient. After you rejected Iris, she married Percival Gillow, a man without prospects and of questionable character. Within a year of her marriage, she was dead. She fell under a train, you told me."

"That is correct," Kimpton confirmed briskly.

Poirot left my side and started to walk around the room as he spoke. "Cleverly—ingeniously—you told me two things one after the other: that Mr. Gillow was an unsavory character, *and that the police were unable to prove that he pushed his wife under a train.* You intended for me to think that if anyone had pushed Iris, it was her husband—that the death of Iris was either murder by Percival Gillow or an accident. *But that is not what you truly believe.*"

"Is that so?" Kimpton smiled. He seemed to be trying for nonchalance, but I was unconvinced.

"Dr. Kimpton, remember that I have been to England. I have spoken to many people, including the police who investigated Iris Gillow's death. They told me about your visits to them, about your insistence that Joseph Scotcher had murdered Iris because she had found out that he was not ill, as he claimed, and had confronted him with what she knew. He feared exposure from her and so he murdered her—that was what you suspected then and still suspect to this day, is it not?"

"Very well—yes, it is. So you have met Inspector Thomas Blakemore, have you? In which case, he will have told you that there was no proof of anything, hence the inquest verdict: accidental death."

"I have a question for you, Dr. Kimpton," said Poirot. "If you believe that Scotcher murdered Iris, why did you encourage me to suspect Percival Gillow?"

"Can't you work it out, Poirot? I would have thought your psychological expertise would make short work of such an easily solvable puzzle. No? All right, I will tell you. In Oxford, when I was a younger man with lots of energy and a fair amount of optimism about people and what sort of stuff they were made of, I tried to convince all the trusting fools, Scotcher's willing dupes. I was as sure as I could be that Scotcher was a liar and a malingerer, with not a scrap wrong with him physically, and so, naturally, I told people. Well, I was as good as ostracized! Scotcher put as much effort into convincing everybody that he was sick as I did into persuading them that he wasn't. He treated a few influential Oxford acquaintances to a meeting with his fake doctor, just as he invited me to one with his fake brother. Both of these nonexistent characters were Joseph Scotcher in disguise: bearded and dark-skinned, at least to the wrist."

"Randall, why on earth have I not heard this story before?" asked Lady Playford.

"Listen and you shall learn why," Kimpton told her. "Between them, Scotcher and his fictitious doctor saw to it that I became extremely unpopular in Oxford. I do not like to be unpopular, and I cannot stand to be outwitted. That was what was happening, and for a very simple reason: people do not care to listen to those who thrust unpalatable scenarios in front of them; they prefer to hear only gilded pleasantries. No one wished to believe that kind, selfless Joseph Scotcher—whom they all worshipped, because he flattered them all so assiduously—would trick them in such a callous fashion, and so they did *not* believe it. Easy! 'Nobody would do such a thing,' they muttered, and they were stupid enough to be convinced by their own platitudes.

"I soon saw that it would not be in my interests to continue with my campaign to reveal what I suspected to be the truth, and have it acknowledged," Kimpton went on. "I am a man who makes decisions and sticks to them, Poirot. I resolved never again to attempt to convince anybody of Scotcher's dishonesty. I had tried and failed to alert people to his true nature. So be it. Let Scotcher thrive or let him go hang, I thought, and with that I washed my hands of him. Athie, you asked why you have not heard my Scotcher stories. That is why. Not even to Claudia did I utter a word. Why, she saw the likely truth for herself, as soon as Scotcher announced at Lillieoak that he was in danger of losing his life to this terrible illness, and then, later, dying for certain. Anybody but a fool could see that he was not the invalid he claimed to be, and my dearest one is no fool.

"She confided in me about her suspicions. Naturally, I admitted that I shared them, though I did not tell her the whole story at that point. I allowed her to believe that I was newly suspicious of Scotcher, as she was.

"*You*, Athie, are every bit as sharp-eyed as your daughter. Day after day, there were no visible signs that Scotcher had any sort of illness—only his word for it. 'I feel weak. I need to rest.' Anyone can say such things! But did you boot him out into the street where he belonged?"

"I did not," Lady Playford said proudly.

"No. Instead, you hired a nurse for him," said Kimpton. "You altered your will for his sake. That is how strong a spell the man cast—on so many. Far from objecting to his lies, you became a willing participant in the game he was playing. Oh, you played with gusto! It was impressive to observe, and also rather sickening."

Kimpton turned to Poirot. "I allowed you to conclude that I suspected Percy Gillow of murdering Iris because if I had suggested it was Scotcher, I would have been back where I was all those years ago at Oxford—trying to convince people he was a bad lot. You would have said, 'But, Kimpton, just because he lied about having a fatal illness, that does not make him a murderer.' The prospect of having that conversation was too wearying, I am afraid, so I took the easy way out. I knew I would have no trouble persuading you that a ne'er-do-well like Percy Gillow might have killed his wife. I hoped you might take it upon yourself to investigate further and establish for certain whether Joseph Scotcher murdered Iris. If anyone can prove it, you can."

"I do not know if anybody can so many years later," Poirot replied. "If it is definitive proof that you hope for—"

"Definitive is the only sort worth having," said Kimpton firmly. "Shall I tell you something? Before I gave up, I made a concerted effort to gather all I could in the way of evidence. I hired a chap like you, Poirot—a detective. Paid him to follow Scotcher for several weeks. During that time, Scotcher went nowhere near any member of the medical profession, though he was busy telling me that he had seen his doctor on this day and that. I could have shared this information with Scotcher's and my mutual acquaintances, but do you know what they would have said? That I was the villain of the piece for arranging for my friend, or former friend, to be pursued by a sleuth. They would have suggested that the detective I hired might have given me incorrect information, or that Scotcher had perhaps not seen his doctor during that particular period, but that this did not mean he was not gravely ill. Which, of course, is quite true! It is unarguable! A chap might be at death's door and still lie about seeing a doctor on this or that occasion. That was when I realized that I could spend hundreds of pounds, and hire all the private detectives in the world, and I would never have enough proof to convince anybody, or to know with absolute certainty myself."

"To return to your possible motives for killing Joseph Scotcher," said Poirot. "It seems that we must add another two to the list: not only revenge for stealing Iris away from you, but also revenge for the murder of Iris, and for having beaten you. Scotcher's lies had fooled everybody. Your attempts to disseminate the truth had met with a hostile reception."

"Wait," said Kimpton. "No, sorry. I forbid you to add revenge for the murder of Iris to that list. Poirot, I fear you do not know me at all! I should not permit myself to murder anybody as revenge for something they might or might not have done, however strongly I suspected they were guilty. Might or might not is not good enough. It is never good enough. And in much the same way, I did not *know* that Scotcher had lied about his illness. I merely suspected it, as I keep trying to impress upon you."

Poirot nodded. "Very well. But there is no might or might not about the next motive on the list: Joseph Scotcher—this man that you so mistrusted and suspected, this fraud, this charlatan—*refused to leave you alone*. I have been, as I said before, to Oxford. I discovered that, like you, before you turned to medicine and before he came to work at Lillieoak for Lady Playford, Scotcher was a scholar of literature—of Shakespeare in particular. Was that the true reason that you abandoned your vocation and entered the field of medicine, Dr. Kimpton? Scotcher was determined to model himself on you, to take what was yours, *to try to be you in any way that he could*— so you decided to let him keep Shakespeare and, meanwhile, you would pursue something altogether different—a career into which you believed Scotcher would not dare to follow you. A healthy man claiming to be dying would surely not choose to go anywhere near the medical profession. Was that your reasoning?"

"It absolutely was not," said Kimpton. "But, I say, isn't it splendid that you could make it fit together so neatly and sound so *likely*? No—I can safely say that when I plumped for a career in medicine, the idea of shaking off Scotcher did not enter into it at all."

"All the same, you must have wished to rid yourself of him," said Poirot. "After Iris, meeting Claudia was a new start for you. Becoming acquainted with her family, the family you hoped one day to marry into . . . and then, who should arrive but Joseph Scotcher! Suddenly he is Lady Playford's new secretary! It dawns on you then that no matter where you go and what you do, he will follow you. You will have to watch people fawn over him, and see them believing his lies! It will be like Oxford all over again. I would call that an excellent motive for murder, Dr. Kimpton."

"I should say so," Kimpton agreed. "So that point goes to you, Poirot. Are you keeping score? How many motives do I have in total?"

"The number does not matter. This is not a parlor game."

"I suppose not, but . . . well, I can't help feeling guilty to have hogged all the attention for so long—especially considering I didn't kill the blighter."

Lady Playford stood up at the back of the room. "It distresses me greatly to hear Joseph described as a fraud and a charlatan, Poirot," she said. "And now we discover he wanted to be a Shakespeare scholar simply to be like Randall? Can you not see, all of you, that the poor man was desperately ill? Not physically, but in his mind! It is quite wrong to apply normal moral standards to a person with Joseph's problems."

"How terribly convenient," said Kimpton.

"Allow me to move on from Dr. Kimpton," said Poirot. "He had many compelling motives—more than anybody else in this room. But remember, he is also, now, a man of science, who has learned to apply the discipline, and the self-control. A different man in his position might have succumbed to a vengeful passion and committed murder; Randall Kimpton did not—not when Iris Morphet first abandoned him in favor of Scotcher and not at any time since then. His pride would not permit him to lash out in that way. Never!"

Kimpton laughed. "Poirot, I take back every insulting remark I have ever made about your methods. Long live psychology—that's what I say!"

"And so . . ." Poirot looked around the room. "We move on . . ."

35

Everyone Could Have but Nobody Did

"THERE ARE THREE PEOPLE here who had no reason to kill Joseph Scotcher: Mr. Hatton, Mrs. Brigid Marsh and Mr. Orville Rolfe. They can all be eliminated."

"A-limmy-what?" Brigid demanded. "Talk English, will you?"

"I am saying, madame, that you did not kill Mr. Scotcher."

"And you think filling my ears with nonsense for hours on end only to tell me what I know fine well already is going to help make tonight's dinner, do you? Instead of telling us what didn't happen, tell us what did! All you've said so far, it's . . . well, it's like me ordering meat for a dozen meals I've no mind to cook!"

"Brigid, do not speak to Monsieur Poirot like that," said Lady Playford. There was a distracted air to her voice, as if her mind were elsewhere, and the reprimand was for form's sake more than anything else.

"Let me get back to me pea and ham soup, then!" came the irate reply. "Is it any wonder folk take things from my kitchen, when I'm not allowed in it all this time?" As she spoke, she glared directly at me, and rather piercingly too, as if she blamed me more than anyone else. I wondered, as I recalled the anecdote about her nephew and the stolen sweets . . . She had seemed angry with me then too. Was it possible that she suspected me of purloining one of her kitchen utensils? Why on earth would she, when I had done no such thing?

"We come next to Sophie Bourlet and Phyllis Chivers," said Poirot.

"Me?" Phyllis sounded aghast. "What d'you wanna talk about me for? I haven't done nothing!"

Sophie had curled herself into a ball in her chair. She made no protest.

"The motive of Mademoiselle Phyllis is clear: she heard, while listening at the dining room door, the proposal of marriage made by Mr. Scotcher to his nurse, Sophie. Envy is a powerful emotion—one that can easily lead to murder."

"I didn't do it, I swear!" Phyllis stood up, clutching at her skirt. "I never killed no one! And if I had, I'd have done her in, not him!"

"Indeed," Poirot said. "You take from my mouth the words. A jealous woman is a hundred times more likely to kill the other woman, her rival in love, than the man, the precious object of her love. Phyllis Chivers did not murder Joseph Scotcher. And as for Sophie Bourlet, what could have been her motive? She loved Scotcher— that is undeniable. I saw it from the first moment that I saw them together. But perhaps knowing that he was soon to die, or believing that to be true—"

"Sophie knew Joseph was as healthy as any of us," Claudia cut in. "It's absurd that she still pretends, as if she imagines she can save his good name even now."

Sophie looked frozen. Still, she maintained her silence.

"Knowing that the man she loved was soon to die from a terrible disease—or else knowing that he would spend the rest of his life pretending he was dying, and forcing her, also, into that same un-bearable pretense—Sophie Bourlet might have become unhappy enough to turn to murder as a solution to her problems," said Poirot. "It is also possible that she loved Scotcher so much that, once she admitted to herself that he had lied to her, she felt betrayed—enough to want to end his life."

"Neither of those theories sounds awfully likely," said Randall Kimpton. "Both are too vague. And yet Sophie must have done it, or else why lie about Claudia and the club and all of that?"

"Neither theory sounds likely, Dr. Kimpton, because Sophie Bourlet *did not murder Joseph Scotcher.*"

"What?" said Kimpton, looking at Claudia. "Come on, old boy, she must have."

"If she didn't, then who did?" Claudia said indignantly.

Sophie stood up. Today, for the first time since Scotcher's death, she was neatly turned out, with her hair brushed and tied back. She looked a little like the old Sophie. "There is something I must confess," she said. "I'm sorry, Monsieur Poirot, for the interruption. I should have told you straightaway—I wish I had! But I didn't, and nor did I tell you at the garda station at Ballygurteen, nor just now in the parlor when we did the experiment—"

"Experiment?" said Lady Playford, as if the word were an ob-scenity, and one she never expected to hear in her own home.

"I will explain about the experiment later," Poirot told her. "Con-tinue, please," he said to Sophie.

She stood with her back perfectly straight, hands neatly folded in front of her. Her comportment brought to mind a diligent schoolgirl, asked to perform a solo at a concert. "I have lied about something important. And I am aware that some of you will think that if I can lie once, I can lie a hundred times, but I am an honest person. I do not like lies. But sometimes . . . Well, on this occasion, I panicked, and made a calculation that proved disastrous."

"What the devil are you talking about, you strange creature?" said Kimpton.

"Shall I tell the story?" Poirot suggested. "You are referring, are you not, to Claudia Playford's white dressing gown?"

Sophie's mouth fell open in disbelief. "How did you know? You cannot possibly have known!"

"Poirot, he knows, mademoiselle. I asked you—it was one of the first things I asked—what Claudia Playford was wearing when you saw her beating Joseph Scotcher's head with the club. You told me she wore a white dressing gown over her nightdress. I knew this was not true. She wore the white dressing gown when she came down the stairs after hearing your screams, to look at Scotcher's body in the parlor. I saw the dressing gown—there was not a spot of blood on it. I notice, always, imperfections of clothing. So, I say to myself, 'Sophie Bourlet lies—either about seeing Claudia Playford attack Scotcher's head with the club, or about the clothing she wore to do so.'"

"I *did* see her do it," Sophie whispered. "I would stake my life upon it."

"You saw her, yes," Poirot agreed. "She was wearing the green dress she wore to dinner, *n'est-ce pas?* Yet you knew that when she reappeared in the parlor in response to your screams, she was wearing a white dressing gown. You did not understand how she could have had time to go upstairs, change her clothes and hide a bloodstained dress in between. So you lied."

"It did not make sense!" Sophie said. "How could Claudia be wearing a green dress to attack Joseph in the parlor one minute, then standing in the hall in a white nightdress and dressing gown the next? The only thing that happened between those two moments was that I screamed—and not for very long before people started to hurry downstairs. There was not enough time—that was the problem. I knew that if I said I had seen her wearing the green dress to beat Joseph, I would appear a liar."

"And so to avoid looking like one, you became one," said Poirot.

"Many times I have encountered this phenomenon. No matter. You added a false detail . . . but once we remove that detail, we are left with what we had before. It is similar—if I may say so, Sergeant O'Dwyer—to your 'Shut up the drawer without the drawer.' Take away this most unconvincing drawer that you and your brother included only to keep yourselves out of trouble, and you are left with the true message, the 'Shut up.'"

"Poirot, what the blazes are you talking about?" asked Lady Playford. "What is this unconvincing drawer, and what does O'Dwyer's brother have to do with any of this?"

"Never mind—it is not important. I only mean that once we take away Sophie Bourlet's embellishment from her story, we are left with the true message that she needed most urgently to communicate to us: that she saw two things which, taken together, appeared to be impossible."

"Excuse me," said Claudia loudly. "Why, might I ask, should I wish to smash up the head of a corpse? I mean, this is all jolly exhilarating, but we must remember to add a little common sense to the mix now and then."

"I am so sorry for lying," said Sophie. "If only I had known . . . but we had not yet done the experiment."

"What blessed experiment?" said Kimpton. "My patience is rapidly evaporating, I'm afraid. Poirot, if Sophie did not kill Scotcher, then who did?"

"All in good time, Dr. Kimpton. Michael Gathercole." Poirot turned to the lawyer. "You have envied Joseph Scotcher ever since Lady Playford employed him as her secretary. You too applied for the job, but you were passed over. What is worse is that Scotcher used *your* knowledge of Lady Playford's mystery stories to curry favor with her. So, you might have killed because of this envy. Or you might have had a more altruistic motive, for I believe that you are a good man who truly cares for others. You might have killed Scotcher *for the sake of Lady Playford, to protect her.* You could see what sort of man he was, and, in your opinion, she could not. She appeared oblivious to the danger of allowing him to remain at Lillieoak at the heart of her home and her family."

Gathercole sighed. "The man was a menace," he said. "I'm sorry, Lady . . . Athie. That is my opinion. I would have given anything to see him sent packing."

Lady Playford had turned pale. "What are you saying, Michael? That you *killed* him?"

"What?" Gathercole looked confused. "No! Of course not. I did nothing of the sort. Monsieur Poirot—"

"Do not distress yourself, monsieur. It is true: Mr. Gathercole did not kill Joseph Scotcher."

"Well, I'm very relieved to hear it!" said Lady Playford. "But, Poirot, the only person left is *me*." She sounded disappointed, as if she had bought tickets for a new play at the theater that had turned out to be a dud.

"You are correct, Lady Playford. You—the protector and defender of Joseph Scotcher, who speaks up for him when no one else will."

Athie Playford sighed. "You're such a tricky customer, Poirot. A deceiver, really. I see what your game is. You are going to talk at length about everything I did for Joseph—how I adored him beyond reason, and how I'm bereft now that he's dead—and you're going to do it in a tone of voice precisely designed to make everyone think there's an enormous 'but' coming. '*But* she killed him because . . .' There is not, though, is there? You know perfectly well that I am not the killer. At least, I hope you do."

She looked doubtful for a moment. "I invited you here—and Catchpool too—because I had read of how brilliantly you solved the Bloxham Hotel murders in London. I was told you were the best. As you know, I feared an attempt might be made upon my life—"

"*Your* life?" Dorro pounced on her words. "But Scotcher was the one—"

"You do not need to tell me, Dorro, that Joseph was murdered and I was not. I am acutely aware of it." Lady Playford took a deep breath. To Poirot and me, she said, "I hoped that, given the choice, Joseph would confide in me fully rather than risk trying to kill me on a night when two of England's finest detectives were staying at Lillieoak. Michael behind the curtain was not my only safety measure; you two were every bit as important."

"Athie, I *demand* that you explain yourself!" Dorro cried. "What curtain? Which Michael? Mr. Gathercole?"

"Oh, do shut up, Dorro," said her mother-in-law. With a small smile, Lady Playford added, "With or without a drawer—whichever you prefer."

"Lady Playford, you worshipped Joseph Scotcher," said Poirot. "I believe you would have given your life for him. You loved him more than you loved either of your two children, and more than you loved your faithful friend and lawyer, Mr. Gathercole."

I struggled to contain my annoyance. Scotcher was dead, and therefore beyond flattery and encouragement; did Poirot care nothing for the prospects of the living, for the harmoniousness or otherwise of relations between them in the future? Solving murders was all very well, but there was no need to explain to the members of an already troubled family how little they cared for one another.

"Lady Playford, if you were to be banished for eternity to a remote place and could take only one person with you, Joseph Scotcher would have been your choice of companion," he continued. "And yet you are an intelligent woman. You could see that he lied to you every single day and took advantage of your generosity. Would a woman like you, proud and powerful, accustomed to writing books in which every blackguard and villain gets punished most harshly . . . would such a woman allow Scotcher's enduring dishonesty to go unpunished?"

Athie Playford waved her hand in a vaguely dismissive gesture. "Get on with it, Poirot," she said. "I'm sure I don't need to tell you that real life is not so neat and tidy as fiction. In real life, the proud woman who, on paper, throws the baddies in prison cells and leaves them to rot—twice a year without fail!—loved a brilliant, beautiful young man who baldly lied to her every single day, and she raised not a murmur of protest! One could not put a story like that in a book. It would be most unsatisfactory."

"You say that life is not as neat and tidy as fiction. In general it is not," Poirot agreed. "But the murder of Joseph Scotcher, at least in its conception, was neater and tidier than any of you, apart from the killer, could possibly imagine."

36

The Experiment

"*Bon*. I will tell you now, so that you can all marvel, as I have been, at the tidiness of the murder of Joseph Scotcher.

"Scotcher committed a murder: that of Iris Gillow. What was his motive? Why, it is obvious: she suspected him of having invented his illness. Do not tell me, Dr. Kimpton, that I cannot prove Scotcher killed Iris, or that his motive was as I describe it. I have not yet said all that I have to say on the matter. You must wait for the evidence, circumstantial though you will undoubtedly claim it is when you hear it.

"For a long time, Scotcher got away with murder. No one was able to prove he pushed Iris Gillow under a train. But his crime caught up with him, and in a satisfyingly tidy way. You see, *the motive for the murder of Joseph Scotcher was exactly the same as the motive for Iris Gillow's murder*. Again I will say it: Iris was killed because she suspected Scotcher was not really dying. And Joseph Scotcher was killed for the very same reason: because his killer suspected that he was not really dying. It could not be tidier or more fitting! Scotcher was killed for the same reason that, some years earlier, had led him to kill. It is simply that he was at a different end of the motive in each instance—the first time, he was the subject of the murder, and the second time, he was its object."

"No, no, no," Kimpton objected. "You are displaying shoddy reasoning, Poirot. First of all, how is suspecting that Scotcher was not really dying a motive for killing him? Many of us suspected it who did *not* kill him."

Poirot smiled, but said nothing.

"And as for him killing Iris because she didn't believe he was dying . . . again, many of us did not. Scotcher killed Iris and not me, for instance."

"That is an interesting observation, Doctor," Poirot conceded. "I cannot be certain, but I believe that Scotcher must have feared a greater threat from Iris Gillow than from you. You have said your-self that you could not persuade anybody in Oxford to believe you, and that you eventually ceased to try. Imagine, then, if Iris came forward in support of your theory . . ."

"All right. Fair point," said Kimpton. "If it was good-natured Iris and not ruthless Randall saying it, doubtless many more would have sat up and paid attention. But, listen, what you said before about the motive for the murder of Scotcher—"

"I will now explain the experiment to which Sophie Bourlet referred," said Poirot. "You have all heard her talk about the problem of time—an impossible conundrum, it seems! From her point of view, assuming she is telling the truth, this is what happened: she saw Claudia Playford, wearing the same green dress she wore to dinner that night, set about Joseph Scotcher's head with the club. Sophie started to scream, at which point Claudia dropped the club and ran away, through the door that leads to the library. A very short time later, people started to come downstairs to see what all the shrieking was about. One of those people was Claudia, in a nightdress and white dressing gown!

"When I first heard that this was the supposed sequence of events, I had the same feeling as Sophie Bourlet: 'Surely this is impossible.' Think, my friends, of how long it would take to go through the library and get as far even as the bottom of the stairs, in order to ascend to the next floor.

"Catchpool and I were talking upstairs when Sophie Bourlet began to scream. You can all see that Catchpool, he has the long legs. Alas, I do not move so quickly, but he does, and he moved as soon as the screaming started. *He did not, on his way down the stairs, meet Claudia Playford, in a blood-spattered green dress, on her way up.* Yet if my nicely developing theory was correct—and I felt certain it was!—that is what must have happened! This problem, this riddle, it was one of great magnitude. And then, finally, I saw that there could be only one explanation, so I arranged an experiment to prove it.

"Sophie Bourlet had originally told us that she had first heard an argument between Claudia Playford and Scotcher—one in which a woman named Iris was mentioned—then seen Claudia start to beat Scotcher with the club, at which point Sophie had started to scream. Based on what I had deduced—the only possible solution to the riddle—I suspected that Sophie's memory of the incident had been distorted by her shock and grief. It simply could not have been as she described. But how to shock her memory, again, into correcting itself?"

"May I ask," Kimpton cut in, "when you say 'shock her memory into correcting itself,' do you in fact mean 'give a liar the chance to tell the truth without losing face'?"

Poirot ignored him. He said, "The experiment went as follows. Sophie stood outside the parlor. At my request, she put on her hat and coat, for a more perfect re-creation of the event. Catchpool and I then performed the same argument had by Claudia and Scotcher on the night of the murder. Catchpool was Scotcher and I was Claudia."

"You should have cast me," said Claudia. "I play the part of

Claudia Playford like no other, let me tell you—heaps better than an old man with a ridiculous mustache. The impertinence of it!"

"I held the club in my hand," Poirot continued. "Catchpool begged for his life—'Stop, stop! Please, Claudia! You don't have to . . .'—and I said, 'This is what Iris should have done—but she was too weak. She let you live and so you killed her.' Exactly the words that Sophie told us she heard. Then I held the club aloft and brought it down with great force—stopping only inches short of Catchpool's head. At that point, I turned to look at Sophie. As I had hoped, she was vigorously shaking her head. 'No,' she tells me. 'No, it did not happen like that.' Mademoiselle, perhaps you could tell us all how it did happen. Ladies and gentlemen: what you are about to hear is the truth. Please pay attention."

Sophie said, "It was all wrong. Suddenly everything fell into place, and it was quite different from what I had told the police and myself and . . . what I had believed. The argument did not happen first, and then the clubbing. I said it was in that order—I thought it was—but I was wrong! As a naturally neat person, I made it neater and more orderly in my memory. The truth was that Claudia was smashing Joseph's head with that . . . *thing* from the first moment. It was already happening! I arrived when it was nearly over. And it was happening—the vicious attack, I mean—*at the same time that the argument was taking place.* And Joseph's head was almost completely destroyed! Which meant . . ." Sophie looked helplessly at Poirot.

He took over. "What it means is that the man apparently begging for his life—the one who cried 'Stop, stop! Please, Claudia! You don't have to . . .'—*could not have been Joseph Scotcher.* He, as we know, was already dead from strychnine poisoning, and nobody could be quite so eloquent with a smashed skull. Therefore . . . the voice Sophie heard belonged to another man, a man who was urging Claudia to desist. This man did not want her to continue to reduce to a pulp the head of the already dead Joseph Scotcher."

"Another man?" Kimpton sounded angry at the suggestion. "Which other man? Are you trying to say that Claudia is in love with somebody else?"

"I did not mention love," said Poirot.

"Don't be absurd, Randall," Claudia told him. "In *love* with? Darling, I would not quicken my pace to prevent a dangerously heavy object from falling on anybody in this world apart from you. You know that."

"Sophie Bourlet made another mistake," Poirot said.

"Yes, she put strychnine in Scotcher's blue pretend-medicine bottle." Kimpton chuckled, apparently happy again now that Claudia had reassured him. "And she's going to hang for it. Right, Poirot?"

"Wrong. As I have made clear already, Sophie Bourlet did not kill Joseph Scotcher."

"Yes, but you've said that about all of us, and someone must have done it," Kimpton pointed out.

"He has not yet said it about me," said Lady Playford in a mournful tone. "I didn't do it, of course. And I fear it might irreparably break my heart if anyone were to suggest that I did."

"You, Lady Playford, are innocent," Poirot told her.

"Thank you, Poirot. Yes, I am."

"Poirot, this is too much!" said Kimpton.

"We demand to know immediately," said Dorro Playford.

"And I am trying to tell you. May I continue? *Merci*. Sophie Bourlet's other mistake was to imagine that she first screamed when Claudia Playford began to beat Scotcher with the club. This was not so! Remember, we have established that Claudia was already bludgeoning Scotcher when Sophie appeared and looked into the parlor, and that the argument with another man was taking place simultaneously. This man, incidentally, was not seen by Sophie. He was, I believe, standing in the darkness of the library. Sophie does not recall whether the door between the library and the parlor was closed or open. I think it must have been open.

"I hope you can all see that if Sophie had started to scream when first she witnessed the clubbing, as she initially told us, she would not have been able to hear the argument over the noise she was making—which was loud enough to raise legions of the dead, if I might be permitted to say.

"Here, then, is what happened: Sophie watched, struck dumb with shock, as Claudia Playford battered Scotcher's head with the club. At the same time, Sophie listened to the argument between Claudia and the man who was concealed in the library but able to see into the parlor. Then Claudia spotted Sophie and ran, and we must assume the man ran away too. For as long as it took the two of them to get to the bottom of the stairs, Sophie stared in horror at the destroyed head and horribly contorted body of her beloved. Some minutes passed; it is impossible to measure time accurately when one is in extreme shock. Claudia and the man with whom she had argued ran up the stairs and were able to conceal themselves before anyone spotted them. *Then,* at that moment, Sophie came to, as if from a nightmare—except for her the nightmare had only just begun. She realized that what lay before her was no apparition, not a dream, but horribly, tragically real. *That* is when she started to scream. Meanwhile, Claudia was swapping her green dress for her white nightdress and dressing gown.

"When Sergeant O'Dwyer arrived at Lillieoak today, I asked him if any of the gardaí who searched the house and grounds found a green dress with bloodstains on it. They did not. The whereabouts of the dress Claudia Playford wore to attack Scotcher remains a mystery."

"I can recall it all now, so clearly," said Sophie tearfully. "I don't know why I didn't straightaway. I was cold—terribly cold in spite of my coat and hat, and being inside. I felt as if I had fallen into a long, dark tunnel, except it was going down and not along, so it couldn't have been a real tunnel. And it was dark and silent and I was quite alone—alone with thoughts of Joseph and how he had been telling the truth all along because he had said he was going to die and now he was dead, except he couldn't be, because it couldn't be real. I wouldn't *let* it be real! When I was thinking all of that, I wasn't screaming. I started to scream because the silence was too frightening after a while."

"Oh, do stop going on, will you?" Claudia said impatiently. "None of this tells us who killed Joseph or why he was killed. Will it speed things up if I admit that it's all true? Yes, I was in the parlor and yes, I was the one who came down rather hard on Joseph's poor old head. Satisfied?"

"*What?*" Kimpton looked aghast. "Dearest one, what do you mean?"

"I did not kill Joseph, though. Did I, Poirot?"

"*Non.* You did not, mademoiselle."

"Then who did?" Kimpton leapt to his feet, angry now. "In the name of all that is holy—"

"You did, Dr. Kimpton—as well you know. You murdered Joseph Scotcher."

"Me? Ha! Balderdash, old boy. You said not thirty minutes ago that I didn't do it—don't you remember? Is your memory as flawed as Sophie's?"

"All of us have imperfect memories, monsieur—Hercule Poirot less so than most. What you say is not accurate. I said that you had many motives to choose from, and that a different man in your position might have succumbed to a vengeful passion and committed murder. I then said that you did not—that you never did. It is true: you did not succumb to a passion of any description. This crime— your murder of Joseph Scotcher—was planned many years ago. It was rational, meticulously planned, driven by logic. One might even say . . . scientific."

"All the good things, eh? What a clever killer I must be!"

"It involved much hard work and discipline on your part," said Poirot. "It was in fact—since we have been using the word—*an experiment.*"

Kimpton sat down again. "I am not at all convinced," he said. "Not yet. I am curious, however, and would like to hear more."

I was not sure that I could have managed to be quite so cavalier if I were accused of murder by a man known to be the world's finest detective—not unless I somehow knew he was bluffing. Kimpton was not one to show weakness in public, however.

"I have now read many times your favorite play: *King John,*" Poirot told him. "I found it fascinating. It helped to put me on the correct path and to shed on me the dawning light."

"I am glad you found it to be a rewarding experience," said Kimpton.

"You see, whichever way I looked at it, the argument about a funeral, overheard by Orville Rolfe, did not make any sense. According to what Mr. Rolfe heard, the point of contention was the open casket versus the closed casket."

"It was," Orville Rolfe confirmed.

"*Bon.* One day when I was thinking about Dr. Kimpton's many motives for murder—he who had known Scotcher far longer than anyone else here—I remembered something to which I had not paid sufficient attention at the time. At dinner, when Scotcher appeared shaken and unsteady after receiving the shocking news of Lady Playford's altered will, Kimpton handed *his own water glass* to Sophie Bourlet and instructed her to make Scotcher drink it. Ladies and gentlemen, whyever should he do this, when Scotcher had a water glass of his own that must still have been full, or almost full? All our water glasses were full when we sat down at the table. The entrée had only just been served when Lady Playford made her announcement, and the first course was soup. Soup is wet; nobody drinks a large amount of water while consuming it."

"Golly!" Harry Playford announced. It was as jarring as if a zebra had strolled gaily into the drawing room. Everybody ignored him, apart from Dorro, who told him to be quiet.

Poirot went on: "Randall Kimpton is an extremely clever man.

He is able to think and act with the speed of lightning. He had been planning the murder of Joseph Scotcher for years, and trying to arrange what he thought were the ideal conditions in which to commit it, and then suddenly he found himself—quite by chance!— surrounded by people who wished Scotcher dead. Kimpton had not known that Lady Playford would alter her will in Scotcher's favor, but she had. She had left to him everything she owned. What policeman would have trouble believing, then, that Harry or Dorro Playford would think to murder Scotcher in order to become immensely wealthy? Or that Michael Gathercole might kill Scotcher out of pure jealousy, or to save Lady Playford from her own foolishness?

"Kimpton knew that *now* was his moment. And so, while everybody was busy staring at Scotcher, or Lady Playford—the players of the main parts in the drama—Kimpton discreetly reached into his pocket and produced the strychnine he had there. He kept it in a small vial, I expect. Why did he always keep the poison about his person? I do not know, but I can guess: if it was always with him, nobody could accidentally find it among his possessions.

"Beneath the table, he opened whatever container the poison was in. Concealing it in a closed fist, he then dropped the strychnine into his own water glass without anybody noticing—a subtle movement of one hand, I imagine, while the other shielded the glass from view—and passed it to Sophie to give to Scotcher."

"But . . . oh!" I could not help exclaiming.

"What is it, Catchpool?" Poirot asked.

"Strychnine has a bitter taste, I believe. Does anybody remember Scotcher saying, 'Oh, that was bitter' after Dorro said something about him rotting in the earth? And then immediately afterwards, Dorro said, 'Well, I *feel* bitter'?"

"You do well to remember that exchange, *mon ami*. Indeed. Scotcher was not in the habit of making direct criticisms of others. Quite the opposite: he was a skilled flatterer of all who crossed his path. Is it more likely, then, that he meant Dorro Playford's words or the water he had drunk when he said, 'That was bitter'?" Without waiting for answers, Poirot said, "I am sure he meant the water: the bitter-tasting water that contained strychnine.

"And now to return to Shakespeare's *King John*, from which Dr. Kimpton quotes so liberally. When we all of us hurried to the parlor and found the deceased Joseph Scotcher, Dr. Kimpton uttered a few words. Perhaps some of you heard him, as I did. It sounded like the final part of a quote: '. . . the jewel of life, by some damn'd hand was robb'd and ta'en away.' I assumed it was from *King John*, as all Dr. Kimpton's quotes seemed to be. I was correct—not only about that, but also in my suspicion that I had missed the beginning of the quote. Dr. Kimpton had mumbled it, and the words were lost. The complete quote is this: 'They found him dead and cast into the streets, an empty casket, where the jewel of life, by some damn'd hand was robb'd and ta'en away.'

"An empty *casket*, ladies and gentlemen. Do you not see? The casket referred to is not a coffin, *it is the human body itself*!"

Poirot looked more excited than I could remember seeing him. I was rather at a loss. While comprehending the immediate point, I could not see what bearing it had upon anything.

"It was Randall Kimpton that Orville Rolfe overheard arguing about the open casket," Poirot said. "Arguing with Claudia Playford. Mr. Rolfe heard a man insisting that somebody must die. Then he said, 'Open casket: it is the only way,' and the woman disagreed. *Joseph Scotcher himself—the body of Joseph Scotcher—was the casket to which Dr. Kimpton referred.* He used the word as it was used in *King John*, as a metaphor for a man's body. And what he meant more generally was this: that there was only one way to establish *with absolute certainty*, the only kind that interested Randall Kimpton, if Scotcher had lied or told the truth about having Bright's disease of the kidneys. Only one way, ladies and gentlemen . . . and that was to open up his body—to make him the subject of a suspicious death so that there would be a postmortem. Only an autopsy would allow a doctor *to look inside the body of Joseph Scotcher* and say—as in fact did happen, precisely according to Dr. Kimpton's plan—'This man has perfectly healthy kidneys.'"

I thought of Kimpton's expression of satisfaction at the inquest, when the truth about Scotcher had been revealed by the coroner. I had misunderstood it—thought he was simply pleased with himself for having known something before I did. Now I understood: according to his own standards of evidence, he had not known for sure—not until the moment he heard the coroner say it: "healthy pink kidneys."

"Dr. Kimpton was almost positive that Scotcher was a liar," said Poirot. "He had been almost positive for many years. As an intelligent man, however, he knew that in science and in medicine, there are anomalies. Most people with failing kidneys do not last as long as Scotcher had (most are not dying once, then some years later dying again), but remission can occur, prognoses change, so one can never rule out absolutely the anomaly that appears to flout the rule—and perhaps, who knows, there is some other scientific cause for this anomaly?

"Randall Kimpton knew some things beyond doubt. He knew that Scotcher had taken Iris from him, had followed him into the study of Shakespeare, had then followed him to the core of the Playford family by installing himself at Lillieoak, the home of the woman Kimpton planned to marry. He believed, also, that Scotcher had murdered Iris Gillow when she had started to suspect he was lying about his health. Kimpton believed this, but he could not prove it. Neither could he prove that Scotcher had impersonated his dead brother, Blake, at Queen's Lane Coffee House, in order to tell the same lies about his health using a different identity. This was maddening to Kimpton, who had grown as obsessed with Scotcher as Scotcher had always been with him. Kimpton suspected that Scotcher had invented his failing kidneys in order to attract Iris's sympathy and lure her away. He wanted to know if he was right.

This wish felt so urgent that it appeared to him as a need, not a desire. He *needed* to solve the mystery of Joseph Scotcher. He needed to know, probably most of all, if Scotcher had murdered Iris or not. After all, if by some remote chance Scotcher was telling the truth about his ill health, then he was unlikely to have murdered Iris for catching him in a lie—for there would have been no lie!

"Eventually it dawned upon him: *he would never truly and fully be able to understand the story of his own life unless he learned the truth about the state of Joseph Scotcher's health.* And what was his response to this realization? I will tell you: Randall Kimpton resolved to know the truth, for certain and beyond doubt. And there was only one way to achieve that: a postmortem. In no other circumstance is one able to look inside the body of another person and see kidneys that are either pink and normal or brown, dry and shrunken. And so . . . the suspicious death of Joseph Scotcher had to be brought about."

Dorro Playford snorted impatiently. "I don't understand what you are saying! You cannot mean—"

"I mean, madame, that it was not excess of emotion that caused Randall Kimpton to murder Joseph Scotcher. It was not jealousy, rage, a thirst for revenge—though I imagine all of those feelings have tormented Dr. Kimpton greatly over the years as he has considered the matter of Joseph Scotcher. But they are not why he killed him. This murder was a scientific experiment. It was a quest for knowledge, for discovery. It was—put as simply as I can put it—*murder for the sake of the autopsy.*"

Poirot Wins Fair and Square

THOUGH I HAVE NO way of proving it, I saw it all, seconds after Poirot had said it. *Murder for the sake of the autopsy. Murder for post-mortem's sake.* Odd that a crime of such enormity can be summed up in as few as four words, isn't it?

Realization after realization flooded my mind. Of course; how did I not see it? Kimpton, the man of science, the man who valued facts and proof above all else, and ridiculed psychology. It made perfect sense.

Nobody in the room moved or spoke for several moments. Then Poirot addressed Kimpton. "You did not turn away from the study of Shakespeare because your favorite theatrical work was deemed unacceptable by your peers," he said. "Nor because Scotcher tres-passed upon your scholarly specialism. No—you chose medicine as a career because you had formulated what you believed was a brilliant plan: you would train as a doctor. Such was the strength of your obsession with Scotcher that you did not care how many years it took. You would take a position, as soon as you were able, that put you in place to perform postmortems in cases of suspicious deaths, and you would do this work very close to where Joseph Scotcher lived. You would murder him close to his home, after setting up an unshakable alibi for yourself, and then he would in due course end up on your autopsy table, ready for you to cut him open to reveal the truth. Opening up his body was essential to your experiment, and how much more satisfying if you were able to perform the procedure yourself?

"At first your plan progressed nicely—within not too many years, thanks to your talent and determination, you were the police's preferred autopsy man in the district of Oxford that was home to Scotcher. Then, suddenly, it all went wrong, did it not? Your new sweetheart, Claudia Playford, to whom you had recently become engaged, told you that Scotcher would soon be living and working here, at Lillieoak. You must have been enraged."

"Well done, old chap," said Kimpton. "Is this the bit where I confirm that my psychological state was as you have described it? It was. I was indeed furious at that point in the narrative. If anyone can make a science out of psychology, it is you, Poirot."

"Randall, he is accusing you of *murder*!" said Claudia. "Will you not deny it?"

"No, dearest one. I'm sorry, but there it is. Poirot won fair and square. I shall not deprive him of his victory."

"Will you not? I would." Claudia stared coldly at Poirot. "You are right to describe Randall as talented and determined—but no man is ever so determined as the most determined woman. I should never give up trying to get away with murder, if I had committed it. Never!"

"I don't think Poirot has finished, dearest one. Though, since you have brought it up . . . as much as it pains me to disagree with my divine girl, I have a different idea about what it means to get away with a thing." Despite his use of endearments, Kimpton's voice was as hard as his face. I noticed that his eyes were no longer flaring and subsiding in their peculiar way; instead they were wild and wide, and apparently set firm that way.

"Please believe me, all of you, when I tell you that I suffer from no lack of determination," he said. "But I prefer to face facts. A murder that one gets away with is one that proves impossible to solve. It is cleanly and perfectly elusive. No one suspects the true culprit—not even the indomitable Hercule Poirot; the killer is eliminated from the ranks of the possibly guilty straightaway, and immune from suspicion and blame thereafter. *That* is the murder I planned to commit. The moment Poirot accuses me, I see that I have bungled the whole thing. I might be able to save my life by trying to talk my way out of it, but I cannot save my plan. I therefore prefer to choose the only other clean and perfect possibility available to me: a full confession. Did I murder Joseph Scotcher? Yes. I did."

"Dr. Kimpton, you were correct when you said that I had not finished," said Poirot, not yet willing to hand the main part to another player. "Where was I? Ah, yes: I had got as far as the problem you faced when Scotcher was appointed as secretary to Lady Playford. If he was no longer to be in Oxford, how could you murder him and be assured of performing the postmortem yourself?"

"That was what I thought at first," said Kimpton. "I was Old Glum-boots for a while, that's for sure."

"And that is why you ended your engagement to Claudia," I heard myself say: thinking aloud. Poirot had not given me permission to speak, but he would have to put up with it, I decided. "Claudia, you told me that when you and Kimpton were engaged first time round, he began to doubt whether he did, after all, wish to marry you. This led to a separation. Five, nearly six years ago, you said—that was when it happened. Joseph Scotcher lived and worked at Lillieoak for six years."

I turned to Kimpton. "These doubts of yours about marrying Claudia were in response to the news that Scotcher had secured the position of private secretary to Lady Playford, I'll wager."

"You are entirely correct." Kimpton was coolly courteous. "I was furious to hear that Scotcher had wormed his way in at Lillieoak. Livid! For a variety of reasons. How could I, pathologist for the police in Oxford, perform a postmortem on Scotcher if he was suddenly in Clonakilty? All the planning I had done, all my medical training . . . Oh, I still wanted to murder the blackguard—more than ever!—but I wanted every bit as much to *thwart* him. He had known nothing of my plan to end his life, you see, but he *had* known of my engagement to my dearest one. Even after Iris—after everything he had done to me by then—he still sought to implant himself on territory that was rightfully mine and ought to have been nothing to do with him.

"I did not know if he wanted to place himself at Lillieoak in order to enrage me or simply to be around me—I kept hearing from Oxford chaps that he still described me as his closest friend, though I had been avoiding him for years. Either way, it was irrelevant. There was plenty of time to kill him and open him up on the table—either in Oxford, or in Clonakilty; I knew I could get a job in County Cork if I had to, for I am demonstrably the best at what I do—but in the meantime, I was determined Scotcher should *suffer*. If I ended my engagement to Claudia, I reasoned, then, in a stroke, the connection between Lillieoak and me would be severed and Scotcher would have to face the fact that he had gone to a great deal of trouble for absolutely no reason."

Kimpton clenched his fists in his lap. "I was a fool. An imbecile. That is what happens when emotional impulses and not solid logic are behind one's actions. I regretted my rashness immediately. I saw that I had, once again, allowed Scotcher to deprive me of a woman I loved. No one, ladies and gentlemen, does that to Randall Kimpton and lives to tell the tale. The final victory, I am sure we can all agree, is mine."

"Your definition of victory is an unusual one," Poirot told him.

"My definition of everything is unusual," Kimpton replied. "I am an unusual person. Where was I? Oh, yes—well, I got down on my knees and *begged* my divine girl to take me back."

"I refused," said Claudia. "It gave me great pleasure to do so."

"But you did agree to enter into a correspondence on the subject of my vileness and your infallibility, dearest one." Kimpton turned to Poirot. "Thanks to Claudia's letters, I discovered that Scotcher had returned to Oxford at least once. It would not have been hard to induce him to do so again. Killing him in Oxford as planned would be the simplest thing, I suspected—barely a challenge at all. Or I could move to County Cork, ingratiate myself with the police and medical establishment here . . . That would be a good way to win Claudia over: a visible willingness to abandon my world and loiter on the fringes of hers, grateful for the most threadbare scraps of attention she might toss my way.

"You all know, of course, that my dearest one was generous enough to give me a second chance." Kimpton looked at Claudia fondly. She turned away. "On the fateful day, until the moment that I dropped the poison into my water glass, I was undecided—about where Claudia and I should live after we married, about where I ought to kill Scotcher. Should it be Oxford, where I knew how the system worked, or Clonakilty, where I imagined—do forgive me, Inspector Conree—that the gardaí would only be able to solve a murder if the culprit handcuffed himself to the gates of the police station and sang, 'I did it,' from sunrise until sunset.

"No, the biggest problem I faced was not the choice between England and County Cork. I'm afraid it was the same boring old dilemma faced by any prospective murderer: how to do it and be absolutely guaranteed of getting away with it? I thought my plan splendid—always had!—but almost foolproof and entirely fool-proof are two very different prospects. You know how I dislike un-certainty, Poirot. Yet I was uncertain myself, I am ashamed to admit. I could not guarantee that I could kill Scotcher and escape detection. And so . . . a date had not been set, and a place had not been decided upon."

"And then at dinner on the evening of what you call 'the fateful day,' *quelle bonne chance*!" Poirot took up the tale. "Lady Playford announces her new testamentary arrangements, and suddenly there are plenty of suspects for a murder, if by chance Scotcher were to die that same night. Never would you have a better chance of getting away with it! You had the poison with you, as always, and so you acted fast."

"I did," Kimpton agreed. "Here, I thought, is the guarantee I have been seeking, that elusive extra layer of security. Who will suspect the richest man in the house, amid hordes of the aggrieved disinherited? Ah, well. 'How oft the sight of means to do ill deeds, make deeds ill done!'" No prizes for guessing where that comes from, Poirot! I might not get to do the autopsy myself, I thought, but never mind—I would certainly be informed of its results and get the definite answer I needed. There would be an inquest that I could attend. One must adapt sometimes—don't you find?"

"Yes," said Poirot. "And having adapted, you continued to think most cunningly."

"You are too kind. I was rash. Impulsive. I made a grievous error. After all my planning, to do the deed in front of all those witnesses—it was insanity!"

"You were cunning," Poirot insisted. "Strychnine takes several hours to kill. Who can tell how many? Who could ever know how much of the poison you put into your glass of water? Later that evening, you made sure to put some strychnine into the blue bottle in Scotcher's bedroom, and then to empty the bottle. You knew that would make it look as if poisoned medicine had been poured away to hide the evidence. In consequence, we all believed that Scotcher had ingested the poison at five o'clock, when Sophie Bourlet gave him the tonic. Suddenly, anybody could have killed him—or so it seemed."

"I am nothing if not ingenious," Kimpton muttered. His air of good cheer had worn off a little.

"No, Dr. Kimpton. In this instance, you were not ingenious but foolish. As you say: suddenly anybody could have poisoned Scotcher if the poison was put into the blue bottle before five o'clock . . . but who would have had a motive before five o'clock? Only you: the man whose first love had been stolen by Joseph Scotcher! The new will of Lady Playford was only announced at the dinner table that evening. By planting misleading evidence about the time of death, you made yourself the only viable suspect."

"Balderdash!" Kimpton said easily. "Pure bunkum! Anyone might have found out about Athie's new will before she announced it—by fair means or foul. She might have confided in somebody, keen on secrets as she is—secrets are much more fun when shared than when kept absolutely to oneself—or the murderer might have come by the information illicitly. Athie had been planning the big announcement for weeks, no doubt—perhaps months. I was confident that the new will would still be viewed as the most likely motive. Even if it had not been, I didn't see that I had much choice. As you pointed out, Poirot, Scotcher had announced to you all at dinner that the water he had drunk was bitter! True, Dorro thought his remark was aimed at her, but that did not make me feel safe at all. You said it yourself, old boy: all the water glasses had been filled before we sat down at the table. Why would I give mine to Scotcher when he had one of his own? And you had all seen me do it! I was afraid that, in due course, one of you would remember, and make the connection between that and Scotcher's 'bitter' remark. It seemed glaringly obvious to me, that . . . well, that *I* had done it, that I was the guilty party."

Kimpton sighed. "I suppose knowledge of one's own guilt will do that to a chap. But, in the hope of rendering it a good deal less obvious to everybody else, I took steps. Once I was confident that everyone had retired for the night—well, all apart from Poirot, who was snoring in a chair on the landing for a reason I couldn't quite fathom, but he was deeply asleep and hardly likely to wake—I put poison in the blue bottle, knowing that was the five-o'clock-every-day bottle. Then I disposed of my water glass from the dinner table, so that no one could later find traces of poison in it. I hunted it down in the kitchen, smashed it and buried the fragments near a pile of broken glass and a smashed jam jar that I had seen in the orangery."

"So it was you who stole my glass!" Brigid Marsh announced loudly, startling us all. "I could have sworn it was Mr. Catchpool." Remarkably, she glowered at me as she said this, not at Kimpton.

Now I understood: she had noticed that a glass was missing and—for some reason best known to herself—decided I had taken it up to my room so that I could drink water in the night. On account of my dry lips—a description I would robustly dispute any day of the week. My lips were entirely normal.

No doubt Brigid had searched my room, failed to find the missing glass, and decided I must have smashed it and hidden the pieces somewhere—hence the anecdote about her thieving nephew who had stolen sweets and broken a bowl.

Poirot said sternly to Kimpton. "I might have been snoring, but everyone had *not* retired for the night, Doctor. Catchpool was in the gardens, looking for Mr. Gathercole and Mademoiselle Sophie, who were at that time missing. He, or they, might have returned at any moment. All three did, a little later, return to the house. That is *three people* who might have seen you coming out of Scotcher's room, or on your way to the orangery to dispose of the glass. You are not as clever as you think you are."

"That is quite apparent." Kimpton threw up his hands. "You, meanwhile, are *far* cleverer than I imagined you could be. The casket business—well, that was an impressive leap you made!"

"It was," Poirot agreed. "And many things started to come together in my mind when I knew the true meaning of the 'open casket' metaphor—the *King John* meaning," he said. "If 'casket' was a person, what did that mean about the argument overheard by Mr. Rolfe? I wondered. I will tell you what it meant. It meant that the disagreement was between Randall Kimpton and Claudia Playford. She knew of his plan to murder Scotcher one day and, maybe fearing that it would go wrong, was trying to talk him out of it. He said, 'Open casket: it's the only way'—in other words, 'I must murder Scotcher if I am to have satisfaction.' She said, 'No, you must do no such thing.'"

"And I was right," said Claudia. "It had already gone wrong—three days earlier, to be precise. I had found the strychnine. Randall took off his jacket rather carelessly and the damned bottle fell out of the pocket. Before that, I was blissfully ignorant of his deranged plan. Had he told me, he would have had the benefit of my opinion a good deal sooner. My opinion was that it was madness—the madness of an unhinged schoolboy."

"Dashed bad luck, the poison falling out of my pocket like that," said Kimpton. "You needn't have known anything about it, dearest one. I'd have gotten away with it if you hadn't found out, you know."

"When I asked Randall what was in the little bottle, he lied to me," Claudia told Poirot. "I could see that he was lying. I made it clear that I would not be fobbed off, and forced him to tell me the truth. Out it all came: Iris Gillow, née Morphet, Oxford; Joseph's first pretense that he was dying, many years earlier; his impersonation of his own brother, to bolster his fakery. And of course, Randall's plan to commit the perfect murder.

"What I heard frightened me, and there's not a lot that does that. I did not want Randall to risk his neck, and besides, there was no need for the whole silly to-do! It was perfectly obvious that Joseph was not dying! No one needed to commit murder in order to prove it!"

"I couldn't make her understand the need for *proof*, Poirot," said Kimpton. "That is why I am so glad that you understand."

"I was frantic with worry and I was careless," said Claudia gravely. "How could I have been so *stupid* as to discuss it in the house, when anyone could have overheard. Well, someone did! Orville Rolfe did.

I thought using the open and closed casket metaphor would provide enough cover—I was wrong. This is all my fault, Randall."

"No, dearest one. The fault is entirely mine. If I had made the perfect plan I ought to have made, I would not have carried a vial of poison around with me for nearly two years—or else I would, at the very least, have put it in a more secure pocket."

"Mademoiselle Claudia, did you see, at the dinner table, what Dr. Kimpton did to the glass of water before he passed it to Sophie Bourlet to give to Mr. Scotcher? You knew he had the poison concealed in his clothing, I assume."

"I knew that, but, no, I did not see him put the poison in the water."

"When, then, did you discover that he had poisoned Mr. Scotcher?" Poirot asked her.

"Later that evening. After dinner, and after Orville Rolfe's digestive system had stirred us all up into a frenzy, Randall and I retired for the night. Immediately, he confessed to me what he had done, with the glass of water. Joseph would be dead by now, he said, and in the morning his body would be found, and so Randall needed to go and remove the relevant glass. There was a chip on its stem, he said, so he would be able to identify it. He also needed to put strychnine in one of the bottles of pretend medicine in Joseph's bedroom. That way, everyone would imagine that the poisoning had taken place much earlier."

Claudia stood and walked over to near where Lady Playford was sitting. "I was incandescent with rage, Mother," she said. "I had not merely suggested that Randall abandon his idea of murdering Joseph—I had *ordered* him to do so, earlier that very same day. And he had disobeyed me! All for the sake of a wretched postmortem that would tell us nothing we did not already know! For that, he risked going to the gallows and leaving me alone. Very well then, I thought to myself. I am going to show him that no future husband of Claudia Playford disobeys her and gets away with it! I told him to go and do his water-glass-stealing and bottle-poisoning. Once he'd gone, I went after him and tiptoed down the stairs. I heard him close the door of Joseph's bedroom after a few minutes—having successfully put the poison in the blue bottle, I assumed. From the sound of his footsteps getting fainter, I guessed he had gone next to the kitchen to look for the glass. I gambled on being able to go to Joseph's room and find no one in it but Joseph.

"Well, don't all look at me as if you can't imagine what's coming next! He was dead, obviously. Stone-cold dead, as you would say, Dorro. I put him in his wheelchair, wheeled him to the parlor, tipped him out, and used that ugly club of Daddy's to try and see to it that Randall was thwarted! He had defied me for the sake of his stupid obsessive need to open the casket that was Joseph Scotcher? Fine! I would punish him by making the cause of death so glaringly obvious that there would be no need for a postmortem—Randall would be deprived of the thing he most wanted, and it would serve him right! It would teach him to listen to me in future."

Claudia paused to compose herself. "I did not realize that a suspicious death always leads to an autopsy. Randall told me that later, when we made up. Oh, yes, we kissed and made up! I made it clear to him that, although I still loved him, I would never forgive him. I am not terribly good at forgiving people. Anyway, that is why I smashed up the skull of an already dead man. And do you know what, Poirot? I thoroughly enjoyed doing it—battering Joseph's head the way I did—because I was livid! With Randall for being so fixated on Joseph and this silly proof that he had been hankering after for *years,* and with Joseph for causing all the trouble in the first place with his needless, idiotic lies, but most of all with myself—for loving Randall and being so fascinated by Joseph, when it had just become abundantly clear that I was better off without either of them!"

"How your words wound my heart, dearest one," Kimpton said with a sigh. For once, he sounded neither pleased with himself nor determined.

"What happened after you had disposed of the glass and put poison in the blue bottle?" Poirot asked him.

"I returned to my bedroom. I expected to find Claudia there, but she had vanished. I looked everywhere, and then I found her—with Scotcher's body, in the parlor, beating his head to a pulp and yelling at him at the same time. I begged her to stop—that was what Sophie heard. And yes, I was in the library, with the door open. I could not bear to go any nearer. Oh, it was not the blood and gore that repelled me. You will laugh, Poirot, but it was at that moment—when I saw Claudia setting about Scotcher with the club, and all that blood, and she was even talking to him, *talking* to a dead man! It was at that moment that it dawned on me how badly—how irreparably, I feared— my plan had gone awry. I stood and stared and could not move—either towards the gruesome scene or away from it. It was the worst moment of my life, the nadir. 'Somehow we have to make this right,' I thought. 'Cover every trace.' I had not been so prudent and restrained for so many years only to have the woman I loved convicted of murder! And then I heard the sound of a door closing, and I knew somebody else was about." Kimpton stared coldly at Sophie Bourlet, as if the predicament in which he found himself were her fault and not his own.

"Poirot, you must tell us how you worked all of this out," said Lady Playford. "I appreciate the aspect about *King John* and the casket reference, but really, was that all it took for you to put it all together?"

"No, it was not all," Poirot told her. "I found a doctor in Oxford who had at one time been Joseph Scotcher's doctor. He furnished me with some very interesting facts. That Scotcher had, to his knowledge, always been healthy was the first. Then, that Iris Gillow had been to see him only two days before she died. She had wanted to know if Scotcher truly suffered from a debilitating kidney disease that would one day kill him. This doctor said, quite properly, that he was unable to disclose information of that sort. He had then contacted Scotcher to ask if Scotcher had any idea why a young lady should make such a peculiar inquiry. Two days later, Iris Gillow was dead—murdered by Scotcher, wearing the same fake beard he wore to impersonate Blake Scotcher for the benefit of Randall Kimpton.

"I also went to a hospital and spoke with another doctor, a Dr. Jowsey—he provided some of your medical training, Dr. Kimpton. He remembers you asking, on your very first day, about the difference, in visual terms, between a healthy kidney and a diseased one, and whether a doctor performing an autopsy would easily be able to distinguish between the two. It struck him as a most unusual question. Also worthy of note is *when* you decided to abandon the study of Shakespeare's plays and pursue medicine. You made your first inquiry only fifteen days after Iris Gillow's death. That was the catalyst that made you feel you *had* to know the truth about Scotcher's health.

"That is almost all of it," said Poirot. "Before I finish, however, I must say that my friend Catchpool helped me a great deal in this matter. You see, there was one thing that would not fit, no matter how much the rest of it made sense: *how could Joseph Scotcher have been, at the same time, dead from poisoning and alive and begging for his life in the parlor?* And then Catchpool made a very useful suggestion to me. He advised me to find the third thing—the one that makes the two things we know to be true not inconsistent with one another! If Scotcher was dead and yet Sophie Bourlet had heard what she claimed to have heard . . . why, then it becomes obvious that the man she heard speaking was not Scotcher! Then it all fell nicely into place, and everything pointed to Randall Kimpton as the murderer. Only one thing remains that I do not understand. Perhaps, Dr. Kimpton . . . ?"

"Ask and ye shall be told," said Kimpton. "And, no, that isn't a quote from anything. I expect it's the green dress, is it? You want to know where it got to?"

"I should like to know," said Claudia quietly. "It was my favorite dress."

"I'm rather proud of myself on the hiding-the-dress front," said Kimpton. "It was covered in blood, and the house was full of gardaí poking around. Then Fate smiled upon me and gave me an inspired idea. I thought of the one place where they would be guaranteed not to look."

"And that was?" Poirot asked.

"The messy leather bag belonging to the even messier police doctor, Clouder," Kimpton told him. "The same doctor who misplaced the key to his car and so could not attend the inquest. The gardaí wouldn't have searched the possessions of their own medical chap, and indeed they did not. I tore up the dress and stuffed it into Clouder's bag, pushing it right down to the bottom. When I saw what else was in there, I knew he wasn't a fellow who was likely to shake it all out onto a table for a good old sorting out anytime soon. That bag was a veritable shrine to detritus and decay! I'm sure the bloodstained strips of green material are still in there, and will remain in situ for years—unless you give him the order to fish them out, Inspector Conree."

Conree bared his teeth at Kimpton, but said nothing.

"That ought to have occurred to me," Poirot muttered. "The doctor's bag—of course. Where else?"

Kimpton pulled a small bottle out of his jacket pocket, removed its lid and swallowed its contents in one gulp. "Never have too little of anything useful, that's my advice, Poirot. Always equip yourself with a spare or two."

I gasped, and heard others do the same. I saw Gathercole shudder. A yelp came from Lady Playford at the back of the room.

"No!" Dorro cried out. "Oh, how ghastly. I can't bear it. Surely something can be done so that . . ." She did not finish her sentence.

"Again, you give up," Claudia said quietly to Kimpton. "So be it. Let us go upstairs, darling. That's allowed, isn't it, Poirot? I'm sure we can spare everybody else yet another gruesome spectacle."

"You should let me go alone, dearest one."

"I shall do no such thing," said Claudia.

"Randall, before you go . . ." Lady Playford began shakily. "I wish to say . . . well, only that it is rather peculiar and fascinating how different people are from one another. For you, the mystery of Joseph Scotcher is now solved, whereas for me what you have done has ensured it can *never* be solved. We knew already, those of us who cared to notice, that Joseph was not truthful about his health. What we did not know was *why,* or if anything could be done about it. I could not have given a fat fiddlestick whether his kidneys were dark and shriveled, plump and pink or purple with yellow stripes! I wanted to find out about his hopes and fears, his loves and losses— whether, underneath all the lies, there was an honest heart waiting to be put to good use! Thanks to you, it is now impossible for me ever to know any of that. I don't mean to make you feel any worse than you already do. It is only that I cannot understand a person who would go to such lengths to prove something of so little interest or importance."

Kimpton appeared to consider this. "Yes," he said after a few moments. "Yes, I can see that you might see it that way. I saw it differently. That, no doubt, is why you enjoy inventing stories and I prefer to establish facts. I'm afraid to say that, in my estimation, my approach is the clear winner. After all, without the occasional solid fact, anyone could ask one to believe anything, and then no story is better than any other." He turned to Claudia. "Come, dearest one. Let us depart."

Hand in hand, they left the room.

Epilogue

THE NEXT MORNING, POIROT and I waited outside the house for the car to be brought round. It was hard to believe that we were about to leave Lillieoak. I made a remark to this effect and got no answer.

"Poirot? Are you all right?"

"I am thinking."

"It looks serious, whatever it is."

"Not particularly. I do, however, find it interesting."

"What?"

"We were invited to Lillieoak, you and I, as an insurance policy. Lady Playford believed that nobody would dare to commit a murder with Hercule Poirot in the house! No one would be so foolish. But someone did dare—Randall Kimpton was foolish enough to attempt it. And now he is dead. He could so easily have waited. In a week, Poirot, he would be gone! In a week, the obsession with opening the closed casket of Joseph Scotcher's body would still have been there, as strong as ever! Why did Kimpton not wait?"

"He saw his chance and made a rash decision." I frowned. "Poirot, you almost sound as if you wish he had got away with it."

"Do not be facetious, Catchpool. I am glad that his crime did not go unpunished, of course, but . . . I am not glad that he underestimated me. That he did not *instantly* decide against committing a murder right in front of the eyes of Hercule Poirot . . . Had he not heard the stories of my achievements? I believe he had, yet he was not impressed. He derided my methods—"

"Poirot," I said firmly. It was not only murderers who tended towards obsessive behavior, I reflected.

"Yes, *mon ami*?"

"Randall Kimpton is dead. It might sound puerile to put it in these terms, but . . . you won and he lost."

Poirot smiled and patted my arm. "Thank you, Catchpool. It is not puerile at all. You are right: I won. He lost."

It struck me then that there were other losers, less deserving ones than Kimpton, and ones I cared more about. Perhaps I was wrong to feel the way I did, but I could not help thinking that whatever lies he might have told and whatever terrible deeds he might have done, Joseph Scotcher had very much wanted to be a good man, and might one day have become one. He had met the dazzling Randall Kimpton at Oxford, had admired him, modeled himself upon him, purloined his sweetheart, followed him into the study of Shakespeare and then into the bosom of the Playford family—but he had not sought to mimic Kimpton's self-regard, his cruel streak, his easy dismissal of the opinions and feelings of others.

I did not like to think that Scotcher had in all probability murdered Iris Gillow. His kind words in the drawing room before dinner on the night he was to die were the most thoughtful and beneficial that any person had ever addressed to me—ever, in my life. That in no way excused murder, I knew. Still—to me it was not insignificant.

"I suppose that while we wait for the car, we might divert ourselves by discussing the one question that remains unanswered," Poirot said.

"I was not aware there was one," I told him.

"Why did Scotcher propose marriage to Sophie Bourlet immediately after hearing about Lady Playford's new will?"

"Oh. Yes, I suppose you're right. I don't know the answer." I refrained from adding, "And neither, surely, do you." It would not do for Hercule Poirot to be underestimated again so soon, and by his good friend too.

"I have a few theories," he said. "One is that he felt that he was at risk of being murdered, for as long as he remained the sole beneficiary of Lady Playford's will. He believed she might change her will back if he could make her angry, or jealous, or both. By becoming engaged to his nurse, he thought he could achieve this."

"I somehow doubt that was his reason," I said.

"Let us, then, try a simpler theory: Scotcher wanted to punish Lady Playford. She had caused serious problems for him by changing her will. He feared imminent exposure as a fraud by somebody at Lillieoak, and he blamed Lady Playford for this. By choosing that moment to declare his romantic love for Sophie Bourlet instead of his loving gratitude towards Lady Playford, he deprives his benefactor of what he knows she wants most: his attention. Suddenly she is no longer the person in the house about whom he cares most."

"More likely than the first theory, but I am still not convinced," I said. "How about this one, since we're speculating: Scotcher proposed marriage in order to be sure of Sophie's silence on the matter of his feigned illness. Previously, he had flattered her in the same way that he had flattered Phyllis, and that was enough for Sophie. But if she knew he was not really dying, as she must have, and suddenly she hears Lady Playford announce that she's leaving all her worldly goods to poor, sick Joseph Scotcher . . . well, a decent girl like Sophie might then feel obliged to speak up. Scotcher's antics might start to look to her rather like fraud. Remember, Lady Playford had confessed to nobody that she knew the truth; she pretended to be fooled by the Bright's disease of the kidneys story."

"So to propose marriage to Sophie was the only way to ensure her loyalty and her continued discretion, Scotcher might have thought," said Poirot. "Yes, that is a good theory. But in the end I prefer a different one. I prefer the theory that Joseph Scotcher loved Sophie Bourlet."

"Does that count as a theory? That was the official explanation, after all."

Poirot ignored my question. "Fear of exposure as a liar—or that he might be killed by someone who did not wish him to inherit the Lillieoak estate—shocked Scotcher into behaving in a way that was more real than it was his custom to be. He loved this woman who accepted him and all his lies without question, who uncomplainingly did all the work for Lady Playford that he was quite well enough to do himself. He had perhaps loved Sophie Bourlet for a long time, but he had never said so in earnest; it was easier for him to say only things that were *not* real. Until that night. Then, in a moment of crisis, it became important to him to declare his love."

"You're a sentimental old soul, Poirot." I smiled. Perhaps I was one too; I could not deny that I felt unambiguously fond of my little Belgian friend at that moment.

"Edward!"

Hearing Gathercole's voice, I turned. He was striding towards us. "Thought I might have missed you," he said.

"No. Not yet."

At that moment, Lady Playford came running outside in her kimono. Her face was pale, and she looked older and smaller than I thought of her as being. She was smiling rather maniacally. "Poirot! Don't dare to escape without letting me grab you first! I have a query about my next bundle, and Michael is *useless* today—aren't you, Michael? Completely inattentive. Poirot, do you remember the disguise storyline I mentioned to you? Listen to my brain wave! What if it's not a disguise but a disfigurement, a facial disfigurement? No noses involved—absolutely not! Noses feature prominently in my bundle-of-the-moment and I can't bear repetition. What about a harelip that has been either corrected or . . . oh! Or *created*—yes, I like that. Why would anyone do it, though? And do I want *all* my books to be propelled by the idea of surgery? I don't think I do. And of course one mustn't alarm one's readers, who, after all, are children. I do think people cosset children too much, don't you? Horrible things do sometimes happen to faces and, really, perhaps the sooner a child learns this, the better!"

Gathercole and I exchanged a smile and moved a little to the side. "I envy you, returning to London," he said. "I'm afraid Lady Playford is not herself. She is pretending to be, of course."

"Volubly," I agreed. "How long will you stay at Lillieoak?"

"I don't know. I want to keep an eye on things for a while. Claudia, for instance . . . I don't think Lady Playford will be of much use to her, nor she to Lady Playford, and I should like to be of assistance to both of them if I can."

We exchanged cards and shook hands. The motorcar pulled up then, as Lady Playford was saying, "Oh, that is *clever*. That is very clever indeed. I see I shall have no choice but to dedicate this particular bundle to you, Poirot."

She turned to me as the driver opened the car door. "Goodbye, Edward, and thank you. I am sorry I disappointed you."

"You did not."

"Oh, yes, I did. By turning out not to be guilty of murder."

"I never believed that you were, Lady Playford."

"You did, I'm afraid. You alone." She looked unutterably sad for a second. Then the frenzied smile reappeared. "I found it amusing—and rather flattering," she said in a high, brittle voice. "You really can admit it, you know. I shan't be in the least offended, and there is no need to feel guilty. You lead a blameless life, I am sure. Too blameless." She gripped my arm. "I am old, but if I were young like you, I would *live,* and I should not mind what anybody thought about me. You sense this in me—I can tell that you do. *That* is why you suspected me of murder. Do you see?" Her eyes glittered with a strange sort of power.

I did not see, and nor did I wish to. It sounded murky and complicated. "Lady Playford, I assure you—"

"Oh, well, never mind that now." She waved my words away to make room for more of her own. "Edward, may I ask you something? Would you mind dreadfully if I put you in a book one day?"

Acknowledgments

I am immensely grateful to the following teams of brilliant, dedicated and inspiring people:

James Prichard, Mathew Prichard, Hilary Strong, Christina Macphail, Julia Wilde, Lydia Stone, Nikki White and everybody at Agatha Christie Limited; David Brawn, Kate Elton, Laura Di Guiseppe, Sarah Hodgson, Fliss Denham and all at HarperCollins UK; Dan Mallory, Kaitlin Harri, Jennifer Hart, Kathryn Gordon, Danielle Bartlett, Liate Stehlik, Margaux Weisman and the team at William Morrow; Peter Straus and Matthew Turner of Rogers, Coleridge & White.

Thank you also to all my international Poirot publishers, too many to name, but thanks to whom this novel will reach readers all over the world. And I'm hugely grateful to everyone who has read and enjoyed *The Monogram Murders* and either written, e-mailed or tweeted to tell me so. Thank you to Adele Geras, Chris Gribble and John Curran, who read early drafts and/or discussed early ideas and made immensely helpful comments. Thank you to Rupert Beale, for his kidney-ailment expertise, and to Guy Martland for his willingness to discuss medical probabilities with me. Thank you to Adrian Poole for sharing his knowledge of Shakespeare's *King John,* and to

Morgan White for gathering together everything I needed to know about Ireland in 1929.

Massive thanks to Jamie Bernthal, who has helped in every possible way from start to finish. Without him, this book would have been worse, less fun to write and—even more worryingly—Lillieoak would have had no ace floor plans!

As always, I am grateful for the support of Dan, Phoebe and Guy Jones, my amazing family. Last but not least, thank you to my dog, Brewster, who used one of my characters as a conduit for his suggestion that Lillieoak ought to have a dog. He's so vain, he probably thinks this Poirot's about him. (Indeed, that very line was the working title of *Closed Casket* for many months, only in the second person.)

Books by Agatha Christie

Mysteries

The Man in the Brown Suit

The Secret of Chimneys

The Seven Dials Mystery

The Mysterious Mr. Quin

The Sittaford Mystery

The Hound of Death

The Listerdale Mystery

Why Didn't They Ask Evans?

Parker Pyne Investigates

Murder Is Easy

And Then There Were None

Towards Zero

Death Comes as the End

Sparkling Cyanide

Crooked House

They Came to Baghdad

Destination Unknown

Spider's Web*

The Unexpected Guest*

Ordeal by Innocence

The Pale Horse

Endless Night

Passenger to Frankfurt

Problem at Pollensa Bay

While the Light Lasts

Poirot

The Mysterious Affair at Styles

The Murder on the Links

Poirot Investigates

The Murder of Roger Ackroyd

*   novelized by Charles Osbourne
†   contributor

The Big Four

The Mystery of the Blue Train

Black Coffee*

Peril at End House

Lord Edgware Dies

Murder on the Orient Express

Three Act Tragedy

Death in the Clouds

The ABC Murders

Murder in Mesopotamia

Cards on the Table

Murder in the Mews

Dumb Witness

Death on the Nile

Appointment with Death

Hercule Poirot's Christmas

Sad Cypress

One, Two, Buckle My Shoe

Evil Under the Sun

Five Little Pigs

The Hollow

The Labours of Hercules

Taken at the Flood

Mrs. McGinty's Dead

After the Funeral

Hickory Dickory Dock

Dead Man's Folly

Cat Among the Pigeons

The Adventure of the Christmas
   Pudding

The Clocks

Third Girl

Hallowe'en Party

Elephants Can Remember

Poirot's Early Cases

Curtain: Poirot's Last Case

MARPLE

The Murder at the Vicarage

The Thirteen Problems

The Body in the Library

The Moving Finger

A Murder Is Announced

They Do It with Mirrors

A Pocket Full of Rye

4:50 from Paddington

The Mirror Crack'd from Side to Side

A Caribbean Mystery

At Bertram's Hotel

Nemesis

Sleeping Murder

Miss Marple's Final Cases

TOMMY & TUPPENCE

The Secret Adversary
Partners in Crime
N or M?

By the Pricking of My Thumbs
Postern of Fate

PUBLISHED AS MARY WESTMACOTT

Giant's Bread
Unfinished Portrait
Absent in the Spring

The Rose and the Yew Tree
A Daughter's a Daughter
The Burden

MEMOIRS

An Autobiography
Come, Tell Me How You Live
The Grand Tour

PLAYS AND STORIES

Akhnaton
The Mousetrap and Other Plays
The Floating Admiral[†]
Star over Bethlehem
Hercule Poirot and the Greenshore Folly

About the Authors

AGATHA CHRISTIE is the most widely published author of all time, outsold only by the Bible and Shakespeare. Her books have sold more than a billion copies in English and another billion in more than a hundred foreign languages. She died in 1976.

SOPHIE HANNAH is the internationally bestselling author of numerous psychological thrillers, which have been published in more than twenty-seven countries and adapted for television. Sophie is an Honorary Fellow of Lucy Cavendish College, Cambridge.